THE JADE HUNTERS

Sinner's Grove Suspense Book Three

A.B. MICHAELS

THE JADE HUNTERS

Sinner's Grove Suspense *Book Three*

ISBN: 978-1-7322361-1-0

For permission requests, please write to:
Red Trumpet Press
P. O. Box 171162
Boise, ID 83716

Design by Tara Mayberry

www.TeaberryCreative.com

Also By A.B. Michaels

"Sinner's Grove Suspense" contemporary series:

Sinner's Grove

The Lair

"The Golden City" historical series:

The Art of Love

The Depth of Beauty

The Promise

The Price of Compassion

Josephine's Daughter

For Beverly

Acknowledgments

When writing fiction, the devil is in the details. Include too little about your characters' expertise or milieu and your reader won't feel confident you know what you're talking about; include too much and the story will bog down. This go-round I send a heartfelt thank-you to gemologist, author and friend Renée Newman, for sharing her extensive knowledge about all aspects of the gem and jewelry trade. I could write a dozen novels based on the technical and historical information she's collected on precious stones and metal. Maybe I will!

Thanks also to my son Adam, a hard-working computer animation student, for taking the time (and having the patience) to explain today's gaming subculture and how the Deep Web works. I doubt I'll ever spend much time there, but it's a fascinating world to contemplate.

As always, a shout-out to my straight-shooting beta reader (and author in her own right) Donna Cook;

graphic designer Tara Mayberry; and editor Andrea Robinson. You are all expert polishers, helping me turn my "uncut" stone of a manuscript into what I hope is a gem of a book!

Then there's Mike, always there, making life so much better for me than it would otherwise be, in too many ways to count.

Thank you all.

Chapter One

The Forbidden City
Peking

August 16, 1900

He found the girl cowering in a trunk.

Colonel Jasper de Kalb of the U.S. Army's Fourteenth Light Infantry Regiment was overseeing a sweep of the Palace of Gathering Essence, one of the many exotic buildings within the Forbidden City of Peking. It was rumored to house some of Emperor Guangxu's favorite concubines. The Chinese monarch and other members of the royal household had already fled the city, leaving a deserted complex of nearly ten thousand rooms, each one of which had to be searched for stragglers and potential assassins. So far, the only ones left behind were aging eunuchs too feeble to escape with the others.

Until now.

Having sent his men down the empty corridors to continue their reconnaissance, De Kalb stood in one of the larger rooms—probably used for taking meals or socializing—and heard what amounted to a broken sigh, as if a child were crying but trying not to make a sound. He stopped and listened.

There it was again. Looking around the room, he spied an intricately carved wooden trunk, the kind one might use for linens. He drew his pistol and lifted the lid.

Two small arms shot up in supplication. "Don't shoot, don't shoot!" the girl cried out in Mandarin, then again in heavily accented English. She had bent her small frame in half to fit into the chest. He wondered if perhaps she was an acrobat or a dancer.

"I won't shoot," he answered. She didn't appear dangerous, so he holstered his weapon and helped her out of the box. She was wearing a high-collared blue satin dress with a cloth belt that held an embroidered pouch.

"What are you doing here?" he asked. "Why didn't you escape with the others?"

The girl, who looked to be barely eighteen, eyed him warily as she brushed herself off. She was mesmerizing, with large eyes, sensuous lips and a pale, almost translucent complexion. What would his son Sander think of her?

"I no belong," she explained in English.

"What do you mean? You're one of the emperor's handmaidens, are you not?"

The girl vehemently shook her head. "I work at British legation. Learn to speak English. But Zaitian—Emperor Guangxu—see me there and want me come to palace."

"He wanted to make you one of his concubines?"

"Yes, but I no want! I love another in my village. Zaitian, he no listen. He . . . he . . ." She started to tear up but swallowed in order to continue. "When you come to rescue your people, Zaitian and everybody around him worry about getting away, forget about me."

"So you hid, hoping none of us would notice you."

The girl sent De Kalb an imploring look. "I am hopeful, yes. Then, when you gone, I escape both you and Zaitian."

Inhaling, De Kalb let out a sigh. "Well, I'm afraid we'll have to report your whereabouts along with everyone else we find. I can't have you running around here unprotected. I don't know how long we're going to be here, and my men lack a pristine record when it comes to local women." *To put it mildly.* Truth be told, the way the forces of the Eight Nation Alliance had treated civilians in their march to Peking was reprehensible.

"No! No is necessary." The girl touched the colonel's arm. "I know special way out beyond Shenwu Gate. Secret passage. You never find on your own. I show you and you let me go licky split, yes, please?"

"Is that how the royals escaped so handily?"

Nodding, the girl took his hand. "Come, I show you."

Caught between mistrust and fascination, De Kalb let the strange girl lead him through a nondescript door that opened to an alley. They crossed the narrow walkway to another entrance that led to a hallway seemingly inaccessible from anywhere else. He could hear his men calling to each other across the central courtyard and reasoned that if he needed help, he could shout and they would eventually find him. That such a slip of a girl could cause him trouble seemed absurd, yet...

They traveled quickly through the phantom corridor which was decorated with brightly painted squares roughly three feet by three feet. About three quarters of the way down, the girl stood on tiptoe and pressed a corner of one of the upper squares. He heard a "click" and watched as one of the lower squares opened. De Kalb bent down and peered inside. It was a landing atop a set of stairs that descended into darkness. A box containing a few candle stubs and matches was set on a shelf against the wall.

"Where does this lead?" he asked.

"North to Summer Palace Road," she said. "But I no go there. I turn east to village along the Chaobai River."

De Kalb debated but a moment before deciding to let the girl go. Why should she be caught up in this international mess? She was just a young girl who deserved to go home to her sweetheart. "All right. If you're certain you'll be safe."

She bestowed a shimmering smile on him. "I am

certain." She took a candle from the box, lit it, and started down. After a brief hesitation, she turned and came back to the entrance to stand in front of him.

"Hold please," she said, handing the candle to De Kalb before unwrapping the embroidered pouch from her belt. She then took the candle back and thrust the pouch into his hands. "Zaitian give me these. He call them his prowling tigers. He say they very old and bring power. Bring good luck. But now I no need. You my good luck today."

Out of reflex, DeKalb stuck the small bag in his pocket. It did not interest him, but she did. "What is your name?" he asked.

"Chen Li Bao. But tell no one." She glanced over his shoulder and her eyes grew wide; then, without another word, she scurried back down the stairs. In a moment she was gone, as if she'd never existed. Silence reigned.

Yes, it was against protocol, but De Kalb decided to wait long enough to give Miss Chen the time she needed to exit the tunnel. After twenty minutes or so he would assign several of his most trustworthy men to investigate the passage and secure it. He turned to retrace his steps and saw at the end of the passage that an old man was watching him. The wizened stranger wore a traditional black tunic and pants, his gray hair straggling down his back. His face was stretched thin over sharp cheekbones and his teeth were crooked with age or perhaps neglect. But his eyes were something else entirely, clear and insightful.

De Kalb calmly placed his hand on his pistol. "Castrato?" he asked.

The old man seemed to know the term and nodded. Then he spoke in what De Kalb recognized as a Manchu dialect. "I was a man once, but no longer. Just as you have the power now, but not for long."

De Kalb stared at the eunuch but didn't reply; it was better to feign ignorance. "I don't understand you," he said.

The servant pointed to the colonel's pocket and spoke in perfect English. "You took a great treasure from the girl."

De Kalb frowned at him. "I asked for nothing. It was a gift."

"A gift." The man nodded. "A gift worth killing for."

De Kalb drew his gun and pointed it calmly at the man. "Well, not today. Today you must accept the fact that your emperor has run away to leave you here as our prisoner." He gestured for the eunuch to precede him back to the main courtyard of the palace. The benevolence he'd felt toward the young girl had dissipated completely. Now De Kalb was on high alert. This old sycophant bore watching, as did the others. He'd be glad when they left this heathen place. They had achieved their mission; they'd rescued the foreign legations and the Christians under siege from the Qing government and its crazy Boxer fanatics. Now it was time to go home. He missed Padma, and he missed his son. This city, forbidden no longer, remained rife with treachery.

The Grove Artists' Retreat
North of San Francisco
February 1906

Sander de Kalb wasn't sure what woke him. A thought, perhaps. A worry. He'd set up a meeting to discuss a major art show for his work and there were still so many details to iron out. Wrapping a silk robe around his naked form, he left his lover sleeping peacefully and padded into the small front parlor of the cottage. He lit a lamp and noticed the time. Three a.m. After pouring himself a sherry, he sat in his favorite chair and once more read the letter that had accompanied the small package delivered that day.

Dearest son, his father wrote, *I hope this letter finds you well. Your mother sends her love and of course asks the perennial question, "When will we see you again?" I find myself wondering the same thing. An entire continent lies between us, which is much too great a distance, and we are living in the same country! I now know how you and my beloved Padma must have felt when I was off fighting in such faraway lands.*

Between military deployments, my life with the two of you was always circumscribed by the next set of orders; now that I have retired, it is difficult to find the structure I have grown used to. But I am working on it.

To that end, I have embarked on a campaign to organize my study. In a drawer I found a memento of my assignment in Peking six years ago. During that operation I met a young woman who left a lasting impression upon me. Indeed, at the time I mused that you might find her fascinating as well. I helped her to exit the city and out of gratitude she gave me the enclosed. Because of the woman's occupation (a concubine), your dear mother would have nothing to do with the gift. Thus, I send it to you in the hope that since the predicament that took you from us is several years in the past, you might meet someone you find worthy and give the baubles to her. I know little about them, only that they were a love token from the emperor, are quite old, and supposedly bring the owner good luck; may they exceed those expectations with you, dear boy.

Your mother and I miss you very much and hope that someday you will return to us, proud to walk the streets of New York and carry on the de Kalb name like your half-brother before you. Until then, I remain your proud and loving father,

Jasper

"Predicament," the artist muttered. He took the pair of earrings out of the box. They were perfect renditions of crouching tigers. Made of milky white stone, the animals' eyes consisted of small diamonds that glinted faintly in the low light. Sander held them up and let them dangle. They were quite unusual, as if the cats considered him prey and were planning to pounce.

"What do you have there?" came a deep, drowsy

voice. Roger, Sandy's lover, stood in the doorway, all glorious six feet two of him, his wide, muscled chest bare, his light blond hair mussed. Sander felt a stirring in his groin, which was common around his partner. He felt sheer joy at the "predicament" his father referred to that had led to his current circumstances; his only regret was that his parents would probably never consider moving across the country to be near him in San Francisco. The Golden City was simply too exotic, even for a man who had chosen a Brahmin from India as his second wife.

Sander held up the stone earrings. "A little something I'm supposed to give to the love of my life. They belonged to a king, and now they're mine."

"Well, I'm afraid they're not my style, but you are every bit a king to me. Come back to bed, darling."

Sander smiled faintly and rose from his chair, putting the tigers back in their square little cage. No, they weren't meant for Roger, but Sander knew someone else who could wear them in style. At The Grove's next life drawing class, it was his turn to pose Mandy Culpepper with whatever props he chose; his dear young friend would look quite striking wearing the small white tigers and nothing else.

Chapter Two

Atherton, California

Present Day

"Which one looks better, the bloodstone or the maw-sit-sit?"

Regina Firestone held up two of her most recent "Fire Stone" creations—dramatic multi-tiered necklaces designed to invoke envy on the part of any style-conscious woman who saw them. Her cousin and close friend Ava Lawrence sat on the bed rendering judgment. A willowy brunette who could have been a model if she'd put her mind to it, Ava was Reggie's trusted source when it came to fashion advice.

"Both are magnificent," Ava said after a moment. "I love the way you aligned the rows of bloodstones to suggest a lava flow. But the maw-sit-sit goes with your hair and eyes better. It reminds me of imperial jade, but with a naughty streak—kind of like you." She smiled, but Reggie was unconvinced.

"Honestly, if I didn't have to present the award this year, I'd much rather be home watching Netflix with Mr. Big."

Ava absently scratched the ear of the infatuated male just mentioned, a rotund, morose-looking basset hound. She addressed the dog. "Your beloved Reggie's so distraught, she has to get all dressed up to crown the next Gem Designer of the Year because she won it hands down last time. *Quelle horreur*!"

Reggie quirked her lips. Ava did have a point. It was petty to grouse about attending the biggest statewide event in her profession. Lapidaries and jewelry designers needed to kick up their heels now and again, didn't they?

She once more held the intricate stone-and-silver necklace just above her cleavage, where she knew it would sit, once she put on her standard little black dress. It really was a lovely piece, and experience told her that someone at the gala would purchase it on the spot despite its multi-thousand-dollar price tag. Ironically, even though she made her living creating jewelry for wealthy men and women, she herself much preferred biking shorts or just chilling in her sweats. It was unusual for her to wear more than small silver hoops and a St. Brigid's cross.

Ava's cell phone chimed to the tune of "The Music of the Night." She glanced at Reggie as she answered; all lightness had left her face. "All right. Of course," she murmured before hanging up. "Austin has to work late again and can't pick up Nia from the sitter," she said, gathering her garment bag and tote. "Which means I have to bail on going with you tonight." She sent Reggie a familiar look of disappointment. "I'm so sorry."

Reggie sat next to her friend and took her hand. "That's no problem, but here's the important thing. It's all going to work out." She noticed the tears starting to form in Ava's eyes. "Listen, you have the legal right to separate from your husband and take your little girl with you. Your plan is a good one. You can do this."

Tomorrow, Reggie was moving to The Grove Center for American Art on the Marin coast for several weeks to help with the grand re-opening of the retreat. She'd been asked by the owners to help put together a major exhibit featuring her grandmother, Amanda Firestone, who had lived, worked, and modeled there at the turn of the twentieth century. A primary element of the exhibit would be the rarely-seen collection of gems owned by the Bay Area matriarch—stones that had resided in bank vaults for the past three decades.

The timing of the Center's re-opening was perfect, enabling Ava and Nia to house-sit Reggie's cottage while Ava initiated divorce proceedings. Uncle Toby, who owned the estate where the cottage was located, lived in the main house nearby and was very protective of all the Firestone progeny. Ava could feel safe here; now all she had to do was work up the courage to leave her philandering prick of a spouse.

Mr. Big sidled up to Reggie and she scratched his fat

belly. "And Biggie here will be overjoyed to have extra female companionship. He may belong to Uncle Toby, but we all know he loves the ladies best."

Ava sent Reggie a grateful smile as she got up to leave. "You're going to knock 'em dead tonight, whichever piece you wear. You're dazzling when you want to be; even Austin says so."

Reggie rolled her eyes. "I suppose I should be flattered, but somehow . . . hey, give little Nia a great big squeeze, will you?"

"Only if I get one first." Ava wrapped her arms around Reggie. "I'm going to miss you," she whispered.

"I'll be back and forth, and I'm only a text away. Remember: You. Can. Do. This."

As Reggie finished dressing, she thought of the many twists and turns that happen in a person's life. Ava thought she'd met Prince Charming when Austin had set his sights on her, but it hadn't taken longer than her cousin's pregnancy for the dashing venture capitalist to start wandering.

And Reggie's own story wasn't much rosier. A year ago, she was engaged to an ambitious gallery owner named Curtis. Plugged into the Bay Area art scene and confident in any social setting, he'd seemed like the perfect counterpart for someone who pretty much stuck to home when she wasn't traveling for work. Sure, she'd had some misgivings about him, and maybe ignored a warning sign or two, like the time he spent nearly three thousand dollars renting a yacht for a dinner cruise to impress a half-dozen art collectors, then borrowed money from her to pay the bill. ("It's an investment, *kära*," he'd told her, using the Swedish nickname for "sweetie.") Back then, she'd told herself it was a small price to pay for furthering her future partner's career.

Thankfully, she'd learned the truth about Curtis before signing on any dotted lines. The Firestone name, shining brightly in society's firmament, attracted all sorts of insects, and her ex-fiancé was one of them. She'd had no clue about his motives until one of her other cousins, a high-level banker, discovered that Curtis had been discussing a deal with an investment firm based on his imminent connection to the family's millions. She'd been devastated. If she couldn't see through Curtis, how would she be able to trust anyone else? Much better to be on her own than stuck in the mire of a failed relationship. Still, she would have liked having a little girl like Nia. Maybe that would have made all the heartache worth it.

But maybe not.

The well-heeled and barely tolerated gem collector Milton Collier cornered Reggie after the award ceremony. "I hear your mysterious gem collection is finally going to see the light of day. About time," he said, taking a long pull from his scotch. In his late forties, Collier was a dot.com millionaire several times over and loved flaunting his financial heft. "Word is you've got some natural triple A emeralds, I-F diamonds, and better yet, some rare jade. I'd like to look at what's in there in case you feel like unloading a piece or two at some point."

This is the downside of going solo. Reggie tried not to let her annoyance show. "First off, it's not my collection, Mr. Collier; the Amanda Firestone Foundation owns it and I'm just the caretaker. Secondly, none of the pieces are for sale. You'll just have to view the exhibit when The Grove Center opens along with everybody else."

Collier pasted on a jovial smile, but his eyes narrowed. "You never know," he said. "Even the best of us get in tight situations now and again." He gave her an appreciative once over. "Like that dress of yours."

Reggie returned his look with a steely-eyed version of her own. "Funny, I had similar thoughts about that jacket you're wearing. If I were tactless, I'd tell you you've been hitting the appetizer circuit a few too many times. But of course, that would be gauche." She ignored his glare as she added, "If you'll excuse me."

Five more minutes and I'm out of here. Mr. Big, here I come. Moments later, as she predicted, an art patron put in a claim for the maw-sit-sit necklace.

"I'll have a check for five thousand deposited into your account tomorrow," Mrs. Abner Wallace said blithely, knowing Reggie wouldn't have charged quite that much. She tapped the piece lightly. "Just send it by courier when you can bear to part with it. I will say, Miss Firestone, you do know your way around gemstones."

"Thank you, Mrs. Wallace; I'll be sure to get it to you right away. I'd give it to you now, in fact, but then I'd feel naked."

Mrs. Wallace tittered at Reggie's lame joke. "Well, I'm sure there are many here tonight who'd be just fine with that. Next week will be soon enough."

Finally extricating herself from the event, Reggie drove back to the cottage and changed into her workout clothes while she finished packing for her stint at The Grove. Mr. Big watched her every move.

"Yeah, I know you're going to miss me, but you'll have Ava and Nia, so that's not so bad, is it, boy?" She scratched behind one of Biggie's enormous ears. He still looked unhappy—but then, wasn't that the sign of a true basset hound?

Her cell phone chirped, and Reggie noticed a text from her Uncle Allen. Strange; he must be a mind reader.

Because of her training in gemology, years ago the family had put Reggie in charge of the jewelry collection. She'd been thrilled with the responsibility, never tiring of spending time with her beloved grandmother's "baubles." However, two signatures were always needed for the box to be opened at the Bank of America's main vault in downtown San Francisco. For as long as Regina could remember, either Uncle Allen or Aunt Patricia had been present when Reggie wanted to visit the vault. Earlier in the evening she'd thought to confirm with her uncle, who two weeks earlier had volunteered to go with her to the bank. The text read:

Know u were planning on viewing the collection before Brinks sent it up to The Grove, but my schedule got hectic, so I thought I'd save u the trouble and get it done. All is well. It will arrive by eleven tomorrow morning. Dr. Wolff has the paperwork and will secure box when it arrives. So, u can thank me for more sleep and no need to fight the city. Love, Uncle Allen

"Huh," Reggie muttered. On the one hand, she was glad not to have to "fight the city," as he put it. San Francisco was indeed a pain in the ass to maneuver in and she often thanked her lucky stars that she lived in a much more resident-friendly town. But she'd been looking forward to seeing the gems before they left. They'd been under her care for so long that, weirdly, she considered them like children—she wanted to make sure they were safe before starting their journey. Logic told her they were, under Brinks' care, much more secure than she could ever make them. Nevertheless . . .

I wasn't until two in the morning that it dawned on her what was odd about the text: the vault teller required two signatures, but Uncle Allen and Aunt Patricia had been separated for the past two years.

Chapter Three

Reggie rose early the next morning and immediately texted her uncle about who had co-signed the gems out of the vault. When he responded, late in the morning, it was to say, simply, that "Because of Brinks there was no problem."

Okay, she could buy that, which was a good thing because her "To Do" list was long. After preparing the cottage for her cousins who'd be arriving the following week, she had to finish some tricky soldering on two commissioned jewelry pieces. She also took Mr. Big on an extended stroll around the estate before reluctantly dropping him off with his rightful owner. The hefty hound gave her a look filled with reproach.

"He's going to miss you terribly," Uncle Toby told her. "I'm a poor substitute, even for a day."

"Ava and Nia will love him to pieces," Reggie said, "and then you and I will both be in the doghouse."

She left Atherton just after lunch, early enough to

reach The Grove in time to greet the Brinks armored car when it delivered the gems by four p.m. The drive took her through San Francisco proper (an hour-long nightmare even during midday); over the Golden Gate Bridge; and through much of western Marin County before she reached the town of Little Eden that lay just down the hill from the art complex. The overcast sky that normally dissipated north of San Francisco had stuck around, but the threat of rain in no way dampened Reggie's excitement. She had lobbied for years to have her grandmother's full story be told; now it was finally going to happen.

This really is a tiny slice of heaven, she mused as she drove through the town. Many of Little Eden's businesses had clever biblical names such as the Manna Market and Dante's Inferno, a bar. The setting itself was outstanding, too, set along Creation Bay with Redwoods and the Pacific Ocean rounding out the topography. An idea ran through her head. *I could be inspired here.*

Dr. Ethan Wolff, a professor emeritus in art history from Stanford University, met Reggie at the Craftsman-style mansion called the "Great House," the retreat founders' original home. Ethan was the grandson of August and Amelia Wolff, and it had been his lifelong dream to re-open the center where he'd spent much of his early childhood.

Now in his eighties, he was surprisingly energetic given his recent brush with death. Apparently, an unbalanced teen working on the renovation crew had fixated on Dr. Wolff's granddaughter Jenna and tried to destroy the family before drowning in his attempt to escape the authorities. Fortunately, the retreat was still on track to re-open in the fall.

The professor ushered her into the library where they settled into comfortable chairs. "I'm sorry Jenna and Brit aren't here to greet you, but they learned of an opportunity to purchase some furniture they felt would work perfectly in the Study Center and said they had to jump on it. I have a feeling they were eyeing some pieces for their own apartment on the upper floor here as well. But no matter. I told them I would get you acclimated to our little retreat."

Ethan beamed in the telling; it was plain he loved having his granddaughter and her intended nearby. Brit Maguire was another descendant of the founders and the architect of the restoration through his firm, Vintage Maguire. He and Jenna had known each other years before but rekindled their relationship during all the chaos just past.

"I'm glad you were available, professor. After all, who knows this place better than you?"

"I can't fault your logic," he said, "nor can I overstate how excited we are to present the full story of your wonderful grandmother. As a little boy I knew her as the author of my favorite book, *Westwind Farm*." He gestured to the walls lined with books. "I think we still have a copy or two here someplace. Oh, how I worshipped her! She was an indelible part of this institution from the beginning."

"I know! Which is why I've always found it aggravating that my family hasn't wanted to share that part of my grandmother's life—especially the time she spent here *before* she became a Firestone. I'm convinced those years made my grandfather fall in love with her; without them, she might never have become a Firestone at all." Reggie sent the professor an impish grin. "Of course, having read some of her diaries, I'm not sure any of us will ever be able to capture the complete Mandy Culpepper Firestone."

Ethan chuckled. "You are right about that. But we will endeavor to honor her as best we can." The good professor cleared his throat. "I ... understand you have talked to our colleague Walker Banks about possibly modeling ..."

Reggie tapped the arm of her chair in irritation. "Ugh. That man. Your colleague is a stick in the mud if ever there was one. We were discussing the flow of the exhibit and when I simply floated the idea of modeling the gems as my grandmother had, he immediately flew off the handle. He—"

"He said you were intending to model them nude. I think the idea rather set him back." The professor was smiling now.

Reggie scrunched her face. "I wasn't even serious about it, but he was so dead set against it that I'm afraid I dug in my heels. If grandmama didn't find it beyond the pale, why should we, more than a century later? Shouldn't we be that much more enlightened?"

"You do have a point. However, I might argue that a near unanimity of opinion exists among the male population when it comes to females they ..." He paused, shook his head slightly. "Well, what do I know, anyway? Perhaps Walker will have softened his stance by the next time you see him."

"Honestly, I don't see why he needs to have much to say about it at all. He's not the museum curator, or even an art historian."

"No, but he is part of the family and does own a significant percentage of this enterprise, which I'm afraid does give him some clout. Besides, he's an acclaimed photographer in his own right; like you, he is an artist of the first order. Perhaps if you two kibitz a bit more on the subject, you might come to a meeting of the minds." The professor rose and took her arm, more to steady himself than to support her. "Now, let me show you where you'll be working before the stars of the show arrive."

They walked from the Great House to the museum building, where Ethan entered an office equipped with a desk and expansive work table. One of the walls held a large whiteboard while two others provided ample space to pin up diagrams, prototypes, and photographs. He pointed to some sketches already posted. "Jenna took the inventory you sent her and worked up some display options based on journal entries and photographs we already possess. Your doubts notwithstanding, I think Walker will be invaluable in helping to shape the look of the exhibit."

"We'll see," Reggie muttered.

Ethan chuckled and once more took her arm. "And

now let's visit your collection's new home." He walked halfway down the hall and opened a door marked "storage."

They're storing a multi-million-dollar gem collection in a closet? Reggie couldn't hide her shock, but it produced only a benign smile on the part of the professor.

"Patience," he said, beckoning her. They entered a small anteroom and Ethan placed his gnarled hands on a flat screen encased in a table near a second door.

"Welcome Dr. Wolff," came the pleasant sound of a woman's voice.

"Establishing new associate. Grove 496," he said.

"Certainly," the voice answered. "Go right ahead."

Ethan turned to Reggie. "Place your hands on the screen like I did, and say your name, slowly and clearly."

"Biometrics, huh?" Reggie glanced at the octogenarian and grinned.

"State of the art, my dear."

Reggie did as she was told and was soon logged in as an acceptable entrant to the real storage room beyond. The facility inside was in fact a fortress, housing several million dollars' worth of artwork created by the retreat's residents during the first half of the twentieth century.

For decades, fledgling artists—many of whom went on to become icons of the art world—spent a year at The Grove, working in their chosen medium completely free of charge. At the end of their stay they were obliged to donate a work of which they were especially proud. Over the years, those donations formed a wide-ranging collection representing not only the era in which they were created, but heralding art trends and movements to come. At The New Grove Center, the historical pieces would be presented in rotating exhibits showcasing their contribution to the ongoing history of American art. In addition, a new generation of artists—painters, sculptors, textile artists, photographers, even lapidaries— would have the same opportunity to add their chapters to the story.

Reggie took in the rows upon rows of canvasses, sculptures, and other pieces. The spirit of creativity flowing in the room set her own imagination humming. She felt at home, even energized here. "This is incredible. A personal guide to half a century of modern American art, just waiting to come to life."

Once again, the old historian beamed. "You understand precisely." He walked over to a section of the storage area that held a large freestanding safe and a work table equipped with several portable light sources. "This facility is beyond secure, but to set your mind at rest, I had a safe installed. It was recommended by Tiffany's, so I assume it must be tamper-proof." He handed her a piece of paper. "You may change the code to whatever you like; I thought that while the collection is here, you could—"

At that moment Ethan's cell phone beeped. He pulled it out of his shirt pocket, put on his glasses, and checked the screen.

"Looks like the treasure has arrived," he said.

The small rosewood chest, for all it contained, was simple yet elegant. Roughly seventeen inches wide and twelve inches tall, it had been created by Erhard and Sohne in 1907 and inlaid with a brass scene of trees and animals. Will Firestone had no doubt chosen that motif because of Mandy's affinity for such things.

It was easily carried in by one of the Brinks guards, who carefully set it down on a table in the museum foyer before standing to the side with his partner (both of them armed) while Reggie checked to see that all was in order. She broke the banker's seal on the chest and opened the door to her grandmother's past.

There was no need to look at the manifest because she knew the contents by heart. The jewelry Mandy wore as an artist's model before she married—the citrine, the gold and crystal collar with headpiece, the perfect white jade earrings, and others—each had its own handmade red velvet pouch. There too were the nine priceless pieces Will had given his wife upon the birth of each child, also in red velvet. Every item had its own small, handwritten note describing when, where, and why Mandy had received such a special gift. Her expressions of gratitude were always heartfelt; time and wealth hadn't eroded her humility and natural grace.

The box even contained the small articles Reggie had stored there years ago: a loupe, a pair of tweezers, and a jeweler's polishing cloth. Nothing at all had been disturbed.

Reggie nodded to Ethan, who sat nearby, then looked back at the guards. "All present and accounted for," she said. "Thank you for taking good care of my grandmother's things."

Papers were signed, the guards departed, and both Reggie and Ethan returned to the security of the inner storage area. "Rest assured, we will know if anything in here has been tampered with," he said. "Why don't you key in your new code now and then I can show you to your lodgings. You'll then be free to return here at any time to work with the collection."

"Sounds like a marvelous plan," Reggie said.

After setting the safe code to Mr. Big's birthday and sending the information to Ava, Reggie deleted her own text and settled into her cottage near the Great House, one of the dozen or so that had been designed to allow an artist of any medium to create without distraction. Each housed a bedroom, a spacious light-filled front parlor, and an efficient kitchen and bath.

By the time she'd unpacked and walked over to have a drink with Ethan, Jenna Bergstrom and Brit Maguire had returned. In her late twenties, Jenna was tall, blond, and fit-looking; Brit, though darker, matched her. He was broad-shouldered with a physique more commonly seen in a construction worker than an architect. It was easy to see how much they were into each other, but thankfully they didn't overdo it on the PDA. *Nothing like watching two people wildly express their love when you aren't in a relationship.*

A storm was coming in, Brit said; they'd brought take-and-bake pizza so no one would need to hoof it down the hill. "Lindy's is known for their incredible pizza dough and they just started selling toppings," he explained. "You can't beat it."

"And the rest of their baked goods are to die for, too," Jenna added. "A word to the wise: if you want to keep your figure, step away from the cinnamon buns. They're legendary."

"Uh oh, one of my favorites." Reggie grinned, feeling at ease with them immediately.

With the rain now falling, the library of the Great House was a cozy place to congregate after dinner. Two bottles of cabernet later, Reggie had to admit it was one of the most enjoyable evenings she'd spent in quite a while. The only missing ingredient was Mr. Big. When the talk turned to the gem exhibit, she let Jenna know she was going to check out the display prototypes first thing in the morning.

Jenna shrugged and took a sip of her wine. "No worries. They're just a first pass; we've got some time yet. Besides, Walker's not due back for a few days, so it can wait."

Ethan must have noticed Reggie's pained expression. "Regina isn't exactly thrilled with Walker's, shall we say, *style*," he offered. "I believe she thinks he might be a bit autocratic."

Jenna laughed. "Yes, I thought that too at first, but

he's actually a very reasonable guy. Low-key. Doesn't throw his weight around. And so talented. Really. I still can't get over the fact that he's colorblind like you are, Da. The landscapes he captures in black and white rival Ansel Adams, and I don't say that lightly."

"If he can't distinguish colors, then how on earth will he be able to capture the gems in the exhibit?" Reggie said.

"You wait and see," Ethan said. "He compensates extremely well."

Brit nodded. "Yeah, I've got to admit, his use of light is truly amazing."

Reggie held her hands up in good-natured surrender. "All right. All right. I see I am outnumbered and outflanked. I will postpone my judgment then, until—"

At that moment the lights went out, throwing the room into almost pitch-black darkness. Reggie's heart sped up, her first thought being, *A security system's only as good as its power source, right?*

Even though he couldn't see her face, Ethan seemed to follow her train of thought, saying, "It's all right. We have auxiliary power."

Several minutes later the power went back on. Brit and Ethan's cell phones immediately started beeping loudly.

"I'll go," Brit said.

Reggie's pulse still hadn't settled down. "Go where?"

"Just to check the storage facility," Jenna said. "The

system lets us know when there's a change back to full power, mainly so we can set our minds at rest."

"That's a very intuitive system," Reggie said. "I'm going with you."

Brit chuckled and went to grab his coat. "Another worrywart like you, Jenna." He touched Jenna's cheek lightly. "You want to drive Ethan home? I'll take Reggie with me."

"Sure. You ready, Da?" At his nod, she held out his coat before putting hers on.

The rain had lightened considerably by the time Brit and Reggie reached the storage room. They both signed in and while Brit checked the perimeter, Reggie went straight to the safe and opened it. The box was there, of course, just as she had left it. She couldn't help it, though—she had to see the contents once again.

Brit came over to her. "All there?"

"Look, I know I'm being paranoid, but I think I'll go over the collection one more time. You don't have to stay; I know the way out."

"Nope, that would completely break Jenna's code of chivalry and I wouldn't hear the end of it. Tell you what; I have some measuring to do for some of the larger canvasses; I'll get that done now and when you're ready to go, I'll escort you to your cottage. It's pretty dark up here at night, and it'll take you a while to get used to it. Sound good? You'd be doing me a favor. I sleep better when I'm on Jenna's good side."

Reggie caught Brit's suppressed grin and sent him a

smirk of her own. "Sure. I'm glad to help. It shouldn't take me too long."

She sat down with the box in front of her and turned on the lights Ethan had thoughtfully provided, one of which was equipped with a magnifier. Out of habit, she took out her jeweler's cloth and began to polish each piece after examining it for signs of wear.

She smiled when she came to the tiger earrings. Removing them from their soft pouch, she held them up to the light. They were her favorites. White and delicate, they never failed to kindle fond memories of her grandmama; Mandy had often let her youngest grandchild play with the stone jungle cats, dangling them as if they were prowling through the grass. Reggie remembered the way their diamond eyes had glittered; she'd asked her grandmother once if the tigers could see them, and Mandy had replied, "Yes, they are looking after all of us."

Those sparkling eyes had inspired Reggie to learn about the other gems in the collection, eventually leading her to her chosen profession. She'd even used many of her grandmother's pieces as a springboard for her own designs, always trying to capture the wonder she'd felt as a child. In the case of the tigers, it was all about the eyes.

The eyes.

Reggie paused. Looked closer. Placed the earrings under the magnifier and found it wasn't strong enough. Pulled her own 10 x loupe from the box and examined first one tiger and then the other.

"It can't be," she muttered.

But it was. The diamond eyes of the jade tigers were brighter, sharper, with more shimmer than she had ever seen before.

Then she examined the bodies, turning each tiger over and using the loupe against the belly. There had been a pale streak of green before, and now there was none.

There was only one explanation.

These were not her grandmother's earrings.

Chapter Four

**Zion National Park
Utah**

Damn, I may not make it out of here. Walker Banks had climbed almost to the top of the narrow crevice, his muscular arms straining harshly in the fading light. His camera pack was dangerously close to getting wedged between the rock walls, and the final stretch was the most difficult by far. He'd nearly slipped on the last hold, a crimp that barely accommodated his large fingertips. Sweat had begun to melt away his hand chalk, but he was in no position to replace it. He flagged his right leg to regain his balance before using momentum to reach up to the next hold with his left arm fully extended. Adrenalin was pumping through him, but he knew that wouldn't last long. He grunted with the effort. *Got it.*

Smearing the rock with the ball of his foot, he

propelled himself upward and finally hoisted himself over the edge. He waited a moment to catch his breath, then reached for his camera one more time.

Click. Click. Click. He caught the last of the golden light as it fell into the slot canyon from above. *Gorgeous. Possibly deadly, but still gorgeous.*

Walker was in Zion on assignment for the magazine *Planet Magnifica*, catching shots of the park's world-famous sandstone striations. Earlier in the afternoon he'd followed the Virgin River along the Narrows; there was so much beauty to capture that time had slipped away before he realized it would be much faster to boulder one of the slots than retrace his steps along the river. No crash pads, no spotters, no one who'd know just what the hell had happened to him if anything had gone wrong. It was an incredibly stupid thing to do, so why had he done it?

He knew why.

Heights didn't bother him. Never had. But tight spaces? Those caused him to shudder. The phobia stemmed from accidentally locking himself in a closet when he was a kid. Now, enclosed areas triggered a sense of panic and the automatic response to Get. Out. *Now.*

As the main canyon narrowed, anxiety had begun to overtake him and because he could climb, he sought the nearest form of escape. He hadn't considered the consequences until it was too late to change course.

Shadows began to lengthen, and he rubbed the back of his neck, sore from looking up so long. Sweat soaked his muscle shirt and cargo pants. In the twilight, the air had cooled considerably.

With a final backward glance, he started in the direction of his rental jeep, more than ready to head back to civilization. By the time he reached his parking spot, it was full-on dark; he tossed his gear in the back and sat a moment to regroup before starting the engine.

It had been a grueling couple of weeks—hot, dry, dusty, and lonely. And yes, capturing the stark beauty of these spectacular desert formations was worth every uncomfortable moment.

As both a venture capitalist and a professional photographer, he'd traveled the globe at all levels of comfort, from cattle cars to the Orient Express. He'd been in dicey situations many times, and almost took up religion as a result of a few of them. He figured his memoirs alone could keep "Nat Geo" in production for several seasons.

But now, a few years shy of forty, he was about to embark on his most treacherous adventure yet: full-time fatherhood.

He was sixteen years behind schedule.

His son, Axel, was the product of an intense but short-lived fling with a woman several years his senior. (At the time, Walker knew nothing about biological clocks.) Although they never married, Walker upheld his end financially, and for the past ten years he'd treated the role of sometime-father as a highlight reel: a week rafting Idaho's River of No Return; ten days hiking the Alps; an expedition to Brazil's Rio Negro.

Walker used exotic locales to co-parent so that by now his son no doubt thought of him more as a tour guide than anything else.

All of that was about to change. Caroline had finally achieved her goal: marriage to a wealthy, international businessman. They'd already had twin girls and were set to move to Brussels. The odd kid out, Axel had dug in his heels and refused to leave American soil.

Enter Walker, the "legal" dad.

"You'll only have to put up with him until he goes back to boarding school," Caroline told him. "Axel really needs a strong male influence, and Jean Paul's just not up to it. He's got his hands full with us girls as it is."

Maybe it's fate, Walker thought. For the first time in many years, he'd made plans to stay in one place, The New Grove Center for American Art, north of San Francisco on the Marin coast. When the center got pummeled by a financial tsunami, Walker had stepped in as an angel investor to help the owner, his distant cousin Ethan Wolff. Originally just a tax write-off, Walker had come to think of The Grove as a challenge he could sink his teeth into.

Why not create an organization that actually turned a profit from a public-private partnership? Why not provide a benefit to the community and be self-sustaining at the same time? That intrigued the capitalist inside him, but what also appealed was The Center's focus on all aspects of American art. Creating something for others to interpret and appreciate separates us from the animals, but being able to create freely, without worrying about paying the bills, was rarely part of the equation. These days, most artists didn't have patrons; they had to get along the best they could, often on a limited budget, or else sell themselves short by going commercial just to make ends meet. The Center's mission was to give juried artists a chance to express themselves fully, with no strings attached, for an entire year.

"Walker, I have a capital idea," Ethan suggested at a recent dinner with his granddaughter Jenna and their mutual cousin Brit. "You don't want to be known as an owner of The Center, but you do want a hand in making it all work. The interest you've taken in putting together the Amanda Firestone exhibit tells me that. But how then to explain your presence? I propose you come and live here at The Grove for the first year. We'll call you—oh, I don't know, how about the "Managing Artist.'"

"How about 'The Big Kahuna,'" Jenna teased.

Walker had chuckled. "I like the sound of that."

"All levity aside," Ethan continued, "I know that the College of Marin would be thrilled to have you teach a class or two in photography, and you could hold some workshops here as well, all the while adding to your own portfolio. And while you're at it, you could analyze the systems in place during our initial year and see how we can improve them moving forward."

"Where would I live?"

"The Great House is huge, and the floor below us is

empty," Brit offered. He'd looked at Jenna, to whom he was all but engaged. "What do you think?"

Jenna grinned. "I think it's a great idea, providing you clean up your mess in the kitchen."

Brit had laughed and kissed her hand playfully. "That's my woman—ever practical."

Thinking back on that conversation, Walker had to admit that moving to The Grove dovetailed perfectly with his new role as father, at least for the short term. He'd asked about adding Axel to the mix and they'd been fine with the idea; in fact, Brit had said they'd figure out a part-time job for the teen if he wanted it. It would be good for Axe to be around creative, positive people who cared about him, and The Grove was certainly a better alternative than the quiet seclusion of Walker's place in northern Idaho.

He'd been driving for ten minutes and reached open space when his cell phone pinged, showing a text from Caroline; he pulled over to read it:

> **Jean Paul has to be in Brussels earlier than we thought, so we're handing Axel over to you a bit sooner. He'll be arriving at SFO at 2 p.m. Tuesday on United Flight 1483. Let me know you got this, and thanks again for taking him. Jean Paul and I really appreciate it.**

Shit. Walker checked his watch. It was a three-hour drive to Vegas, so he'd have to crash somewhere near McCarran International if he wanted to catch the first flight to San Francisco. Then he'd head to The Grove to get settled before driving back the next afternoon to pick up Axel. Best case, that would give him approximately forty-four hours to prepare for full-time parenthood.

Right.

An hour down the road he received another text alert, this one from someone whose message was more unsettling than Caroline's:

This is Regina Firestone. Sorry to bother you, but Professor Wolff felt you ought to know: I discovered that a piece of my grandmother's collection is counterfeit and am almost positive the switch was made recently. Going to verify my analysis with a colleague and investigate any leads from there. Will keep you informed.

Walker's blood began a slow simmer. Ever since they'd met, that woman had pushed all his buttons. If what she said was true, there's no way she should "investigate any leads." Why didn't she just go to the police? Bad enough she wanted to model the gems in the nude like her grandmother had; now she was turning detective? Grim-faced, he rapidly typed out a reply.

After you have checked your hunch, do not, repeat DO NOT start investigating on your own! I will meet you tomorrow to discuss; will let you know when and where as soon as I book the flight.

It didn't take long before his phone pinged again, but Walker ignored Regina's response. Instead he called his virtual assistant and got the ball rolling on a Vegas airport hotel and a sunrise flight to San Francisco. Maybe he'd make it to Ms. "I Can Do It On My Own" Firestone before she even had time for breakfast. It would serve her right.

When it rains, it pours, he thought with a curse, and headed off into the night.

Chapter Five

V ihaan Chaudry looked like a cyborg with the magnifier attached to one eye. He described precisely what he saw. "The eyes are Tolkowsky brilliants, post 1919. Thirty-three facets on the crown, twenty-four on the pavilion. They didn't even bother to facet the culet, which was much more common pre-twentieth century." Reggie's colleague removed his lens and handed the earrings back to her. One of San Francisco's most esteemed diamond cutters, he was an expert in both historical and modern styles.

"Any way at all to tell who might have cut it?" she asked.

"None, I'm afraid. The cuts are not without flaws, so whoever did it must have been in a hurry, using the style he or she was most comfortable with. They might have even fit the sockets with pre-cut stones, which tells me they felt confident their clients wouldn't be the wiser. Indeed, a lay person would not have been able to tell the difference. It may very well have been an opportunity for a local cutter to make a quick dollar."

Reggie took a moment to absorb her colleague's analysis. Last night, when she'd examined the earrings, she'd been ninety-five percent certain they were fake. She'd immediately alerted the professor and, reluctantly, Walker Banks. On the off chance she was wrong, however, she'd called Vihaan first thing this morning to make an appointment at his North Beach studio for a second opinion. The other step she'd taken was to arrange for an appraisal team from Sotheby's to come to The Grove and examine every other piece in the collection. It was bad enough if one piece was counterfeit; she wouldn't sleep until she knew the rest, at least, were genuine.

Reggie's worst fears about the tigers were now realized, and she dreaded having to bring up the topic with Walker Banks again. Their initial texts about it last night were barely civil and she'd ignored his subsequent messages.

"Thank you for your insight, Vihaan," she said, placing the earrings back in their pouch. "Would it be asking too much for a list of local cutters you feel might be tempted by such an assignment?"

Vihaan frowned. "Far be it from me to look into the hearts of my professional counterparts, but ..." He paused and opened a drawer in his desk. Inside were a slew of business cards, which he shuffled through before picking out three of them. "I am forever receiving cards from fellow cutters who hope I will send them my overflow. Although I would deny ever having said it, these are three I would not recommend, some for quality reasons, and some out of simple mistrust." He handed them over and added, "But it's the jade carver I would be more interested in if I were you. There are far fewer of them in the city, if indeed the replica was made here."

"I know," Reggie said, pocketing the cards. "I'm in the process of figuring out when the switch took place; that will help me determine if it was done locally or not." She turned to leave, but Vihaan touched her arm.

"Be careful, my friend. Whoever's behind this has money to spend, which means the outcome is very important to them."

Reggie sent Vihaan a grim smile. "The outcome— the right outcome—is important to me as well."

As she left Vihaan's inner studio, Reggie tugged on the forest green jacket of her business suit. She didn't like the snugness of it and seldom wore it, but it did lend her stylish gravitas when she had to represent the Fire- stone family. The Bank of America was her next stop. She had an appointment at two, and it wouldn't do to walk into the branch in her usual cargo pants and crop top, especially when she was about to determine if they'd cheated her family out of a million-dollar heirloom.

She was so busy smoothing down her trim skirt that she didn't notice the man waiting in the anteroom until she looked up.

He was the last person she expected or wanted to

see. Guilt, attraction, and irritation swirled through her, as if she were a cheeky teenager caught by a truant officer she thought was cute. *Regina, this is not acceptable*, she told herself.

"I'll make a deal with you," Walker Banks said. "I'll start answering your text messages if you'll start answering mine."

Damn, she looks good. Walker kept his expression neutral as he took in the sight of Regina Firestone dressed in a stylish dark suit and silk blouse that emphasized her perfectly proportioned body. She wore her hair in a respectable-looking chignon that showcased her fine bone structure and wore classic high heels that looked so good on her that they could have been Christian Louboutins but probably weren't. Walker had photographed hundreds of good-looking models in the early days of his career, but few carried their charms as well, or as unconsciously, as Ms. Firestone did.

The expression on her face was something else entirely. "What on earth are you doing here?"

Walker shrugged. "I told you I wanted to connect before you traveled too far down this road, but you didn't return my calls. Fortunately, Ethan was more responsive. He told me you had an appointment here this morning, so I took a cab straight from the airport, hoping I'd catch you. So, what'd you find out?"

He watched her hesitate; clearly, she was weighing the pros and cons of being open with him.

"Look, I'm going to get the full story sooner or later. Right now, I'm running on empty, so let's have something to eat and you can fill me in."

After a moment, Regina reluctantly agreed. "There's a good cafe on Market Street. Have you got any food issues?"

Walker snorted. "If it can be eaten, I've probably eaten it. Yak, muktuk, milt. Although I'd probably pass on the latter. Fish semen's no longer on my bucket list."

With a delicate grimace, Regina agreed. "I tried it in Jakarta—didn't like it, either."

Walker slung his ever-present backpack filled with camera and field equipment over his shoulder, picked up his worn leather duffel, and followed Regina to her car. She drove them to Millie's on Market and they settled in for the chef's renowned stuffed French toast.

As he dug into his meal, Walker caught Regina staring at him. "I know I look like a piece of—well, like something the cat dragged in. I was down to my last shirt, but at least it's clean."

The woman had the grace to look embarrassed—but only slightly. "Sorry. It wasn't that. I'm just wondering why you made this a priority. Surely you have more important things to do. Ethan said you were on assignment, and I know you're involved in the re-opening of The Grove, so …"

"So, your grandmother's collection is an important

part of that opening, and it sounds like something got seriously screwed up."

She bristled like a porcupine rattling its quills. "I believe a crime was committed, yes."

"Tell me what you think happened. It's a pair of earrings, right?" Walker continued to demolish his French toast as he listened.

Regina began by recounting her suspicions about the quality of the light reflected in the tigers' eyes.

"Sounds pretty obscure. Sure that's enough evidence?"

She speared him with her gaze. "In this case, yes. Like you being able to determine the exposure differential between the F16 and F18 stops on your camera. Most lay people wouldn't be able to see the difference. In my case, I think that's what the thieves were counting on."

"But you saw it."

"Yes. What's more, Vihaan knows the styles of diamond cutting and how they've evolved; he could tell right away that the cut was much too modern for the age of the piece."

"What about the carvings themselves? Seems unlikely, but maybe someone simply swapped out the diamonds."

Regina sipped her coffee; she took it with cream, no sugar. "I wish it were that simple, but the more I looked at them, the more I realized the jade was slightly different as well. The originals are carved from what they call 'mutton fat' jade."

"Appetizing," Walker said dryly.

"I know. Sounds gross, but it's actually a good description." She pulled out the earrings to show Walker what she meant. "The originals are carved out of a type of jade thousands of years old from the Hotan River Valley in northwest China. The royals loved it; it was their 'stone of heaven.' I've had our tigers appraised and they're most likely from the early Qing Dynasty, which puts them at mid-sixteen hundreds. It took another century before the deposits were mined out and jadeite imported from Burma became the more common form. I can't tell where this jade came from, but I know these are copies because they lack the pale green belly stripe of the original pair."

"How did your family end up with them?"

Reggie smiled. She obviously had a soft spot for the stone cats. "I guess love is reckless. The tenth emperor gave the tigers as a love token to a new concubine in 1900, but she loved somebody else, and during the Boxer Rebellion, she gave them to an American colonel who helped her escape the palace. Several years later he gave them to his son who was one of the first artists at The Grove, and *he* gave them to my grandmother as a wedding gift."

Walker didn't want to pick a fight, but ..."Did she ever model them?"

Regina's hackles rose again. "Yes, she did, which is a very good reason to get them back in time for the re-opening. I'm hoping I'll be able to track down whoever carved the counterfeit pair, but I have to nail down when the originals were taken first."

"Sounds complicated," he said, finishing his meal. "How do you propose to do it?"

"I have an appointment at two with the manager of the bank where the collection was vaulted. That may shed some light on what happened."

Walker checked his watch and reached for his wallet. "Well, we'd better get going, then." He watched with half a smile as Regina frowned and went for her purse. "No need," he said, signaling for her to keep her money. "I was the one who had to be fed; you were just being courteous."

"Thank you," she said stiffly. "I'll make sure to pay for the next one."

Walker rose and left his usual cash plus generous tip. "It warms my heart you think there might be a 'next one.'"

She gave him a look that said *Don't press your luck.* "Listen, you don't need to be there. "I can drop you—"

"Regina, let's get something straight. I may not be a professional cop or bodyguard, but there is no way in hell I want you traipsing all over the city scaring up counterfeiters and thieves all by yourself. In fact, I think we ought to get the authorities in on this as soon as possible, preferably right after we talk to the guy at the bank."

The woman looked like she was going brain him before she dialed it back. "No! I mean, let's just wait for a bit, at least until we have a few more facts. The Grove has already gone through hell, what with all the sabotage during reconstruction. Let's just ... let's see if we can nail down a bit more before we go that route. Okay?"

She really did have the most arresting eyes, he thought. He'd seen photographs of her grandmother; they could have been twins.

Those eyes were staring at him now, imploring him. What color were they? He shook his head to get clear. "Okay, but not for long. This is not a game for amateurs like us."

"Fair enough."

She waited for him to gather his equipment and was silent as they walked to the car. She seemed to have accepted the fact of his presence, but looks, even lovely ones, could be deceiving.

Randall Cherrington, manager of the Bank of America branch that had held her family's gem collection, looked animated, as if he'd had a drink or two at lunch. He shook Reggie's hand. It felt damp. "Miss Firestone, so nice to see you."

Reggie gave him a perfunctory smile. "Mr. Cherrington." Not knowing exactly how to explain Walker's presence, she went with just his name. "This is my ... colleague, Walker Banks. Walker, this is—"

"Randall Cherrington, at your service. Your holding company is a well-respected investment partner at the corporate level. It's nice to meet the man behind the name. Welcome, sir."

Walker raised an eyebrow to Reggie before shaking Cherrington's hand. *Obviously dressing up doesn't mean diddly if you have enough money,* she thought irritably. *I could have worn my cargos and been totally fine.*

"I was given word that all went well with the transfer," Cherrington said smoothly. "Is there something else I can help you with?"

"Well, Mr. Cherrington, the transfer is what I wanted to talk to you about."

Cherrington frowned; apparently, he wasn't used to service hiccups. "By all means. Let's speak in my office, shall we?"

Ten minutes later, at Reggie's request, Cherrington left to retrieve the sign-in log. For the past several years, during her biannual visits to the vault, Reggie had inspected each jewelry piece carefully and systematically; to her they were treasured heirlooms to be lovingly cared for. The last time she'd signed in, two months ago, all was well. That meant that sometime between then and now, the switch had been made. But how?

"Here you go," Cherrington said, handing her the sheet for the Firestone account. She could feel both his and Walker's eyes on her as she scanned the document. "Is there something wrong?" the manager asked.

My God. There most certainly is. "I don't see Donna's signature." Donna was the bank vault manager —the person who, for as far back as Reggie could remember, had been in charge of signing customers into and out of the vault.

"Uh, no. Donna's been using up some of her vacation for the past six weeks. It was either that or lose it." Cherrington smiled nervously. "You know Donna. It was tough to get her to take some time off, but she had an opportunity she couldn't refuse."

"According to this log, my uncle and I signed in to the vault five weeks ago, two weeks ago, and yesterday."

Cherrington glanced at the sheet. "That seems to be the case, yes."

"There's only one problem. The last time I was here, Donna was working."

The manager took the log again and perused it. "No, I'm afraid Rod Myers was the vault teller. See, there's his signature."

Count to ten. "Yes, I see his signature, Mr. Cherrington. I see my uncle's, and I also see mine. Only that isn't my signature because I wasn't here."

Cherrington looked completely befuddled. He studied the sheet again as if willing a different result. "I think perhaps you're—"

"No, I'm not—"

Walker cut her off. "Um, Mr. Cherrington, is there someplace we can go for a bit of privacy? It might help Ms. Firestone if she checked her appointment book against the sheet."

"Certainly. Feel free to stay where you are. I'll step outside for a few minutes."

Realizing she'd almost aired the family's dirty laundry, Reggie threw Walker a grateful glance before answering the banker. "Thank you. We'll just be a moment."

After Cherrington left, Reggie muttered five words. "I'm going to kill him."

"I can see now why you don't want to take this wide just yet. I assume you're referring to your uncle?"

"Dear old Uncle Allen," she said. "I thought something was strange when he told me he'd handled the paperwork for the transfer. It always takes two signatures and he's been divorced from my aunt for two years." She could feel her pulse ticking up, a sense of outrage building.

"You're sure you're not mistaken about when you were last here."

"Well I certainly wasn't here yesterday. The last time I saw the collection was with my aunt, and Donna signed us in." She pointed to the date on the log-in sheet. "I checked each piece like I always do, and they were fine."

"Is there something else in the vault he could have been checking?"

"No, in that particular account there is only the collection."

Walker scanned the sheet. "So, it looks like your uncle accessed the jewels without you, and three weeks later checked on them again."

"Yes, but why?" What on earth was Uncle Allen up to? He'd always been one of her favorite relatives, a close and respected member of the Firestone clan until his mid-life crisis caused the break-up of his marriage. Had he really changed so much? Was she ready to accuse him of stealing from the family? After so many years, she couldn't believe him capable of such a betrayal, even if he wasn't a Firestone by blood.

She fought the urge to hop on the phone and read her uncle the riot act. But common sense and a dose of trepidation stopped her. Although she'd never admit it, she was somewhat relieved to have Walker around to puzzle it out with her.

"What does your uncle do for a living? I assume 'jewel thief' isn't on his resume."

"He's a real estate broker and he has several rental properties. He's intelligent, but no, I don't think he could pull something like this off. Then again, I haven't seen him much since he and my aunt split up. Maybe he's changed."

"There's only one way to find out. Let's pay your uncle a visit."

"Now?"

"Right now."

Chapter Six

They drove across the Golden Gate Bridge, heading up to Sausalito, where Reggie's uncle had moved after his divorce. "How do you want me to play this?" Walker asked.

Reggie appreciated the question, even if she didn't know quite how to answer it. "I'm not sure. I don't think I gave anything away when I called to say I wanted to stop by. Since he's on my way back to The Grove, it sounded innocent enough."

"But you didn't mention *me*."

"No. I figured that would make him uneasy, especially if he knew your connection to the retreat."

She glanced at Walker before concentrating again on the freeway. Unfortunately, he set her hormones humming: tall and rangy, with the kind of lean muscles a man gets from physical activity besides lifting weights. She caught his profile—strong, with a day's worth of stubble and slightly long, slightly wavy dark hair that was just showing a bit of gray. She was pretty sure he wasn't married—no ring—but wondered if he lived with anyone. *Don't go there.* The electricity she'd felt the first time they'd met had bothered her; to be attracted to someone so pig-headed was *not* a good thing. Assuming he was off limits would make it easier to have sensible discussions about a lot of things, including how they were going to track down her earrings.

"So?" he asked.

"Oh. Sorry. I was ... just had a squirrel moment."

Walker smiled. Even his teeth looked good. "I can be low-key or in his face, whatever you want me to be. It's your call."

"I think ... I think I'll just introduce you as my friend and we'll take it from there."

She took the Monte Mar Drive exit and wound her way up the hill to her uncle's house, a one-bedroom bungalow overlooking the harbor. As they parked, he came out to greet them. Allen was in his mid-fifties, with thinning hair, a slight paunch, and an unfortunate belief that he deserved a much younger, much prettier companion than his wife of thirty years. Aunt Pat had indulged him through one affair but finding out about the second one sent her straight to a lawyer known for securing extremely generous settlements—hence the one-bedroom bungalow. It was the same attorney, in fact, that Reggie had recommended to her cousin Ava.

True to form, he was not alone; his latest girlfriend, or so Reggie assumed, stepped out with him. She looked to be in her early forties, with a spiky lavender haircut and a tan, toned body with zero percent body fat. She wore a tight turquoise dress and chunky jewelry that was part of the "Sante Fe" look.

"Reggie, honey," her uncle gushed. "Glad you dropped by. Oh, and who do we have here? I haven't seen you with anyone since Curtis. Good to see you're moving on." Her uncle looked a bit wary beneath his genial façade.

"It's not what you think, uncle. Walker's just a friend."

Allen shook hands and patted Walker on the shoulder. "I know Reggie can be a bit intimidating—she scares the hell out of me, sometimes   but she's a sweetheart underneath it all."

"Hi, I'm Halona," said Allen's companion. She held out her hand to Walker, wearing no less than four rings. "It means 'Happy Fortune' in Iroquois."

Of course, it does, Reggie thought. *If you knew how much of a fortune Walker had, you'd be very happy indeed.*

"We were just about to have some cocktails on the terrace," her uncle said. "Why don't you join us?"

"Actually, I need to speak to you about something ... something I don't think you want to share with—"

"Is your Aunt Pat asking for an increase again? She send you to plead her case? I told her she was bleeding me dry, but that ass of an attorney she's got—"

Reggie put her hand on her uncle's arm. She was already beginning to feel sorry for him and she hadn't even confronted him yet! "No. It's something else. Something much more important." She held his gaze until it dawned on him that something was seriously wrong. She could see uncertainty and even fear cloud his features, even though he tried to mask them.

He pulled a hundred dollar bill out of his wallet. "Halona, honey, do me a favor, would you, and go have your nails done or something? I've got to talk to my niece here about some family business, and—"

"Oh, don't mind me. I can visit with your friend here." Halona gave Walker a suggestive smile.

Uncle Allen looked at Reggie, who discreetly indicated that Walker was part of the conversation they were about to have. That, she could tell, shook her uncle more than anything. "No, babe, I'm afraid that's not going to work," he said shakily. "You'd best head down the hill now."

Halona sent them all a pretty pout, no doubt annoyed that her happy fortune had dissipated for the day. After she left, the three of them sat on the small back patio. Allen didn't bother offering drinks.

"What's this all about?" he asked.

"That's something you need to tell me," Reggie said. "Walker is working with me on grandmama's jewelry exhibit. It's come to our attention that a piece of that collection was stolen before it reached The Grove."

Uncle Allen looked genuinely perplexed. "That can't be. I checked the inventory. Every piece was accounted for when it was loaded onto the Brinks armored transport. I watched them put it in and lock the doors myself."

"Yes, every item listed on the manifest arrived; it was only after I examined them at The Grove that I noticed the jade earrings were counterfeit."

"That's simply not possible," he said. That—"

Time to cut to the chase. "Uncle Allen, who posed as me when you took the collection out of the vault five weeks ago? Was it Halona?"

"My god, no! I mean, what are you implying?"

Reggie pursed her lips in frustration. "I'm not implying anything. I'm telling you I saw the log-in sheet at the bank. I know that you came in on three occasions when I wasn't present, and I know that someone else forged my signature. Did you wait until Donna went on vacation? Wait, did you *encourage* her to go on vacation? You probably offered her one of your rentals up at Tahoe free of charge, didn't you?"

If one had to photograph the definition of guilt, it would be Uncle Allen's face. He looked completely deflated, as if the congeniality that had served him so well throughout his life had suddenly decided to leave town. Still, he didn't speak.

"Mr. Willis," Walker said calmly, "you didn't just take the gem collection out to check it, did you? You took something from it and returned it three weeks later."

"Yes, I returned it. There were three pieces, actually. I returned all of them. She told me—"

"Who told you?" Reggie asked.

"Her name's Sandi. I met her at the Rickhouse on Kearny. We went out a few times. I even took her to Tahoe. And, well, I got in a tight spot and asked if she knew anybody who could help me. She set me up and said there was nothing to worry about. They'd only hold the pieces until I—"

"Until you what?" Reggie was growing more alarmed as the story unfolded.

"Until you paid a debt?" Walker asked. "A gambling debt?"

Uncle Allen looked at Walker as if in a trance and nodded. "I'd gotten into a bit of a jam in a private poker game and needed quick cash. I had an escrow closing on one of my properties in two weeks, but they wouldn't take my word. So, I ..."

"So you let them have a few pieces as collateral until you could pay them back? Uncle, how could you have done that?!"

Fear was front and center on his face now. "You don't know these people. They're ruthless! And your aunt was asking for so much and the fucking judge was on her side, and, well, I needed it, that's all. I've got expenses, too. Sandi's contact said he'd give me a bridge loan as long as I gave them some easy collateral. My money came through, I paid up, and they returned them, end of story."

"But that's not the end of the story, is it? What on earth did you think they were going to do with something that valuable for three weeks?"

"I don't know. I don't know! All I know is, Sandi

said not to worry, it was just insurance on their part, in case I decided to skip town or something. As if I would. But it all worked out."

Walker leaned forward. "Did this woman Sandi fill in for Regina at the bank?"

"No. Sandi runs a modeling agency downtown—Beauty for Hire, I think she called it—so she sent a girl over that looked a lot like you, Reggie; Her name was Chandra, I remember that, and we went to the bank and, well, she'd been practicing your signature and we made it happen. She picked out three pieces and she brought them back three weeks later."

Reggie was beside herself. "What on earth made you think you could trust these people?"

"I didn't have much choice, now, did I? But I wasn't a complete idiot about it. I told them I'd written a letter telling everything I knew about them and if anything happened to me or to the gems, the authorities would be alerted. Of course, I didn't really write the letter, but they didn't know that."

Reggie met Walker's eyes and it seemed they had a rare meeting of the minds: *This man is beyond gullible.*

"What's the name of the man you borrowed money from?" Walker asked.

"Frank. Frank Somebody. I never caught his last name. Sandi gave me his phone number. He's some kind of loan shark, I guess. I never met him in person; it was all handled by the women."

Reggie felt sick to her stomach. "Besides the earrings, what other pieces were 'borrowed'?"

"I think the citrine and the emerald choker," he said.

"You think or you *know?*" Reggie shot back. Walker sent her a look which probably meant *calm down,* but for God's sake, what a screwed-up mess! She took a deep breath and got up to leave. "I want the names and numbers of everyone you had contact with related to this theft, and you'd better not leave anything out, because I am very close to taking this to the police."

"Oh Jesus, Reggie, honey, don't do that. They're going to think I ratted on them or something. I mean, how bad is it, really? Nobody got hurt. And let's face it, no one will know the difference, and—"

Reggie's eyebrows shot nearly off her head. "But *I* know!" She was milliseconds away from reaming him yet knew in her heart that he wasn't a monster. He had put the family in a terrible situation, but it was out of desperation, not malice or greed. He truly thought that what he'd done was harmless, at least until now. To get the police involved at this point could ruin him. She had to leave before she said something she'd regret. "I don't want to continue this conversation. Just get me the information, *now.*"

"If you don't mind, I'll drive," Walker offered as they left her uncle chugging his highball a few minutes later.

Reggie didn't mind one bit; she couldn't focus on anything other than the lunacy of what her uncle had done. After a few minutes she couldn't help it; she dialed Jenna to see if she had an update on the appraisal.

"Good news on that front," Jenna told her. "The

team from Sotheby's brought in a mess of equipment and started first thing this morning. Every piece seemed to pass muster; it all matched its provenance data."

"Thank you, thank you, thank you," Reggie said, relief flooding through her. She nodded to Walker. "Your cousin Walker is with me and we're headed to The Grove now."

"Good. Tell him the Explorer he ordered was delivered this afternoon. It's a handsome shade of blue." Reggie signed off and looked over at him. "Jenna says your new car looks great."

"Glad to hear it; I didn't have the time to drive mine from Idaho."

Reggie's mind was elsewhere. "I really could kill him, you know."

"Yeah, I don't blame you. It's frustrating as hell when people we care about disappoint us."

"That's putting the best possible light on it. I mean, my uncle's got to have a screw loose if he thinks that whole thing just happened by chance."

Walker nodded. "My guess is they'd been watching him for a while, knowing his connection to your family, and probably to the collection itself."

"And he fell right into it. But there must be some way we can handle this without having it be splashed all over the media. Even if my uncle can avoid legal trouble, the publicity will eviscerate him, and they'll drag my aunt through the muck. Then there's The Grove and..."

"Look, I have a suggestion," Walker said. "Not sure

if you ever met Gabe de la Torre. He's a detective with the Marin County Bureau of Investigations. Since the switch happened in the city, it's not his jurisdiction, but that's good. I think he's still recovering from a wound he got on vacation in Italy, so I can call him, see if he's got some time to help us out—at least point us in the right direction."

It struck Reggie that this was a ploy to get her to turn this mess over to the authorities, which she was not going to do, at least not yet. "It's all right. You don't have bother."

"You're kidding, right?" Walker's tone was anything but playful.

She saw the set of his jaw. "No, I'm not kidding. You were nice to go through the motions with me today. I don't know, maybe you feel responsible because you're part of The Grove now. But there's no reason you should put yourself out any more on account of me and my family's screw-up. I can handle it on my own."

They'd driven through San Rafael by this point and were now on Sir Francis Drake Boulevard heading west. Walker took the first opportunity to pull over and stop the car. He then turned toward Reggie, his hand running along the back of her seat. His eyes burned into hers.

"I hope we don't have to keep having this conversation," he said with unmasked irritation. "You're right about one thing: The Grove doesn't need any more headaches than it's already had, so I think we can agree we want to get to the bottom of this as soon as possible. I can help you do that. If that means asking a few more questions around town, fine. If it means getting the police involved—and I hope it does—so much the better. It is both ridiculous and dangerous for you to handle this by yourself. So, do you want me to call Gabe or not?"

Reggie looked at him and blinked. Much as she detested the idea, Walker was right. She could use all the help she could get. But on her terms, not his. She would lead the expedition, not follow; she owed her family that much.

She sent him her most professional look. "Well, if you think the detective might be able to give us some useful information, then yes, please do."

"All right, I will," he replied tersely, and started the car again. He said nothing more, so she turned and gazed out the window for the rest of the trip. It was now late afternoon. By the time they reached The Grove she'd be ready to grab a bite and then be *more* than ready to snuggle in for the night. Tomorrow she'd start the search for the missing tigers...and it looked like she wouldn't be doing it alone. She let out a gentle sigh that only she could hear.

Chapter Seven

At ten the next morning, Reggie met Walker in front of the Great House, once more dressed in business attire, assuming they'd drive into Little Eden together for the meeting he'd set up with Detective de la Torre. Instead, Walker announced with an air of apology that he needed to drive separately. "I've got some errands to run."

Annoyed with herself for feeling let down, Reggie cloaked her disappointment with a "Sure, no problem. I'd want to drive too if I had a brand spankin' new car." He sent her a crooked smile and they drove separately down the hill.

Reggie's spirits revived as she and Walker entered the Havenwood Inn. Originally a turn-of-the-twentieth-century, Queen Anne-style home, it had been lovingly renovated and turned into a small hotel and Italian-themed restaurant. Gabe's significant other, Dani Dunn, owned the inn and Gabe was known to take most of his meals there.

"Smells delicious," Walker said as they surveyed the airy dining room. It was half filled with customers, but Gabe was nowhere in sight. As they looked around, the door to the kitchen opened and the sound of animated Italian wafted through. Dani, petite with short mahogany curls, walked toward them shaking her head and smiling.

"Good morning! Gabe said he was meeting you here, but he's in the midst of, shall we say, a lively discussion about the proper ratio of thyme to oregano for Chef Paolo's newest pasta sauce."

The volume of the conversation had now increased so that it could be heard through the door.

Dani chuckled. "I love him to pieces, but I can't wait for him to be taken off the injured list. He is driving poor Paolo around the bend."

Reggie reflected on the first time she'd met Dani. The innkeeper and Jenna had driven down to Reggie's cottage in Atherton to learn about her grandmother's time at The Grove. Back then Dani had been much more somber and reserved. Love had a way of bringing out the best in people, but Dani's change seemed to go even deeper than that. She'd recently returned from her father's funeral in Italy, and apparently she'd worked through some very difficult issues with her family that must have been weighing on her. She was obviously in a much happier place now.

At that moment, the detective walked through the swinging door, looking like a Giorgio Armani model on his day off—tall, trim, and broad-shouldered, his midnight-black hair mussed, wearing a cobalt blue golf shirt and jeans. His left arm was encased in a sling.

"I should have been a chef," he muttered, whipping his good arm around Dani's waist for a brief squeeze and kissing her on the top of her head. He then used the same arm to shake hands with Walker. "Good to see you; how's it going?"

"I'm not sure you've met Regina Firestone," Walker said.

"I don't think I have; I would certainly have remembered." He bestowed a heart-stopping smile on Reggie, but there was nothing flirtatious about it.

Dani is one lucky lady. "Are you sure you have time to talk with us?" she said. "We don't want to be a bother."

"I've got nothing but time for the next ten days. Time enough to drive Dani crazy and her pig-headed chef as well. How can I help?"

Dani showed them to a corner table and took their drink orders. Reggie got right down to it. "Maybe you've been alerted that part of the Grand Opening of the New Grove Center will include my grandmother's jewel collection."

Gabe nodded. "I've been discussing security protocols with Brit and Ethan related to it, yes."

"Good. Well, the collection arrived at The Grove by

Brinks Armored Courier two days ago and one of the pieces—actually two, if you consider it's a pair of earrings—has been stolen, and a counterfeit pair put in its place."

Gabe looked from one to the other. "What's the value?"

"The latest appraisal put them at three quarters of a million dollars," Reggie said, "but it could be even more now. The value is tied mainly to their historical significance."

"It wasn't Brinks' fault, by the way," added Walker. "It happened while the collection was held in a B of A vault in downtown San Francisco."

"An inside job?"

"I wish," Reggie said. "Unfortunately, my uncle, who had access to the collection along with me, unwittingly helped orchestrate the theft. The vault needs two signatures, so he and a woman posing as me signed in and took several pieces, which he thought his so-called friends were only 'borrowing' for a few weeks as collateral for a loan they'd given him. Once he repaid them, they returned the pieces, and he and the woman put them back in the vault. But the earrings had been switched. He had no idea."

Dani brought coffee and pastries to the table, along with an espresso for Gabe. "*Sei la mia luce,*" he murmured to her in thanks.

Reggie reflexively looked at Walker, who returned her gaze. She sensed he already knew what Gabe was saying: *You are my light.* "So." She pulled out her notebook to get her thoughts back on track. "We have a rough timeline and my uncle gave us a few names."

"That's good, but I take it the collection's been in the vault for a while." He pointed to Reggie's notes. "What makes you think the switch happened during the time you've indicated?"

"The entire collection, including the earrings, has provenance and appraisal analytics," Walker explained. "Regina checked the pieces regularly. It was only after the transfer to The Grove that she noticed something was off."

Reggie nodded. "I've had Sotheby's in to re-verify the authenticity of the rest of the collection, which they have certified. And I took the earrings to a colleague of mine, a professional diamond cutter, who examined the eyes. Here, let me show you." She handed the tigers to Gabe. "Diamonds glitter a certain way depending on how they're cut. Most people wouldn't notice the difference, but trust me, there is one. I had it confirmed: these are cut in a style that didn't exist when the original earrings were made."

Gabe held up a tiger to examine it in the light. "Okay, so the eyes are different. What about the bodies?"

"I'm almost positive they're different, too, but I need to take them to a jade carver for verification."

"So, you're looking at a three-week period in which you think the thieves took the originals, copied them and returned the fakes to the collection. And you say that other pieces were also taken and returned that *are* original. Why go to all that trouble?"

"I've been asking myself that," Walker said. "The log-in sheet shows Regina's uncle and the imposter weren't in the vault for very long. The pieces they took could have been random. Maybe the woman just took what she thought they could reproduce quickly, and the earrings won out. But maybe not. Maybe they knew beforehand which piece they wanted, and taking the others was just part of the scam. But how would they know what was even in the collection?" He turned to Reggie. "Has the collection been displayed in public before?"

"Never. My grandmother wore the pieces individually, of course, but she passed away decades ago, and my family didn't really want the full story of her collection to be widely known...although why they're so worried about it is beyond me."

"Could be your uncle mentioned the collection in passing, and someone got him to talk about it," Gabe offered.

"That's a possibility; he's pretty gregarious. Too gregarious, in fact, which is why my Aunt Pat divorced him. He mentioned someone named Sandi that he met at a bar and hooked up with. Apparently, she runs a modeling agency called Beauty for Hire. Maybe his big mouth started the wheels in motion."

Walker frowned. "Yeah, but what are the chances that this Sandi person would know someone involved in stealing or counterfeiting jewels?"

"I don't believe in coincidences, myself," Gabe said. "I can run the name of the establishment through the system and see if anything turns up, but instinct tells me his lady love was in on it from the beginning."

"Then how did they know to target him?" Reggie was back to having homicidal thoughts about her uncle. How could he have been so stupid?!

"Answers like that pop up eventually. Excuse me one second." Gabe pulled out his phone and began to scroll through it. When he found what he was looking for, he asked Reggie to jot down a telephone number. "That's the number for Dr. Leo Brunt. He's ... well, he's a lot of things, but the important thing for you is that he's an art expert. He knows the San Francisco art scene inside and out. He's also a private investigator. I've worked with him on a few cases. Smart guy. Good at what he does. If these tigers are on a collector's wish list, he'll likely know about it." Gabe paused before adding, "One more thing..."

"I already know where you're going," Walker said. "But it won't do you any good."

Reggie looked at both men. "What?"

"In a situation like this," Gabe said, "where a crime has been committed but the law doesn't know about it yet, it's not a good idea to go around turning over rocks to see what's underneath. The bad guys want the opposite of what you want, *capisce?* And given the sophistication of this heist, I imagine there's some money behind it, so...perhaps the best course is to call your insurance company."

Reggie had begun shaking her head before Gabe even finished. "I've already been over this with Walker," she said. "I have to do all I can to solve this quietly before it drags my family and The New Grove Center into a cesspool of tabloid goo. As to the insurance money, the bottom line is, I don't want it. I want my family's property back. And I'm going to do all I can to make that happen. End of story." Reggie patted the purse where she'd put her notebook. "Maybe your man can help me make it happen."

Walker gave the detective one those *you know women* looks that make women want to slug the men who give them.

Ugh. Reggie rose and shook Gabe's hand. "Thanks so much for your time; I'll be sure to keep you in the loop."

She marched out the door without bothering to pay for the coffee.

One step forward, two steps back. The woman was destined to drive him off the cliff. Walker exchanged looks with Gabe, who shrugged and said, "You need to watch her back."

"I know, but that one's got a mind of her own."

"The best ones always do." Gabe waved off Walker's attempt to pay for the drinks and pointed him to the door.

"Thanks, Gabe." With that, Walker strode after

Reggie, hoping to catch her before she took off without telling him what she was up to.

He found her just outside the hotel, talking on her cell.

"That's fantastic. I can be there in an hour, tops." Reggie's smile contained a hint of smugness as she hung up. "That was Professor Brunt. He happens to be home —lives in Larkspur—and he's willing to chat right now. You're welcome to come with me."

"Can you reschedule? I ... I've got to pick someone up from the airport." He glanced at his watch. *Damn. Already eleven o'clock.*

She caught him checking the time and frowned. "Uh, no. You said you wanted to help, and that's fine, but that doesn't mean I work around your schedule. You have something else to do. I get it. But I'm moving ahead on this while I can. And it looks like you'd better get on the road to pick up whoever's flying in. I'll see you back at The Grove."

With that she hopped in her car, a ten-year old, slightly dinged-up Honda, and headed off.

Walker started up the Explorer but wasn't even distracted by his "brand spankin' new" car. That had him worried. He'd always been easily able to compartmentalize his life: work, women, pleasure, the annual "dad" gig. But Regina Firestone was messing him up. Her single-mindedness both enthralled and frankly, terrified him. Most women he'd been attracted to were strong, and had definite ideas about how to meet their personal needs. He could understand that, even if it didn't make for long-lasting relationships.

Regina didn't fit that mold. She wasn't hung up on money, or status, or even bling, at least for herself. Instead she was hellbent on avenging her family and doing so in such a way as to not harm them or The Grove in the process. It was obviously personal: those cats were her babies and she was determined to do whatever she could to protect them.

But Gabe was right: this was no time to be snooping around on her own. If Regina did discover proof of a crime, he didn't doubt whoever was behind all this would try to silence her. The thought sent a shudder of foreboding through him.

Dammit. He should be there to make sure she didn't make any rash decisions. Then again, wasn't that high-handed of him? Who was he to be telling her what to do? She was a grown woman (*God, yes*), fully capable of thinking straight and acting accordingly. She didn't need some jerk she hardly knew telling her what to do. Still...

Okay. Reality check. Regardless of whether he should be with her, he couldn't be. Axel was flying in and he needed to be there for the boy. He could no longer put fatherhood in its little box. It was past time for him to stop delegating and start being a dad. A real dad.

It dawned on him why he hadn't told Reggie just who he was picking up: because he was still trying to keep the compartments of his life separate.

Those days are over, he thought with a grimace. That idea unsettled him even more.

He checked his watch. Three hours to fight the traffic down to the airport.

Fatherhood, here I come.

Chapter Eight

"You certainly don't look like a college professor," Reggie remarked over Subway sandwiches and a couple of beers. She and Dr. Leo Brunt were sitting on the back terrace of his third-story flat, part of another renovated mansion (this one a Greek Revival), just off the main street of the village named for the wild blue and white flowers called larkspur that grew around the area.

Leo had greeted her an hour earlier looking sort of like the actor Jason Momoa, but with short hair and no eyebrow scar. Handsome, but imposing. She'd brought lunch and he'd provided ice-cold Tecates on what was turning out to be a rather warm day. She'd explained the facts of the case and he'd listened attentively. She liked him.

"Well, at the risk of sounding trite," he said, "one should never judge a book by its cover..."

"...except on Amazon," Reggie said, smiling.

"Sometimes that's the only way to judge it...along with the reviews, of course."

Leo grinned. "You've got a point." He finished off his beer and got down to business. "Do you know Thomas Ling?"

"By reputation. He worked on the Olympic Medals for the Beijing Olympics back in 2008."

"Yes. Back then he was known as Ling Qiang Mao. He was one of the carvers in Kunlun, became a hero in his own right. After the Games they let him emigrate here, to "retire," they said, although he's not that old. He still works and has built quite a following for his jade carving. As you probably know, since the Games, the demand for nephrite has shot through the roof."

"Is he the only jade carver in the city?"

"There are a few, but he's by far the best."

Reggie handed her tigers to Leo to examine. "So, do you think he could have carved these?"

Leo held them up to the light. "They're precise enough to be his work, yes."

"But how good are they compared to the original?"

"That's the million-dollar question, isn't it?" He brought a loupe from his study and examined one of the earrings from all sides. "Usually a carver will leave a discreet mark to identify his work. It's a bit of an ego thing, but it helps with provenance, as well. Ling uses a tiny feather, but I don't see one anywhere."

"I see your point. I use a mark on my creations, too. It's a little flame. But I can't imagine putting it on something like this."

"You'd be surprised," Leo said. "When the work is exceptional, no matter its purpose, the artist often wants at least a smidgeon of credit for it, even if he's the only one who knows about it. You mind if I take a picture?"

"No, go ahead." She watched as Leo propped the tigers up and took a few shots with his cell phone. "So, without the mark, how do I find out if he carved them?"

Leo handed the earrings back to her. "Well, you don't ask him straight out, that's for sure. I imagine the best you could do would be to get him to open up about his recent projects—if you were so inclined."

"Hmm. If I were so inclined." She cocked her head in thought. "But what about collectors; do you happen to know of any voracious ones? All of the characters in this play seem to be actors. I'm thinking there's a director out there somewhere."

"I'm inclined to agree with you. Theoretically it could be anyone, based anywhere; it's just that this switch seems to have required an unusual amount of local coordination; it's not the typical anonymous online transaction. So, yes, there are a few major jade collectors in the area, from high to low. The Consul General for the People's Republic of China here in San Francisco is one, which stands to reason. And a retired movie star from Hong Kong named Lily Quan. She's in her seventies now but is still quite active in promoting Chinese culture in the city. Lives in Presidio Heights. And of course, Milton Collier. He's down in Hillsborough."

"Milton Collier? I know him."

"Lucky you," Leo said wryly. "He's somewhat of a blowhard, but tenacious. He can get a bee up his butt about something and will stop at virtually nothing to achieve his goal. He bears watching."

Reggie remembered Collier's words from the gala. He seemed to know something about her grandmother's collection. How had he found out about it, and how far was he willing to go to obtain what he wanted? "I thought he collected all types of gems."

"Oh, he does, but he knows what he likes and he has a favorite."

"What's that?"

"Antique mutton fat jade."

Who did Walker have to pick up at the airport? Reggie couldn't help wondering as she left Dr. Brunt's place and headed into the city. Was it a friend? Girlfriend? Significant Other? He said he had a place in Idaho; was the person flying in from there?

Okay, you should be grateful he's not in your way. Now you're free to find out what happened to the tigers without any interference, which is just what you wanted.

Buoyed by her mental pep talk, Reggie headed toward Brannan Street in the city's wholesale jewelry district south of Market. Having worked in the trade for some time, she was familiar with the area; two of the three cards Vihaan had given her were on Brannan.

Her plan was to present herself as a customer in

need of a "special" cutting. She'd already found her bait by scrolling through the Jewelers Security Alliance's missing gem and jewelry database and choosing an extremely valuable diamond and emerald choker. Now it was time to set the trap.

First stop: Elite Diamond Enhancers, run by "licensed premier diamond cutter" Mr. Adit Khatri. It was a good bet Mr. Khatri had come up with the title "licensed premier" himself because she'd never heard of it.

After donning a hat and sunglasses, Reggie entered the drab-looking office suite and stepped up to the small counter where a middle-aged Indian woman dressed in a sari looked to be updating her accounts using an old-style adding machine.

"I'm wondering if I may speak to Mr. Khatri," Reggie said when the woman paused in her tapping. She leaned closer and lowered her voice. "I have a special job I'd like him to do."

The woman looked intrigued and spoke the Queen's English. "Mr. Khatri is currently at his workshop finishing up a commission, but I am a co-owner of this establishment and can speak for him. What are you looking for?"

Hmmm. Okay, let's jiggle the hook. Reggie pulled out her cell phone and showed the woman the picture of the stolen necklace. "I'd like to know if ... given the right circumstances ... and incentives ... he could duplicate this piece. Just the diamond portion, of course; I would have the emeralds cut separately. But I would need it quickly, in, say, two weeks?"

The woman looked at the picture and frowned; her voice was authoritative. "This is part of the JSA database; it is stolen property, and even if it weren't stolen, the design is proprietary. It would be unethical to duplicate it." She looked up at Reggie as if memorizing her face for a possible future police lineup. "We do not do that kind of thing here, Miss..."

"Oh, well, all right then. Never mind." Reggie beat a hasty retreat, chuckling as she reached her car. *Good for you, lady.* It was encouraging to know that some people had standards; she'd make a point to tell Vihaan; maybe he'd change his mind and send some work over to Elite.

Two blocks away, Diamond Cutters Unlimited yielded similar results but for different reasons. Reggie met the cutter himself, Raju Lagari, who was in his late twenties, charming, and unabashedly ambitious. He reminded her of the character played by the actor Dev Patel in that movie about the hotel in India for English retirees.

"I'd consider your proposition in a heartbeat, miss, but I am afraid my schedule has been tied up for the past five weeks. I have been working on a very big assignment, but it should be wrapping up in a week or two. If you could but reconsider your timing...we could talk about it over dinner, perhaps."

Reggie' eyes narrowed. "If you're so tied up with work, how is there time to go out to dinner with me?"

"A man ...and a woman... must always find time to

eat." He gave her what some would consider a swoon-worthy smile.

"Uh, thanks, but no thanks. Good luck with your project," she said and turned to go.

"My name is Raju, by the way. And yours?"

He had caressed her shoulder lightly and Reggie looked at his hand long enough for him to reluctantly let go. "It's of no importance to you. Thank you for your time."

She felt far less upbeat after that encounter, and ten times worse when she realized the location of the final diamond cutter Vihaan had given her. "Surat of San Francisco" was located on the forty-second floor of "Triple Five," the office building at Five Fifty-Five California Street, in the heart of the financial district. It was one of the tallest commercial buildings in the city and Reggie *detested* skyscrapers.

Because high places scared her to death.

You can do this, she told herself repeatedly as she waited for the express elevator in the lobby. Already she could feel her adrenalin kicking in and her palms start to sweat. She began her usual deep breathing protocol: in through the nose for five counts, out through discreetly pursed lips for ten.

Luckily it was an express elevator to the thirty-fifth floor, then she'd take a "local" the remaining seven flights. The elevator was spacious, which was good, but a lot of people crowded in behind her, which was bad. The horror of being stuck between floors in a hot, crowded elevator car—and even worse, of panicking out loud if such an event were to occur—jumped to its favorite spot at the front of her brain. When the door shut, she concentrated on the floor and kept up her measured breathing as the box shot skyward. After roughly a minute of mental hell, the doors opened onto the thirty-fifth floor and she switched to another bank of elevators. One of them was an express to the top of the building, which had once housed the famed Carnelian Room restaurant. Sad to say she'd never dined there because she couldn't imagine being able to eat a bite knowing she was so high off the ground. Instead she followed the crowd to one of the "milk run" elevators and once more stepped inside what she morbidly considered a "box of death."

Why did people have to get off on every damned floor? It seemed to take forever, and by the time she reached floor forty-two, she was the last person exiting the car. Yet the minute she stepped outside she could feel her system rapidly returning to normal. As long as she didn't look outside, she was fine; moreover, she knew she wouldn't mind getting back in the elevator at all. It didn't make any sense, but descending—the faster, the better—was always a relief.

She checked the directory and followed the signs toward suite 4217. Any diamond cutter with an office here must make a hell of a lot of money to afford the rent.

As she turned the last corner, a group of people almost filled the hall coming toward her. They were all Asian, and she couldn't tell if they were part of the same group or not. She felt like a salmon swimming upstream, out of place in more ways than one.

She checked her watch. Four thirty. Almost quitting time. *No wonder everyone's leaving at once. I hope Argawal's still working.*

"I think you can still catch the elevator," she called out to the group as they passed by. One of them, a conservative-looking accountant-type, glanced at her with surprise, then briefly returned her smile. "Thank you, I hope so," he said with a slight accent.

When she entered the office at the end of the long hall, she was surprised to see a very young woman, who looked East Indian, rapidly clearing out files and putting them in boxes, as if she were spring cleaning or even closing down the operation. It looked like she was holding the side of her face with one hand as she worked.

"Hello, I'm sorry to bother you so late in the day, but I was wondering if I could speak to Jay Argawal about a ... a special diamond cutting commission."

Strangely, the young woman didn't turn around, but continued working as she replied, "He has left for Surat. No telling when he will return. I am sorry."

"Oh." Reggie walked closer to the woman. "When did he leave?"

"Two weeks ago," the woman said.

Two weeks. The timing was perfect.

"Miss, can you tell me by any chance what project he was working on before he left?"

At that the woman turned around, her eyes wide and

fearful. "I don't *know*," she cried. "I don't know *anything*. I've already said so! Now, please, if you'll excuse me, I have work to do." She turned back and began shoving files in boxes even more haphazardly than before.

Reggie was glad the young woman had turned away, because she couldn't hide her own shocked reaction, not to what the woman had said, but to what she looked like. Her right eye was beginning to swell and one of her cheeks sported a large red welt, as if someone had just smacked her across the face.

In that moment, Reggie realized she could very well have passed the woman's attacker in the hall, and whoever it was probably knew she'd seen *them*.

She did not want to go back into that hallway alone.

Chapter Nine

Walker waited for Axel just outside the "ticketed passengers only" section of the United Airlines terminal where they'd agreed by text to meet. It was now thirty minutes after the plane had landed and several planeloads of travelers from various flights had passed by on their way down to the baggage area. Where in the hell was he?

Walker was about to text his son for the third time when he finally spotted the teen ambling down the wide corridor by himself, seemingly oblivious to the world around him. He wore baggy board shorts and a T-shirt that said "Sarcasm: Just Another Service I Offer." With a backpack slung carelessly over his shoulder and wearing headphones, he was scrolling through his cellphone as he walked.

"Axel!" Walker called, just to get his son's attention before he passed on by.

Axel John Madera resembled neither Walker nor his

mother. He was five foot nine, give or take, with pale, clear skin and bushy dark red hair that fell to his shoulders under a Mets baseball cap turned backwards. Moreover, though he had a nice-looking face, he looked like he weighed considerably less than a hundred and fifty pounds.

My God, haven't they been feeding him? Then Walker remembered their last vacation together, a tour of the Pyramids a year earlier. When it came to eating Egyptian food, Axe had pretty much stuck to rice and pita bread. He didn't even care for the dates that were so often served for dessert. Walker himself tended to take the path of least resistance when it came to meals: whatever was available, no matter how plain or exotic, was fine with him—and that had sometimes included MRE's. He could tell he was going to have to put a bit more effort into mealtime where Axel was concerned, at least when it came to the green stuff.

"How was the flight?" he asked.

Axel looked up, almost an afterthought. "Gucci." He looked down at his phone, apparently thought better of it, and shoved it in his back pocket. "So, where are we off to this time? Timbuktu? Zanzibar? The North Pole? Mom said it was a surprise."

They headed toward Baggage Claim. "Uh, no. I thought she told you. We're staying here until you go back to your school. Actually, not here in the city, but north a ways. At a place called The Grove."

"What is it? A resort or something?"

"No, it's an artists' retreat, or will be once it opens. I'm part owner and I'm working on getting it ready."

Axel stopped and looked at Walker, his expression shifting from laid-back to uncertain. "You mean we aren't going any place cool? What am I supposed to do while you work?"

"Believe it or not, I've got you lined up with a job." Walker watched as uncertainty turned to near panic on his son's face.

"A job?"

"You know, where you work at something and they pay you?"

Axel took his headphones off and set his jaw. "I never agreed to that."

Barely swallowing his annoyance, Walker muttered, "Yeah, well, shit happens." He paused, realizing why his son might be a touch defensive. "Have you ever *had* a job?"

Axel shook his head.

What were they teaching this kid? "Well, it's not going to kill you, and you may even like it. Come on, let's get your gear and get out of this place."

Instead of walking, Axel immediately pulled out his phone and started tapping. Walker put a hand on his shoulder. "You'll have plenty of time to let the world know the sad turn your life has taken. How about you take a break from that for a while."

Glaring with resentment, Axel once more pocketed his phone. "This sucks."

Mentally, Walker wavered between *Give him a*

break; he's leaving his comfort zone and *What a spoiled jerk.* He opted to ignore the remark.

They picked up Axel's duffle and found the car before heading up through San Francisco.

After driving several miles, Axel broke the silence. "So, what exactly are you gonna be doing while I'm slaving away at some so-called job?"

"Among other things, I'm putting together a multimedia exhibit that includes a very special collection of gems and jewelry. There's a woman—"

"Ah. I get it."

Walker frowned. "What do you mean, you 'get it'?"

"You're not married. You got boatloads of money. Women like that shit."

Walker checked the time on the car's dashboard. Was it normal to want to throttle your kid within an hour of picking him up? "The woman—her name was Amanda Firestone—was part of the retreat when it first opened back in the early 1900's. It's her collection we're featuring. I'm working with her granddaughter to design the exhibit."

"Oh. So, you're just working with this lady to put on the show, is that it?"

He wasn't about to share what else was going on. "That's it."

So ended *that* conversation. After a few more silent miles, Walker offered an olive branch. "So, who do you listen to?" His son wasted no time hooking his phone up to Walker's state-of-the-art car audio system.

"This set-up is wicked," Axel said.

Walker knew enough to accept the compliment. "Glad you like it." They continued driving north to the sounds of Flaural, a psychedelic rock band from Denver.

Just over the Golden Gate bridge, Walker's cell phone pinged. It was Gabe de la Torre. Hoping he wouldn't be pulled over for using his cell, he turned down the stereo and took the call.

"Just wanted you to know I checked out that modeling agency Beauty for Hire that Regina mentioned. We were right to be skeptical. Turns out, it's a legitimate agency, but the real moneymaker is the side business, a high-end call girl operation run by a madam named Sandra Bollocks."

Walker smirked. "Stage name, no doubt."

"No doubt. Anyway, she's tied to a fixer named Frank Hatteras. They lay pretty low and the board of supervisors turns the other cheek because Frank and Sandi provide all kinds of 'special services' for that crowd. Because the pair knows too much about the high and mighty, the law looks the other way, too."

"Figures. So, Allen Willis was a mark from the get-go."

"Looks like it."

"Think there's any chance one or the other might sing?"

"I'd say somewhere between extremely slim and none."

"I'll let Regina know not to go knocking on that door, then."

"That's what I was hoping you'd say."

"Yeah, well, telling her and having her listen are two different things."

"Welcome to my world, *amico*. I'll catch you later."

Walker hung up and Axel immediately increased the volume. It didn't matter, because Walker's concern about Regina had leapt from the back of his mind to the front. Where had she gone after her meeting with the detective? Where was she now? He glanced at Axel who was nodding to the music as he stared out the window. Between reining in Regina and dealing with his son, his life had suddenly gotten a whole lot more complicated.

Despite the crap news his dad had laid on him when he got off the plane, Axel was impressed. If he was going to be parked someplace until his dad could dump him back in school, it may as well be someplace cool. "This place is sick," he said, dropping his backpack and duffle in one of the bedrooms upstairs. "You think it's haunted?"

"I don't think so," his dad said. "No restless spirits waiting to go to the Other Side if only we can solve the mystery of their deaths. Sorry to disappoint you."

Axel ignored the sarcasm. "Hey, no problem. I bet if there are, they're chill, anyway. So, where can I get something to eat?"

"Did we not just have burgers and fries at the Milk and Honey? Or is my memory failing me?"

"Nah, you're not going senile ... yet." Axel snickered as he pulled out his laptop. "I just like to know where I can find a snack in the middle of the night."

"Well, follow me, then."

They headed down to a big-ass kitchen, where a fine-looking female, some guy who looked like he was probably her boyfriend, and an old man were playing cards. When they walked in, the younger guy held up a bottle to Axel's dad.

"Sure, I'm in for the night." Walker pulled a beer from the refrigerator, not bothering to offer Axel anything—the putz—and said to the group, "Everyone, this is my son, Axel. He'll be staying with me until he goes back to school. Axel, meet Jenna Bergstrom, Brit Maguire and Dr. Ethan Wolff."

Axel shook hands all around and his dad looked impressed with that. *Geeze, his expectations are pretty fucking low if that gets his motor running.*

"Oh, I'm so glad you're here," Jenna said to Axel. "You're just the person I need."

Axel glanced at his dad and frowned. Why would a babe like her be interested in him? "I am? How come?"

"Because I understand you're a whiz with computers, and I need a computer whiz, that's why."

"What do you need help with?" Axel felt kind of stupid. "I mean, I'm not a repairman or anything."

Jenna grinned. "No, the system's fine, but I've lost my partner in crime for a few weeks. Dani's mom in Phoenix needs to have a procedure done," she explained to his dad, "and her step-dad's still out of commission with his broken hip, and, well, you get the picture." She turned back to Axel. "So, I need a researcher for three or four hours a day to help me finish up some background material. Pay's not much—twelve bucks an hour—but it'll give you something to do. What do you say?"

"Well, it's either that or you can work with me out on the construction site," the guy named Brit said. "We can always use another strong back."

Axel looked at his dad before addressing first the guy and then Jenna. "Ah, I think that would be a no to you, and a yes to her," he said with a lopsided grin. "If that's okay with you."

"Smart man," his dad said. "Fruit doesn't fall far from the tree."

Everybody laughed and Jenna piped in with, "That's great. We'll get started at nine in the morning. In the meantime, I picked up some staples for you guys: bread, milk, cereal, oranges, I think. Enough to get you by until tomorrow."

Axel's dad leaned over and gave Jenna a kiss on the head. "Thank you, cousin. Greatly appreciated." *Wait, she's dad's cousin?*

Then his dad asked what game they were playing, and the old guy said, "Bezeek. I just took seventeen tricks." Axel had never heard of it.

"Actually, it's pinochle," said Brit, "but that sounds too much like an old lady's game, so the professor likes to ratchet up the class a notch."

Axel's dad smiled, but he didn't seem like he cared

that much. Instead he asked, "Have you seen Regina this evening?"

Who in the hell was she?

Brit put his empty beer on the table. "No. We thought she might have tagged along with you today." He checked his watch. "It's getting kind of late. Jenna, do you have Reggie's cell number?"

"I do," Axel's dad said, and immediately started dialing. Axel wondered if that was the lady he was working with. His dad looked nervous. "She's not answering," he said. "I think we should—"

At that moment everybody heard the crunch of tires on the driveway behind the house. A car door closed, and Axel watched his dad's face as he focused like a laser on the kitchen door.

Chapter Ten

Watching Regina walk through that door in her prim little suit was like someone lifting a two hundred-pound barbell off Walker's chest. She looked weary and he forced himself not to gather her in his arms and let her know precisely how glad he was to see her. As it was, he couldn't stop the release of a long exhale.

Walker watched as Regina's eyes scanned the group and rested on Axel. She smiled, but Walker could see the question mark in her gaze.

"Regina, I'd like you to meet my son, Axel. Axel, this is Regina Firestone. She's the lady I told you about who I'm working with on the new exhibit." In case she was unclear about any of it, he added, "Axel's mother and her new family are moving to Belgium, but Axe is going to finish out high school here in the States. He's even got a job helping Jenna with her computer research starting tomorrow."

"Ah," Reggie said, extending her hand. "I think you're going to like it around here. It's pretty sick."

Axel glanced at Walker and raised his eyebrows as he shook her hand.

"We were about to call the Highway Patrol," Brit said lightly. "Where you been?"

"Oh, I had some ... appointments and then my uncle Toby met me in the city for dinner. He brought Mr. Big, so I could love on him for a little while."

"Oh, Mr. Big," crooned Jenna. "How is he?"

"The usual: fat, smelly, adorable." She turned to Axel, "Mr. Big is my uncle's basset hound who's infatuated with me." She batted her eyes. "What can I say?" She sent everyone a half-smile and turned to go. "I'm pretty whipped, so I'm going to call it a night."

"Wait, I'll walk you over. I want to go over a few things." Walker turned to his son. "Axel? You good?"

"Yeah, sure. I'll just—"

Ethan broke in with, "Young man, you look like a sharp card player. We could use a fourth hand. Would you like to join us?"

Axel hesitated. "I, uh, don't know the game."

"Nonsense. You'll pick it up in no time. You can be my partner." He sent Axel such a warm nod of encouragement that Walker wanted to hug the old man on the spot. Bringing his son here, even for a little while, was one of the best decisions Walker could have made.

But Axel's response threw that decision into question. In a bored, bordering-on-sarcastic tone, the boy said, "Yeah, no thanks. Not my thing. I'm just gonna chillax upstairs."

An awkward silence filled the void as Axel left the room. "I'm sorry," Walker said to the group. "That was rude."

"Don't worry, he'll come around," Jenna said as she shuffled the cards. She knew teens, especially those going through tough times. "He's just had a lot of changes thrown at him; he probably needs to decompress." She pushed the deck over to Brit. "Cut, please."

"Thanks for the thought," Walker said. Part of him wanted to sit Axel down and teach him some manners, but now was not the time. He placed his guilt-laced irritation into its own little compartment and shut the door on it. He'd deal with Axel later.

The night was bordering on cold, but he didn't feel it as he headed down the lit path alongside Regina. She was subdued, pulling her jacket closed against the dropping temperature, and said nothing until they reached her cabin.

"Would you like to come in?" she asked. They both knew it wasn't a come on.

"Yes," he said immediately.

Once inside he turned on the small gas fireplace, apparently converted from the original wood-burning variety.

Regina dropped her satchel on the little dining room table and rubbed her arms before pointing to the kitchen counter. "I've got some port, if you like; would you mind pouring me some while I change out of this chain mail? It's driving me bonkers."

"Sure." Walker had to smile. At least they agreed on one thing: neither of them liked dressing up if they could help it.

A few minutes later she came out in leggings, flats, and an oversized sweatshirt. She looked troubled, but delicious all the same. *I need to quit thinking that way. It's not helpful.* He handed her the drink. "Something happened today that's got you spooked. What was it?"

"That obvious, huh? I don't know exactly what's going on, but whatever it is, it's not good."

Reggie curled up on the couch in the little parlor of the cabin and watched Walker as he settled into one of the chairs opposite her. She couldn't deny her attraction to the man, but what did she know of him, really? Why hadn't he told her he had a son? Not that it mattered, but what else wasn't he telling her? *No, not important; too many bigger fish to fry.*

She took a sip of the port, savoring its sweetness, and began with the easy part. "The meeting with Dr. Brunt went well. He gave me the name of a potential jade carver as well as three local collectors who might be obsessed enough to try and pull off something like this." She took another sip and shivered. "I even happen to know one of them."

Walker focused his dark blue eyes completely on

her. He seemed to be reading her, perhaps trying to figure out what she was feeling as well as saying. She didn't feel invaded, however; she felt valued.

"But that's not concerning you right now," he said.

"No, it was what happened later. I didn't tell you, but Vihaan Chaudhry gave me more than his expert opinion on the authenticity of the diamond cuts; he also gave me the names of three cutters in the city who might be tempted to take on a job like that."

"Don't tell me you tracked them down on your own." Walker's expression was stark.

"No excuses. I did. You were busy, and, well, I checked out the first two by posing as someone who wanted to get a 'special' cutting job done quickly. I implied that it wouldn't exactly be on the up and up."

Walker exhaled heavily. "Regina," he said in warning, but she held up her hand to stop his lecture.

"I know. In hindsight it was a bit risky. The first one almost had me arrested—which I considered a good thing—and the second said he'd been tied up with a big job since well before the tigers went missing. That was just before he came on to me."

"My God," Walter muttered.

Reggie barreled on. "But I think I hit pay dirt, if you can call it that, on the third cutter. According to his assistant, he'd left for India and she didn't know when he was returning. As she was telling me this, it was obvious she was scared stiff, and after I got a good look at her face, I saw why."

"What was wrong with her face?"

"I can't swear to it, but I think someone had just been in to see her. She must not have given him or her the answer they wanted, so they let her have it."

"What, you mean, yelled at her?"

"No, I mean slugged her in the face. She was frantic to get out of there. And I realized I may have seen who did it."

"What?!"

"I don't know for certain, but as I was heading down the hall to her office, several people were walking toward me. Some accountant-looking guy; this attractive but edgy-looking woman, I'd say in her early forties, who looked pissed at God knows what; and two hulking guys dressed in black who were arguing about something. They were all Asian, but I couldn't tell if they had come from the same office suite or not."

"So, if you saw them, it means they saw you."

She nodded; he really seemed to be on her wave length. "I'm not going to lie, I was scared to death heading back down that high rise. I kept thinking the worst, that he or she was going to come at me in the elevator or something. It was stupid—"

"Yes, what you did was stupid."

Okay, well maybe not on quite *the same wave length.* "I meant it was stupid to think I was going to be attacked in a hallway. It's a public building, after all, with a lot of people running around. Whoever it was didn't make themselves known, but yes, I've been jittery ever since. Even seeing Mr. Big didn't help much."

"Why didn't you tell me about the cutters?"

She shrugged. "Because I knew you wouldn't like it." She held his eyes. "So how come you didn't tell me you had a son?"

Walker snorted. "It's hardly the same thing."

"Isn't it? There's a matter of trust involved in either case. I don't want you putting up roadblocks, and you … you obviously have a part of your life you're uncomfortable sharing, at least with me."

Walker sought to brush it off. "It's not that. I just … well, it's an old story. Old as the hills really."

"I'm listening."

"Okay, well, I grew up in southern California, part of a ranching family. Pretty successful. Actually, make that *very* successful. There was pressure on me to continue in my father's footsteps. Only I didn't want to go that route—my sister's a fantastic foreman, she runs the place now—so I got my folks to lend me some money, and ...." He paused, almost with embarrassment, "—and I made several good investments, paid them back, and made even more money. Then I *really* threw them for a loop by getting into photography. Went to school, became an apprentice, started in the fashion biz—"

"Ah, know your way around Jimmy Choo and Tom Ford, do you?"

He smiled. "Yes, ma'am. But I was young and somewhat naïve about the lengths women will go to in order to fulfill their own agendas. I was also full of, shall we say, 'natural drive.' Axel's mom was several years older and very pretty—not a model, but in charge of them, which I thought was great. So, we did what people do, and she got pregnant with Axel."

"So, you married..."

Walker shook his head. "No. I asked—out of guilt, I'm afraid—but she declined, saying she was going to have him on her own. She moved to the East Coast and it was only after Axel was born that she contacted me again and said she'd changed her mind, that she wanted to 'make it work' between us. I found out through mutual friends that she'd been sleeping with someone else at the same time and figured he was a better bet, so she'd followed him back east. Obviously, he didn't come through like she hoped, so I was the consolation prize. But by then I'd moved on, grateful as hell that I didn't catch anything from her. I knew there wouldn't be a good outcome if we made it legal, so I declined." His voice took on a slightly defensive tone. "I have fully supported Axel all his life, however; I consider him my son, whether there's DNA to prove it or not."

"Wow. Sounds like being a single parent wasn't exactly on her list of priorities."

"No, but she did a good job with Axe, and eventually found someone suitable to marry. They have twin girls and are on their way to live in Brussels as we speak."

He downed the rest of his port.

Poor Axel, Reggie thought. *What would it be like to feel unwanted within your own family?* Having been born into a large and loving extended clan, she couldn't imagine it. "Must be a bummer for your son. I bet he feels like a fifth wheel. Maybe that's why he felt so uncomfortable tonight."

"No, I'm sure he was just tired from the trip."

He sounded protective—of himself or of Axel, she couldn't tell. Maybe it was a case of *I can rag on my family members, but nobody else better do it.* That trust issue again. "Well, he seems like a nice young man."

"Yeah, he is, most of the time."

Reggie got up and went to the kitchenette to drop off her now-empty wine glass and drink some water. Walker obviously didn't want to reveal any more of himself than he had to; it was probably better to keep things on a professional level. She needed to remember that.

Walker brought his glass over too and rinsed it out. "With what you went through today, are you okay now with getting the authorities to step in on this? Nothing is worth getting hurt over." He gently tipped her chin up. "Nothing."

She took a breath, knowing he was only trying to emphasize a point, but feeling that pull all the same. *Professional. Keep it professional.* "I suppose you're right—"

At that moment the satchel she'd dropped on the dining room table began to buzz.

"That's probably my Aunt Beth. She's been trying to reach me off and on today, but she's a talker, and I just don't have the energy, so I haven't returned the call."

Walker dropped his hand but didn't move. "Best to check," he said.

She leaned over him to pull the phone out. "Oh, it's my cousin Ava," she said. "Let me get it."

It took less than a minute for Reggie to feel the earth drop underneath her.

"Oh my God," she cried.

"What?" Walker touched her again. "What's wrong?"

"I can't believe it. No, it can't be. Are you sure?"

On the other end of the line, Ava didn't sugar coat it. "They found him stabbed to death in the Tenderloin along with some call girl, Chandra somebody. Just thought you ought to know."

"Th ... thanks. I'll get back to you." Stunned, Reggie ended the call.

"For God's sake, tell me what happened," Walker demanded.

"It's Uncle Allen," she said, tears beginning to fall. "He's been murdered, along with that model he told us about, only they're saying she was a prostitute."

"Makes sense. Gabe called me earlier to tell me that modeling agency's a front for a call-girl operation."

"So she was setting my uncle up for the slaughter from the very beginning? Who would do something like that?"

"Somebody who likes money a whole lot more than human life. You see now why we've got to get the police in on this? Even if murder wasn't in the original plan—"

"What do you mean?"

Walker stared at her but didn't immediately answer, and Reggie realized why. He was probably thinking, "Maybe if the switch had never been discovered..."

He was right. Maybe if she hadn't figured out there'd been a switch, maybe if she hadn't confronted her uncle...

What had Uncle Allen said? "How bad is it really? Nobody got hurt" and "No one'll know the difference."

But Reggie had known the difference, and she'd opened her big mouth about it—to her uncle, to the banker, and indirectly to the gem cutters.

And now her uncle was dead.

"Oh my God," she said, and a new flood of tears followed.

"Goddammit all to hell," Walker said.

Chapter Eleven

W alker couldn't help it; he folded Reggie into his arms and held her as she wept for her hapless uncle and her unwitting role in his death. She didn't push him away; in fact, she clutched him tightly, accepting without apology the solace he was willing to give.

"He ... he wasn't perfect, but he didn't deserve that," she protested. "He didn't deserve to die, for God's sake! And that poor girl. She was probably only following orders and look what happened to her. She was just a pawn. They were both pawns. And I ... I..."

That admission brought on a new onslaught of tears, and Walker did the best he could, stroking Reggie's hair and telling her it was going to be okay, that it wasn't her fault, when, really, his anxiety level had just shot up a hundredfold. After a moment, she raised her head and looked at him with such grief and vulnerability that he took her face in his hands and kissed her gently on the forehead, her cheek, and then lightly on her mouth.

Immediately he realized he'd crossed a line and made to stand back, but she held him and whispered, "It's okay. I know what this is." After a moment she stepped away, wiping her tears. "I don't know about you, but I could use another drink."

They both settled on the couch this time, and Regina talked more about her uncle, sharing little stories about him and processing what had happened out loud, but with fewer tears. When her eyelids began to droop, Walker tucked her into bed, but not before asking, "Do you want me to have Jenna come over to be with you? Or do you want to come back to the Great House for the night? And I don't mean—"

She gave him a sad smile. "I know what you meant. And no, I'll be okay. But tomorrow—"

"Tomorrow you should be with family. I know your uncle wasn't part of the fold anymore, but he had been for a long time, and that counts for something."

"You're right. But do I tell them about the theft? At this point they haven't a clue. I'm just afraid—"

"You make that call after you've slept awhile," Walker said, gently placing a strand of her long curling hair behind her ear. "But we need to contact the police, and soon. When you're ready we can check with Gabe. Maybe he can fill us in on what happened, tell us where to go next."

"I'll talk to him and decide from there," she said, and yawned. "Goodnight, Walker."

"Regina, I—"

"Lock the door on your way out, please," she said, turning on her side. Within a minute she was asleep. Walker pulled her covers up a little and secured the cottage before he left.

Filled with turbulent emotions, he headed back to the Great House and upstairs. It was well past eleven and the kitchen was dark. *Just as well*, he thought. Tomorrow was soon enough to impart the bad news to everyone about the death of Regina's uncle. *What a mess.*

He noticed a light under Axel's door, so he knocked slightly. Hearing no response, he entered, thinking perhaps his son had fallen asleep with the light on. But no, Axe was wearing headphones and a mic, playing a video game.

Time to lay down a few rules. He tapped Axel on his shoulder. "Wrap it up," he said.

Axel frowned. "I'm playing a game."

"I said wrap it up. *Now*," Walker repeated, using a calm but "don't mess with me" tone.

"Fuck, I gotta go," Axel spoke into his microphone. "Sorry, guys." He disconnected and laid his laptop to the side of the bed. "Thanks a lot; you just lost the game for us."

"And the operant word in that sentence is 'game,' as in, it's just a game."

"Maybe to you," Axel grumbled.

"Definitely to me. So, I know you're probably not used to being dictated to, but we've got to lay down a few rules, one of which is, while you're here with me, living in this house, you're going to have to turn off the electronics at ten."

"Ten?!"

"Yeah, Ten. It takes a while for your brain to calm down after you've been amped up with your video games."

Axel snorted. "What do you know about it?"

"Enough to know you're starting a job tomorrow—a job you're damn lucky to have, I might add—and that job requires you to be on your A game. And you can't be on your A game if you've been up until one or two in the morning. It just doesn't work that way... and if you're honest, you'll admit I'm right."

Axel sat mulishly silent. How had Caroline handled all the video game playing? When she was single she'd probably used it as a baby sitter, and habits like those were hard to break. Axel was no doubt used to his mother or step-father complaining but never doing anything about it. But he really did need to change it up, and Walker figured it was best to start out as he meant to continue. "Well?"

"Okay," Axe said. "I get it."

"So, you're going to let me take the laptop after ten at night, no pushback?"

"I said I get it!"

Walker's irritation got the better of him. "Good, because having to give it up at ten is better than not being able to use it at all, which is your only other option."

Axel glared at him, finally letting out a long breath. "Take the fucking laptop, then," he said, shoving it toward Walker. "See if I care." He rolled away from Walker dismissively.

Laptop in hand, Walker was about to leave the room when Axel rolled over again and asked mockingly, "So, did you do the nasty with Regina? I mean, she's hot, but not nearly as hot as Jenna."

Okay, that does it. "Are you kidding me? How old are you? Men with any smarts or class whatsoever just don't talk about women that way. They don't 'kiss and tell.' For your information, Regina lost an uncle today, so you need to be kind to her. As for Jenna, you'd better not make her feel uncomfortable in any way, shape, or form. She used to teach troubled teens, and one of them, a kid not much older than you, stalked her and almost killed her before he himself was killed. I'm surprised she's even willing to take a chance on somebody your age after what she went through. So, trust me, she won't take kindly to any move on your part that even hints at a repeat of that scenario. And that doesn't even factor in Brit, who will tear anyone who messes with her limb from limb. She's his partner, his mate; do you understand?"

Axel blinked a few times and nodded slowly. He looked shocked. *Good.*

"I didn't know that happened to her," he said.

"Why would you? I'm just saying, tread lightly there. And if she happens to bring it up, listen to what she's saying and learn from it. You'll stay healthier that way."

Walker was about to leave when he remembered their dinner at the Milk and Honey; a group of girls about Axel's age had been sitting in the booth across the aisle. "There are plenty of girls your age around here," he said. "What about that group sitting across from us tonight—any of them float your boat?"

Axel snickered. "'Float my boat'? What is that, some kind of sailing term?"

Patience. Give me patience. "I have no idea where the phrase came from. Do you know what it means, or do I have to spell it out for you?"

"Some of them seem cool," he said with a shrug.

"Good, then you can spend an hour before bed figuring out how to go about meeting them." He reached over, took Axel's headphones, and added, "We're all sharing wi-fi in this house and there's a baseline, so if the data usage spikes, I'll know who caused it. So, don't be sitting on your phone all night, or that'll go, too."

"What bullshit," Axel muttered.

"And clean up your mouth, too."

Yeah, that went well, Walker thought as he retreated to his own room. *I oughta teach parenting classes, I'm so good.*

In order to relax, he tried to practice what he'd just preached to his son; he'd focused on Regina. But thinking about her didn't set his mind to rest at all; on the contrary, it revved him up as if he'd been single-handedly killing the enemy in *League of Legends*, or whatever game Axel had been playing. Yes, he wanted her, but it went much deeper than that.

While she spent time grieving with her family, Walker would work on the exhibit. Soon enough, however, she'd be back seeking justice. Now that matters had turned deadly, he hoped she'd agree once and for all to let the police take over the case.

But here was the kicker: he totally understood her desire to take matters into her own hands if necessary. If it had been his stolen heirloom and his relative who'd been killed, he'd be doing everything he could to seek justice, whether the police were involved or not.

In her hunt for the thieves—and now more likely killers—Walker had to make sure Regina didn't inadvertently become the prey.

It took him far too long to fall into a restless sleep, and when he did, he dreamed he was tightrope-walking across a deep gorge. On one side stood a teenage boy and on the other, a mysterious woman. Both were calling to him, and he had just dropped his balancing pole.

Chapter Twelve

Axel sucked in air and let it out. Did it again. It helped to keep the jitters down, which had started several months ago when his life started to get tossed around like a football.

God, he'd had them bad a few days ago when he'd started working for Jenna. She must have thought he was gonna have a seizure or somethin'. But she didn't say a word; she just told him what she needed and left him alone to get it done. Yesterday was better, and today, well, one or two deep breaths and he was already feelin' pretty chill.

He settled into his chair in front of the PC in Jenna's office and logged on. His crush on her had died down pretty quickly. She was hot, yeah, but she was old—not to mention, she was totally into Brit Maguire, which was understandable because, shit, the guy was *built.* Axel examined his own arms, which were skinny and pale. *Maybe I ought to do more stuff outside.*

"How'd you sleep last night?" Jenna asked from her side of the room. "I heard your dad has a no-screen policy after ten. How's that working out?"

"You promise not to rat me out?"

"Scout's honor."

"I slept pretty good last night."

Jenna grinned as she turned back to her machine. "Yeah, don't you hate it when your parent gets it right?"

"I'm not worried—doesn't happen very often."

"So says every kid that was ever born."

Axel snickered, but inside it hit him: he had a parent who gave a shit. Sort of. It felt weird. It wasn't that his mom didn't care, she just had other things to do right now, like live the life she always wanted, without him messing things up.

It hadn't always been that way. He had to give her credit—she'd tried to hook up with whoever Axel's dad was. First it was that guy Phil somebody, but he wasn't interested. Then it was Plan B: Walker Banks. He'd stepped up with the moolah and at least Axel could say he had a dad, which made him no different than all the other kids he knew whose parents had split up. But one thing was always lurking in the back of Axel's mind: Did his dad even know he might not be the real deal? Axel wasn't about to tell him because God knows, he might split altogether.

But it had blown him away when his father said Axel could stay with him and didn't even use some weird vacation as a buffer. And the dude was sort of making an effort. He worked during the day, but he showed up and stuck around at night. They didn't talk much, and he was still on Axel's case about the laptop, but it was tolerable. And he wasn't shoving fast food down Axel's gullet three times a day, either. They'd even gone grocery shopping together.

"I'm afraid I suck in the kitchen," he'd said, "Your mom teach you anything about cooking?"

"Sort of, but she was always wanting to put weird shit in everything, like shitake mushrooms—"

"Hence the name," his dad had joked.

His dad. So, they'd gotten plain food and he'd negotiated, letting Axel get certain snacks like Dinamita Chile Limon Doritos in exchange for promising to eat crap broccoli or salad with dinner.

Screen time was still a big-time issue. It pissed him off royally that his dad held the laptop out there like some sort of trained monkey shit. "Do what I tell you and I'll give you a treat!" Fuuuuck. So Axel had to use his phone under the covers, which sucked so bad that he usually shut if off after a half hour or so. And yeah, sure, fine, he was sleeping better. But still…not gonna tell *him* that.

They'd had a truce goin' these past few days except for one thing, which wasn't over food or screen time. And it wasn't even Axel's fault.

"What do you mean you don't have a driver's license?" his dad had fumed when Axel told him he couldn't drive down to Little Eden and pick up some toothpaste for himself. "You're sixteen, aren't you?"

Instinctively Axel had run to his mom's defense.

"Uh, *hello*, we live in New York City. Who needs a car?"

His dad looked like he might have a cow or something. "Are you serious? Are you saying you don't care about learning how to drive a car?"

"I didn't say that." In fact, he'd asked his mom and Jean Paul several times to let him get a permit and sign him up for driver's ed. They'd never had the time.

"Well then, they damn well should have taken you out to the burbs and taught you how to drive."

It felt good that his dad would have gone to bat for him, but then he had to spoil it by saying, "Listen, I don't have time right now, but I promise you, when I get through with this project..."

Yeah, right. Heard that one before.

Hell, you can't have everything, right? It was enough that he had the jitters under control for a while. He'd take what he could get.

He picked up the online trail where he'd left off yesterday. Jenna had him researching the Chinese gangs that hung out in San Francisco around 1900. How sick was that? Apparently, the lady whose photographs and stuff was being shown in the new museum had been kidnapped by one of the gangs—they called them 'tongs'—when she was younger than Axel!

It reminded him of a video game he'd played a while back called *Sleeping Dogs*. That one took place in Hong Kong and was all about, like, the Chinese mafia. He told Jenna about it. In the game, you can be one of the gang members and those guys are badass, like they don't care, they chop people up and stuff. And it turns out that's what they used to do in real life.

"Check this out," he called over to Jenna. "These Chinese gangs were like the MS-13 of today. They were into the same illegal stuff, like drugs and prostitution and gambling. And they had certain enforcers they called "boo how doy" who went around with these little hatchets and knives and shit, and whoever the leaders said to cut up, they'd cut up. Some guys even wore chain mail to protect themselves. We're talkin' some bad juju goin' down."

Jenna turned around in her chair. "You know, I always wondered what happened to all those gangs after the 1906 earthquake. The entire neighborhood was destroyed, so, where did all those bad guys go?"

"I've been reading about that, too," Axel said. "A lot of people disappeared. I mean, the Chinese didn't get much help from the government, but they didn't ask for much, either. They were pretty much on their own. The head honchos, those guys they called the Six Companies, fought like crazy to get the place re-built, and part of that meant cracking down on all the illegal stuff that went on. So that pretty much meant the death of the gangs.

"But here's the weird part. Along about the Sixties, there started to be more guys coming in from Hong Kong and China, and they started mixing it up with the local guys, so gangs started springing up again. I mean, some of them exist even today."

"Where's Bruce Lee when you need him?" Jenna asked.

"No shit," Axel said.

After working at his job (which he had to admit was pretty cool), Axel usually went back to his room at the Great House to play video games while he waited for his dad to get home. Games were great for getting rid of the jitters. For one thing, you could count on them; they were always available, and they had a clear-cut set of rules that everybody had to play by. Plus, there was a whole slew of people—other gamers—you got to know online. Axel had even met a guy named Bystander who was a badass hacker in the Deep Web; he'd already shown Axe a few tricks he could use to find information that the regular web didn't have. Of course, Axel's dad would no doubt shit a brick if he knew what his son was doing; he'd probably take Axel's laptop and drop it off the nearest cliff. Some things were better left private.

Reggie stared at the clock on the nightstand: it was two a.m. It had been three days and she still couldn't wrap her head around the fact that someone would kill another person over something as trivial as money. Because that's what all this was about, wasn't it? Someone—a collector, or maybe a broker—somehow learned that the earrings were part of the Firestone collection. He or she wanted them badly enough to pay a team of thieves to steal them. But to murder two people in cold blood over them? It just didn't seem possible.

But it *was* possible. In fact, it had already happened. And Reggie burned to know why.

Pulling the tigers from their soft leather pouch, she examined them by the light of her LED magnifier. "What do you have to tell me, gentlemen?" she murmured. "Who made you?"

She inspected each animal carefully with her loupe one more time, just as Dr. Brunt had done, but saw no identifying marks. The animals were hiding something from her; she could feel it. It was in their strangely glittering eyes. Reggie paused.

Their eyes.

Of course.

She took out her jeweler's kit, and, donning the glasses she used for her close-up work, pulled a pair of prong lifters—it looked like a miniature can opener— and applied the proper-sized notch to one of the tiny prongs holding the diamond eyes in place. With just the tiniest bit of pressure, the prong lifted. Two more prongs followed, and she was able to remove the diamond from its socket. The first eye revealed nothing, so she carefully removed the second.

And there it was.

The tiny feather etching that signified Thomas Ling's work. If one didn't know what to look for, they might think it a small scratch caused by the diamond itself. No doubt the carver figured no one but he would ever see it.

Well, he was wrong.

She added Mr. Ling's name to the list of players involved in this deadly heist. Hopefully the police could track him down and compel him to talk. They simply had to find the bastards who did this.

She wouldn't sleep until they did.

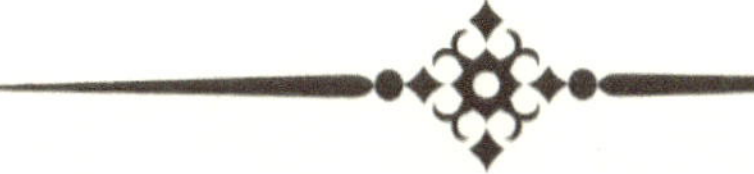

Chapter Thirteen

"The initial report has the hallmarks of a random hit," Gabe explained the next morning over coffee.

The night before, Regina had texted Walker, asking him to set up the meeting with the detective, which Walker had been more than happy to do. Gabe had clearly done his research before their arrival today.

"There's no way it was random," Regina said. She was dressed for comfort, as if she had a long list of things to do. She looked more determined than ever, which had Walker worried.

"The story's common as dirt, I'm afraid. A wealthy older man picks up a prostitute, or in this case, a higher-priced call girl. They're out on the town and some perp sizes them up, figures there's money to be had. Maybe he follows them for a while. Eventually they enter a witness-free area—it could be just a block or two that's darker than usual—and he holds them up. Doesn't even need a gun—a knife'll do just fine in most cases. Maybe one of them balks, and the guy makes good on his threat. He kills one of them. Then he has to kill the other to keep him or her quiet, and he takes off. Simple, but deadly all the same."

"But we know her uncle knew the woman before that night," Walker said.

Gabe leaned back in his chair. "Sure, they'll assume he's a repeat customer."

"What if someone could swear that they were together at the bank?" Reggie turned to Walker. "Maybe we could get the bank manager, Randall Cherrington, or how about the vault teller who waited on them—Rod Meyers, I think his name was—to testify that Uncle Allen and the lady were in the bank on the dates we're talking about. I'm sure I could find something to show I wasn't there that day. That would give the police a solid connection between the theft and the murder, wouldn't it?"

"Yes, it would, but don't be surprised if they cover their asses," said Gabe. "No bank is going to want it known they let an imposter into their vault not once but three times."

Walker knew well the power of photographic images. "How about bringing the vault teller in to identify the two victims by their photographs—see if he puts them together in his memory without putting him on the spot to say whether or not he's looking at the real Regina Firestone?"

"He may find himself between a rock and a hard

place," Reggie said. "If he identifies the woman as being me, it's obvious she wasn't me, because I'm still here. And if he doesn't identify her as me, then he's lying or incompetent, because she's the one who was in the bank. Heck, maybe he'll think *I'm* a suspect and did them both in."

"Doubtful, but I'd say lay it all out for the case detective and let him run with it." Gabe finished off his espresso.

"How about the FBI?" Reggie was on a roll. "Can we get them in on it? I know they have a Jewelry and Gem Theft Program."

Gabe quickly squelched that idea. "I don't think so, not at this point, at least. The Feds generally get involved with crimes like this that cross state lines and involve property worth over a million bucks; otherwise it's going to be handled by the local jurisdiction, in this case the SFPD."

"Even with my uncle's murder?"

"You'll have to prove a connection, and even then, the locals may retain the right to handle it on their own without outside help."

"So, who's the detective in charge? Do you know him?" Walker asked.

"Yeah. Afraid I do. Roger Liu. He's touchy about all things Chinese, so he may not be excited about helping you retrieve a priceless artifact that he thinks ought to belong to the Chinese people anyway."

Reggie looked affronted. "Well, he believes in property rights, doesn't he?"

"Sure. He's a 'by the book' kind of guy. I'm just saying he has latitude in how he approaches his cases and he may not want to bend over backward for you."

Reggie was already up and collecting her purse. "Well, he'd better do something; we're not just talking a jewelry theft anymore."

As he rose, Walker sent Gabe another long-suffering look. It was getting to be a habit. "We'll keep you posted," he said, already feeling uneasy about the day ahead.

Reggie had to admit Gabe had pegged the encounter with Detective Liu perfectly. He was the poster child for skeptics.

She and Walker were sitting in spindly chairs at a scarred table in a plain vanilla conference room located in the SFPD's Tenderloin Station. A large mirror hung on one wall, which Reggie guessed was two-way. How many other victims, not to mention bad guys, had sat here telling their own sad stories to the law?

Despite his busy schedule, Liu had at least agreed to hear what they had to say. "Whatever light you can shed on this case would be much appreciated," he'd said, and Reggie had laid out the facts as they knew them.

"All right, let me get this straight," he said after she finished. "You're telling me that you're missing a set of earrings and you think it has something to do with the murder of Mr. Willis and Miss Ramirez." He looked at the initial report on his laptop. "It says the female victim was wearing a pair of imitation gold hoops."

Reggie sensed the detective's disbelief and could feel her temper rising. "Mr. Liu, these are not just any earrings and Chandra would not have been wearing them. I don't know if you quite understand, but they are both a work of art and a priceless artifact. Their last appraisal came in at seven hundred and fifty thousand dollars, and that was three years ago. My uncle did a stupid thing by engaging with a nefarious group of people—"

Liu suppressed a smirk at the word "nefarious" as he took his notes.

Keep it steady. "All right, how about duplicitous? Larcenous? *Murderous?* Because I can show you the provenance. I can show you that the substitute gems are fake, and I can point you in the direction of the woman whom my uncle said organized the swap—the woman who employed the other murder victim."

"And that woman is?"

"Sandi—" Reggie turned to Walker. "Did Gabe give you her last name?"

Walker shifted uncomfortably in his seat. "Uh, Bollocks. He gave the name 'Sandra Bollocks.'"

"What?! You're joking. That's ... That's ..." she looked over at Detective Liu, assuming he'd be guffawing at that one, but he looked stone-faced as he wrote down the information.

"You know who she is, don't you?" she said.

"Her name has crossed our desk from time to time, yes."

Detective Liu was about to say more when a sergeant knocked on the door and entered, giving Liu a piece of paper. After the officer left, he read the report and placed it face-down on the table. He considered Reggie and Walker briefly in silence, but there was an undercurrent now, as if the case had taken on an entirely new dimension for him.

"Look," he finally said, closing his book. "I am going to be perfectly honest with you. Under normal circumstances I wouldn't share information until after you had both been interviewed, your whereabouts last night verified, etc., but I am going on gut instinct here, partly because you volunteered to share what you know, and partly because Detective de la Torre called before-hand and vouched for you. Right now, I have to treat the theft of your *artifact* as a lower priority until the evidence we gather connects the two. I will assign an officer to take down your information, but candidly, we don't have much time to devote to crimes like these. You've been on the streets. You've seen what we're up against. Our homeless problem is growing and main-taining the safety of all our citizens is stretching us extremely thin. This double homicide is a perfect example of what we're dealing with, and now it's going to claim even more of our attention."

Walker frowned. "What do you mean 'now'?"

"I just received a preliminary report from the medical examiner and there are certain similarities between this case and another that happened about a month ago."

"Similar in what way?" Reggie asked.

"In the manner in which the bodies were found," he said.

What is he talking about? Reggie looked at Walker quizzically, then back at the detective. "You're saying the same person that killed Allen Willis and Chandra Ramirez probably killed somebody *else?*"

Detective Liu nodded. "We're still analyzing the evidence, but yes, that's precisely what I'm saying."

After sharing their information again with another officer, including the names of the vault teller and bank manager, Reggie agreed to have her picture taken for a possible photo lineup. Once she'd done that, she couldn't get out of that station quick enough.

"I don't know what just happened in there. Could we be wrong about all this?" she asked as Walker, who'd driven that day, pulled out his keys in the parking lot. "I mean, could my uncle and Chandra have just happened to be at the wrong place at the wrong time? Speaking of which, why were they in the Tenderloin to begin with? Did she live there? Because I can guarantee you my uncle did not generally hang out in that part of town."

Walker sent her a brief smile before unlocking their doors. "I don't know. I don't believe in coincidences any more than Gabe does. The only other explanation is that the third victim is somehow connected to them."

"Detective Liu said he was a young guy, right? Some low-level staffer to Amy Jin on the city's board of supervisors. Supposedly he was attacked near his apartment in the Richmond district. What kind of connection could there be—gambling? Real estate? A love triangle?"

She paused in the midst of buckling herself in. Reality had just smacked her in the face. "The police don't have the time or the resources to find the link any time soon, do they?"

Walker hesitated before answering. "It doesn't look like it," he said. "But—"

"But what? We're supposed to sit on our hands and wait for them to get their act together when we could be doing something ourselves, right now?"

"Regina, we agreed…"

"No, I didn't agree to anything. I said I'd decide what to do after I'd talked to Gabe. Well, I've talked to him, *and* to the police. And now I'm going to do whatever else I can to find out who these monsters are."

"Even if it puts your life in danger?"

She paused, asked herself the same question. Answered it. "Even if." She reached over to touch Walker's arm. "I'm sorry."

It wasn't the answer Walker wanted to hear, she knew. He looked dour but determined. "So, what do you have in mind?"

Gazing at the man awaiting her lead, she felt an

enormous sense of power, as if she were a queen and he the Captain of the Guard, a sworn protector. The notion sent a frisson of excitement through her. *Dammit, I really like this guy.*

She pulled out her notebook and flipped through it before finding the page she wanted.

"Last night, when I couldn't sleep, I examined the earrings one more time, and you'll never guess what I found."

"The Secret of the Mummy's Curse."

Ha! At least he still has a sense of humor. "That's Egyptian folklore, not Chinese. No, I found the identity of the man who carved the fake earrings."

"You're kidding."

"Nope. Leo told me what to look for, but neither of us saw it the first time around because it was hidden behind one of the eyes."

"The carver put his name on a forgery? That sounds ridiculous."

"Not according to Leo. It would be like a master painter or a sculptor—or *photographer*—or even a jewelry designer like me, creating something magnificent and marking it in some secret way to claim it as our own." She found Thomas Ling's address and showed it to Walker, who punched it into his GPS.

"Chinatown it is," he said. "I'll even spring for dim sum."

Chapter Fourteen

He was irritated, preferring to take his time when they had sex. She was very responsive and the feel of her satiny skin rubbing rhythmically against his always got him more worked up than when he was obliged to perform during these stolen moments. But her other lover was due back at any time from his meeting, and as so often happened, they'd had to make do in the confines of the back office. He clutched her midnight-colored hair to keep her steady. She was wearing the simple jade necklace he'd given her. It was a dragon.

He glanced at the clock on the wall. Two p.m. "When is he due back from lunch?"

"Two ... thirty ... give or take," she panted. "I don't want him anymore. I want to be with you only."

"It will happen ... someday soon," he ground out. "You'll see. Don't leave him until the time is right." With that he increased his tempo until they both finished. She moaned her release quietly.

Within moments he had thrown away his condom and the proof of their tryst. As he zipped up his pants, he watched her put herself to rights. She really was an attractive woman, and even though she hadn't confided in him yet, he had no doubt she loved him. When the time was right, she might even give up everything for him. Too bad she'd be disappointed.

Too bad she was his enemy.

Chapter Fifteen

The GPS had directed them to the small storefront upon which the words "Asian Carvings" were stenciled on the window. A note taped to the window said "Closed," but a door next to the shop was open, leading to a staircase. Families often lived above retail space in neighborhoods like this.

"What you want?" an elderly Chinese woman said from a partially-opened door on the landing. *She sounds scared*, Walker thought, and it put him on edge. Older people and children should never have to feel frightened.

"We're here to see Mr. Ling," Regina said. "May we come in, ma'am?"

Now the woman sounded more angry than alarmed. "You know he gone, go away now."

"Who do you think we are, *Zumu*?" Walker asked.

Her voice softened slightly at the endearment. "You from government, like the others."

"No, Zumu, we are not," he assured her. "We are friends of Mr. Ling and we want to help him. I assume you are his mother? If so, you are of great importance in this matter. Will you help us?"

The woman hesitated before opening the door wide enough to let them in. She appeared as frail as she sounded—small and slightly stooped, her white hair scraped back in a bun. Her translucent, papery cheeks were slightly red and puffy. *From crying?*

She led them to a small living room and gestured to two upholstered chairs facing the sofa. The space was compact, but well-appointed; a small ancestral shrine graced one of the corners by the far window over-looking the street.

"You want tea?" she asked.

"No, that would be too much to ask, but we would like to talk to you, with your permission." Reggie seemed to be on the same track as Walker; moreover, she was a natural at putting people at ease.

The old woman inclined her head and sat down primly on the sofa. Her fidgeting hands gave away the emotion roiling beneath the surface.

"You say the government took Mr. Ling away?" Walker asked. "How long ago was this?"

"Three days," she said. "They say he was selling secrets to the Chinese government and they took him. But that not true! He only jade carver. Where would he find secrets to tell?"

Regina looked as puzzled as Walker before asking,

"Ma'am—Zumu—can you tell us what they looked like?"

The old woman waved her hand in disgust. "They big and wear dark suits like all government men, but they worse, much worse!"

Frowning, Walker asked her why.

"Because they Chinese! I tell them their ancestors would be ashamed of them, turning on people from same place they came from. But they tell me be quiet and they take my Qiang Mao away and he did nothing ... nothing."

Regina quickly sat on the couch next to the distraught old woman and took her hand. Consoling someone who was hurting crossed all cultures.

"Zumu," Walker said gently, "do you happen to know what your son was carving a few weeks ago?"

The woman looked up at Walker with rheumy eyes. "They were tigers. Special white tigers. *Bai lao hu.* They bring powerful energy and strength. In here." She pointed to her stomach.

"Who was he carving the tigers for?" Walker saw that Regina was tight with anticipation as she asked the question.

"He tell me for someone in the government. So why they come and take him away after he do what they ask?"

"I don't know," Regina said, "but maybe we can find out."

"You can bring my Qiang Mao back to me?" The

woman looked so hopeful that Walker couldn't bear to disappoint her. Reality, however, reared its head.

"We can make no promises," he said, "only that we will try."

The woman paused before asking, "Why you do this for my son? If you not the government, who are you?"

Walker didn't need to make something up because Regina stepped right in with the truth. "We are artists, like your son, and we want him to remain free to create more beautiful things."

The old woman, tears in her eyes, smiled at them for the first time. "My son more beautiful than any jade carving. You bring him back, please. Tell him I make him special egg foo young."

"We will do our best, Zumu," Walker said as they left.

Once back on the street, Regina muttered, "If those were government men who took him, I'll eat my hat."

"You're not wearing a hat," Walker observed.

"Doesn't matter; I still wouldn't have to eat it. I'd bet money that he was forced to carve the tigers, and once he finished, they contrived a way to get him out of the picture so that he wouldn't talk. I just hope they haven't harmed him."

"That's a bet I wouldn't take," Walker said grimly. "Where to now?"

Regina was already consulting her book. "Uncle Allen's friend Halona manages a boutique at 1845 Green Street. I think it's time to see what she knows about where Uncle Allen was headed."

"Green Street here we come," Walker said.

The dress, long and body-embracing with a slit up one side, was made of pure off-white silk; down the front, a panel of delicate cream embroidery gave it a rich, tapestried look. It was sleeveless with a mandarin collar and a teardrop neckline--and it was the absolute last dress the customer Halona was showing it to should be wearing.

"I think it could look marvelous on you," Halona gushed. "Look at the detail on this overlay."

The woman, in her mid-sixties and carrying the weight of her life experience in her hips, looked skeptical. She turned to see Reggie and Walker standing nearby. "What do you think, young man?" She held the dress, still on its hanger, in front of her.

Reggie hid a smile as Walker, caught like a deer in the headlights, quickly regrouped. He tilted his head as if considering the possibility, then shook his head.

"No, I don't see you in that. You need something much more vibrant—" He smiled at her. "—like you undoubtedly are."

The matron grinned, then looked at Reggie. "He's a charmer, that one. Better watch out for him." She turned to Halona. "I think he's right. What have you got in a red chiffon?"

Halona had recognized them and frowned but didn't say anything until the woman left with a design in royal blue that really did flatter her. Walker's nod of approval had made the sale.

"What are you doing here?" Halona asked without a trace of the conviviality she'd shown the first time they'd met. The three of them were alone in the shop.

"You don't seem that distraught that my uncle was murdered," Reggie said bluntly. "Why is that?"

Halona busied herself straightening the blouses and sweaters hanging on the circular sales rack. They didn't need straightening. "What, you think I had something to do with it? That's absurd. It's just..."

"Just what, Halona?" Walker took on the voice of a concerned friend. "Did something happen between you and Allen that upset you?"

"Well, you might say that." Unconsciously Halona began sliding the hangers more forcefully; one of the blouses slid off and she jerkily restored it. "The night he was killed he got another call from that bitch Sandi. He told me she was a real estate client of his; seemed she was always calling him at odd hours. I mean, you don't go looking at houses at ten o'clock at night, do you?"

Reggie had to admit that was sketchy. "So, you're saying that night Sandi called him and what, asked him to meet her someplace?"

"No, it wasn't her he was meeting. He said she'd referred him to someone else and set up a time and place for them to meet in the city. He says to me, 'Never know what these things lead to, baby; might be a commission down the road big enough to buy us that condo in Cabo.' Come to find out he's meeting a hooker.

A hooker!" Halona did tear up then; Reggie wondered if it was out of grief, anger that he'd lied to her, or just the frustration of having lost a potentially fine Sugar Daddy. None of it mattered now, though; Halona was back to selling high-end dresses and saving up her own commissions for that elusive condo.

They'd left the shop and were almost back to where they'd parked the car when Walker patted his jacket and said, "I think I left my phone back there." He handed her the car keys. "Wait here and I'll go back for it."

"You sure?" Reggie peeked inside the car through the window. "I didn't see you with it. Maybe you left it in the car. Let me call you and see if it's here."

"No, it'll just take a minute," he said, and quickly jogged back up the street.

A few minutes later he returned, opened the driver's side and slid in. "All is well. By the way, you don't need to say it."

"Say what? You should keep track of your phone better?"

Walker rolled his eyes. "No. I'm assuming you now want to see Sandi Bollocks, right? Confront the lioness in her den and ask her why she stole your family heirloom and led your uncle to his death?"

Reggie slowly smiled. "I hadn't thought of it in quite those terms, but yes, that is precisely what I would like to do."

"I figured as much," Walker muttered. "I'd like to go on record that I don't think we should be turning over these particular rocks."

"And if we don't, who's going to? You heard Detective Liu. He could care less about the theft of those earrings. But if we can give him a lead that pertains to my uncle's murder, he'll have to put some resources toward it."

"And the other victim? The one who has nothing to do with any of it?"

"We don't know that yet. There's got to be a link somewhere. We just have to find it."

Walker checked for oncoming traffic before pulling out. His voice was resigned. "So, where's this Beauty for Hire?"

Chapter Sixteen

Regina said little on the way to the modeling agency, but as Walker was parking in front of the building on California Street, she turned to him and said, "I have an idea, so just go along with me, okay?"

That didn't sound good. "What kind of idea?"

"Trust me," she said, and got out of the car.

The "Beauty for Hire" agency looked legitimate enough: the receptionist's area had both color and black-and-white glossies of very attractive young women and men adorning its walls. A white board listed several companies who were currently hiring models for print or video advertising productions. "Asian male, mid-twenties, exotic yet all-American look" ... "Petite redhead female with spitfire personality" ... "Leggy blond with come-hither expression..."

"They all fit into their little boxes, don't they?" Reggie murmured. "How about 'happy expression, plays well with others'?"

Walker threw her a look of *yeah, that's not how the game is played* and walked up to the receptionist, who fell smack into the "sultry brunette" slot. "We're here to see Mrs. Bollocks," he said. "Regina Firestone."

The girl, who didn't even appear to be of drinking age, pressed an intercom button on her desk. "A Miss Firestone and some guy to see you, ma'am."

They heard no response from the intercom, but after a moment, Sandra Bollocks herself walked through the door at the back of the reception area. She was a hard-edged bleached blond who kept a trim but curvaceous figure despite the fact that she was flirting with fifty. Her current expression wasn't exactly cordial. She was obviously smart enough to know there was only one reason Regina would be knocking on her door.

"May I help you with something?" she asked coldly.

Regina matched her icicle for icicle. "I certainly hope so. It's about my uncle, the one who was recently murdered, along with one of your girls."

Sandra glanced at the receptionist, who was busy acting as if she hadn't heard anything. "Hold my calls, Cindy." She then beckoned to Reggie and Walker. "Come this way."

They followed the woman down a narrow corridor to the office at the end of the hall. Once inside, Sandra wasted no time on niceties. "I need you to strip, please," she said.

Walker hadn't expected *that*. "What the hell for?"

Regina hadn't taken her eyes off the madam, but she

calmly began unbuttoning her blouse. "Because she wants to see if we're wearing wires. Is that correct?"

Sandra indicated that it was and waited while Regina took off her blouse completely.

My God, Walker thought. Regina was wearing a simple white bra with lace trim on the straps. Her breasts were a perfect size: peeking out beyond their confines but not spilling out indiscriminately. He took a breath.

"And the slacks," Sandra said.

Stoney-faced, Regina complied, and Walker was treated to matching whities that hid her innermost secrets while advertising just how spectacular her body really was. Sandra stepped up to her and slid her arms along Regina's sides and legs. "All right, then," she said before turning to Walker. "Now you."

"Oh, for God's sake," he said, and pulled his t-shirt over his head. He glanced over at Regina to see her looking at him. She quickly turned away.

"And the pants."

"I am not dropping trou in front of you, lady."

Sandra shrugged. "Okay, but I'm still gonna check." She proceeded to run her hands ever so slowly up both sides of his legs. When she got to his groin area, she didn't hesitate to feel him up.

"Shit!" he said.

"Hmm. You sure that's all you?"

"I'm sure," he gritted out. Another glance at Regina caught her looking at the side wall. Crap, he felt about fourteen.

Sandra stepped away and, as if it were any other business meeting, she indicated two chairs in front of her desk. "Sit, please," she offered.

Now dressed again, Walker and Reggie sat down.

"Was that really necessary?" he asked.

"You are obviously not here to hire or be models, and if we're going to talk about private matters, then the meeting should be private. I'm asking you again, why are you here?"

Regina started right in. "Before he died, it came to light that my uncle had had money problems, and at one point in our conversation, he indicated that he had met you, and that you had helped him 'out of a jam' as he put it."

Sandra kept her expression bland. "Yes, so what? No law against that, is there?"

"Well, that depends," Regina said. "He also mentioned one of your so-called 'models' who, it turns out, was something slightly more than a model."

"Yes, well, maybe your uncle liked a little kink." She tilted her head and observed Regina before adding coyly, "You do look a lot like her, you know."

Walker flinched at the crude inference, but it didn't faze Regina in the slightest.

"Yes, the dead woman did resemble me, which is precisely why you set her up with him. She needed to impersonate me for reasons other than a little role playing in the bedroom, didn't she?"

That took Sandra back a few steps. "I don't know what you're talking about."

"Yes, you do," Regina said, leaning forward. "And if you don't, your partner Frank Hatteras certainly does. He's the fixer in all this, isn't he? He's the one who figured out how to wrap my poor hapless uncle up in such a bind that he had to go along with your ridiculous plan to steal a piece from my family's gem collection and replace it with a fake. It's a good thing he blew it."

Walker fought the urge to look at Regina and ask her, even by a raise in his eyebrows, what she was talking about.

Sandra, on the other hand, was completely gob smacked. "What exactly are you implying?"

Regina went in for the kill. "I'm not implying anything. I'm telling you outright that you all thought you were so clever in swapping out the white jade earrings. So clever, in fact, that whoever made them for you didn't even notice that they were already dealing with fakes—meticulous fakes, but fakes nonetheless. My father had a copy made of them fifteen years ago for this very reason. And I keep the real ones where no one can find them. So, I want you to go back to whoever hired you for this dirty little job and tell them you failed. Utterly. Completely."

"I ... I don't see ..."

Regina rose from her chair. "You don't see," she repeated contemptuously. "That's an understatement. You don't see that you botched it. But I'm here to tell you that you did."

Walker said nothing as he made to follow her. He didn't know what she was up to, but *whoa*.

"Wait," Sandra said when they were halfway to the door. Her voice had a speculative tone to it. "If we failed, then why bother coming to talk to me about it? You should be gleeful you pulled one over on us."

Regina whirled around and stalked back to Sandra's desk, slamming her hands down on top of it. "Gleeful? *Gleeful?* You know as well as I do that my uncle's murder was no random mugging. You caused the death of someone in *my family,* not to mention another person who was certainly innocent of any crime requiring a death sentence. My god, she even worked for you. She trusted you! If you ordered that hit, you are beyond despicable. If you didn't, then you are a complete fool for hooking up with someone who would. Whichever one you are, you'd better check your back—because so help me, if I can find a way to pin this whole sorry, sordid mess on your shoulders, I will damn well do it!"

The look on Sandra Bollocks' face told the story: shame, confusion, and fear all fought for supremacy.

Regina's face was stoic but streaked with tears. Walker followed her out the door.

God, that felt good. Reggie slowed her breathing as she sat waiting for Walker to buckle up and start the car. She'd wanted to haul off and slug that woman, but that would have been a bit over the top.

"Damn," Walker said, looking at her. "I didn't know I was driving around with Diana Prince."

Reggie sniffed. "Wonder Woman, I'm not."

"Well, you came across as Fury, then. But the question is, why? Why make it sound like you double-crossed *them?*"

"Because of the tigers' eyes. I kept thinking about them. Whoever ordered them made didn't know enough about creating a foolproof forgery, or he or she would have ordered the right diamond cut. Which means that without some kind of mark, like the one Thomas Ling hid on the carving, they probably wouldn't know the real from the fake. I got to thinking, if we start telling everyone, even outside the law, that the earrings have been stolen, that will only drive whoever took them underground. But if we can inject a little doubt into the equation, then we might flush them out. They may want to try again, you know, to get the ones they now believe are real."

Rather than agree with what she considered to be quite logical thinking, Walker looked angry.

"So, you decided to stake yourself in the middle of the forest and wait for the bad guys to pounce, in the hope you can escape in the nick of time," he said. "For God's sake, Regina."

All right, so she hadn't quite extended her reasoning that far. But still ... "I'm not an idiot. I'm not about to run upstairs to the attic when the creepy guy invades the house. But I have to do *something.*" She looked out the window, appalled that she'd started to tear up again.

"I know, but this is something for the professionals—"

She turned back to him, infuriated at her own lack of power. "Who will do nothing! And by the time they track down whoever did this, if they even do, my family's heirloom will have vanished forever. I didn't spend the last several years of my life taking care of my grandmother's legacy just to have it slip away without trying my best to get it back. That is not who I am."

Walker seemed taken aback by her outburst. "Okay, all right, but until we figure out who's behind this, I ask just one thing."

"What?"

"You move into The Great House with the rest of us. There are plenty of guest rooms and the place is wired for security. And you tell Ethan, Brit, and Jenna why. No more holding back. Even if the authorities slow walk it, at least the family will be up to speed."

"I was going to suggest that very thing," Reggie said. "There's safety in numbers, which is why you should explain things to Axel, too."

"No," Walker said firmly. "Not yet. He's too young to have to worry about things like this."

"He's old enough to—"

"I said no."

Walker wasn't about to budge; she could tell he would do just about anything to keep his son out of harm's way, but sometimes that kind of reasoning backfired. Still, he was Walker's child, not hers. "Okay."

He looked at her, as if surprised she wasn't going to keep arguing. "Let's head back now and fill everybody in."

"Sounds good."

Reggie watched Walker's profile as he drove. "Two out of three," he muttered. "Not bad."

Chapter Seventeen

S andi's townhouse was cast in shadow, the late afternoon sun making a half-hearted attempt to peek through the venetian blinds. The bedroom smelled of stale smoke and the lavender of her favorite candle. Frank Hatteras slid his bulk to the side of the bed and exhaled heavily.

"That was so good, baby." she crooned, rubbing his gray-haired, barrel-shaped chest. "You're always so good. You're my Lover Bear."

Lover Bear grunted. "Hand me my cigs, babe, will ya?"

Sandi took one for herself and handed him the pack. They each took a moment to light up before she said, "So what do you think?"

She'd called Frank shortly after Regina Firestone and her well-hung escort left and asked him to meet her at her townhouse. When he arrived, she played for him the conversation she'd recorded of the bitch and her claims that they had screwed up. The crack Sandi'd made about Allen Willis maybe wanting to fuck his niece had gotten Frank all riled up, but now he was focused again on the part that mattered. They listened to the recording again.

"She could be lyin' through her teeth," he said afterward.

"Or she could be telling the truth. I mean, how would we know? The thing is, she was pretty pissed off that Allen had died for nothing, and Chandra, too. And she's right about that part. Everything had worked out fine. So how come they killed them? How come?"

Frank took a hit on his cigarette. "I don't get that part, neither. I mean, the deed was done. So far as all of us knew, the switch came off perfectly."

"And what about Chris Fung? All he did was link us up, and he ends up on the wrong end of a shiv, too. I don't like it, Frank."

"Look, the two of us don't need to worry. We got too much to sing about to ruffle our feathers. But this twist does have me thinkin.'"

"Thinking how? Like, how you're going to tell the client we screwed up?"

Frank took another hit and exhaled. "Hell no," he said and started to cough. He gestured for the bottled water that Sandi always kept on her nightstand and gulped some down. "Hell no," he repeated. "The last thing we want is to tell them we fucked up. No, I'm thinkin' of something else..."

Chapter Eighteen

A xel had been surprised as hell—as well as kind of scared—when his dad came home and asked if he wanted to have a hands-on driving lesson before dinner. Shit yeah, he did. Sort of.

"Brake. *Brake*!" his dad yelled now.

"Okay. Okay!" Axel slammed his foot down on the Explorer's brake pedal a little too hard and jolted both him and his dad as the SUV lurched to a stop. "Geez, if you weren't such a maniac about it..."

His dad scrubbed his face and took a breath. "Yeah, you're right. I just didn't want you to slam into that tree, is all. Don't mind me."

Fuck. This was not going well at all. After the talk they'd had about driving, his dad had given Axel the go-ahead to take an online course to learn the rules of the road. That was going fine. But it was the real-world part that scared the shit out of him. I mean, this was a giant lethal weapon! And here he was just driving it around the parking lot behind the school at the bottom of the hill—thank God school wasn't in session.

Maybe he just wasn't cut out for this. "Hey, well, okay, so you tried, and—"

"Put the car in reverse, like I showed you," his dad cut in. "Now turn around ... slowly ... and let's get to the other side in a reasonable amount of time. No great hurry. Just feed it a little bit of gas. Not too much ... that's good."

Okay. Okay. I can do this. Axel wiped his sweaty hands on his jeans and gripped the wheel again. He made it to the opposite end of the lot with just a couple of starts and stops.

"Better," his dad said. "You'll get the hang of it eventually."

"Yeah, sure." Axel wasn't so sure about that; his dad was probably just giving him props.

"So, you want to take it up the hill?"

Axel looked at his father with surprise. "You ... you trust me to do it?"

His dad shrugged. "What's the worst the can happen?"

"Uh, we fall off the side of the cliff."

"Not gonna happen. Come on. Let's go."

They headed back up and Axel creeped along slowly but still lurched twice. Inside he was freaking out that they were going to roll back down, but he kept his foot on the brake and it seemed to be okay. His dad just sat there, looking straight ahead, not saying much except "Take it slow" and "That's it." They finally entered the big gate of the retreat and Axel drove around to their usual parking space by The Great House. He pulled in kind of crooked and turned off the engine. Never had he felt such relief! They both sat there for a minute until his dad turned, gave Axel a quick smile and said "Good job" before quickly going inside.

"No, it wasn't," Axel muttered to the empty car. "I sucked."

"And that, in a nutshell, is why I'm crashing your party," Reggie said to the group assembled in front of her later that evening. She and Walker had put together a simple dinner of spaghetti and salad for everyone, with ice cream served in the library. Axel had eaten his quickly and gone upstairs, saying he was scheduled to play a video game with his online team members.

Ethan, Brit and Jenna had listened attentively to her story about the switch of the tigers and her uncle's role in it, along with the steps she and Walker had taken since then to find out who was behind it all.

"I can see why you wouldn't think it was a random attack on your uncle," Jenna said. She shivered and Brit reached for one of the soft throws off the back of the couch and gave it to her.

Ethan sat on a comfortable reading chair by the fireplace with a small afghan of his own spread across his spindly legs. "My dear, I very much appreciate your unwillingness to have The Grove subjected to any more bad publicity, but really, this does seem to be something for the authorities to deal with."

"If only they would," Reggie said. "Did you know that under the best of circumstances, less than five percent of stolen jewelry is ever recovered?"

Brit shook his head. "It's not that much higher for stolen art, which is why we have our own version of Fort Knox here."

"Besides which, the detective assigned to the case isn't all that keen to put a lot of resources toward mere theft," added Walker. "He says he's got more important cases and I can't blame him. He suspects the death of Regina's uncle and the call girl, along with another man, is the work of a possible serial killer."

"Oh my God," Jenna said. "Why do they think that?"

"Something to do with a mark the killer left on all three victims," Reggie explained. "We don't know how that third guy was involved in all this, but I'm sure he was. We've just got to find out how."

"It's not really your job, you know," Brit said.

Reggie looked at Walker. "He sounds a lot like you. Were you two separated at birth or something?" They all laughed, which broke the tension a little, but Reggie knew it was going to tense up again when she told them her latest plan.

"Technically you're right, Brit. But I'm the one with the most at stake. To me, it's personal. So, I've staked myself right in the middle of it, as Walker put it."

Ethan looked intrigued. "How so?"

"I led one of the players, whom we know helped orchestrate the switch, to believe that she and her partner had stolen the wrong piece of jewelry, and that I personally possessed what they wanted."

"In other words, you set yourself up as bait." Brit sounded as disapproving of her idea as Walker had.

"Pretty much, yes."

"Which is why she's staying in the Great House for the duration. Sorry, I should have asked first, but—"

Jenna huffed. "As if you'd have to. You're more than welcome, you know that, right?"

Reggie reached over to squeeze her friend's hand. "I do and thank you."

Jenna then turned to Ethan. "But what about you, Da? Maybe you should—"

He waved her concern away. "I've already had my allotment of terror for one lifetime, thank you. No one's going to bother with a rickety old man." He smiled complacently. "Besides, I've now got a concealed carry permit."

"What?!"

"You're kidding."

"Da!" Brit, Walker and Jenna all protested at once.

"Yep. It's been in the works for a while, and your very obliging foreman, Mr. Rodriguez, helped me get precisely the firearm I needed. Not too big, but big enough."

"I don't want to know," Jenna muttered.

"No, you don't. But rest assured, I'll be perfectly

fine. There is one thing, however; if one of you would be so kind as to give me a ride back to my cottage..."

Brit hopped up. "I'll give you a lift." He kissed Jenna briefly. "See you shortly."

Jenna rose and headed toward the stairs. "I think the third room on the right's open," she said. "I'll make sure you've got towels and stuff."

"Oh, don't go to any bother. I'll just—"

"No worries," Jenna said. "Glad you're going to be here to help balance out all this testosterone." She grinned at Walker as she said it.

"Yeah, we're toxic, all right," he said.

"My kind of poison," Jenna called out as she headed to the second floor.

Reggie started to gather the ice cream bowls. "Help me clean up?" she asked Walker.

"Oh, you're going to fit in just fine." He chuckled as he followed her into the kitchen.

They fell into an easy routine of doing the dishes, as if they were a team, as if they had always been together. She found herself remembering what he'd looked like without his shirt earlier in the day. He could have been one of the models whose glossies decorated the walls of that agency; he was that good-looking. *Down, girl; he's taken a million photos of stunning women and had his pick of them.*

As if he'd read her thoughts, he said, "Pretty strange today, wasn't it?"

"You mean, about the—"

"Yeah, I'm not used to stripping on command."

She smiled at him. "You're no Magic Mike, huh?"

"No, more like Unwilling Walker."

She couldn't help herself. "I'm glad you didn't say 'withered.'"

At that, he caught her gaze and held it. "Not an issue," he said. "Not an issue at all."

Oh. Oh my. Reggie's imagination began to take flight, so she tamped it down with a "Well, I'd better scoot over to my cabin and get my things."

"I'll come with you."

"You don't have to—"

Walker raised one eyebrow and said nothing; instead he reached for his jacket hanging on a peg near the back door and waited.

"Fine, be that way," she said without heat, and preceded him into the dark.

By half past eight the next morning, Brit was already gone and Axel had left for the museum with Jenna to work for a few hours even though it was Saturday. That left Reggie alone with Walker in the kitchen again, this time clearing the remains of breakfast. With the sun shining through the room's large greenhouse window, it promised to be a lovely day. Reggie was feeling optimistic.

"We've got to stop meeting like this," Walker joked.

She took a half-empty cereal box from the table and

put it back in the cupboard. "You mean over Fruit Loops and cinnamon toast?"

Just then the toaster popped up with two more pieces and as they were chuckling, Reggie's phone rang from her vest pocket. Time stopped as they stared at each other. The last phone call they'd received together had not been a good one.

After a charged moment, Reggie swallowed and answered the call.

"Oh dammit," she said after listening for a moment. She mouthed the words *My Uncle Toby* to Walker. "Any structural damage? ... Good, good … I'll be down there around eleven to clean up ... They don't move in until tomorrow, I believe, but I'll double check. Yes, I know it was lucky … Yes, all right. Love you."

She hung up the phone, looked at Walker and shook her head. "I don't know whether to be mad as hell or pleased as punch."

Walker frowned. "Why? What happened?"

"My cottage was ransacked last night."

"Shit. No way."

"Way. My guess is Sandi told Frank I had the real tigers. Somebody broke into my place and tore it apart, which means they bought my story."

Walker didn't look happy. "You could have been there."

"But I wasn't. The good news is, my cousin Ava and her daughter aren't moving in to house sit the place until tomorrow. Turns out Uncle Toby had an alarm system installed for them two days ago and was just waiting to arm it until my cousin got there. Lousy timing for me, but great for them."

"How bad was the damage?"

"Nothing major; it's all just stuff. I'm going to drive down and deal with it this morning."

"I'll come with you," Walker said. "We'll clean it up in no time."

Oh yes, I really *like this guy*. Reggie smiled her thanks before posing the question she'd been grappling with. "If Sandi and Frank are to blame for this stunt, do you honestly think they're the brains behind this whole operation?"

"No. Gabe said Hatteras was a fixer, and that's the kind of stuff someone like him would try to pull off. But murder? That's on a whole different level."

"That's what I thought, too. Did you see Sandi's face when I called her on it? I don't think killing one of her girls was ever part of her plan."

Walker rubbed his chin; he hadn't shaved, and the stubble looked right at home on him. "I agree. It wouldn't make sense to take such chances when you've already got a sweet deal going with the suits in power." He finished buttering the toast and gave a piece to Reggie. "Remember, Gabe said Hatteras was in tight with the city government."

Discouraged, Reggie had been sitting with her chin in hand, but Walker's words struck a chord. She popped up in her chair. "That's it—that's the link with the third victim! He'd been an aide to someone on the board of supervisors, right?"

"Amy Jin, I think, yes. Are you suggesting she—?"

"No, not necessarily. I don't know anything about her. But it stands to reason that everybody knows *somebody* in that place. Like an exclusive little club, you know? So maybe someone at a higher level contacted the staffer, who put them in touch with Hatteras."

She pondered while she chewed her toast. *A higher level*. Something kept tickling her memory. "*Leo*."

Walker gave her an odd look. "Leo?"

Reggie smiled the satisfaction of one who has just filled in the outer frame of a thousand-piece puzzle. "I just remembered what Dr. Brunt told me about the local jade collectors he knew. One of them is plugged into the city's cultural affairs, and the other is much higher than even that." Her smile faded as she realized where this whole search was headed.

Who is it?"

"The Consul General of San Francisco."

For what country?"

She swallowed. "The People's Republic of China."

Walker stopped mid-bite. "You're serious?"

"Afraid so. The question is, if it was someone that high up, do you think Sandi or Hatteras would have relayed my message to them?"

"Not in a million years," Walker said. "What I *can* see is those two trying an end run. They probably figure what the client doesn't know won't hurt them."

"But their client *is* going to know, because we're going to tell them."

Walker frowned. "How do you propose we do that?"

Reggie took a deep breath. "We're going to invite every collector Dr. Brunt can think of to see the 'real' Firestone tigers."

"What, you're putting on a party?"

"Yes, and though I never thought I'd ever say this, I want to make sure I'm the belle of the ball."

Chapter Nineteen

The Palace of the Legion of Honor was a small but elegant museum located on the headlands of San Francisco, west of the Presidio and east of the Cliff House. It had an impressive view of the Golden Gate Bridge and was known for its impressive Rodin collection. Nearly a hundred of the French sculptor's works, not to mention the museum itself, had been donated to the city by Alma de Bretteville Spreckles, one of the most flamboyant characters of the Gilded Age.

From what little he'd read about her, Walker wished he'd been able to capture "Big Alma" on film. Even in the old black-and-white prints he'd seen, her outsized personality came through without apology. She was known throughout her life as both a great beauty and a woman of implacable will; both of those traits reminded him of the woman he was now sitting next to.

The afternoon turned out to be as warm and as mild as promised, even in the city, which by all accounts was rare. Regina leaned back on the stone balustrade that encircled the museum's garden, her eyes closed and her face tilted toward the sun. She was dressed in jeans that fit her like a cherished glove, and a roomy, loosely woven cotton sweater that hid the charms he knew existed beneath. She wore brightly stitched ankle boots; he wondered idly what color they were.

It was almost three p.m. and they could see that Dr. Leo Brunt was wrapping up a tour of the museum's permanent exhibits for a group of college students by discussing some of the garden sculptures. Regina said he was an adjunct professor of art curation at the University of San Francisco, although you'd never know it to look at him. He came across as a slightly more civilized version of The Rock, with the same passable-looking, vaguely exotic head placed on top of a physique that looked like it could hold its own in just about any dicey situation.

Walker muttered a mild expletive and felt small for doing so.

"Did you say something?" Regina asked.

"Me? No. Just wondering when class is getting out. Seems strange to take a field trip on a Saturday. The whole point is to get out of school, isn't it?"

Regina rolled her eyes. "It's not fifth grade, you know. Besides, he says Saturdays are good for showing students how the public views a museum collection." She checked her watch. "He said to meet him here at 3 p.m., so it should be any time now." She was paying the professor the same rapt attention as his students, which irritated Walker even more.

"I'd love to take a class from him sometime; he is so dialed into the art scene. I wonder if he ever teaches adults?"

"Haven't a clue. You could ask him. I'm sure he could accommodate you."

His energy was starting to slip its tether, so he got up and examined the huge bronze statue of El Cid overlooking the lawn. Only one of the horse's front legs was raised. Wasn't that supposed to mean something in terms of how the subject astride the horse died? He wasn't sure. The learned professor would probably know … of course he would.

Dr. Brunt gestured for his students to exit back through the main entrance and walked over to Regina, taking her shoulders and giving her a quick peck on the cheek. Walker set his jaw. Brunt had met her, like once, hadn't he? Wasn't that a bit—

"And you must be Walker Banks," he said, extending his hand. "I love your work, man; what you do with form, shadow, and light is incredible."

Okay, well, maybe he's not so bad. Walker returned the handshake. "Thanks, Dr. Brunt. Coming from you, that's quite a compliment, since Regina says you're the go-to guy for art in the city."

"Call me Leo, please. I'm not sure how far my expertise takes me, but I'm willing to help. Let's grab a coffee in the museum and get down to business."

Regina cordially slipped her arm through Leo's as

they walked ahead; Walker tried not to be even more out of sorts than he already was.

Was something wrong? Walker sounded clipped as he offered to stand in line to get coffee. *Well, maybe he just needs some caffeine.* Reggie took advantage of the time to fill Leo in on the latest developments regarding the theft.

He was astonished. "Your whole house was trashed?"

"Well, it's just a cottage, but yes, they did a number on the place. Walker and I were down there this morning cleaning up; Fortunately, they didn't take anything of real value, just a small gold necklace I'd been working on. I'm staying at The Grove for the time being, and I usually keep the tigers with me."

"May I see them again?"

"Sure." She pulled them out of her purse and handed them over. "You were right, by the way. Thomas Ling made his mark, but it's hidden behind one of the eyes. And I'm not sure whether you've heard, but he's nowhere to be found. His mother says he was taken away by government agents for some espionage-related charge, but I don't buy it, not for a second."

Leo rubbed his chin just like Walker; neither man would have a problem growing a beard. She liked it.

"No, that doesn't sound like Thomas. How long ago did she say he was taken?"

"Four or five days ago, I think."

"I'll make some discreet inquiries; see what's what." He examined the earrings again, then held her gaze. "So, you really want to do this, huh?" He was referring to her request on the phone earlier that day.

"What? You mean stick a sign on myself that says 'Come and get me?'"

He smiled as he handed the tigers back. "Something like that."

"You have officially joined the chorus of naysayers who think I'm crazy."

"And Walker Banks is one of them, I trust."

Reggie snorted. "The chief naysayer."

"Good man," he murmured.

"But my answer is still an unqualified yes. I think the culprits who broke into my home last night are underlings, trying to take advantage of the confusion regarding which pair is real, perhaps. But someone higher up the food chain orchestrated the original switch. I'm almost sure of it."

Leo was about to respond when Walker came back with three coffees and some tasty looking cinnamon buns. "I couldn't resist," he said, handing out the cups and pastries.

"Ironically these come from Lindy's in Little Eden," Leo said. "That little bakery right down the hill from The Grove."

"I am doomed," Reggie said, biting into the sweetly satisfying confection.

"So, Regina tells me you have a list of who's who in the jade collection world."

"Pretty much," Leo said. "And surprisingly, a number of them are open to showing their collections to each other. They like to preen about what they've acquired, and possibly do some wheeling and dealing on the side."

Walker looked skeptical. "But would they come just to see the tigers?"

"Certainly, knowing they were from the Firestone collection, which hasn't surfaced in decades. But I think I can do you one better."

"What do you mean?" asked Reggie.

"You said you knew Milton Collier, right? I saw him at an auction last week and he mentioned your collection. He already knew you had moved to The Grove to set it up—said he read a blurb about it in the trades. He also knew the tigers were part of the collection and he said he'd love to see them 'up close and personal,' which would indicate he didn't instigate the switch. It would be no stretch at all to get him to agree to host a collectors' reception in your honor. Collectors do that all the time."

"Really? I pretty much insulted him the last time I saw him."

"Let me guess: he came on to you," Walker said. He sounded disgruntled.

Reggie nodded. "Yep. But Leo, if you think he'd still be willing, could we invite the other collectors you spoke of—the retired actress and the Consul General?

We think there may be some type of government connection, so they should be at the top of the list."

"Absolutely," Leo said. "Serious collectors rarely miss an opportunity to scout out their next purchase, so don't be surprised if you get several offers, whispered to you in passing."

"Well, at least we can eliminate Collier as a suspect," Walker said.

"Perhaps," mused Leo, "But even if he took them, planting a seed of doubt about their authenticity would entice him to do a little double-checking on his own, 'up close and personal.'"

"Or maybe he'd see it as an opportunity to secretly gloat about what he'd stolen," Reggie suggested.

Leo shrugged. "Or he could be exactly as he seems, an interested connoisseur."

Walker took a sip of his black coffee and shook his head. "I don't like it. It's one thing to have control over a venue; it's another to be operating on someone else's turf."

"Yes and no," Leo said. "A lot of these people are friends, or at least friendly enemies, and they'll relax a bit more in a private setting. We might hear something that leads us where we want to go."

"As long as we can maintain some control over the environment, I think it's a great idea," Reggie said. "Go ahead and float the idea by Mr. Collier. If he bites, tell him you're sure I'd be flattered to have him host the reception in my honor. We could tout it as a 'tease' for the Grand Re-Opening of The Grove." She turned to

Walker. "Could you pay the upfront costs—catering and so forth—so we can at least have that much control? Maybe we can use that as an excuse to poke around beforehand and see if he's up to something. I promise to pay you back every penny."

Leo looked at Walker, an amused expression on his face. "That work for you?"

"Whatever she needs," Walker said, but he wasn't smiling.

"Well then, while you're at it, you'd best have some added security; I can line up some of my cohorts to work the event, if you like."

Walker nodded. "By all means. I'm sure you know the priorities."

Leo glanced at Reggie. "Yes, I do."

As they all got ready to leave, Walker asked Leo the strangest thing. "So, about El Cid in the courtyard," he said, "the hoofs..."

"Urban legend, I'm afraid. Works with El Cid but there are two dozen or so in Washington that don't fit the bill."

"What on earth are you guys talking about?" Reggie asked.

"Nothing much," Walker said. "Just something I read about horse statues." He and Leo headed out together and Reggie couldn't help admiring them from behind. *Guys are sexiest when they're just being ... guys,* she thought with a grin.

As for her beloved earrings, she felt more optimistic

than she had in days. Maybe she'd find the answers she'd been looking for.

But another thought followed on the heels of the first, and it wiped the smile off her face: once she knew who'd taken her family's treasure, what on earth could she do to get it back?

Chapter Twenty

You know it's a rockin' idea. Just ask her what she thinks. What's she gonna do, fire you? Axel warred with himself as he sat across from Jenna in the museum office. He'd uncovered some really sick shit about the tongs and he figured a lot of people would be interested in it, especially these days.

"So, uh, I found some cool stuff," he said, trying to sound like it didn't matter whether he shared the stuff or not, even though he was dying to.

Jenna was peering at her screen and didn't look up. "Oh yeah? What?" She tapped on her keyboard a few more times, then turned to him and smiled.

"Well, you know how today everybody's tatted up..."

"I'm not," she said.

"Yeah, well, I'm not, either, but that's just because I'm a chickenshit." He grinned at her.

"Ha! Me too. But go on."

"Well, lots of people love gettin' tats and I been reading about how the Chinese have been doing it for centuries, only Confucius said you shouldn't mess with the body that your parents gave you 'cause it's disrespectful to them. So, they used tattoos to punish people who broke laws and that ended up being a sign you were a criminal."

"Kind of like a permanent version of The Scarlet Letter," Jenna said.

"What's that?"

Jenna looked surprised. "What? They didn't teach you *The Scarlet Letter*? Nathanial Hawthorne? What's this world coming to?"

She said it like a joke, but Axel still didn't know what she was riffing on, so he went on. "After a while the bad dudes started to dig the idea of tats, plus, when they started gangs like the tongs in Chinatown, they each had their own tats that said what group they belonged to. Like, you had to get one to prove you were loyal and everything. I'm pretty sure that gangs do that today. And the *boo how doy* marked other people up, too. Plus, the Chinese have had these, like secret societies *forever*. They were mainly poor people and they were always giving the emperors shit. Like, they were the Resistance. And *they* had secret tats. So it might be kind of cool to mention that stuff in the museum part about the tongs, and when people read it, if they have tats, they can see what a long tradition they're part of. I even found some old pictures of some of them. Maybe they'll want to read some more about it, too."

"That's a great idea. Come to think of it, I remember reading somewhere in Amanda Firestone's diary about her husband's tattoo. Apparently Will Firestone got one in Hong Kong or someplace. That was long before they got married."

"Hey, maybe he joined a secret society there or something."

Jenna chuckled. "Nah, I don't think so. As I recall, it had something to do with missing his family. It was a reminder of what was waiting for him back home in San Francisco. So, we could add that as a tie-in, along with the tattoo background. You know something? You've got the makings of a natural born museum curator."

"Yeah, right." But Axel couldn't keep the grin off his face. Sometimes his ideas were pretty damn good!

He worked on getting more facts for another hour or so until Jenna announced that they were done for the day, which was cool because it was Saturday, and who works all day on Saturdays? *Well, except my dad,* he thought.

"Hey, I've got to go down to Lindy's to re-stock the cinnamon bread and run a few more errands. You want to come with me and get the lay of the land? There's a cinnamon bun in it for you," she said.

Axel could tell she was just being nice, but it beat just hanging out by himself. "Yeah, I'm in."

"I'm just getting to know Little Eden again myself," Jenna explained as they drove down the hill a short time later. "The last time I was here I was around your age. But Lindy's Bakery has been in business for more than a hundred years, can you believe that? And it's still owned by the same family."

There was no parking spot nearby, so they'd had to drive around until Jenna spotted a space that required parallel parking. Axel watched carefully as she maneuvered into it.

"That was *epic*," he said. "How long did it take you to learn that?"

"What, parallel parking? No time at all. You just need to take a couple of tries and then you get it. I hear your dad's giving you lessons. He'll show you."

That'll be the day. "Yeah, I don't think so. He was pretty irritated the one time he tried to teach me."

"Well, he's got a lot on his mind. If you want, when we go back up to The Grove, I can show you in the parking lot up there."

"Really?"

"Sure. No worries."

They walked back up the street and entered the store, which was real homey looking but still modern. There were three cases filled with pies and cinnamon rolls and loaves of bread and all kinds of cookies. And behind the counter was one of the girls from the cafe where Axel had eaten with his dad. She was about the same height as Axel but was a lot curvier and she had really pretty light hair and some freckles that were kind of cute. She looked around his age, too.

But the most incredible thing was her t-shirt. It said, "Sorry for the things I said during Settlers of Catan."

Axel pointed to her shirt. "You play?"

The girl grinned at him. "Does a bear shit in the woods?"

"Kaitlyn!" an older lady, also working behind the counter, ragged on her.

Kaitlyn shrugged and chuckled. "Sorry. How about you?" she asked.

"Oh, well, I like to play, but I just moved here, and ..."

"Hey, you wanna play in about—" She looked at the clock and he followed her gaze. It was one p.m. "—two hours? A group of us play on Saturday afternoons at the Hang Out. It's like an all ages place."

"Uh, I don't know where that is. I—"

"It's on Holloway Road. Three blocks down, one block over. About ten minutes' walk from here."

Axel reviewed his options. He could say no, go back to The Grove and hang out online ... or he could play the game and maybe meet some people. It was a no brainer. He glanced at Jenna, who was getting her bread and the cinnamon rolls from the older lady, then turned back to Kaitlyn. "Uh, sure, if you think it's okay."

"Oh yeah, it's fine. We have extensions, so we can have different players. And, um, we order pizza afterward, so bring some money for that."

Axel sent her what he hoped was a cool smile. "Okay. Gucci."

Once they'd left the bakery, Jenna playfully thumped Axel on the shoulder. "Way to go, bro!"

"You sure you don't mind? I figured you probably didn't really want to, you know—"

"What, give you the parking lesson? Sure, I will, but it can wait. Let's make my other stops so we can get back to The Grove in time for you to walk down the hill again."

"Uh, walk?"

Jenna laughed. "Yeah, weird concept, I know. Or maybe you could ride a bike; you know how to ride?"

Axel took offense at that. "Of course I know how to ride!"

"Hey, I went to art school in New York and I know from experience you take your life in your hands riding there. Anyway, I think my brother—he's off at college—has one you can use. When I was a little kid, I used to ride my bike down the hill all the time."

"Sweet. No, I was just kind of thinking I didn't know where it was, so I didn't want to get lost."

Jenna nodded. "You're like me. You want to know what you're getting into. So, let's drive around and find the place so you'll know right where to go."

They stopped by the Manna Market and a few other places before finding the Hang Out, which really was pretty close to the bakery. Then they returned to The Grove. His dad and Regina still weren't home, but he was used to being on his own, so that was no big deal.

He ran upstairs, sniffed under his arm, and decided he'd better take a quick shower and change shirts. Turns out Jenna's brother Jason had an old beater, but it still worked okay. Good thing he'd be sweating getting back up the hill after the gaming session and not before.

It was turning out to be a great day.

Chapter Twenty-One

Sandi Bollocks sat in her office chair rubbing one of her feet. "What a godawful day this has been. We spend half the night looking for those damn tigers and come up empty. I get about three hours' sleep, then I've got to spend the whole day coordinating the escorts for that IT convention. 'I want a blond with big boobs,' 'Gimme a black Asian gender neutral who likes it rough.' For heaven's sakes, I've got variety, but come on! Have you seen some of those guys? Beggars can't be choosers."

Frank Hatteras was paying more attention to his phone than her.

"Hey, Earth to Frank," Sandi said.

He looked up. "Huh? Oh, sorry. Listen, I think I've got an idea how we can make some lemonade here. Plan A: we tail the broad—I'll find out where she's living—and at some point relieve her of the bling."

"How do we know she'll even have them with her?"

"We don't. If she doesn't have them, we 'persuade' her to get them for us."

"I'm not so sure about that. That specimen she was with looked like he wasn't leaving her side anytime soon, so no, I'm not thrilled with that one. Too dangerous. What's Plan B?"

"Plan B is I tell the client we've got word a certain unnamed person has information of vital importance regarding the tigers, but they need ten G's to spill the beans. We collect and share what we know."

Sandi put her shoe back on. "I like that one a whole lot better."

"Yeah, but that's peanuts compared to what those tigers are worth."

"True, but if you screw up, I'm stuck visiting you in the Q or else paying for a fancy funeral."

Frank got up, leaned over the desk and gave Sandi a quick kiss. "I'm touched you'd even put on a funeral, baby. Leave it to me. I'll be in touch."

Sandi sat rocking in her chair for a few minutes after he left. This whole job had gotten way out of hand, and she didn't even know who they were dealing with! Frank had kept the client to himself, if he even knew who it was, and she wondered if he wasn't planning a double cross. No, they'd been together too long for that, hadn't they? But never trust a bullshitter, right? She ought to know; she was one, after all.

The intercom buzzed. "The guy in room fourteen eighty-three says Marla didn't show. He'll take whoever else you got, but you gotta move fast."

"Tell him we're on it," Sandi said. "And if Marla shows, let him know the threesome's on us."

She dialed one of her most reliable girls. *Frank and I agree on one thing, at least: you've got to keep the customer happy.*

Chapter Twenty-Two

Was the time racing by or moving like sludge? A little of both, Reggie decided.

The "sting," if you could call it that, was shaping up nicely. Leo had called Milton Collier, who said he'd be delighted to host the gathering a week from the following Tuesday, leaving them ten days in which to prepare. Between Collier's list and Leo's there were already fifty-five rsvp's, including the Consul General, his wife, and two staff members. The actress/activist Lily Quan would also make an appearance. Collier had offered to pay for the caterer, but at Reggie's insistence he'd deferred and settled for opening his expansive home for set-up on Tuesday morning. He would love to give Reggie a personal tour of his collection, he'd said.

Leo had also hired a contingent of security personnel. Some of them would act as servers, and others would be in plain clothes, ubiquitous "art lovers" who'd roam the premises and keep their eyes peeled. Collier had said it wasn't necessary because he employed his own security staff whenever he had a party. Again, however, Reggie insisted—or so relayed Leo—because of the earrings' value as well as a "previous attempt at theft which had fortunately been thwarted." Leo had purposefully kept the details of the failed heist ambiguous.

"We want these players to believe you're wearing the equivalent of the Crown Jewels," Leo told her. "We're getting the idea across."

With all the tumblers clicking into place, Reggie was anxious to get on with the performance. Were any of the guests the quarry they sought? And if so, would they overplay their hand? She was impatient to find out, and spent every evening researching the likely suspects to see if she could glean any useful information about them.

The Consul General, for example, was in his early fifties and had been educated in England before returning to China to serve in the government. He was an ambitious man and already wealthy, as so many high-level bureaucrats were in the People's Republic. His wife had also been educated in the west but was a practicing physician and usually stayed home in Beijing with their two children. Apparently, however, she was visiting her husband in the States—perhaps, Reggie mused, on a buying trip. They were connoisseurs of both Hotan and Burmese jade and supposedly had a growing collection that included nephrite specimens from Alaska and Wyoming.

Lily Quan, the retired actress who lived in the exclusive San Francisco neighborhood of Presidio Heights, was an admitted devotee of all things Chinese; she gravitated toward hand-painted porcelain from both the Ming and Qing dynasties, along with carvings and jade jewelry.

And Milton Collier, the host, seemed like a spoiler: his acquisition record (which, unlike many collectors, he wasn't afraid to share with the public) showed that he often stepped in with an inflated bid to thwart his colleagues. He had amassed quite a fortune in historic gems from several different countries, but he had a real fondness for old jade—*very* old jade.

On top of would-be thieves, Reggie had a stubborn photographer to deal with who vexed her on several levels, some of which she didn't want to think about.

Walker was definitely getting under her skin. He was not comfortable with the upcoming event and her part in it, and he let her know it one evening as she sat working alone on her laptop in the library of the Great House. Jenna and Brit were out and Walker had left sometime earlier to "run some errands." He and Axel had just returned together, arguing as they entered the house.

"You've been out until after ten p.m. almost every night this week," Walker said. "I drove around all over looking for you. What's this all about?"

"I'm just hangin' with friends, that's all." Axel sounded defiant. "What do you care, anyway? I'm not using the laptop you're so worried about."

"Well, it's dark out, and you're on a bike."

"Yeah, well, not much I can do about that until I get a car," Axel shot back before leaving the room. "Gotta get to sleep. Work tomorrow." He glanced at Reggie on his way upstairs. "Hey," he said without much enthusiasm.

"It's not safe!" Walker called to his son's retreating back. They both watched Axel disappear and Walker let out a frustrated sigh. "That kid," he said.

"Hey, he's got friends, though, right? That's a good thing."

Walker shot her a disgruntled look. "Yeah, but who are they? They could be anybody."

Reggie was careful not to smile. "Yep, anybody. Like really great kids, for instance."

"You're one to talk," he responded, walking around the sofa to face her directly. He practically shook his finger at her. "You're putting yourself out there, just asking to be preyed upon by whoever's behind this."

Reggie started to argue but thought better of it; Walker was loaded for bear right now and nothing she could argue was going to change that. It dawned on her that even though he put on a stoic front, inside he was probably afraid that he couldn't protect those he cared about. The idea that he might feel that way about *her* sent her heart skittering.

"Aren't you going to say anything?"

Yes, he is absolutely spoiling for a fight. "No. Nothing I can say will make you feel any better, about me or about Axel. Sorry."

He stared at her for a long, charged minute, the tension between them stretching so taut she thought it might snap and hurt one of them. Without realizing it, she took in a shuddered breath and held it. They were partners in one sense, adversaries in another, but these days, holding his gaze for any length of time was bound to churn up emotions, desire heading the list, that didn't fit in either category.

He broke eye contact first and ran his hands through his already disheveled hair, a quirk she noticed happened regularly around her. "Women and teenagers," he muttered before heading toward the kitchen. "I need a beer."

Reggie slowly exhaled, her heart returning to normal.

Walker Banks was taking up way too much of her mental space. They were merely reluctant colleagues with a common goal, right? He cared for her safety as he would for anyone he worked with.

But what about the kiss? He must have felt something. *Purely a response to my distress,* she argued. *It probably meant nothing ... at least to him.*

Better to focus on matters she could control, if that was even possible. Truth be told, she didn't feel the same level of anxiety that Walker did about the reception. Intuition told her that it would be a reconnaissance mission for the thief as much as for her, if the culprit even showed up. She was confident that Walker, Leo and the security team would protect her on the off chance she needed them.

No, it was the uncertainty that had her spooked. The not knowing who it was, or what they might do later on if they believed the ruse.

Whether Walker approved of it or not, she'd chosen the path. It might be dark, but she was committed to following it.

During the days before the reception, both Reggie and Walker had worked on the Amanda Firestone exhibit. One thing Reggie came to realize right away was that Walker Banks thoroughly understood the visual arts. He'd expanded upon Jenna's initial layout so that now, for the first time ever, visitors could truly understand and appreciate the life of Mandy Culpepper *before* she became the Bay Area's social and literary icon Amanda Firestone. For years, Reggie had lobbied her family to make this happen, and by God, she would *not* let the theft of her grandmother's jewels spoil it in any way.

She'd finished going over the draft of the major didactic labels that would go on the walls and paused to watch Walker working on another section of the display. He had sinewy arms and strong, sure hands; he didn't hesitate to move the large hanging panels around until he was satisfied with their placement. Ninety-nine percent of the time he was right; Reggie knew, because she was always looking for that one percent, just to keep him honest.

"I think you've got those two up too high," she

admonished him the afternoon after his tirade. "Just because you're six feet tall, doesn't mean the rest of the world should have to stand on tip toes."

Unperturbed by her dissent, he was focused, professional. "Nope. These are transitional images, and if you're viewing them from the other side, they must be higher, or they'll be blocked by the partition wall."

She purposefully walked across the exhibit space to view it from the perspective he'd laid out. Dammit, he was right. He shrugged his shoulders before turning back to the wall display.

"I do love the way this flows," she admitted as she walked along the right side aisle following the inline display the way visitors would see it. A timeline showed historic photographs of Little Eden and The Grove before and during construction of the retreat at the turn of the twentieth century. The founders August and Lia Wolff were profiled and their vision clearly explained. Images already collected depicted Mandy as a wide-eyed, fifteen-year-old mother's helper from the village, dressed in an old-fashioned pinafore and shoes; a case displayed similar clothing, loaned by estates, worn by the working class during that time.

As she walked, Reggie began to imagine the transformation of Mandy into a talented young writer who championed the slave girls of San Francisco's Chinatown. Here there were photographs of the young girls and other immigrants going about their daily lives, as well as the "dens of iniquity" that whites during that time feared and ridiculed. Original documents showed the practice of posing as "paper sons," the way many Chinese got around the highly restrictive immigration laws. The presentation didn't glorify the story for either side: Jenna, Dani, and Axel's research revealed both the good and the bad aspects of San Francisco society during the Gilded Age.

The latter part of the exhibit featured one of the most captivating parts of Mandy Culpepper's early life. On the cusp of adulthood, she had served briefly as a life model, posing nude for the retreat artists so they could learn to recreate the human form in their chosen medium. And what a sublime human form it was, reproduced by the artists in sketches, paintings, sculpture and even a few photographs. Mandy was obviously an exceptional woman both inside and out; Reggie admired her, and envied her a little, too.

Every ten feet or so, an interactive audio console was placed that would encourage listeners to steep themselves in the era through original sounds: the clip clop of the horse and buggies sharing the road with the occasional honk of a new-fangled automobile ... the call of a newsboy proclaiming the headlines of the day ... the talk of everyday Americans gleaned from audio archives around the country. Adding a unique touch were clips from a nostalgic interview with Amanda Firestone herself, taped by an enterprising relative when Reggie was just a child; her grandmother's recollections dovetailed perfectly with the entries the woman had written in her lifelong diary. Neither the written nor spoken memories of her life before marrying Will Firestone had ever been shared with the public.

Then there were the jewels, the highlight of the exhibit.

Right now, several empty pedestal cases armed with silent sensors dotted the spacious display room. Each already had labels describing the piece of jewelry that would eventually be placed inside. One of them would contain the jade tigers—when they were returned. *But what if we don't find them?* she thought in a brief burst of panic. Would they have to put Thomas Ling's reproductions in the case instead and pretend they were the originals? And where was the carver, anyway? Nothing had turned up about him since his "arrest." Had they gotten rid of him, too? She tried to ignore the profound sadness she felt at the thought that someone else might have lost their life over the theft of the earrings. *Don't borrow worry*, she told herself.

Focusing again on the exhibit, she couldn't help but admire the large black and white photographic reproductions on the walls that showed Mandy wearing some of the pieces—and nothing else.

What didn't exist was a place for a live model. Secretly, Reggie heaved a sigh of relief, but felt a need to protest on principle. She preferred anger to sadness anyway. She grit her teeth, trying but failing to minimize her irritation. "I don't see a place for a live model," she said. "You can't just ignore me and think that I'm going to go away."

With an air of resignation, Walker climbed down the

ladder he'd been perched on and beckoned Reggie over to one of the many benches set strategically for visitors to rest their feet while perusing a specific work of art. In this case it was the bench with the best view of the jade tigers' display case.

"Can we talk about this sensibly?" he asked.

Oh, that was the wrong thing to say, Mr. Banks. "Sensibly?"

Walker held up his hand. "I'm sorry. I meant without emotion, on either side. If you'll indulge me, I'd like to share some thoughts."

Reggie tilted her head. She could be sober and judicious about this. She could. "Go right ahead. I'm listening."

"When your grandmother posed nude more than a century ago, she was doing so for the benefit of a very limited, very specific audience. She knew those men and women. They were her friends. They were not interested in exploiting her—well, maybe the photographer was, but luckily, he never attempted to cash in on the photographs he took of her. The point is, her audience was small and friendly; yours would be totally different. Today it would essentially be the world."

"Oh, come on," she began, but stopped when Walker asked with a pointed look to continue.

"I know you want to pay homage to your grandmother, and I respect and admire that. However, if you pose naked as a publicity stunt or out of some harebrained notion that you're helping The Grove off to a better start, you're wrong. You will saddle The Grove with a prurient first impression that the tabloids will latch on to and not let go of."

What did she ever see in him? He was a prude. "It's not a harebrained idea."

Walker paused as if collecting his thoughts. "Okay, you're right. The word 'harebrained' is hereby withdrawn, your Honor. What I meant was, even if you skirted public indecency laws and were allowed to model as you've imagined, it would be captured forever on every visitor's cell phone. Within seconds, you'd become the new darling of Instagram, and if you didn't go along with the crowd, you'd be savaged on Twitter and every other form of social media. And that *would* hurt The Grove and what it's trying to achieve." He looked at her intensely. "I have a better idea."

Reggie narrowed her eyes. "What's your better idea?"

"Why not do a series of photographs, instead? Just like your grandmother did. That way it's private and tasteful. And you're not physically on display."

Reggie wasn't too sure how she felt about her body being captured on film. Before she could stop herself, her insecurities bubbled up. "That's so permanent. I don't know if I measure up. My grandmother was so…" Beautiful. Exotic. Elegant. She didn't know if she'd suffer by comparison.

Walker seemed to understand her unspoken concerns. His voice softened. "You are every bit as capable of wearing the jewels *au naturel* as your grandmother was. You have nothing to fear."

Walker's words felt like a caress and Reggie sensed warmth rushing upward from her toes. Was she going to mortify herself by blushing? "So, you're saying, as a compromise, I should have some photographs taken as part of the exhibit?"

"Precisely. I love the idea of recapturing those moments from your grandmother's story, showing the timelessness of both the gems and the beauty of the human form. And I think there's only one photographer who can do that justice."

"Who do you have in mind?"

"Me."

Chapter Twenty-Three

"You?"

If he hadn't been so invested in her reaction, Walker would have laughed at the shocked expression on Regina's face. "I am a professional, you know." He couldn't help the slight edge to his words.

"I ... I know that. Of course, I know that. It's just ... I didn't think..." She sent him a rueful smile. "I guess I didn't think beyond the 'I should do this' part to the 'How am I going to do this' part."

"Well, I've been thinking about that, too. I've studied the historical photos of your grandmother's modeling, and I think we'll be able to recreate the set-up in the front room of your cottage. That way you will have complete control over how many people you want to be present during the photography session."

Regina's expression looked faintly horrified. "I'm not sure how comfortable I'd be with others in the room."

Walker couldn't help chuckling. "Uh, what did you think was going to happen with a live modeling session?"

She had the grace to look sheepish. "You've got me there. I guess I thought of it as a one-shot deal. But you're right, of course. Still, I think maybe it should just be the two of us."

The two of them, alone? He was already beginning to harden at the thought. *No, that can't happen; we do not need that complication.* "Well ..."

"Wait. I could ask my cousin Ava. She'd be happy to help me out."

Thank you, Ava, whoever you are. "Yes, that'd be fine. I was thinking we could combine shots that reflect the originals, along with others that put a modern twist on things. And in each, I could use color selectivity to highlight the gems on an otherwise black-and-white image."

Regina impulsively reached for his arm. "I love that! The original photographs are lovely, but they don't capture the vibrant color of the citrine or the gold collar or, well, any of them. The most eye-catching photo is the one where she's wearing the tigers, I guess because they're white."

"Color wasn't available to most photographers until the year after those photos of your grandmother were taken. In fact, I'm surprised Peter Raines didn't paint some of the shots afterward for that very reason."

"Well, we'll be able to show how brilliant they are

—" she stopped then, embarrassed. "Oh, I'm sorry, I heard you don't distinguish colors very well."

He shrugged. "Certain ones, but I manage. And it's good you'll be with me, so you can help me figure out what colors they should be." And, God help him, he was looking forward to it.

"So, um, when would we do this?"

"I was thinking this weekend, if that works for you. Saturday after dinner? I'm going to need several weeks to work with the photographs afterward; I don't want to rush it. But if you're worried about the reception, I totally get it. We can wait—"

"No, let's get it done. I'd like to have it out of the way so we can concentrate on what needs to happen after Tuesday."

Walker's lips quirked. "You make it sound like a dental appointment."

And then she graced him with a look—part guile, part innocence—that nearly blinded him with desire. He thought of the cliff he'd barely crawled out of back in Zion and realized he was on the brink of another abyss of a very different type.

"No, I wouldn't exactly call it that," she said.

They gazed at each other, each sending the other bemused smiles. She absently placed a strand of her long curling hair behind her ear. It took an enormous amount of concentration to keep from leaning over and kissing her. He could already imagine her taste: fresh and natural and spicy. It would be so easy to—

"So, like is anybody here?"

Walker's thoughts were interrupted by the sound of Axel's voice, calling from the other side of the exhibit hall. "Yeah, down here around the corner," Walker called back.

In a matter of moments, Axel, dressed in his usual shorts and mocking t-shirt ("See, another day when I didn't use algebra") came up to them. But he wasn't alone. Glued to his side was one of the girls Walker recognized from their first night at the Milk and Honey Cafe. She was almost as tall as Axel, with thick blond hair and a few scattered freckles. She had a sweet, wholesome face and wore a disarming smile.

"Uh, Dad, this is Kaitlyn O'Roarke. Her family owns Lindy's Bakery. You know, where we get that totally sick cinnamon bread?" Axel glanced at Kaitlyn, who giggled. "Uh, and this is Reggie Firestone. She makes jewelry."

"Cool." Kaitlyn looked around the nearly-empty space. "So, this is the exhibit you've been designing, huh?"

She had addressed her question to Axel and Walker caught Regina's eye. It was universal that when a boy wanted to impress a girl, he tended to exaggerate his achievements. Kaitlyn must be the reason Axel had been coming home late.

"Uh, yeah," Axel said, glancing at Walker, no doubt hoping he wouldn't put the lie to Axel's words.

"Why don't you tell Kaitlyn about the part you're

working on now?" Walker asked. "I'm sure Regina would like to hear about it, too."

Axel frowned but hesitated only slightly before saying, "Well, there's this whole section in the show that's about the Chinese gangs and their badass societies. They had some weird sh—uh, stuff going on, like all these secret passwords and tattoos and even some underground hideouts. The lady who's the star of this show got kidnapped by one of them."

"Oh my God," said Kaitlyn, suitably spellbound.

"Yeah, she was even younger than us, but the good news is, she escaped, even though her Chinese buddy at the time was beaten almost to death."

"Wow, that's some gruesome stuff," Regina said.

"Yeah, totally." Axel then took Kaitlyn by the hand. "Come on, I'll show you how it goes from the beginning. My dad's the installer." The two teens wandered back through the exhibit, Axel's voice growing fainter as he continued to enthrall his audience of one.

"Guess we know where Axel's been every night." Reggie looked amused.

Walker wasn't as sanguine. "Please don't tell me I've got to start worrying about hormones now; I've got enough on my plate as it is."

Reggie stood up and pulled on Walker's hand much like his son had done with his girlfriend. "Come on, let's get out of here. Maybe the kids will deign to join us for pizza."

Walker stopped and pulled out his phone. "Wait, I'd

better mark the occasion. The two of us have agreed for going on fifteen minutes now."

"Very funny. If you're so impressed with that, let's obliterate that record and see if we can make it last through dinner."

"You're on."

They'd eaten dinner at Papa Giuseppe's over in Bellam Cove, but their pizza didn't hold a candle to Lindy's. Kaitlyn had suggested it because it was a welcome change of venue for her and it was obvious Axel was eager to please his lady love.

Kaitlyn, it turned out, was an avid board and video game player; she also liked art and practiced calligraphy. Best of all, she loved the outdoors and had already taken Axel on several hikes around the area. He was even beginning to sport a bit of a tan. For that alone, Walker was grateful. But the way Axel looked at Kaitlyn reminded him of his sixteen-year-old self and that gave him pause.

After dropping the girl at her home and returning to the Great House, Regina called it a night and Walker stopped by Axel's room to pick up his son's laptop. "I really like Kaitlyn," he said. "She seems like she's got her act together."

Axel nodded as he hung up his jacket. "Yeah, she's cool." He stopped and looked Walker in the eye, a surprisingly mature move. "So, I was sort of hoping you could take me to get my license here pretty soon, since I'm already sixteen and all. And then, you know..."

"Let me guess. You want to borrow the car and take her out on a proper date?"

Axe smiled sheepishly. "Yeah, maybe."

"I don't know. There's a lot of stuff we haven't gone over—"

"Well, uh, I've been learning stuff from Jenna. Like she taught me to parallel park and shit like that."

"What? Have you been bugging her?"

Axel bristled. "No! She offered. And she's really cool and nice, and most important—she's *around*."

Shit. The parental noose tightened a little. Axe was right; Walker had canceled their next couple driving lessons in favor of getting materials for the exhibit or working with Regina. Axel hadn't bugged him about them since; now Walker knew why. "Okay, yeah, I'm sorry about that. Things came up—" *like me dropping the ball.*

"Sure, I get it. You and Reggie 'working together.'" He used air quotes. "But hey, it's okay because Jenna came through. And even the Professor drove around with me once, giving me tips. So, it's all good. I just want to get it *done*."

"All right. Let's set a time to see if you're ready, and we'll take it from there, okay?"

"Yeah, sure. When?"

"Ah, how about Sunday, early?" There was one

more thing he needed to get out in the open. "And, Axe, we need to talk about you going back to school—"

"I don't want to talk about that now," he said fiercely. "I'm really tired. Just let me enjoy this time for once, okay? *Okay?*"

Okay, I hit a nerve there. He held up his hands in mock surrender. "Okay. Duly noted. Goodnight."

On his way back to his room, Walker ran a mental inventory of all the situations competing for front row center in his brain: The Grove. The exhibit. Axel driving. Axel getting involved with a girl. Axel feeling abandoned. Axel being in school three thousand miles away. Regina. The stolen tigers. The dangerous game she was willing to play. How to protect her. The reception. What he needed for that. What it meant that he needed just to be with her. Photographing her naked. God, photographing her *naked*.

Okay. One problem at a time. One day at a time.

Once inside, he saw that the package he'd ordered had been delivered and someone—Jenna, probably—had brought it up to his room. He took the smaller white box out of the larger brown one. Regina might not like it, but it would come in handy for the reception—she'd have to agree with that, at least. And even if she didn't, he had no regrets; it was just something he'd needed to do.

He stripped and went to bed, knowing it would be a while before he slept.

"You agreed to do *what?*"

Reggie, lying in bed, paused on the phone to let Ava absorb what she'd described she was going to do with Walker Banks.

"You heard me. He's going to take some photographs of me modeling grandmother's jewels."

"Naked."

"Naked."

Reggie could hear her cousin's audible sigh on the line. "Do you really think that's a good idea? I mean, you don't even like the guy."

Reggie thought about the kiss and the pull she experienced whenever she was near him, which was decidedly *not* what an enemy would feel. "Well ... that's not *exactly* true. We get along most, well, a lot of the time; we just have disagreements about certain things. I even agreed to go to an art reception with him on Tuesday, so that says something, right?" She hadn't told Ava about the stolen earrings and her plan to flush out the thief, knowing her cousin would be as vocal in her opposition as Walker was.

"All right, I'll concede that point," Ava said in a dubious tone.

"Then you'll come and help out?" Reggie asked.

Ava snorted. "I don't think Walker Banks needs any help. As I recall, he's done this a million times."

"It's not for him; it's for me," Reggie said. "I ... I'd like you to be with me during the session."

Ava's tone turned serious. "Why, are you afraid he might try to pull something?"

"No," Reggie said with a sigh. "I'm afraid I might try to pull something on *him*."

"Oh, girl, that is so not good."

"I know. So, would you, could you, pretty please?"

"Yes, of course. Austin is insisting on taking her that night, so that should work out fine."

"Speaking of Austin, how did he respond to you moving out? It's been a few days now."

Ava sounded concerned. "Austin was surprised—shocked is more like it. I don't think he expected me to have the courage to leave him. He's pissed, and now he's trying to be super dad, wanting Nia all the time. You know he's going overboard when he asks for her on a Saturday night."

"Listen, I know you don't want him back—at least I hope you don't—but this should be a great learning experience for him. Maybe he'll come to appreciate what it's like to be in a loving, two-person relationship."

"We can only hope," Ava said. "I'll just be happy if he keeps things civil during the divorce proceedings, but I have a feeling it's going to get messy. Have I told you lately how happy I am that you found out about Curtis before it was too late? If it weren't for Nia, I'd be kicking myself over the mistakes I've made."

Reggie and Ava talked for a few more minutes about the cottage and how Mr. Big was holding up. When they said their goodbyes, Reggie insisted that Ava give the hound a sloppy kiss for her. "Scratch behind his right ear when you hug him, and he'll know it's from me." She hung up to the sound of Ava's chuckle.

Some things are just not meant to be ... and some things are. Reggie spent the next two days worrying that Ava wouldn't be able to make it, and sure enough, around mid-afternoon on Saturday her cousin called to tell her that once again, Austin had pulled the rug out from under her.

"I could kill the man," Ava groused. "I am so very, very sorry. I could bring Nia down with me..."

"No, that's okay, really. I just hope the whole custody thing gets worked out so you can eventually get some order back into your life."

"Listen, I'm sure Walker will postpone the session. I'll line up a sitter."

"I can't do that; I mean, I could, but he's spent the entire morning setting up the shoot and he's still there. Besides, he's only doing this as a courtesy to me, so I'm not going to pull an Austin on him."

"Yes, but you were worried..."

Reggie huffed. "I know, but as I said, not about him. He's a big boy, though, right? If I get out of line, he can take care of himself. He can just say no."

Reggie could tell her cousin was trying not to laugh. "Uh huh. I'm sure he'll just say no." Her voice turned serious. "Listen, I truly am sorry about this."

"I know you are, and I am officially letting you off the hook."

Reggie hung up the phone and paused to let it sink in. She'd worried that her cousin couldn't help her out, and now that it was a reality, she was glad. *Glad.* What was wrong with her? Was she so desperate that she'd fling herself at a man simply because he was so damn attractive?

No, it was more than that, and she knew it. She hadn't known Walker Banks for very long, but what she knew about him now pushed all the right buttons. He was intelligent and creative and disciplined. And even though he hadn't always been a hands-on dad, he was certainly trying now. Best of all, though he didn't like her tactics, he'd been very helpful when it came to investigating the theft of the tigers.

One question remained: was he involved with anyone? He hadn't brought up Axel right away, and who knew if maybe he kept his relationships separate, too?

Reggie tried her best to focus on what really mattered. She didn't need to be obsessing about this, especially now.

Instead, she drew up a list of questions to ask the collectors in order to draw them out or possibly trip the culprit up. The reception was just three days away and it was critical that she be able to weed out at least some of the suspects.

When she tired of that, she spent time with her drawing tablet, sketching out potential designs for a new collection she'd been thinking of, called "Oh Natural." She'd create images of nature—trees, leaves, flowers, mountains—but present them in more abstract ways. The tattoos Axel had been researching were an odd sort of inspiration in that each image stood for something meaningful, even if you didn't know right off the bat what the meaning was.

Something meaningful. In the end, that's what it all came down to.

Chapter Twenty-Four

The camera lens doesn't lie. It has no reason or ability to. It simply records what it sees depending on the amount of light available to it. Walker had always been in awe of that simple fact: that in a world where the worst images so often took center stage, there was a way to capture tangible beauty and know it was real, that it existed, even for a moment as brief as the click of a shutter. The earth was filled with moments like those that most people were never able to witness firsthand: the glint of the sun against a striated canyon ... the rush of a mountain stream as it breaks through the ice during spring thaw... the spin of a worshipper's prayer wheel on a mountaintop in Tibet. Walker took pride in knowing that his work had brought many such moments to light.

Of course, what sometimes happened *after* the truth was captured was something else; Walker's start in the fashion industry had taught him that. Through filters, lighting techniques and other flaw-erasing digital tricks, an image that started out saying one thing could end up saying something completely different, and all for the sake of the client's current ideal of perfection. "Buy this dress or wear this make up and you can be as flawless/hip/unique (the ideal changed for every ad campaign) as we are."

Preferring the truth was one of the main reasons Walker had left the fashion world. Today, although he was working in a similar environment, his objectives were entirely different. Instead of selling a product, he was honoring a historic life and illustrating the timeless beauty of the human form.

He'd spent the better part of two days setting up his equipment and furnishing the impromptu studio. The couch was adequate, but with Jenna's help he brought in some extra furniture and a large free-standing panel that they draped with fabric to mimic what had been the backdrop for many of the old prints. Throughout the process he couldn't help imagining Regina sitting, standing, kneeling, dressed in absolutely nothing. It was a wonder he got anything done.

You've got it bad, he thought as he re-positioned one of the lights near the sofa and turned on the small space heater.

He'd set up the props to mirror those in the historical photographs of Mandy Culpepper which he'd taken from an out-of-print coffee table book Ethan had given him weeks earlier. Called *The Grove's First Year*, it was the only artistic work the disgraced photographer Peter

Raines had ever created, and it contained a few photographs of an unidentified "life model," which the family knew to be Mandy. Walker had found the corresponding negatives in a box Raine's father had sent to The Grove after his son's death from alcoholism. Most of the negs were decent yeoman's work, nothing to get excited about. But there were others that Walker felt compelled to print out because of the unparalleled beauty they portrayed in a time before Photoshop.

Last night he'd reviewed the prints one more time so that he'd know what to recreate. In them, Mandy was nearly eighteen and admittedly gorgeous. He would bet she hadn't been a blond, or a brunette; her hair seemed to be some shade in between, like Regina's. Were they the same? For once he found himself irritated at the black and white medium, and his own limitations, that hid the information from him.

Mandy was naked or nearly so in every photograph, and every shot told a story. In one she wore a studded collar that conjured visions of a proud harem slave. In another she wore the jade tiger earrings as if she were the royal concubine they were meant for. And in a third, she held a large apple as if she were about to devour it.

In every image he saw not Mandy, however, but Regina, and it rankled that his attraction to her might impact the shoot. And he was worried about *Axel's* hormones? Thank God her cousin was going to be in the room.

To possibly dissuade her from this folly, he'd dropped off a copy of the prints so that she could see what he'd be asking of her. He half expected her to text him and tell him the whole thing was off, but she hadn't. In fact, he hadn't heard from her or seen her at all. He was about to text her when he heard a knock; maybe her cousin had arrived early and come straight over.

But no. When he opened the door, Regina stood on the small front porch alone, carrying a tote bag on her shoulder and holding the antique jewelry box that contained her only adornment for the shoot.

"Sorry I'm late. Ava called and her loathsome soon-to-be ex-husband screwed her over like he often does, so she can't come. Are you still okay with doing the shoot?"

Walker's mind said *Danger, Will Robinson!* but his body reacted much more affirmatively.

He ignored his mind; he'd lost it, anyway.

"Yes, of course." He held the door open while she came in; her long, thick hair, pulled back with two clips, brushed his arm as she passed by. She smelled like violets. He noticed Brit's truck head back down the road. "Brit give you a ride?"

Regina patted the box. "He gave these lovelies an escort per my request." She put the box on the small kitchen table and took off her sweater. "It's warm in here."

"Uh, yep. I think you're going to need the heat in a little bit, but we can play it by ear. Did you have a chance to look at the photos of your grandmother that I'd like to recreate?"

Regina nodded. "I hope I can do her justice. I know

our coloring is similar, but she really carried herself well, don't you think?"

"I have no doubt you'll do the same. So, tell me, have you ever been photographed professionally before?"

"Yes, when I was about five and my mother wanted to commemorate my first year in school. If you don't count that or the yearly class pictures, then, no."

Walker took up his camera. "All right then, to get you used to the process, let's just talk while I take some pictures of you, okay? Have a seat."

"Don't you want me to..."

"Disrobe? No, not yet. We've got plenty of time." He walked over to the kitchen counter, poured a glass of a rich Malbec from the bottle he'd brought, and handed it to her. "You like Malbec, right? I noticed you had wine with pizza the other night."

She smiled, looking pleased that he remembered, and took a sip.

"So, tell me, how'd you get interested in gems and designing jewelry?"

Regina hesitated, no doubt feeling awkward, but quickly seemed to get over it as she related the story of being Mandy's youngest grandchild, and how her grandmother often let her play with the contents of her "box of baubles." She remembered how joyful and spirited her grandmother was when she'd relate the story attached to each gem.

Regina also loved playing outdoors, she told Walker, and even had an artistic bent, so when she was in her teens, she figured the best way to combine all three interests would be to become a jewelry designer who researched the various types of stones she used.

"Where were you trained?" Walker asked, all the while clicking away from different angles. Every so often he'd stop and adjust the lighting, then begin shooting again. It was reassuring to be in this familiar creative headspace. Form. Lighting. Composition. He could do this.

"Oh, the Gemological Institute in Carlsbad," Regina answered. "I loved it. We got to do a lot of caving there, too, which was great because you get a feel for the natural forces that create many types of gems. It's beautiful deep inside the earth."

Walker tried to suppress a slight shudder, but Regina caught it. Taking another sip, she asked, "Ever been caving?"

"Not my idea of a good time. Give me the wide-open spaces any day."

She smiled. "I like those, too—most of them, anyway. Heights I can do without."

"Ah. No bungee jumping for you, then." He watched her eyes light up as she grinned at him. *Those dimples. Wow. She really is exquisite.* He paused to regroup. *Focus.* "What aspect of your art gives you the most joy?"

"Hmm. That's a very good question. I think it's the creation of something special, out of nothing but little rocks and whatever I've used to connect them."

"Yes, I can totally see that." Walker put his camera

down and smiled. "Something beautiful. Something meaningful."

Regina gazed at him now, tilting her head slightly as if she were trying to figure him out. "Do you mind if I ask *you* a question?"

"Shoot," Walker said.

"How did you come to be a photographer with … with your eyesight issues?"

"You mean being color blind? Let's just say when you're born not knowing anything different, it's a not a problem. You compensate without even thinking about it. I look at images in a way that makes sense to me, emphasizing light and shadow, for instance, or form. It only becomes a problem when other people tell you it is."

"I see what you mean," she said thoughtfully. "In a way it sets you apart from the crowd, when you can bring another perspective to the same set of conditions."

He nodded, and then admitted something he'd never told another person. "I do wish that I could see my woman's true hair and eye color, though. That would be something."

She blinked at him, her eyes wide. "You … have a woman?"

"No," he replied, their eyes locking. He hesitated before giving her a half-smile. "Who would have me?"

A silence grew between them and the energy subtly shifted. It seemed as if they both understood that something was going on here besides a photo shoot.

Finally, she said, "Do you … should I?"

He swallowed hard but spoke calmly, determined to be professional about this, for both their sakes. "You should."

She stepped into the bedroom then, and a few minutes later she came out again, this time dressed in a short silk robe. He knew she wore nothing underneath and that the robe too would soon be gone.

Keep it together, man. Focus on the work. Just. Stay. Focused.

"Where do you want me?" she asked.

And he hesitated, wishing he could tell her the true answer to that question.

She felt the air charge between them as Walker paused, sending her one of those searching looks, but this one seemed almost fierce. Maybe she imagined it, because it left as quickly as it came. Wishful thinking on her part, perhaps? He blinked and shook his head slightly, turning away from her to check his notes.

"Let's begin by recreating some original poses," he said in a neutral voice. "I think we'll start with the citrine necklace."

Acutely aware of the silk robe brushing against her body, Reggie went to the kitchen to take the necklace out of the box; at that point she realized that Walker had pulled the sofa out slightly from against the wall and placed a narrow sofa table behind it, where he'd put a simple vase filled with yellow narcissus. "Where'd you get the flowers on such short notice?" she asked.

"I had to call around. I figure if we're going to mirror the original photographs, we should be as accurate as possible. I'm hoping the color works."

"They're perfect." Still feeling a tad self-conscious, she nevertheless sent him a grateful smile. "I really appreciate how much thought you're putting into this."

"These photographs are going to be part of history. They should be done right. Besides…" His eyes softened slightly. "I know how important this is to you."

Her heart softened, too. Here he was, yet again, working to turn her desires into reality. There was so much to like about this man.

If only she were in this state of undress for a different reason.

Taking a breath and turning to the box, Reggie put on the necklace. The bright yellow citrine was cold against her breast, a welcome chill to the flame building inside of her.

"Now, if you'll sit on the couch and hand me your robe, we can get started."

She did as Walker instructed, foolishly turning away from him as she took off her covering, as if doing so would shield her any more than facing him would. When she turned back, he was adjusting a nearby lamp and re-checking his camera, which he'd set on a tripod. She waited for him to finish, and when he looked up, she handed him the robe.

Those eyes again. Focused on her. "Are you ready, then?"

She smiled nervously. "As I'll ever be."

The professional in Walker took over at that point. He began to instruct her in a tone that could only be called "matter-of-fact."

"Sit with the vase behind your right shoulder; cross your legs, look to the left ... *click click click* ... now the right *click click* ...now straight at me. You ... you are meeting your lover and you are wondering where he is ... *click click* ... now you are confident he is coming home to you..."

At one point he moved his tripod closer, adjusted one of the standing lights and leaned in to adjust the stone, which nestled within her cleavage. His hands brushed her skin as he straightened the chain and her body responded immediately, her nipples tightening. Fortunately, he didn't comment on it.

He continued in that manner, directing her in a calm, dispassionate voice. She, on the other hand, was positively humming inside, titillated beyond belief that he was fully-clothed and she was completely naked. What did he think of her? He had to be comparing her to the photos of her grandmother. Was she measuring up? She shivered involuntarily.

"Would you like me to turn up the heat?" he asked.

It can't get much hotter than this, can it? Except if maybe you were naked, too. "No, I'm warm enough," she managed.

After the citrine shot came the tigers. He retrieved

them from the jewelry box, asked her to stand while she put them on. They reminded her of the theft and her simmering anger bubbled to the surface. "Will anyone know they aren't the originals? I would be mortified if they could tell."

He smiled slightly. "No one but us will know and I promise we'll re-shoot with the real tigers once we get them back, all right?"

She smiled her relief. "That was the absolutely right thing to say."

Then she froze because Walker had begun to put his hands in her hair. To do so he moved very close to her, close enough that their bodies almost touched.

"The original had Mandy's hair up like so," he said, carefully twisting and arranging her tresses.

Oh, she thought, but said nothing.

The scant space between them arced with electricity.

As he continued to fold her mane into a loose chignon, she took in his scent; it was a cross between leather and wood and male. She fought the urge to close the distance. How could he stand this? Was she the only one feeling this way?

He stepped back from her for a moment and tilted his head while he perused her. Then, smiling faintly, he pulled a few long hairpins out of his back pocket. She held her breath as he strategically placed them out of sight, his arms encircling her. She knew it wasn't his intent, but still she felt protected; sheltered; even treasured.

Then it was over, and he stepped back, once again

examining his work. She let out a careful breath and cast about for something to say that wouldn't betray how she was feeling. "How do you know how to do that?" she asked, almost afraid of the answer.

"Tricks of the trade. On a fashion shoot you're working with two diametrically opposed concepts: perfection and time constraints. Fixing hair quickly helps bridge that gap. I always keep a few pins in my camera case out of habit." His eyes gleaming wickedly, he leaned in as if to let her in on a secret. "They're also good for keeping ties from flapping, applying glue to false eyelashes, and most importantly, closing half-empty Dorito bags." He matched her smile briefly before stepping back and once again assuming a professional demeanor. "That should do it. Ready to continue?"

She nodded, unsure how much more of this she could take.

He captured several poses and then, as he'd done with the first stone, took the camera off its stand and took a series of hand-held shots from various angles. As he moved, he'd call out a running patter of gentle commands and comments like, "Look here," "Turn quickly," "That's it" and "Give me sultry."

Reggie thought back to the expressions her grandmother had used while modeling and tried to emulate them. A chuckle burst out instead.

Walker lowered his camera. "What's so funny?"

"I was trying for 'sultry' like grandmama, but I can't do it. I wouldn't know how to do it."

He paused with his camera by his side. "You really have no idea, do you?" His voice held a touch of wonder and he murmured, almost to himself, "No idea at all." He turned away suddenly and placed his camera back on its stand before facing her again. That neutral expression of his had returned. "Please take off the earrings and we'll go to the collar."

She handed him the tigers, which he returned to the box before bringing back the ornate gold, bronze and crystal dog collar with matching headpiece. Once more he asked her to stand, and this time he removed the pins and let her long hair flow down one side of her neck, running his long fingers slowly through the strands. "Do you remember what your grandmother wrote in her diary about modeling this jewelry?" he asked while carefully placing the headpiece on her hair.

She could tell it was a leading question: he already knew the answer. She nodded.

"What did she write?" As he spoke, he leaned over her to fasten the collar around her neck. The scent of him was driving her crazy.

"She ... she wrote that the artist—it was Frieda Mallock— told her to play the role of an Egyptian royal consort."

"A favored concubine to the king," he whispered. "His lover." His fingers brushed softly against her skin as he closed the latch with a resolute *click*.

Reggie's heartbeat sped up along with the insistent throbbing she was feeling everywhere else. "Yes."

"What else?"

They stared at each other.

Then she understood what he was doing, what he wanted from her. "She said she asked Frieda if it was all about the power of being so close to the King."

He took her gently by the elbow, her skin surging with his touch as he led her to the draped panel. "And was it?"

"Yes," she said, sure of herself now. "But there was more."

"And what was that?"

"He was also a superior lover, and that made it all worthwhile."

Walker adjusted her slightly by the shoulders so that she was standing the way he wanted her, then stood back. His eyes remained firm on hers. "You show me that."

And she did.

Somehow, in response to Walker's calmly renewed commands, she began channeling her grandmother. At least it felt that way, standing tall, full of confidence, with a sense of her own identity and self-worth. How had he brought that out in her? She wasn't sure, but she understood now what he meant by "sultry."

Never had she felt that way with Curtis; in fact, she'd always felt vaguely inadequate, even though, toward the end, many of his personal habits had begun to bother her, such as the fact that he wore too much cologne. Tonight, for the first time in her life, she felt she could hold any man in thrall, including the one staring at her now.

Walker once again took the camera in hand and moved closer. "She wrote one more thing, didn't she?"

Reggie looked him in the eye. "She did."

"What was it?"

"She said that Will watched her from the back of the room and..."

"And what?" Their eyes had not left each other and Walker's voice had turned rough.

Her breath caught. "And wanted her. He wanted her."

"Yes. He did."

Chapter Twenty-Five

My God, I'm losing control. At the start of the shoot, Walker had warned himself to keep it professional and not do anything to make her think he was taking advantage. But from the moment they began, it had been a struggle to keep that promise, to put his desires aside and think like an artist, only that.

But dammit, when he asked for sultry, she'd given it in spades. And yes, the artist inside him admired the play of light across her gently rounded stomach, the shadows accenting angles and form, and the striking image of a woman fully aware of her power.

But this was not just another woman. It was Regina. And he couldn't help but react to the sensual beauty that was hers and hers alone.

The curve of her breasts.

The scent of her skin.

The feel of her soft hair in his hands.

It all simmered under the surface, barely contained, until she looked at him like she desired him, too, and could damn well have him if she wanted him.

In a moment of pure, primal instinct, he nearly stopped all the pretense to let her know in no uncertain terms that he wanted her, too.

I have got to end this now or we're both in trouble. Walker took a deep breath and abruptly headed back to the table. "I think that's a wrap."

"What?" Regina sounded surprised.

He turned to face her and said, curtly, "I said we're finished."

She frowned at him. "Did you get what you wanted?"

What a loaded question. "Not everything, but I have enough material to work with for now. And you ... you must have other things you have to do. And there's Axel, and..."

She tipped her head. "And you're tempted by me."

Well, that's what I get for unlocking her inner goddess. It didn't help matters that she was still naked and beautiful and mere inches away.

My God, I'm drowning in lust here and she's calling me on it. He ran his hands through his hair. "Listen, I'm sorry if I misled you. This was just a photo shoot, like a thousand other photo shoots. That's all." *And that's a crock if ever I heard one.*

"I see."

He watched the confidence drain out of her lovely

face and wanted to kick himself for causing that. But he had never succumbed while in a professional setting, and he couldn't allow himself to do it now.

She stumbled through the rest of her words. "I'm sorry if I made you feel uncomfortable."

He turned away and busied himself with packing his equipment, feeling like an ass. "It happens," he said. "Why don't you get changed and we'll take the box back to the storage facility." When he looked up, she had already gone into the bedroom, shutting the door.

A few minutes later she reappeared, fully dressed and looking composed. She checked the contents of the box and gathered it, along with her sweater and tote bag.

"Ready when you are," she said.

Walker's insides were churning as they walked along the path to the museum building. He was reluctant to say anything for fear he might say something hurtful again, or something completely inappropriate, like "I want you more than I've ever wanted anyone."

She was obviously ready to move on. "I think I've narrowed down our suspects to three or four. Leo says—"

"With all due respect, Leo doesn't know shit. Because if he did, we wouldn't be putting you at risk like we're going to do in three days." Absurdly, he was happy she'd changed to a topic he could get mad about. Anger was much more satisfying than frustration.

"Leo—Dr. Brunt—set this reception up at my request and I'm grateful for his help." She sounded peeved. "I've told you from the beginning that you don't have to get involved with this."

"And I've told you I'm tired of you saying that because I'm not bailing."

Neither of them spoke while Regina put the box back in the safe, nor on the walk back to the Great House. As they approached the mansion, they saw Axel wheeling his bike over to its usual parking place where he unceremoniously dropped it. Walker checked his watch. It was five minutes to ten.

"Let me guess," he said. "A 'Settlers of Catan' party with Kaitlyn?"

"No, a two-hour hike, practically straight uphill, then the party. I'm beat."

Walker glanced at Regina and saw her indulgent smile. Dammit, she even liked his kid. She didn't deserve the put down he'd given her, especially since it wasn't true. "Well, goodnight, then."

"Yeah, hasta later," the boy said on his way around the back of the house. "I'll drop the laptop in your room, so you won't have to bitch at me about it."

"Appreciate it," Walker called to him, but Axel was already gone from sight.

"I think Kaitlyn's good for him," Regina said.

"I agree. Maybe she'll keep him so tired he won't be thinking what I'm afraid he's been thinking."

"You think too much, yourself," she said, and followed Axel, leaving Walker to ruminate on that remark on his own.

It was nearing midnight, and Walker was still strung tight as a piano wire. Never had a woman gotten so deeply under his skin. With Caroline it had been lust, then guilt, then measured acceptance; women after her had come and gone. But there had never been such *yearning*, a sense that he was meant to be with this woman and she with him.

He had to see her. Come what may, he had to tell her the truth about the session, had to lay his cards on the table. She was entitled to that honesty and so much more.

He put on a t-shirt and jeans and ventured down the hall. Regina's room was on the other side of the landing, far enough that they never had to run into one another if they didn't want to. He wanted to.

Passing Axel's room, the sounds of heavy sleep drifted through the door. His son had dutifully dropped the laptop off earlier and was now apparently out like a light.

Walker crossed over the stairs leading to the down-stairs, but all was quiet now. Three doors down, he checked to see if any lights were still on in her room; they weren't. He felt momentarily guilty for waking her up, but it couldn't be helped. He knocked softly on the door.

No response.

He rapped again, whispering loudly, "Regina?"

Still nothing. He was about to increase the volume when the door opened. His heart tightened at the sight of her.

"Walker? What is it? Is something wrong?" she asked. "Is Axel okay?"

"Yes, yes. Everyone's fine. Well, except me. I need to talk to you."

For the space of three seconds, she gave him a questioning look. "Now?"

"Right now. *Please.*"

She opened the door and stepped back. Her hair was mussed, and she wore a little camisole with spaghetti straps and soft looking harem pants. She stood holding his gaze and he returned the stare, deliberately closing the door behind him.

"I need to tell you something. About the shoot."

There was a catch to her breath. "You mean the one that was like a thousand others?"

He walked slowly toward her, shaking his head. "I lied. It was like no other shoot I've ever done. It was all I could do to stay on task. You are ..."

She smiled then, slowly, a sultry look.

Between that and knowing exactly what she looked like underneath her clothes, he turned hard as a post. Because he was allowed now. There was no more holding back.

"And you want me," she said slowly.

"Oh, I want you," he said, taking her by the waist and pulling her gently to him. "Desperately."

"Then take me."

Walker wasted no time and Reggie's pulse began to thrum at the thought of what was to come. He threaded one hand through her hair as before, but this time to anchor her for his kiss, which was deep. It was a claiming kiss, a kiss that demanded she participate, and she did, letting him know how much she wanted him back.

When they came up for air, he quickly pulled down the strap of her camisole, exposing her breast first to his view and then to his mouth. Her knees slackened and she gripped his broad shoulder for support. The feel of his tongue circling her made her dizzy.

"God, I have wanted to taste you just like this," he said. "You are delectable."

Then he was on her again and she had no words. Only pleasure. At last she was free to touch him as she pleased, but it was all she could do to hang on while he tended to her breasts, her neck, her mouth.

All the while, he was moving her toward the bed, and they were soon on it. He took but a moment to remove her top and slip her pants past her hips so that now she lay completely open to him, her breath hitching as she let his hands roam expertly along her body, touching her, exploring her, invading her.

"Oh my God," she panted, not quite believing what

was happening to her so quickly, this possession that unleashed an unbearable electricity shooting through her body, sizzling and sparking, leaping, pulsing. Once more she was at his mercy, he who was still completely dressed.

But not for long.

She reached for his shirt and he reared up, pulling it from behind his neck in one frenzied motion. "Skin to skin," he said, breathing hard. "I want every part of you."

In between gasps she managed to say, "Then your jeans need to go, too."

He sent her a grin that touched her core and quickly obliged, yanking them off. "I'm clean but I don't have any protection with me. Tell me what I can do."

"Anything. Everything," she replied. "I'm protected."

"Thank God." He crawled above her and settled in, skin to skin, as he'd said. Raising her arms above her head, he gripped her hands in his as he kissed her passionately and rocked his body back and forth along hers.

She hooked her calves behind his knees, wanting more. Answering her need, he reached between their bodies and stroked her in time to his rocking. She shuddered at his touch, her head falling back.

He nipped her earlobe, his breath hot on her neck, and she thought of the concubine's words about the king: "a superior lover." *Surely the king was no match for this.*

Still holding her arms above her head with one hand, Walker increased the pace with the other until she started to cry out, approaching her peak. Only then did he enter her, stealing her breath as he thrust deep inside. The fullness of him, the friction and the heat of his invasion, brought her quickly to climax. The moment lasted longer than she thought possible, extended by the pleasure of his hard taking of her.

They completed their journey together, matching each other's frenzied hunger, and as their bodies stilled, their hearts continued to beat hard against one another.

Walker waited several moments before pulling out, reluctantly, it seemed. But as he lay back, he pulled her close to him. She settled comfortably on his sturdy chest, his arm warm around her, his hand absently playing with her hair.

Finally, he said, "I have wanted to be inside you for such a long time."

She smiled, pretended to check her watch. "All of two hours, huh?"

He chuckled, and the sound of it rumbling in his chest tickled her ear. "No, I'd say a bit longer than that," he said. "Try the first time we met."

She pulled up slightly to look up at him. "Even when I was driving you insane about modeling the jewels?"

"Even then." He gave her a satisfied smile. "Especially then."

She lay back down, grinning at the ceiling. "I guess I should have tried being sultry earlier. "But I ..." She bit back her words, not knowing if she could say them, especially now that they'd been so intimate together.

"What?" he prompted gently.

She hesitated, then came out with it. "I know this sounds ridiculous, but I was worried you might be thinking Mandy Firestone pulled off sultry better than I did. I don't think I'd come out ahead with that comparison."

He turned this time, propping himself on his elbow. The look on his face was serious. "Your grandmother was a beautiful woman and led a life we can all aspire to. I'm happy to play a small role in sharing that life with the world." He gently tucked her hair behind her ear, afterward trailing his fingers along her jawline. "I can understand why you'd wonder if you live up to her legacy, but no good ever comes from comparing ourselves like that. Her life was extraordinary, but her time on earth is over. It's our time. You are here, you are real, and you are living your own extraordinary life—in *your* way, not hers."

His words brought tears to her eyes and she reached up to touch his cheek, the bristles gently prickling her fingertips.

He leaned in and kissed her again. It was tender at first, but soon changed, a more insistent demand born of hunger, of desire.

As his hand started to caress her already-warm body, she was astonished to feel his erection hard against her hip.

Superior lover, indeed.

But more than that. She was coming to feel that Walker Banks was a superior man. She stroked the muscled planes of his chest. "You're here, too," she whispered.

"And I'm very, very real. Let me show you."

And he proceeded to do just that.

Chapter Twenty-Six

Axel woke up early and checked his phone. Barely six in the morning. *Shit*. He didn't think his dad meant they should go out *this* early. He checked his messages and saw a text from Kaitlyn from last night:

Did I wear you out going up that mountain, AJ? Hope so - lol! K8

He smiled and texted back:

Neva—could go on 4eva.

There was no response, which meant she was probably still asleep. Damn, she was so sweet. And the way she gave him his own nickname, "A.J." after he told her his middle name was John. Friggin' cool. He liked it. He liked her. A lot.

He scrolled through Reddit to see what was happening. SOS. Then he checked Imgur to see the latest memes. The one with the black lab sitting on the can was still high in the rankings. It *was* pretty funny.

He checked the time again. Six-forty.

Crap. He flopped back down to see if he could fall asleep again. A half hour later he was still checking the time.

He was so pumped up, it felt like Christmas morning! Only Christmas morning had never been all that great, because his mom was usually trying to impress some potential Sugar Daddy by making a big dinner, and it stressed her out so bad she usually ended up yelling at Axel to turn down the t.v. or go out and play (even though December twenty-fifth in New York City isn't exactly a kid's playground).

Still, the way he'd heard Christmas morning usually went, this is what it must feel like.

He felt good about the driving. No, make that *great*. Even though the professor reminded him that no matter how good a driver he was, it was the other guy you had to watch out for.

He had it all figured out: he'd show his dad how good he'd gotten, make the DMV appointment, and before he knew it, bam! He'd be a licensed driver! He'd be able to take Kaitlyn out, maybe go over to Bellam Cove for pizza, maybe even go into San Francisco to a concert or something.

He took out the rules of the road booklet and went over the signs again. Those were the tough ones. He thought of the secret signs that gangs everywhere seem to have and how far back people been makin' up that shit. Everybody needs some sign that hooks them together with their own people. Everybody wants to belong. And why wouldn't they?

Seven thirty rolled around—*finally*—and Axel got completely dressed, jacket and all, and went two doors down. Time to get the old man up. He knocked, not so loud that he'd wake everybody up, but loud enough so his dad would hear.

No answer.

He knocked again and when there was still no response, he got worried and checked the door. It was unlocked so he opened it and went inside. "Dad?" he called quietly.

Still nothing. The room was like a suite where you had a small front room and then the bedroom and bath toward the back. A feeling of dread coiled in his gut as he moved toward the door. *Be okay. Be okay. Be okay.* Slowly he approached the door, which was half open, his pulse starting to hammer. He opened it wider and looked inside.

Empty.

Where the hell was he? *Maybe he's an early riser after all.*

He headed down the stairs and into the kitchen, but all was quiet. No one was up, and it didn't look like anyone had *been* up—no coffee brewing, no cereal out, nothing.

Feeling a small sense of panic, Axel's jitters started up. He crept quietly upstairs again, trying not to wake anybody while he figured out what to do, but when he reached the landing, he saw his dad coming out of Regina's room. Relief surged through him until he saw the change in his dad's face. He'd looked fine until he saw Axel, but then his expression turned to shit.

"Where have you been?" his dad barked. "You were in at ten. Did you sneak out again?" He stood there in nothing but a pair of pants that he hadn't even buttoned all the way. He held a shirt in his hands.

Had his dad forgotten about their driving session? Shit, he had! And in that second, Axel was back being the third wheel, the *inconvenience*, the kid who had to be dealt with. His disappointment turned to anger, toward himself, mainly, for thinking this time things were going to be any different. "Well, I sure as hell ain't getting any pussy like you are."

He saw Regina come into the hall; she was dressed in a robe.

What's going on?" she said, and his dad turned back and told her, "Don't worry about it. It's my problem, not yours." Then he faced Axel and said in a cold, hard voice, "That comment was uncalled for. You need to go to your room *now*."

And that just broke it. He was going to be ragged on by a guy who probably wasn't even his real father? A guy who played dad once or twice a year and only took Axel in because his mom dumped him? "I don't think so," he sneered, and took off.

He heard his dad yell, "Come back here!" but he

stop. He just grabbed his bike and headed down
ll.

What in the hell just happened? Walker had just spent one of the most incredible nights of his life, with a woman whom he knew could easily become an addiction. They'd made love three times, fallen asleep wrapped around each other, and he'd awakened in the morning, more than ready for a fourth go at it. But it was already after seven and he knew Axel was counting on him, so he'd reluctantly left Regina's bed, only to find his son, fully dressed, sneaking back up to his room like he'd been out all night. God, if he was with Kaitlyn, if that kind of stuff was going on … he knew more than anybody where it could lead. *Shit, how am I gonna deal with that?*

He quickly got dressed, intending to find the boy, but his gut soon told him to wait downstairs just a bit to let them both calm down. He didn't want to let loose with anything more that he'd regret later. As he was about to leave his room, he heard a light knock. Regina was standing in the doorway, dressed in a pretty top and running shorts. "What happened with Axel?" she asked softly.

Walker was too embarrassed to level with her; "I told you it was nothing," he said.

She walked over and laid her hand on his arm. "It

wasn't nothing if he stormed out of here like that. What did you say to him that set him off?"

"What makes you think I said anything to *him?* Christ." He ran his hands through his hair in frustration. "He's just a punk kid, he mouthed off, end of story."

"But what was he doing?"

Walker felt cornered; he couldn't tell her he suspected his son had been out all night until he talked to Axe, so he selfishly turned it around on her. "I don't know, okay? Can you just drop it?" He watched with sickening dread as the light left her eyes and her jaw tightened.

"I'm sorry if you think I'm harping," she said calmly. "I'm just suggesting there might be a reason for your son to go off on you. Did you accuse him of something? Maybe he didn't do it. Maybe he was disappointed in *you.*" With that, she turned and left the room.

Stunned, Walker stood there rolling the idea around in his head. Could she be right? Maybe Axe hadn't been sneaking around; maybe he was just trying to be quiet. *And I immediately jumped to the worst possible conclusion. What kind of a shit parent am I?*

A split second later he realized that Regina was dressed for running, which meant she'd be going off, possibly into the woods, by herself. Did the killers know that she had moved temporarily to The Grove? If so, was she safe? *Come on, don't go overboard,* he thought. *She'll be fine.* Still…

"Regina, wait!" he called after her.

There was no answer, because she was already gone.

"There's a path that runs behind your cottage. Follow it around and you'll eventually come to a deer trail that leads down to the prettiest little cove you've ever seen."

Jenna had told Reggie about the path a few days earlier, and now was the perfect time for Reggie to explore it. She wasn't an avid runner—more like an enthusiastic walker/hiker—but this morning she needed to work off the hurt she was feeling since her altercation with Walker.

Last night had been magical, almost too good to be true. And the light of morning had borne that out. By rights she should have been angry at his rejection of her, but what she felt was much worse: a soul-deep sense of disappointment.

The simple term for what Walker had was "baggage." But by his and Reggie's age, didn't most people have some? Reggie was thirty-four, and after her last romantic fiasco, she'd pretty much figured she wasn't meant to connect with anyone. She'd made peace with that; after all, there were lots of advantages to the single life, and she'd always been one to focus more on what she had than what she lacked.

Then Walker Banks had entered her life, storming her senses and challenging her at almost every turn. If she could believe him, he'd been equally drawn to her.

But could she believe him? Right now, she felt like Walker was an expert angler, teasing her until she took the bait, hooking her, and then throwing her back in the water.

The only mitigating factor was knowing that Walker was hurting, too. Not because of her, but because he was learning the hard way what it takes to be a good parent. Obviously, he and Axel had issues to work out and he'd let Reggie know more than once that her input regarding his son wasn't appreciated. The smart thing would be to step away.

But how could she? From the beginning he'd disagreed with her decision to recover her family's heirlooms, but whenever she tried to let *him* off the hook, he'd insisted on continuing to work with her. Given what they'd just experienced, how on earth were they going to keep the tension between them under wraps enough to pull off the reception and ferret out the thief?

All these thoughts swirled through her head as she found the steep trail and headed down toward the cove. The morning was cool, but clear, and a slight chill settled on her skin as she wove in and out of the shady pine and eucalyptus trees that marked the trail.

As she neared the bottom, the scent of the ocean overtook that of the forest. Once she reached the water, she could see why Jenna had recommended it: the spot was dazzling—a beautifully soft, sandy beach protected by rock outcroppings that at low tide, according to Jenna, left behind all sorts of little sea treasures. *Yes, I could be inspired here,* Reggie thought, not for the first time since she'd come to The Grove. She imagined her grandmother walking along the same path; had Mandy looked for sea shells or gazed at the horizon? Had she thought about Will? Had she had doubts about what she was feeling for him or what he was feeling for her? Maybe. Probably. It gave Reggie a sense of connection to think so.

At the other end of the cove, another trail led upward in the opposite direction from which she'd come. Jenna had told her it led to Puerta Del Mar, an estate older than The Grove. The former owner, Boyce Wheeler, had been murdered not long ago and his niece, who had been in line to inherit the property, was being held in connection with the crime. Apparently, the property would be put up for sale at some point, but in the meantime, it needed a lot of work.

Out of curiosity she worked her way up to the top of that side of the hill. Other than the cove, the only way to get from one estate to the other was to drive inland to the main road that connected the turnoffs to the two properties.

The grounds at Puerta del Mar were wildly overgrown; it was obvious they hadn't been tended in years. Beyond them loomed the estate's Victorian-style mansion, a sad-looking relic that at one time must have been a magnificent Painted Lady, but now looked more like Miss Havisham's domicile. Reggie looked up at the turrets and dormers; there was even a small Widow's walk along the side facing the ocean. The overall structure looked sound, but the ornate trim that identified the Victorian style was on its last legs, with missing spindles and flaking gingerbread cutouts. She thought of her

Uncle Toby's impeccably maintained mansion, built in the same era but light years away from this crumbling piece of history. "What a shame," she muttered. "A little TLC and you'd be a beauty."

Rounding the corner to the front of the house, she saw that it had a wide wraparound porch. She *loved* verandas like that. So much potential.

It wasn't until she got up to the front entrance that she noticed a white car parked on the far side of the house. That was odd; the front door was padlocked, so it was a sure bet no one was living there. She noticed a "For Sale" sign leaning against the railing. A realtor starting to prep the place, maybe? "Hello?" she called out. She lifted the door knocker and banged it a few times. No response.

A too-small window was set to the right of the front door, so Reggie pressed up against it to peer inside. The foyer looked large, but dreary and at the far end she could see a thick, arched entry way with wide-open double doors that led to a study or an office of some sort. At the far end of that room was a large picture window which had to overlook the coast. "Must be spectacular," she mused out loud.

She still had her face pressed against the window when she heard footsteps behind her. Reggie turned, assuming it was the realtor, and was shocked to see Sandi Bollocks...

...who was equally shocked to see her. The only difference between them was that Sandi had a gun and Reggie didn't.

Chapter Twenty-Seven

I've got to make this right. Walker drove down the main street of Little Eden looking for signs of Axel until it dawned on him that his son was probably at Lindy's. Sure enough, when he pulled in front of the bakery, he saw Axel's beater bike propped against the side of the building. *Only in a place called Little Eden would you not think twice about leaving your bike unlocked.*

As usual, there was already a group of stalwart Lindy Lovers waiting in line for their fix of fresh-from-the-oven cinnamon rolls, bread, and other baked goods. Walker was familiar with the routine; he'd stood in line more than once himself. The owner of the shop, Kaitlyn's father, made eye contact with Walker and nodded his head in the direction of a table at the back of the dining area where Axel sat eating one of the coveted rolls while talking quietly with Kaitlyn. Walker went up to him, causing Axel to stand abruptly, as if to storm out.

"Wait," Walker said quietly. "Please. If it's all right with you, I'd like to talk."

Kaitlyn was astute enough to see that he and Axe should be alone, so she got Axe to sit back down and rose instead. "I'm gonna go help Dad at the counter," she told him. The underlying message was *I'm here if you need me*, which Walker both admired and envied. His son must have picked up some worthwhile traits—no thanks to Walker—for a girl like Kaitlyn to be so supportive. He thought briefly of Regina and how he'd rejected her attempts to be there for him. How stupid could one man be?

Once they were alone, Walker wasted no time. "I'm here to apologize."

Axel looked him warily. "For what? Being a dickwad?"

"Yeah, basically. I shouldn't have lit into you before finding out what you were doing."

"Yeah, I was just looking for you."

Walker nodded. "Instead I jumped the gun and accused you of doing something that I had done."

Axel looked puzzled and Walker, despite feeling ashamed, forged ahead. "I spent the night with Regina, and when I saw you, up and dressed so early in the morning, I thought you were sneaking back in after having done the same with Kaitlyn. I'm sorry. That was wrong."

"Huh," Axel said. "So, you were, like, projecting?"

Walker snorted. "Sounds like you've seen a therapist or two. Yes, I guess I was, but it's part of something bigger, I've come to realize. I'm just feeling my way about this parenting stuff. It's a whole new gig for me and obviously I've got a ways to go. And I need to remember where you are in all of this."

"What do you mean?"

"Well, I never bothered to ask how you feel about your mom and everybody moving overseas. My guess is, you said you didn't want to go, and she didn't try very hard to convince you otherwise."

He could see he'd hit the mark by his son's tightened expression. "It's cool. Whatever." Axel had begun tapping his thigh rapidly, like a chain smoker dying to get to his next cigarette. Walker had noticed that his son became more jumpy at certain times, usually when he was under stress.

"Really?" Walker said. "I think I'd be royally pissed."

"You would? Why?"

"Come on. If I'd been living in the same place all my life, even a rat hole like New York City, and my mom and stepdad were tolerable, and I'd even got to liking my new little sisters, I'd be mad as hell if they pulled the rug out from under me."

Axel's eyes were suspiciously moist before he turned away to look out the window near their table. "Yeah, well, maybe. A little."

"Add to that you get sent to Outer Slobovia to be with your slacker dad..."

Axel snickered and looked back at Walker. "'Outer Slobovia?'"

"What, you never heard of that place?"

"Uh, nope."

"Ah. Well. Okay, Northern California then. Same difference."

Axel chuckled again, then paused. "What makes you think you've been a slacker?"

"Because I haven't been there for you enough. I should have spent more time with you, bein' a dad. I mean, a real dad. Not just for a couple of weeks at some exotic location. And I'm sorry for that."

"It's no big deal. I get it," Axel mumbled.

"You do? Because I don't. Except to chalk it up to, I think they call it the Peter Pan Syndrome. You know, staying a boy when you ought to be man and all that."

"Peter Pan's a pussy," he grumbled. "Any guy that wears tights and flits around like that..."

Walker grinned. "Hold on now. Don't go saying that kind of stuff in public. Pan's entitled to his own lifestyle, just like the rest of us."

Axel sniffed. "Yeah, well...he's still a pussy."

With a chuckle, Walker agreed. "So, listen, I'm not gonna say it's going to be smooth sailing from now on, because, let's face it, you're a little rough around the edges, too. I mean, that comment you made..."

"Yeah, that was uncool; I didn't realize she was standing there. I'm kind of sorry about that."

"Okay, good. Because I really care for that woman, I want you to know. I mean, more than I've cared for another woman in a quite a while." *As in* ever.

"More than my mom?"

Walker let out a sigh. *How do I answer that?* "Let's just say I cared a lot for your mom, too, but it was a long time ago and I think she's much happier now, which is the important thing."

"Yeah, that's the important thing," Axel said with tinge of bitterness.

"And Regina? She's argued your case more than once with me, and more importantly, she knew better than I did about how involved you ought to be in what's been going on at The Grove."

"What, you mean with the re-opening?"

"No. I'm talking about the theft of an important part of her family's jewelry collection, and even worse crimes. In fact, she took off on a run and I'm worried about her safety, so if you'll come with me back to The Grove, I'll fill you in. You game?"

Axel nodded and gave Kaitlyn a short wave as he and Walker left the bakery. They loaded his bike into the back of the SUV and Walker let Axel drive up the hill, telling him along the way about all that had happened. They parked in their usual spot and Walker stopped at the Great House to see if Regina had returned. She was still out, so he and Axel jogged down to her cottage in case she was there. She wasn't, but someone had been. The place was trashed.

"Jesus, you weren't shittin' me," Axel said.

"No, I wasn't." His heart beginning to pound, Walker checked the time on his phone. "Regina's been gone for more than an hour. We need to find her, and we need to find her *now*."

Chapter Twenty-Eight

With shaking hands, Sandi pointed her small caliber handgun at Reggie. "What in the hell are you doing here?" she screeched.

Reggie's heart caught in her throat. *Do not scream. Do not do anything to set her off.*

"Sandi—may I call you Sandi? Listen. You don't need that gun. Let's just talk, okay? I was out hiking and heard about this place. That's why *I'm* here. But why are you here? Could you tell me?"

She watched as Sandi's hand shook; the woman was a bundle of nerves. *Keep it together, Sandi. Please keep it together.*

After staring at Reggie for what seemed like an eternity, Sandi looked at the gun and finally lowered it. "You're right, dammit. I've got no business being here. I came to see you, but I lost my nerve."

"You came to see me? Why?"

Sandi laid the gun down and put her hands on the porch railing, trying, it appeared, to pull herself together. Then she pulled a pack of cigarettes out of her purse and lit one with her still-shaking hands. When she turned back to Reggie, tears were running down her cheeks. "They killed my Frank," she said. "And it was all my fault!"

"Mr. Hatteras? And what do you mean 'your fault'?"

The woman started pacing the deck. "He was putting on the pounds and I told him he needed to go to the gym, so he started going. Only he told me he liked sweating off the pounds in the sauna rather than sweating them off on a treadmill." She chuckled through her tears. "He called it a 'road going nowhere.' But then somebody waited until he was alone in there and cut his throat. They even propped him up and wrapped a towel around him." She looked imploringly at Reggie. "It was bad enough they took out Chris Fung. Then they told Frank they wanted to set up Chandra and your uncle one more time after the switch— I had no idea they were going to get rid of them, too! I should have known we'd be next, but I was stupid. I just didn't think it would come to that. Frank said he was going to tell them about your double cross, and I think they somehow got wind that we tried to go around them."

"*My* double cross?"

"Yes, you know, swapping the tigers before we did."

"Oh. Right. But who is 'them?' Who's your client, Sandi?"

"That's just it—I don't know!" Sandi waved the

hand holding the cigarette. "Frank was contacted by Chris Fung on behalf of someone in the government—someone pretty high up, or at least a power player. The only way to communicate was through a closed Facebook group called 'The Jade Hunters.' Supposedly it was for jade collectors to talk about pieces they wanted to buy or sell, or the latest news on jade prices, that sort of thing. Frank didn't even have email, so we had to get him a cheap tablet and a gmail address." Her voice cracked. "He picked 'Big Frank 56' for his password because that's how old he was."

"In order to join the group, he had to have a Facebook profile," Reggie said. "Who fixed him up with one of those?"

"I did. We made it totally private, under the name 'Francis Pierre Montelban.' We figured no one would make the connection."

"So, 'Francis' joins the Jade Hunters private group and then what happens?"

"Chris had told him to check the group online every day for a direct message, and that's how he was given instructions."

Reggie couldn't believe a crime could be so blatantly discussed online. "Do you mean to tell me they said things like, 'Once you take the jade pieces, drop them off at 'such and such.'?"

"God, no, it was all in doublespeak. Things like, 'Here's an art dealer who might be able to find what you're looking for. He's single, etc. etc.' But Chris had put it all in context with Frank, so it was easy to figure out what they wanted us to do."

"How long ago was this?"

"Must have started, oh, at least four months ago." Sandi heaved a sigh. "Frank brought me in, and I was told to strike up a conversation with your uncle at the Rickhouse. They knew all about his real estate holdings and his gambling habit. My job was to get him to take me to Tahoe, where I maneuvered him into the private poker game that got him in trouble and needing the loan."

The pieces of the puzzle were starting to fit together, but there were still a lot of holes. "So how did you make the eventual swap?"

"That part was easy. We were told to open a P.O. box at the Pine Street office, and Chris gave Frank another box number at the same place to mail to. So, when we got the goods, Frank mailed them to their box, and a few weeks later we were given the replacements and later paid through ours. After Chris, neither of us ever dealt with anybody in person."

God, how frustrating! "What about notes or records? Did Frank keep any?"

"Frank had what he called the 'front office' on McCallister," Sandi said, "a couple blocks from City Hall. But that was only for show; he never kept anything important there. He had a back office on Eddy Street in the Tenderloin, but I never went to it. So, either Frank knew who they were and never let on, or he never found out, either. At this point, I don't even care who it is, I just want to get the hell out of dodge before they come looking for *me*."

"What about your, uh, businesses?"

"I sold the modeling agency and the escort brokerage to Cindy for a thousand dollars each and left her enough to pay this month's bills. She's smarter than she looks; she'll keep it going." She paused. "Chandra was a good girl, and she didn't deserve what happened to her. If I had known what was going to happen, I never would have—but that's water under the bridge now. I figured I'd better make myself scarce and let you know so you could do the same thing if you wanted to."

"What are you doing in this place, then?"

"Well, I drove through The Grove, but I started to worry that maybe you'd have me arrested for what we did, so I chickened out. Saw this place was on the market, so I came here to figure out what to do next, maybe get up my nerve again. And then you show up. If that's not karma, I don't know what is." She pulled a small pouch out of her purse and handed it to Reggie. "I wanted to return this, too. I should never have taken it, so here it is."

Reggie opened the bag to reveal the reticulated gold necklace she'd been working on. It crossed her mind that some people had truly bizarre sets of ethics. Sandi didn't think twice about stealing jewelry worth nearly a million dollars but felt guilty just for lifting one of Reggie's unfinished works. Go figure. "Thank you. So, where are you headed now?"

"I've got a cousin who lives in—wait, it's probably

better if you don't know. Suffice to say I'll be all right, but this is way more serious than stealing a couple of jade earrings. I'm telling you, you and that man of yours have got to beware. If I knew where to find you, *they* certainly do, and they'll be coming for you next."

No, we're going after them, Reggie thought defiantly. Instead she said, "I appreciate the heads up, and, well, I wish you the best of luck, Sandi." Reggie meant it, which was pretty bizarre, too, considering what Sandi and Frank Hatteras had done.

After the woman left, Reggie took a quick look around the perimeter of Puerta del Mar and headed back to The Great House via the cove.

The situation, she realized, was crazy on many levels. By rights she should have figured out a way to have Sandi arrested, but Reggie couldn't admit they'd succeeded without wrecking her plan to draw out the *real* thief. Furthermore, Sandi was right to disappear: it made total sense that she would be the next victim. Reggie would never forgive herself if she'd kept the woman in town, only to have her murdered by God knows who.

A major problem remained, however: with Sandi out of the picture, the next logical target was Reggie herself,

Shuddering slightly at the thought, she made her way back down to the cove, but it was no longer unoccupied. From the far end, a man was running toward her which after a split second she realized was Walker. He shouted out to her. Lagging behind him was another person, Axel.

She froze as Walker came closer. Was he going to berate her again? If so, she was going to give him a piece of her—

But she had no time to say a word, because as soon as he reached her, Walker took her face in his hands and kissed her within an inch of her life.

The moment Walker saw Regina coming through the trees onto the beach, his only goal was to get to her and make sure she was all right. Kissing her felt as natural to him as saying hello to anyone else.

"You're okay?" he asked when they finally broke apart. "Nobody...?"

"I'll tell you about it," she said quietly, and stepped back to greet Axel. "Did you think I was lost?" she asked the teen.

"We didn't know what to think. Dad told me what's been going on, and when we checked your cottage and found out it was trashed—"

"Trashed?" She looked at Walker. "Really?"

He nodded as Axel continued. "Yeah. So Dad said we all gotta drop everything and start looking for you. He said if you weren't down at the cove he was calling the cops."

Regina looked surprised, but Walker merely shrugged. "I was ... concerned."

Axel scoffed. "Concerned? He was totally wigged out. Trust me."

Walker sent his son a quelling look. "Yeah, okay, Mr. Observation. Look, go on ahead and let the others know to call off the search, okay?"

"You could just call them," Axel said with a grin.

Axe was milking it. "Go on, get out of here," Walker said, waving him off.

"Yes, Herr Father." Axel gave a mock salute and headed back up the hill.

Between patching things up with Axel and seeing that Regina was safe, Walker was almost euphoric. He couldn't resist lightly caressing her cheek. "Are you truly all right?"

"Well, aside from being held at gunpoint ..."

"What?!"

"It was Sandi Bollocks, of all people." Regina filled him in on the death of Frank Hatteras and Sandi's fears that she might be next.

"Why didn't she go to Detective Liu? He probably would have cut a deal in exchange for some leads to the killer."

"She doesn't even know who their client was; everything was handled online and through p.o. boxes, so she figured her safest bet was to leave town."

"Was she the one who rifled through your place?"

"The first time yes, but not the cottage here at The Grove. She actually returned the one little necklace she'd taken before. So that means..."

"Whoever we're looking for knows where you are, and that where you are, the tigers are."

He watched as Regina's face tightened, not from

fear, but from determination. "It's time we updated everyone," she said, "including Gabe de la Torre. It feels like the enemy is getting closer and I can't let anyone get caught up in this unawares."

"*We* can't let that happen. Let's go have that talk."

Chapter Twenty-Nine

Walker was torn. He owed Regina an apology for his boorish behavior and he hoped like hell that she'd forgive him. But the death of Frank Hatteras and the vandalism of her cottage here at The Grove had him more worried than ever. He'd just as soon call off the reception, give what evidence they had to Detective Liu, and call it a day. But he knew Regina would get her back up if he lobbied against it. Still, he had to make his case.

"You can make the report online—call it vandalism —and I'll make sure I'm assigned to it," Gabe said later that afternoon after Walker and Regina had updated everyone on the situation. The detective's arm was no longer in a sling and he seemed ready to spring into action. "I'll be able to assign a patrol car to make the rounds at night, at least for a week or so. I can also connect with Detective Liu without raising too many eyebrows. And if you don't mind, I'll get Leo to put me on Tuesday's guest list. We'll keep it low-key since I shouldn't be encouraging you all to be proactive about this investigation."

"Is this reception really needed? Walker asked. "We already have several leads. Perhaps there's enough to turn over to the police before putting Regina out there where she could get hurt."

"He has a point," Gabe said. "That would be the easiest and the safest thing to do."

"I know you're all worried, but I'm not going to get hurt," Regina insisted. "We've planned for every contingency, and I feel we can make some real progress if we just stick to the game plan." She set Walker a look that said, *Sorry, I'm not going to budge on this one.*

The professor addressed Regina directly. "I have given this a bit of thought, my dear, and I find I am of a more positive mind about what you are attempting to do. As long as you remain vigilant, you are right to try and expose the perpetrators. So much valuable art has been lost to public view over the years because victims throw up their hands and wipe their tears with insurance money. It is both disgraceful and sad."

Walker reached for Reggie's hand. "Well, certainly no one can put Regina in that category, although at times—like right now—I sure as hell wish I could." He smiled gamely and gave her hand a squeeze. If he couldn't stop her, he was damn well going to protect her.

He glanced at Axel, who had a thoughtful look on his face. Regina had been right all along that his son should be included in the discussion. Walker could tell the boy felt far more respected than he had when the day began.

It helped bolster his son's confidence that Walker finally made good on his promise to review Axel's driving ability. He'd done so while they waited for Gabe to show up and the boy had surpassed Walker's expectations. He'd even parallel parked! They'd agreed to make an appointment at the DMV in San Rafael for the following day.

"So, basically, some badass dude is trying to clean up his mess and now he's not sure if he got what he wanted in the first place," Axel now summarized.

"That's it," Regina said. "And we're pretty sure these aren't random killings because the first three supposedly have some sort of mark on them."

"What kind of mark?" Jenna asked.

Gabe explained that a detail like that usually wasn't disclosed early in the investigation because the team didn't want copycats to muddy the water. He pulled out his phone. "But let's see if they at least found one on Hatteras." The answer came within minutes. "The ME's preliminary report says yes, there's a similar mark behind his ear."

"How long before you guys start looking for what the victims have in common besides the mark?" Brit asked.

"Oh, they're looking; they just haven't found a link that satisfies them yet."

Regina showed her frustration. "But we've tried to

explain to Detective Liu how they're connected; he doesn't seem interested in the facts."

"I know it seems that way, and maybe Hatteras will help him turn the corner. But he has no evidence at this point to place the first victim in your scenario, which is why he has to keep casting the widest possible net. And frankly, sometimes killers pull stuff like this just to throw off the investigators. The marks could be a complete hoax."

"Or they could really mean something," Axel said. "Maybe there's some gang involved or something."

"Anything's possible, I guess. Once I talk to Detective Liu, I'll see if he'll make an exception and let me disclose more details. I think I can vouch for you all not to run to the press. The more heads we put together on this, the better." Gabe got up to leave, pulled out some business cards from his wallet and handed them out to everyone. "Call me anytime, day or night, if you need something."

After he left, Reggie volunteered to upload the police report while Brit and Jenna took the professor back to his cottage to get some of his personal items. "I don't care whether you have a concealed cannon, you're still moving in here until we get this straightened out," Jenna said. That left Walker and Axel to clean up the coffee cups from the meeting. Axel wasted no time putting in his two cents. "This is some serious shit," he said.

"Yeah, it is, which is why I don't want you spilling

your gut to Kaitlyn. She doesn't need to be involved in something that could turn dangerous at some point."

"Oh, but it's okay for me?" he asked with a smirk.

"Listen, if I could, I'd ship you someplace else until all this was over. The idea of you being in harm's way doesn't do a damn thing for my peace of mind. But for some strange reason, Regina thinks you can handle it. I don't know why, but she actually likes you."

"And as you said, you obviously like her."

Once again Axe turned thoughtful. He avoided Walker's gaze as he stacked the cups and saucers. "Well, since it's pretty clear she feels the same way, you'd better not do anything to screw it up ... like get hurt or anything."

The tone of Axel's words gave Walker pause. His son wanted to be treated like an adult, but part of him was still a kid—a kid who might be worried his dad was going away just like his mom had.

"Axel," Walker said, and waited for Axel to look at him. "I'm not going anywhere, and I'm sure not planning on getting hurt."

Axel held Walker's gaze, holding him to his promise. After a moment he nodded slightly. "That's good."

"Yeah. Hey, let's go upstairs and see if we can book a DMV appointment online."

"I'm down with that," Axel said, and this time he grinned from ear to ear.

Walker didn't knock on Reggie's door later that night, which was a good thing. They'd come to a tentative truce, but the underlying tension between them remained. She couldn't be sure if it was because of his feelings for her, or more that she was putting all of them at greater risk.

She feared it was the latter, and that he was right. Despite the blessing that Ethan had given for her quest, was she in fact being selfish about wanting to catch the thieves? Four lives had already been sacrificed to the cause, lives that might have been spared if she hadn't stirred the hornet's nest. Just because her uncle and the others had been part of the original crime, didn't mean they deserved to die for it. And how would she feel if someone else was hurt, if someone completely innocent became "collateral damage"? She couldn't live with herself if that happened.

They were just little jade tigers, after all. Not worth risking anything for.

Or were they? When do you take a stand against bad behavior and say, "No, this is wrong. I'm not going to slink away and just let it keep happening. I'm not going to take money to make it all go away. Even if—especially if—law enforcement doesn't have the time or the resources to do anything about it, I'm going to do all I can to retrieve what belongs to my family, even if there's risk involved."

That thought led to another, equally uncomfortable notion. Why hadn't she told Walker about the Facebook group? She'd vagued him out by saying "online."

She knew why. Because he wouldn't agree with what she was about to do.

She pulled out her laptop and looked up "The Jade Hunters" on Facebook. It was indeed an invitation-only group, and when she checked the members, she saw that there were only twelve. One of those listed was "Francis Pierre Montelban." Three more were listed as "administrators." They included "Cheri Lynn Holmes," "Arthur of The Jade Shop," and "Carl Smith."

If she asked to join the group, she knew that one of the three administrators would take on the task of evaluating her to see if she was worthy of joining them.

And one of those three could very well be the thief, if not the killer.

She began to type:

Gina Culpepper, jewelry designer. I have valuable information about a famous pair of jade earrings and would like to join the group. I come highly recommended by Francis.

After a brief hesitation, she hit "enter" and closed her laptop.

When sleep finally came, she was still wondering if she'd done the right thing.

Chapter Thirty

The following two days were a list-maker's dream. Walker worked on the exhibit, met with Gabe, and ordered a tuxedo in nearby San Rafael while Reggie plowed through her own tasks in preparation for the reception. She also checked and re-checked her Facebook account to see if she'd been accepted to the Jade Hunters group. So far, nothing had turned up. "One way or another, I'm going to connect," she muttered, checking off each item on her list with a fervor driven by the stress of knowing she would soon have to perform in front of a room full of people.

In truth, Reggie hated being on display, especially if it entailed being anything other than herself, which made the entire dust up with Walker over her modeling seem ridiculous in hindsight. It was amazing the lengths one would go to just to save face or prove a point.

... and maybe the same held true for catching a killer.

She'd thought long and hard about what to do if and when she determined who the culprit was. Once they knew for sure she was on to them, she couldn't just wait around to see if they would make a move. Somehow, she had to get them so worked up that they'd expose the real tigers to compare them to the fakes.

The complexity of the situation hit her at three a.m. on Monday. There weren't just two pairs in play—there were three: the originals (that Reggie said she still had), the fakes created by the thieves (which Reggie also had), and the "fakes" the thieves now thought that perhaps *they* had. Reggie should have in her possession two pairs, not one, which meant coming up with a second set, fast.

She waited until seven a.m. and called Leo. He answered gruffly and it sounded like a woman's voice in the background asking, "Who is it?"

"Sorry to wake you, but I just realized our plan is missing a key element," Reggie said.

"What's that?"

"If I have the originals like I say I do, then I must have the fakes they put in the vault as well. If all I have is the one pair, it's pretty much an admission that they're fake."

There was a pause, then, "Damn, you're right."

"So, I was thinking..."

"I see where you're going. Look, I know a cutter who's good—not as good as Thomas Ling, but still competent. More important, Liane can be trusted. I'll send her those photos I took, see what she can do on short notice."

"And I can get the eyes from Vihaan. I'll have him cut them in the proper style and attach them. We won't have them in time for the party, but if there are any follow-up connections, we'll be ready."

"Sounds like a plan."

"Thanks, Leo ... now go back to doing whatever it was you were doing." She couldn't help smiling as she said it.

She heard a chuckle. "Uh huh," he said.

His guards kept the lantern on the dimmest setting for most of the day, to save on batteries, they said. At night there was no light at all, which threw Thomas Ling's prison chamber into a coffin-like blackness that only a subterranean location could manage.

So, the jade carver had learned by the end of the first week to gauge his surroundings more by sound and touch and smell than sight. He was becoming adept at it, even as he sat on a damp-smelling sleeping bag in a small stone room, unable to walk because he'd sprained his ankle while being manhandled by the goons.

He knew, for instance, that his guards were in the next chamber over eating egg foo young. Was it as good as the dish his mother made? It couldn't be. Hers was light and filled with the freshest vegetables and bits of chicken. It was an American dish, yes, but she had quickly made it her own. She could open a restaurant and serve it, it was that good.

Thoughts of her sent a wave of panic and despair through him. She was old and by herself, and not able to get around very well. He had to escape, somehow, but it would help to know why he was here in the first place. Hadn't he done what they'd asked of him? Had something gone wrong? His captor was not the woman who had forced him to complete the forgery, but a man in his late thirties. The man had been to see him only twice—each time, apparently, to make sure he was still in good health.

"Please, sir," Thomas had asked him, "Why are you doing this?"

"The man had said only, "You will see," and walked out. But each time he'd seemed nervous. Time, Thomas sensed, was pressing down upon him, upon all of them.

Perhaps his one idea of rescue, born of desperation, would bear fruit. He called out to the thugs in respectful Cantonese, "Were you able to find the alabaster?"

After a moment the taller one, Chow Li Jun, came around the corner. He pulled several stones, each about the size of an apricot, out of his pocket. Handing them over, he asked, "Will these do?"

"They are perfect. And the carving blades?"

Chow pulled out a small zippered pouch but hesitated. "These could become weapons."

"Where would that get me?" Thomas asked. "I have no idea where I am or how to escape. My captor seems to want me alive, and you have taken good care of me. Why would I want to harm you?"

"The boss would not like us giving you these things."

"The boss does not need to know. Now do you want me to carve the amulets for you? Because I need both the stone and the tools to do it."

Reluctantly Chow handed the pouch over. "You say they will have power?"

"Most definitely. They will have Olympic power, like the medals I created years ago. I will carve one for you, and one for your brother. They will protect you in your noble cause. And I will do more than that."

"What do you mean?"

I must tread carefully here, Thomas thought. *Appeal to his greed, but not overmuch.* "I think your quest is just, but there is no reason why you shouldn't earn a little extra along the way. I am known for my carving; with my mark, the experts know it came from me and will price it accordingly."

Chow looked skeptical. "I would have no idea where to sell such a thing."

"I can help you there, too. I know a man, a broker. He is very discreet, and sympathetic to your cause. All you have to do is tell him I sent you and show him the piece, and he will accommodate you. You can trust him."

The beefy young idealist didn't get angry. *Thank God he's at least somewhat pragmatic.* "First you show me one of these carvings; then we'll see."

"That is fair enough."

Chow left the room and Thomas wasted no time in beginning to carve the symbol the two brothers had showed him. If he could get them to take one or two to Dr. Leo Brunt, if the man could put two and two together. If, if, if...

Axel couldn't get his DMV appointment until the morning of the reception, but it was early enough that Reggie was confident Walker could get back in time to drive with her down to the Hyatt Regency near the airport. There they'd change for the evening's event after meeting with Leo to hear about anything unusual he'd come across when visiting Collier's estate.

At a quarter to two in the afternoon, Walker returned with an elated Axel, who leapt out of the driver's seat and ran into the Great House, waving his new license. "I got it!" he crowed.

Walker followed behind, reminding his son that it wasn't a good idea to race out of a car while leaving the keys in it.

"Yeah, whatever," Axel said and ran upstairs to spread the word of his newfound independence.

"That's one happy camper there," Reggie said from the library where she'd been working. "Now, did *you* get what you needed?"

Walker held up the garment bag he'd carried in. "Ready to go." He put the bag down across the back of a chair and sat down across from her. "I've been meaning to talk to you."

Reggie's pulse immediately shot up. Whenever men said they wanted to "talk," it usually didn't end well. "What about?" she asked carefully. "Are you worried about tonight?"

"Yes," he said. "You know I'd scrap this plan if I could, but I've committed to seeing it through and I've been telling myself that you know what you're doing."

"... and that Leo and Gabe know what they're doing."

"That, too. But no, this is about us."

Oh, this could be bad. "About us."

"Yes. I'm sorry it's taken so long, but I owe you an apology."

Interesting. "You do, huh?"

He nodded. "On Sunday I bit your head off for no good reason, and in the process, I ruined what had been an incredible night. I'm very sorry."

Reggie couldn't believe the relief surging through her. She felt almost giddy. "You were upset about Axel and I was butting in."

"No, you weren't. You were merely suggesting a reason for his behavior and I wasn't willing to listen." He reached over to take one of her hands. "And then, when you went on your run, and I couldn't find you, and saw the cottage ..." He shook his head.

She reached up and touched his cheek. "Well, I accept your apology. It's all good."

Walker took a deep breath and kissed her palm. "It's

all *very* good." He stood and tugged on her hand. "Come with me. I have something for you."

He held her hand all the way up the stairs and into his room. On the bed was a white box, which he handed to her.

Puzzled, she looked at him.

"Go ahead, open it."

"You didn't have to—"

"This is not a 'get-out-of-the-doghouse' gift. I bought it over a week ago. The moment I saw it, I knew I wanted you to have it."

She untied the ribbon and lifted the lid. Inside was the breathtaking white dress they'd seen in the boutique where Halona worked. It came with a matching clutch and was even in Reggie's size. "Oh my," she said, her heart lifting.

"I know it's presumptuous of me, but I can't imagine anyone else in that dress, and with your hair up, and wearing the tigers, you will make the impression you want to make tonight. Believe me."

She smiled slowly, trying for sultry once again. "But will I impress you?"

He drew her closer, until their bodies were pressed together, and touched his forehead to hers. "Sweetheart, you impress me whether you're wearing running shorts, a beautiful gown, or nothing at all ... especially nothing at all." With that, he kissed her deeply. And in that moment, the almost frenzied motion that had driven her the past two days transformed into another kind of energy altogether.

They barely made it on the road in time to make the meeting with Leo.

What a monstrosity, Walker thought.

Milton Collier lived in a thirteen-thousand-square-foot, ultra-modern home in the millionaire enclave of Hillsborough, thirty minutes south of San Francisco. To take advantage of the hilltop location and views of San Francisco Bay, the prevailing building materials used were steel and glass. His estate was surrounded by geometric, immaculately maintained landscaping which was in turn enclosed by a twelve-foot-high electronic security fence. When a visitor reached the gate to the estate, they were instructed by a disembodied voice to alert Security who, if they were on the guest list, would in turn send them a special code to allow them entry. They had to be quick about punching it in, however, because the voice warned them it would be obsolete in three minutes.

"We should have rented a limo to be worthy of the place," Regina quipped as she and Walker drove up in his Explorer. "Imagine if we'd taken *my* car."

Walker tapped the steering wheel, waiting for the massive gate to swing open.

Their meeting with Leo at the Hyatt had been both encouraging and frustrating. Encouraging because the investigator had thoroughly scoped out the place and determined the best strategy for keeping Regina in someone's sight the entire evening. But it was frustrating because there were still too many unknowns. Regina may soon be having a conversation with someone who had ordered the deaths of four people, and she could very well be next on the hit list.

The two of them had made love in their hotel room after Leo left, but the contentment he'd felt after that interlude was now gone, replaced by an underlying fear for Regina's safety. He was no longer in a jovial frame of mind.

"You look very nice," Regina said, no doubt hoping to distract him.

Walker glanced at her in her form-fitting new gown. "There's no comparison."

She smoothed the sensuous material along her lap before tapping one of her earrings. "You were right, it really does display the tigers well."

"No, it displays *you* well. Hopefully not too well."

"I do think you're worrying too much," she said. "You heard Leo; he's placed his team where it needs to be. My main concern is finding out who we're up against and pushing them to make a mistake."

The massive gate swung open. "Well, then, we'd damn well better get started."

Chapter Thirty-One

"**M**agnificent."

"Captivating."

"Superb."

Reggie had been responding to accolades like that for the past hour, as guest after guest, champagne or cocktail in hand, approached her to view the rare piece of history she wore like a queen. With her hair pulled back in an elegant chignon, the tigers were highly visible against her skin, and Walker was right—both she and the dress set them off perfectly.

She graciously accepted each compliment, taking the opportunity to talk about her grandmother's legacy and tout the upcoming re-opening of The Grove Center. She made a mental note of anyone who seemed to be inordinately interested in the shape and design of the tigers, but so far no one had given any obvious indication that they believed the earrings were anything other than original.

Walker stood stoically by her side, an impeccable consort in his perfectly tailored tuxedo. He was all but ignored by Milton Collier, who acted as though Reggie were some exotic creature Collier alone had discovered. Only his hosting duties kept him from fawning over her.

Reggie was anxiously waiting to meet the collectors Leo had marked as possibilities when an unexpected guest showed up, turning her insides cold.

Curtis Black was tall, Nordic-looking, and dressed in a deep red tuxedo jacket with a snakeskin cummerbund and bow tie. His need to be hip had been one of her concerns about him; this evening he seemed to be trying for an edgy, artistic look. Instead, he came across as a wannabe pimp. Did he have any idea of the impression he made?

"Reggie," he said, taking one of her hands and leaning in to kiss her so hastily that she couldn't step back in time. As usual he had worn too much cologne. "You look positively ravishing."

"Hello, Curtis," she said flatly, quickly regaining her composure. She discreetly put her arm through Walker's. "Walker, I'd like you to meet Curtis Black, who runs a gallery on Chestnut Street."

Curtis and Walker seemed to size up the situation simultaneously; their eyes dueled while they shook hands.

Curtis lobbed the first salvo. "I don't know whether Reggie mentioned it, but she and I go way back ... don't we, *Kära*? At one point we were as close as it's possible to be."

Walker countered smoothly, putting his arm around Reggie's waist. "I'm afraid you just didn't come up," he said. "Of course, we've had other things to do, haven't we, sweetheart?"

Curtis frowned. "Really? I'm surprised she didn't tell you we were once engaged."

"Out of sight, out of mind, I guess," he said, gently drawing Reggie closer.

She wanted to kiss him but figured that would be cruel. Instead she gave Curtis the same bland smile and watched him reluctantly concede the field.

As Curtis walked away, Walker murmured, "Looks like you dodged a bullet with that one."

She grinned at him. "I couldn't have said it better."

They were still smiling at each other when Collier walked up with four people in tow.

"Reggie, I'd like to present Mr. Jiang Wei, the Consul General of San Francisco for the People's Republic of China, and his wife, his chief of staff Daniel Long, and his interpreter Sharilyn Huang. Mr. Jiang and his wife are avid collectors of antique jade. We've been known to haggle a time or two over particular pieces, haven't we, Jiang?" Collier gave the diplomat's shoulder a friendly squeeze.

Jiang looked to be in his late fifties; he was of medium height with a receding hairline and a soft-looking belly. His wife was petite but sharp-edged, dressed in a blue satin sheath adorned with Cantonese-style embroidery.

"It is a pleasure to meet you, Miss Firestone," Jiang

said. "Your tigers are indeed beautiful and a fitting symbol of my country's history and culture. I would love to talk to you sometime about perhaps returning them to their homeland."

Ah, now there's a motive. She gave the diplomat a look of kind but firm resolve. "Thank you, sir, but these have been in my family for over a century; I promise you we will continue to take excellent care of them."

As Walker joined the introductions, several thoughts occurred to Reggie in rapid succession: Jiang seemed like much more than your average government bureaucrat. Why did the man need an interpreter, since he seemed to speak English perfectly well, and did Jiang's wife, who stood stone-faced next to her husband, wonder the same thing? Was Sharilyn Huang just a colleague of Daniel Long, or was there something else between them? Reggie couldn't help but speculate whether Sharilyn Huang served Jiang in another more "informal" capacity.

She wouldn't be surprised if it were true, because the woman was stunning. She looked about Reggie's age, and was slightly taller than both Jiang and even Jiang's aide de camp. Possessed of a dancer's body and a flawless face, she wore a simple black sheath that provided the perfect backdrop for her dramatic necklace. It was a hammered bronze choker that Reggie knew well—because she had created it.

"I'm honored, Ms. Huang."

The woman smiled apologetically. "Why is that,

may I ask?" She spoke English without a trace of accent.

Reggie pointed to the necklace. "Because you're wearing one of my Fire Stone creations. I designed it to echo one of the other pieces from my grandmother's collection."

The woman instinctively reached up to touch the strands. "It ... it was a gift. I didn't know. I'm sorry."

"No apology needed. I love to see others displaying and enjoying my work, whether they know it's mine or not." Reggie leaned forward. "I always give my works a name; that one I called 'Possession' because the piece my grandmother modeled gave her the aura of a royal Egyptian slave. Of course, she was nude at the time."

Reggie smiled as she told what she thought was an amusing anecdote, but to her surprise, Sharilyn was not smiling back. She looked, in fact, as if she might rip the necklace off and fling it across the room.

Reggie drew in a breath. *Awkward.*

Daniel Long stepped into the breech. "If you'll excuse us, Sharilyn and I came straight from work. We have a stern task master and have been dying to check out tonight's delicious buffet."

"By all means," Reggie said.

Sharilyn composed herself quickly; she addressed Jiang in soft Cantonese before bowing slightly to the man and his wife and heading toward the far side of the room with Daniel.

"She thanked me for allowing her to come and view

your beautiful tigers," Jiang said, watching his two assistants leave. His wife, who still had not spoken a word, watched her husband watch them.

Something's going on, but is it related to what's important? Reggie glanced at Walker who raised his eyebrows in acknowledgment.

Then, as if someone had turned on a switch in her head, Mrs. Jiang broke into a lovely smile at the sight of something behind Reggie's shoulder. Leo Brunt was approaching with retired film star Lily Quan. The seventy-something celebrity still maintained the arresting looks that had taken her to the heights of the Hong Kong film industry five decades earlier. Wearing a satin brocade jacket, she carried an ornate hand-painted fan. She and Mrs. Jiang embraced and spoke rapidly in their native language; they were obviously dear friends.

The actress then addressed Reggie and Walker. "I'm sorry, I haven't seen my good friend Changying since the last time she visited her husband here in the States—what was that, a year ago? We have been friends for a very long time." She held out her hand. "You must be Regina Firestone, the 'tiger lady' we have all been waiting to meet." She stepped closer and looked carefully at the dangling jade earrings. "Yes, they are quite exquisite, are they not?"

Reggie decided to test the level of the woman's interest. "You are familiar with their provenance, Ms. Quan?"

"Oh yes," she said. "I know their history very well. I

know where they came from, and I can tell you where I hope they're going."

"Where would that be?" asked Leo.

"Why, straight into my collection, of course!" That elicited a round of chuckles.

"I'm afraid you'll have to stand in line, Lily," Collier said. "Jiang stands ready to best any offer you might make, and I of course am ready to blow both of you out of the water."

Aside from some nervous titters, Collier's tactless grandstanding quelled the joviality of the conversation. Reggie noticed that Daniel Long had returned alone carrying a small plate of appetizers.

Standing close to Walker for courage, Reggie felt compelled to go out on a limb. "As I've already told you, Mr. Collier, the tigers are not for sale. Not the originals, and not even the replicas that we had made for security purposes."

That stunned everyone into silence.

"Are you saying that the tigers you are wearing are not real?" Mrs. Jiang asked, faintly horrified. It was the first time she'd spoken English.

"No, I'm not, ma'am," Reggie said. "I am saying that none of the pieces in the Amanda Firestone Foundation jewelry collection are for sale, including her jade earrings."

"Well, that's definitive," Leo Brunt said. "Milton, tell us about your most recent acquisition."

Thanks to Leo's finessing, the conversation turned to more general topics of jade artifacts and collectibles, a subject on which Collier was happy to hold court. Afterward he led a tour of his private collection, which took up most of the lower level of the mansion. He stuck like glue to Reggie, touching the small of her back as he pointed out various acquisitions. Walker, she noticed, kept a respectful distance but was never out of sight.

"I know what you've said about those tigers," Collier whispered to her at one point when the rest of the group was commenting on a particularly fine Ming vase. He rubbed her back slowly. "But I can truly make you an offer you can't refuse."

Reggie turned to face him and said matter-of-factly, "You have watched me refuse repeatedly, Mr. Collier, on any number of levels. Don't you find that tedious? I know I certainly do." And with that she purposefully moved to Walker and slipped her arm through his. "It's feeling a bit stuffy in here; would you mind if we ventured outside and admired the view?"

Walker sent Collier a look of feigned apology; the collector frowned but could do nothing except watch Reggie and Walker head back up the stairs.

On the upper level there were still several dozen guests milling about, and a group of white-coated waiters bustled back and forth dispensing drinks and hors d'oeuvres. She could see Gabe across the large reception room talking with Leo; he took an appetizer off a passing tray before continuing his own circulation of the room.

Reggie and Walker stepped onto the expansive

terrace overlooking the pool and garden; the evening was cool, and Walker automatically took off his jacket to put it around Reggie. She was smiling her thanks when Lily Quan came up to them.

"I'm sorry to be stalking you," she said with a thinly veiled sense of urgency, "but I have some information about your grandmother and those earrings that I think you'll be very interested in."

"What kind of information?" Walker asked.

Lily tapped him lightly on his bicep with her fan, gracing him with the smile that had lit up thousands of movie screens over the years. "You'll just have to come and find out. Shall we say noon tomorrow? I will even treat you to lunch." With that she pressed a card into Reggie's hand and glided back the way she'd come.

"What do you suppose that was all about?" Walker asked.

Reggie gazed at the woman's retreating figure. "I don't know." She looked down at the card Lily Quan had given her. It listed the woman's address, and on the back, she'd written: "Bring the earrings." She showed the card to Walker. "We may be getting somewhere."

"Good. Now will you do me a favor and let me take the cats?"

"What? Why?"

"Because you've done what you came to do, and my stress level will drop significantly if you're not advertising that you're wearing a fortune in jewels."

"You're such a worrywart," she said lightly, but reached up take off the tigers. She pulled their pouch out of the clutch she carried, replaced the earrings and started to put them back into her purse, but Walker beckoned with his fingers, so she handed the pouch to him.

It was a good thing she did.

Chapter Thirty-Two

Walker was right: They'd done all they could to advertise that the original jade tigers were still in Reggie's possession. Neither Gabe nor Leo had reported anything amiss and Gabe had gone home for the night. As the guests started to exit, Leo indicated he'd be discreetly letting members of his team leave as well.

Reggie was more than ready to leave, but asked Walker to wait while she made a dash to the ladies' room.

"I'll come with you," he said.

Such a worrier, that man. She shook her head. "I'll be two minutes." She took the stairs to the second floor where Collier had turned over one of his massive bedrooms for female guests. The *en suite* bathroom had a fifteen-foot vanity, reminding Reggie of the type actors use backstage.

When she reemerged from using the restroom, Sharilyn Huang was standing in front of the mirror applying lipstick. The two of them were alone.

Sharilyn looked at Reggie's refection in the mirror and said, "Oh, you're not wearing the tigers. Did Mr. Jiang or Mr. Collier make you an irresistible offer?"

"Ah, no, much to their disappointment." Reggie checked to see that her chignon was still firmly in place. "The tigers are just a bit too heavy to wear for long."

Sharilyn glanced at Reggie's clutch on the counter. "I would imagine so." She caught Reggie's eye and once again touched the gold necklace she was wearing. "Thank you for the information concerning this necklace. I hadn't realized it had such an interesting backstory." She smiled, then, and left.

Beautiful, but odd, Reggie thought as she finished her ablutions and reapplied her own lipstick. She'd bet a week's pay that something was going on with that woman and the married diplomat; the wife suspected something, at least. Reggie couldn't imagine such a conundrum in her own life.

The thought of Walker waiting below gave her pause. Was it hormones, or was something important happening between them? Did she *want* something to happen? Her luck in the romance department had never been that great. But maybe this time...

She was still focused on those thoughts as she headed back down the elaborate staircase. Halfway down she looked up to see a man with a white jacket and dark hair running toward her, carrying a large food tray high enough that she couldn't see his face, nor could he see hers. He obviously wasn't paying attention because he ran into her at full speed, causing the tray to ram into her and splatter the contents all over her dress and the steps.

"Oh!" she cried as she began to slip on the stairs.

But instead of stopping to help her, the man paused only briefly, then continued to run past her.

"What the hell?!" Walker cried. He'd apparently seen the collision from the bottom of the staircase and quickly ran up to help Reggie. "Are you all right?"

"Y... yes, I think so," she said, rubbing the side of her face where the tray had smacked her. Already it felt like it was beginning to swell. She looked down at her beautiful dress: red stains—cherry or strawberry juice, she couldn't tell—had already soaked through the embroidered front, leaving what looked like a trail of blood down the length of the garment.

By now several people had heard the commotion. Leo came running. "What just happened?"

"A waiter just plowed into Regina," Walker said.

"Here on the stairs?"

"Yeah. He was headed up and just kept going. I don't think he's on your crew."

Reggie watched Walker and Leo exchange looks; the two of them immediately bolted up the stairs. *God, what is going on?*

Several female guests gathered round to help her;

Sharilyn Huang even brought her a cold pack that she'd apparently scrounged from the kitchen.

"That could have been me," she said," but I'm so sorry it was you."

After several minutes, Walker and Leo came back down empty-handed. "He escaped through a window," Walker said. "We missed him."

Leo took a couple of men to see if they could catch the imposter on the grounds of the estate. Notified of the assault, Milton Collier cut his personal museum tour short and came barreling upstairs. "He ran full speed into you and kept on going?" he asked Reggie. "Why would he do such a thing?"

"It's obvious he wanted the tigers," Walker said.

Sharilyn looked puzzled. "But she wasn't wearing them. She'd taken them off."

"He probably thought I'd put them elsewhere," Reggie said. She looked around on the staircase and the floor below. "Like in my purse ... which is gone."

Milton Collier insisted on calling the Hillsborough Police Department, who sent over a patrol officer to take down names and fill out a report. While the rest of the guests were permitted to leave (with the caveat that they might be asked to give statements later), Walker and Regina sat on the couch in Collier's library, recounting what had happened. Walker could tell the adrenalin had left Regina some time earlier;

she no doubt felt twice as tired as he did. She also looked bedraggled, with her chignon half undone and her dress stained all down the front, probably beyond repair. Yet she answered every question patiently and without rancor. He wanted to kiss her in the worst way.

Collier was not happy with either the caterer or Leo Brunt. "You said you would handle security for this event, and look what happened," he complained to Leo after the officer had left.

"I can't argue with that," Leo said, contrite to a point. "But don't go blaming Elite Eats; they had nothing to do with it."

"Well, somebody let a thief pose as a server, and it certainly wasn't me."

He looked Collier squarely in the eye. "We don't know anything except that there were several people at this event who would like nothing more than to get their hands on those tigers, and that includes you."

Walker half expected Collier to blow a gasket over such an accusation, but he didn't. In fact, the notion seemed to appease him. "You're right; I suppose one can't dangle candy in front of a toddler and expect them not to try and grab it. I may even have some ideas along those lines..."

Walker had had enough; he stood up and gently took Regina's hand. "We'd love to hear your theories, but we've had a very long day, so we'll be saying good night."

Regina looked grateful for the exit strategy. "Thank

you again for hosting the reception, Mr. Collier; I'm sure we'll be hearing about this in the local news."

Collier beamed at that idea. "Yes, I bet we sure as hell will."

It wasn't until they reached the car that Walker took Regina into his arms. She came willingly. "I could throttle you for taking such a chance tonight," he murmured, inhaling her unique, intoxicating scent. "If it's the same thief we've been after, he could have had a knife..."

Regina pulled back to look at him. "We don't know if it was the same man—and I think you need to let Leo know what really happened."

"You're right." Walker strapped himself in and called Leo to explain everything. "Have Gabe tell the police Regina was so shocked by what happened that she didn't remember until just now that I had taken the tigers for safekeeping, so we called you right away to pass along the update. We need to make sure that detail gets put in the report before it goes to the press."

Leo assured him he'd take care of it and Walker hung up. Then he turned to Regina. "I was hoping you'd play along and let everyone think the thief had taken the earrings, and you did. The question is why?"

"Great minds think alike, I guess. I didn't like the idea of everyone knowing they were in your jacket, plus I was thinking they might be taken as evidence and our entire plan would be stopped in its tracks."

Walker glanced at her as he drove through the estate gates and headed back to the hotel. Her cheek was swollen, and he fought the overwhelming urge to seriously injure whoever had done that to her. Instead he asked if she'd like to stay at the hotel or go on back to The Grove.

She closed her eyes for a moment, then turned toward Walker. "Would you mind if we stayed the night? I would like nothing more than to sleep in and have a leisurely breakfast before we visit Lily Quan."

"About that: do you really want to bring the tigers with us? We know they aren't genuine, but she doesn't."

Regina took a minute to answer. "I think I would, if only to gauge her level of curiosity. If she pulls out a loupe and starts poring over them, then I'll worry. Are you all right with that—staying over and bringing them to her?"

Regina's reasoning made sense, besides which he was too tired to argue. "More than all right. I'll call Axe when we get to the hotel to let him know what's going on."

"You're a good dad," Regina said, and closed her eyes again.

Back at the Hyatt, Axe's phone went to voicemail, which it often did when the boy was playing a video game with friends. *When the cat's away*, Walker thought. He sent Axe a separate email just to make sure, and for good measure sent one to Brit as well.

We're back tomorrow after lunch; until then keep us posted; we're just a phone call away.

Ten minutes later the two of them were ensconced in the king-size bed, Regina tucked under Walker's arm.

She fell asleep almost immediately, her arm draped securely across his bare chest.

He took longer to drop off, his mind filled with possible scenarios regarding Regina and the tigers … none of them comforting.

Chapter Thirty-Three

As soon as she was able, she dialed the special number. He answered on the first ring and what he told her made her want to scream. "What do you mean they weren't in there?" she said in rapid Cantonese.

"I'm telling you, there was only some tissue, a lipstick, and a notebook and pencil. The tigers were not there."

"You would be telling me the truth, yes?"

"Why wouldn't I? Haven't we been in this together since the beginning?"

She rubbed her forehead. "Yes, yes, I'm sorry. You're right. It's just—this is becoming far too complicated. What about the other?"

"The crone left town. Sold her brothel and left for places unknown, just like the diamond cutter we used. I couldn't get anything out of that little tart who answers the phone, except a discount on a whore. She's already drumming up new business."

"Maybe you should take her up on it. It might do you some good to let off steam in a different sort of way."

"No, what I need—what we both need—is to secure the tigers sooner rather than later. Time is no longer on our side."

"Of that we are in complete agreement. But we need leverage. Let me think how best to achieve it."

"I have ideas of my own."

"Good. Then between us we will make it happen. I will be in touch."

"I will be ready."

Chapter Thirty-Four

I t was a modest home by Presidio Heights standards: Mediterranean-style, perhaps four thousand square feet with white stucco walls hung with Asian art and memorabilia collected throughout a successful, high-profile career. Lily Quan had been a darling of the jet set, a player during Hong Kong's zenith as a film mecca. She'd won several accolades, including a Golden Globe nomination for her portrayal of a female triad leader in the movie *Dragon Tears*.

The housekeeper led Reggie and Walker to an enclosed courtyard rimmed with large terra cotta vessels filled with blooming zinnias, daisies, and petunias. Lily Quan seemed to have garnered more than her share of summer sun in a normally fog-enshrouded city.

"What on earth happened to you?" Lily asked upon first seeing Reggie.

Reggie self-consciously touched her cheek. Walker

had told her it didn't look bad, but obviously he'd been lying. She sent him a look that said she was on to him. "I had a run-in with a serving tray."

"And a thief posing as a waiter who stole her purse," Walker added.

"At the reception?"

"Yes, you missed all the fun," Reggie said wryly.

Lily tsked and beckoned them to sit around a table set for lunch. "I hope you don't mind sitting out here. The older I get, the colder I get, so any time I can soak up the sun, that's where I am."

Over iced tea, Reggie filled the celebrity in on what had happened. "I have to say, Sharilyn Huang was very helpful; she was right there with a cold compress, or I'd probably look like I'd been bludgeoned instead of just smacked."

Lily sniffed. "Ah, Sharilyn. Thank God that's coming to an end very soon."

"What do you mean?" asked Walker.

"I mean she's been sharing Jiang's bed for the past year and a half, but he'll be returning to the homeland in two weeks—that's why Changying is here—and that piece of fluff will have to find another sugar daddy."

"I wondered about that," Reggie said. "But why on earth would his wife put up with that in the first place?"

Lily shrugged. "Not much she can do about it, is there? She has a medical practice and two children to look after. He travels a lot and has a roving eye for both jade and pretty women. Apparently, he met Ms. Huang at a gem show and was so smitten, he brought her over as a staff member. Changying has been biding her time until the end of this assignment." Lily took a sip of her tea. "And people wonder why I never married."

Reggie shuddered. "I have a cousin who's going through a similar situation, except that she's finally decided she's not going to take it anymore and is getting a divorce."

"Don't think Chiangying hasn't considered it. But her husband is a rising star, and in China's government, that's who you want to—how do you put it—hitch your wagon to. It's not as if he's asked for a separation; he's content to have his cake and eat it too. *Men*—present company excluded, of course."

"For what it's worth," Walker said, "I've always subscribed to Paul Newman's philosophy: 'Why go out for hamburger when you can stay home and have steak?'" He looked at Reggie as he said it and her pulse skittered in response.

"Smart boy," Lily said, raising her glass of tea.

The housekeeper came to the doorway, indicating that lunch was ready. She brought out chicken curry salad with sourdough baguettes and cold marinated asparagus, paired with a crisp Riesling.

"I'll bet you were expecting dim sum," Lily said. "Don't tell anyone, but I do so much Asian cultural advocacy that every organization seems to feel that's what I need to eat. I get tired of it, especially if it's not cooked right."

This woman is delightful. I hope she isn't also a thief. "Your secret is safe with us," Reggie said. "I adore curry."

"But never milt," Walker muttered, which got a snicker out of Reggie.

"Milt? What's that?" Lily asked. "Something I should try?"

"I wouldn't," Walker said. "It's fish semen."

The woman let out a guffaw that didn't match her graceful demeanor. "I thought I'd heard everything by now; I guess not."

The meal proceeded with light banter, but after the dishes were cleared away, Lily got down to business. She picked up a scrapbook that she'd propped next to her chair. Placing it on the table, she leafed through to a page marked with a sticky note then turned the book around so Reggie could see it.

"That's my grandmother," Reggie said. It was a photo of Amanda Firestone and Lily Quan from a 1965 Hong Kong newspaper. More importantly, Reggie's grandmother was wearing the jade earrings.

"I thought you might be interested in seeing that, which is why I invited you today. I found Amanda Firestone to be a completely down-to-earth, gracious human being, which is rare among those who have as much money as she did. She was in Hong Kong to accept a humanitarian award on behalf of the work she'd done for Chinatown immigrants, and I think that's what saved her from having the tigers stolen then."

"You've obviously known about the tigers for a long time," Walker said.

"As has everyone else who collects quality and antique jade, not to mention other players. Word gets around."

"Wait, are you saying there was an attempt to steal the tigers back in the Sixties?" No one in Reggie's family had ever mentioned such a thing.

Lily paused as if weighing her answer. "Precisely what do you know about these earrings of yours?"

"I know they were a gift from one of the last emperors to a concubine, that she gave them to an American Army colonel, and that they were given to my grandmother by that man's son."

"And the tigers themselves?"

"Only that they were carved from hotan jade, possibly in the 17th century at the beginning of the Qing dynasty."

"All of that is true, but there is even more to it. What makes the pieces so valuable today isn't just their antiquity, but the story behind them. Tigers symbolize authority and power in China, more so than the lion. If you look at the markings on a real tiger's head, for example, it's similar to the Chinese symbol for 'king.' It is said the carved tigers contained the essence of the Qing monarchy, and that when they left the emperor's hands, so too did all his power."

"But the dynasty was already crumbling by that time," Walker said. "The calligraphy was already on the wall, so to speak."

"It's true. The Boxer Rebellion was really a last-ditch effort to throw the foreigners out and cling to power, but it was too little, too late." Lily's words were somber; it was obviously a painful topic for her. "We all know what happened. A revolution, a generation let down by a weak republic, and the post-war communist takeover. Now we have what we have, and China has blossomed in many ways. But that doesn't mean there aren't those who wish things were different, and still others who actively work for change."

Reggie was perplexed. "But why are the jade tigers so relevant today?"

"Symbols, you will admit, are powerful. Your American flag, for instance, helped bind your colonies together; even today it is painful for most Americans to see anyone mistreating it."

Reggie followed Lily's train of thought. "So, the tiger still stands for power and authority."

"Yes, but not just authority," Lily stressed, "the *king*, and by extension, the monarchy."

Walker seemed incredulous. "There are those who want to restore the old dynasty?"

"Or create a new one. Imagine if Britain did away with their monarchy tomorrow. Can you imagine how many citizens would be hell-bent on restoring it? Monarchies are comforting to many people for the sense of continuity and identity they bestow. It is the same with many of the Chinese people, only they have been longing for that to happen for more than a hundred years. So, to answer your earlier question, Regina, yes, there were rumblings about 'repatriating' the tigers. It didn't come to pass because certain powerful individuals decided it was not a good idea."

Lily calmly took a sip of her wine and in the silence, Reggie realized that Lily herself must have had something to do with it. Their eyes met and Reggie nodded slightly in comprehension. Lily replied with a half-smile.

"And you're saying that even now, in the hands of certain people, the tigers would still be a call to arms."

"Yes, Mr. Banks. That's what I'm saying. Or, to put it in more modern terms: they would become the Nike symbol—the "Just do it' of not only fundraising, but ultimately, revolution. All the factions know this, and depending on who they are, they either want to promote the symbol or suppress it."

Reggie let out a breath. "Why tell us all this?"

The older woman leaned forward, her voice compelling. "I want you to be aware that you could be dealing with much more than an avaricious gem collector. The stakes are likely much higher, and therefore much more dangerous. I liked your grandmother very much, and I would hate to see her granddaughter become a victim like so many others." She took the scrapbook off the table. "Now, did you bring the tigers?"

Reggie glanced at Walker before meeting Lily's gaze. "Yes. Do you want to see them?"

Lily merely grinned, a Cheshire cat. "No. I just wanted to see how much you trusted me." She then turned toward the house and called out, "Rosa? We would love to have our dessert now." The venerable star was back to her light-hearted, charming self. "I'm sorry, but the Chinese do not have a handle on the best desserts. I serve lemon meringue pie whenever the situation warrants, and this is one of those times."

It was mid-morning and Axel covered his mouth yet again. His eyes had started to water.

"Third time's a charm," Jenna called from her desk to his.

"What?"

"Yawning. I'm surprised you haven't caught some flies over there."

"Ha ha." She was right, though; he'd finally gotten to sleep around two in the morning, and it was super tough to get up after just five hours and be ready to go to work. How did people do it day after day? "I'm just kinda tired, is all."

"You mean to tell me that even though your dad wasn't home, you didn't shut down your laptop at ten pm.? I'm shocked, I tell you. Shocked."

"Yeah, well, you probably think I was playing video games, but I wasn't—not the whole time, anyway. I was also doing some research."

"Really? On what?"

Axel swung his chair around. "Okay, so you know we were talking about gangs and secret societies and stuff? I been curious about any that might still exist today that were around a long time ago. You know, *Da Vinci Code* kind of stuff. So, I was talking to this guy I know who knows his way around the Deep Web—"

Jenna stopped to look at him. "Wait, you go on the Deep Web? That sounds dangerous."

"It can be. You gotta know what you're doing. I'm not a hacker or anything, if that's what you're thinking. But my friend's a Gray Hat—that means he's not a good or a bad guy— and he's been explaining places I can go to find out certain things that I can't find on the surface. I'm thinkin' if my dad and Reggie are right, then there's gotta be some connection between those weird marks they're finding on the bodies, and the stolen tigers. So, I've been looking for wacko groups that have anything to do with tigers and there're a shitload of them, more than you might think. And I've been looking for symbols 'cause we were talkin' about tats and every-thing. But there's a lot of freakin' weird stuff out there. Some of these guys are like super-sophisticated; they've got websites and shit, and they link up with members all over the world."

"If these groups are supposed to be secret, why put themselves on websites where people can track them down?"

"Oh, these aren't websites that just anybody can log

on to. You need to have keys to encryption codes and passwords and shit that changes every couple of minutes. Think of it like a vault that has like ten locks you have to go through before you get to the money. It's a whole different world down there."

Jenna shook her head like she couldn't believe what he was saying. "I don't think you ought to be doing that, Axel. Really. You should tell your dad about it. Better yet, you ought to leave it to the police."

"Hey, even the police don't know about a lot of this stuff, and Deep Web users want to keep it that way. They don't trust any authority. Period. But believe me, I'm not going to do anything stupid. I haven't gone on any illegal sites and I don't plan to. I'm a chickenshit, remember?"

Jenna sent him a half smile that showed she wasn't convinced he knew what he was doing and then turned back to her screen. But Axel knew. He yawned again before getting back to work.

Reggie was deflated, a tire gone flat. All she'd heard since her tigers were stolen were warnings—from Walker, Gabe, the police, and now Lily Quan. In so many words, they'd all said the same thing: Don't dig too deep; you may not like what you find.

It wasn't the digging she minded; it was the frustration of not finding anything under those rocks Gabe talked about! At this point she had a list of suspects that seemed to be growing, not shrinking, and no evidence that pointed strongly in one direction. The only thing that had worked was planting a seed of doubt in the mind of whoever stole the earrings to begin with, and that assumed the thief who took her clutch last night worked for the same mastermind who'd orchestrated the switch in the first place.

"What did you think of Lily Quan?" Reggie asked as Walker headed west on Sir Francisco Drake Boulevard back to The Grove.

"I think if she's not telling the truth, then she should have won the Golden Globe for Best Actress."

"I feel the same way. She could have easily asked to examine the earrings to see if she'd stolen the right ones. But all she really did was warn us the tigers were vulnerable and that we could be heading into dangerous territory."

"So, does that mean we can at least take her off the list?"

"Arrggh! I don't *know*! Maybe it was all an act to scare us off. Then there's Milton Collier and the consul general ..."

Walker tapped on the steering wheel as he drove; she noticed it was a nervous habit of his; she tried to imagine what inner rhythm he was following.

"I'd bet money that Collier's not brave enough to pull off a switch like that," Walker said, glancing at her. "He's got too much to lose if he got caught; he'd rather just pay for his candy, including you."

Reggie frowned. "Well, I'm not feeling particularly

sweet right now. I look like a prizefighter and my dress is probably ruined."

Walker reached over and squeezed her hand. "You want that dress replaced, I'll replace it. It's nothing. As for your cheek, I think I'll call you Rocky. That guy had heart and courage, and he won in the end, didn't he?" He raised her hand and kissed it. "Besides which, I think you're absolutely beautiful."

Reggie found herself tearing up and looked out the window but was saved from further embarrassment when her cell phone rang. It was Leo with an update. Thanks to Gabe, the corrected version of the story was hitting the papers. He'd also had word from his friend Liane, the jade carver. She'd started on the tigers early this morning and they'd probably be ready the following day, thanks to her skill with water, sand, and, of all things, a dentist's drill.

"That's fantastic. Please tell her to put her mark behind the eye socket so we can tell it apart, then if you could send them by courier to Vihaan Chaudhry, I'll let him know what we need. Oh, and Leo? Don't beat yourself up about last night, okay?"

"Thanks," Leo told her. "At least I found out what happened. Collier had told Elite that he'd be adding one or two undercovers as servers, and I'd said the same. It was a case of too many cooks."

Leo promised to update her on the progress of the tiger reproductions and signed off.

"The big question is, what's next?" Walker asked. "Short of sending each suspect a memo saying,

'Regina Firestone will be holding court alone, with just her authentic tiger earrings for company between midnight and three a.m. the next three nights'—not going to happen, by the way—what do you have in mind?"

They'd reached The Grove and Walker pulled into his regular parking spot.

"Well, my game plan for the next little while is to see if I can get the stain out of that dress, put another cold compress on my cheek, and hope that someone will take pity on me and come up with dinner so I don't have to think about it."

Walker grinned. "I think that can be arranged."

They entered the kitchen which was devoid of people but had a note on the counter along with a small box from Fed Ex. The note was from Jenna. It said that she and Brit were "resting" upstairs (Reggie smiled at that one) and that Axel was hiking, then having dinner with Kaitlyn down at Lindy's. Jenna also mentioned she'd signed for the package.

Reggie checked the return address. It said "F. Hatteras, P.O. Box 17111 San Francisco, CA 94109. She opened the box to find two keys along with a note which read:

The more I drive, the madder I get. Whoever killed Frank ought to pay for it. I remembered he gave me an extra key to his back office in case he ever lost his, so here it is. It goes to 482 Eddy Street Suite C. For what it's worth, the other key goes to the P.O. box we used at Pine Street. The number's in the return address. Maybe you can find something and put the assholes away. Good luck and stay safe.

Sandi

Reggie handed the note to Walker. "I think I know what's next."

Chapter Thirty-Five

The following afternoon, Regina insisted on driving her car into San Francisco. Even though the Tenderloin district sat on the flats just below the wealthy enclave of Nob Hill, it was historically one of the diciest neighborhoods of the city; unfortunately, it hadn't gentrified with the times.

Some said the Tenderloin got its name from the anatomy of the prostitutes who used to ply their trade out of "cribs" along its streets; others said it was so named because the area's corrupt police officers could afford the best cuts of meat based on the kickbacks they got for turning a blind eye to all the vice taking place beneath their noses. Either way, the Tenderloin was not high on Walker's list of places to visit, especially with Regina.

The four hundred block of Eddy Street was classified as mixed use, with body shops and corner groceries sharing street access with run-down apartment buildings and the occasional shabby hotel. Homeless individuals and drug users also called the area home. Prevailing wisdom said never go to the Tenderloin at night, and if you had to go there during the day, for God's sake, don't drive.

They drove.

Regina pointed out that her ancient Civic, complete with slightly dented fender she'd never bothered to have repaired, would be much less conspicuous than Walker's brand-new Explorer. She had a point, but it still didn't sit right. *Pick your battles*, he thought, and slid into the passenger side of her car.

Frank Hatteras maintained his "back office" in a narrow, shotgun-style building wedged between a coin laundry and a shop called "Glamour Tan." Walker didn't want to think about the extra services provided to users of the tanning beds.

They entered the small vestibule of the building and Regina used Sandi's spare key on the door marked "C" at the end of the hall. It already showed signs of an attempted break-in, but it looked like the dead bolt had held firm; apparently word had gotten out that the fixer wasn't coming back.

The office didn't seem like it had been searched, but by the look of things, Frank Hatteras had not been a tidy man. In addition to a small, grimy bathroom and a cluttered storage closet, his workplace consisted of a grim, windowless room with a large, black metal desk, most of which was piled high with papers that left barely enough space for a coaster which held a stained, empty coffee cup and a cheap-looking, Garfield wannabe ceramic cat statue. The desk itself was defaced by the dents and scratches that decades of careless use had left behind. *And Hatteras needed a coaster because...?*

Next to Frank's office chair was a paper shredder, its receptacle almost full and its jaws stuck with the fibrous taffy of incriminating details. Across from the desk were two battered folding chairs, and on one wall a lateral file in gunmetal gray provided a sideboard of sorts, upon which a couple of framed photos sat. One was of a young girl—a long-lost daughter, maybe? The other was of Frank and Sandi on a beach somewhere, him grinning at the camera with a stogie between his teeth and a tropical drink in hand, not worried a whit that his gut was overhanging his suit or that Sandi's charms were spilling out of hers.

Between the two photos was a bowl of rotting fruit whose sweet, pungent decay mixed with the general mustiness of an old, run-down enterprise.

"I can see why Sandi stayed away from here," Regina said, looking around. "This is gross."

Walker also scanned the room. "Yeah, he gives 'man cave' a bad name. There's no computer, so I guess he kept records the old-fashioned way."

"Or maybe he carried a laptop."

"Could be. Let's hope he was technophobic. Why don't we start with the filing cabinet?" Walker pulled out two pairs of disposable latex gloves from his jacket. "I use these when I'm dealing with my camera lenses; I don't think we want to leave any signs we've been here."

"I hadn't thought of that. Thanks," she said, pulling on her pair.

They each took one side, Regina pulling out several unrelated files to kneel on so they wouldn't have to touch the matted carpet. The hope was that Frank used some logic when it came to labeling the "projects" that he and Sandi had worked on.

One file, labeled "Tiger Balm," looked promising until Walker started to read the notes inside. Apparently the "Tiger" referred to the Madison Wisconsin Tigers, a minor league baseball team whose batting coach had arranged for "massages with benefits" as a bonus for his best hitters during a road trip to the West Coast.

"I'm going to need to wash my hands after reading this stuff," Walker said.

"Well, don't use the bathroom; you'll probably catch something," Regina quipped.

After twenty minutes she released a frustrated sigh. "Most of these records pertain to deals that are several years old; I haven't found anything more recent than three years ago, and *nothing* that pertains to the earrings or the switch or any of it. Maybe he didn't keep any records for that one."

Walker spied the pile on the desk. "Or maybe he hadn't gotten around to filing it yet." He started sifting through the overflowing inbox; from all the receipts, flyers, profit and loss statements, letters, and scribbled notes, it seemed Hatteras had dipped his toe in lots of little enterprises, giving out micro loans at high interest rates. No doubt the entrepreneurs he mentored were into businesses that rarely passed the sniff test. Still, nothing in the pile turned out to be relevant.

"What about the desk itself?" Regina asked.

Walker sat down in the squeaky, tattered office chair and started opening drawers. He found the usual flotsam and jetsam—an opened pack of cigarettes, a pair of gloves ... some nail clippers, a roll of scotch tape ... and a few boxes that looked like they contained bank checks. Nothing, however, pertained to the tigers. As he looked over the desk to where Regina was straightening up the lateral file, he noticed the back of the ceramic cat. God, it was an ugly thing. He reached over to turn it around and saw there was a hole in the bottom of it from which a narrow black cord extended into a hole drilled into the desk.

"There's something here." Tapping his phone's flashlight app, he looked underneath and saw a small shelf which held a recorder. "This looks promising," he muttered. He looked back at the cat again and saw that the "grin" of the cat's mouth was open (originally a kid's bank perhaps?) but covered with a dark mesh screen from the inside. Within the hollow statue was a small microphone attached to the cord and taped to the inside cheek of the garish feline.

"I guess Hatteras wasn't so retro after all," Walker said. "Check this out." He brought up a small micro cassette voice recorder from the hidden shelf. It wasn't the most sophisticated bug in town, but it beat the hell out of pen and paper.

He hit the record button and said in a normal voice, "Four score and seven years ago, our fathers brought forth on this continent a new nation." He hit stop, then rewind, then play, and his voice came clearly through the tinny speaker: "Four score and seven years ago..."

Regina looked at him and smiled. "Hatteras didn't worry about keeping notes; he let the little black box do it for him. Now all we have to do is find the tapes that correspond to the time before the switch happened."

They hadn't found any tapes in their search of the lateral filing cabinet, so Regina went back to the storage closet and began pulling items out that might contain the little cassettes. Walker, meanwhile, continued searching the desk, checking for false bottoms or any secret location that would hide the evidence that had kept Hatteras in business for so many years.

He didn't find a thing.

Frustrated, he lifted the boxes of checks to see if something might be behind them and heard a rattle.

Checks don't rattle, he thought with a smile. But as he was about to call out to Regina, he heard another voice instead.

"Who the hell are you and what are you doing in Frank's office?"

Don't freak out. Despite her stampeding heart, Reggie

stood up and looked directly at the intruder, a thin, middle-aged Hispanic man holding a baseball bat. In this neighborhood, that bat probably came in handy. One good thing: he looked almost as scared as she felt.

The best defense is offense, right? She took a breath. "I'm Gina." She picked up the photograph of the girl as her proof. "Who in the heck are you?"

The man hesitated, as if someone had switched the script on him mid-scene. "Jorge Mendoza. I have the office next door. I—"

"Then you knew my Uncle Frank." Reggie tried for a tentative, emotional smile. "Hey, do you mind lowering that thing?" She pointed to the bat. "This is hard enough without having to worry about you bashing my brains in."

Jorge hesitated a moment more before lowering the weapon. "Yeah, I knew Frank." He nodded toward the photograph in her hand. "He told me he had a daughter, not some niece." He frowned and raised the bat again.

Shit. In for a penny, in for a pound. "Well, that's funny, because that's most definitely a picture of me. Of course, I was a lot younger then. But you know my uncle. A real storyteller. Maybe he was trying for a little sympathy. Do you have daughters?"

"Yes, one," Jorge said guardedly. "Why?"

"I rest my case." She sniffed. "But I guess it doesn't matter anymore."

Jorge looked more confused than ever. "You never said what you're doing here ... and who is this *güey*?" He indicated Walker with the bat.

Walker looked at Reggie and nodded ever so slightly.

"Well, I'm the trustee for my uncle"—she held up the key—"hence the key, which means I've got to clear this place out by the end of the month. And since this isn't the safest part of town, my boyfriend said he'd come with me while I figure out what has to be moved, thrown out, and fixed up. I've hired a cleaning service and I gotta tell them the scope of the job."

He looked suspicious. "So, if you're not doing the cleaning, what's with the gloves?"

Reggie shrugged. "I loved my uncle, but he was a real slob." She gestured around the room. "I mean, look at this place. You never know what's going to crawl out around here. Germs are not our friends. But hey, we were just leaving, so if you'll head on out, I can lock the door behind you."

Walker calmly walked toward the door and waited for Jorge to pass him by. Reggie brought up the rear, turned off the lights, and locked the door.

"We'll be back," she said without inflection. "It was nice meeting you, Mr. Mendoza."

She felt the man's eyes on her and Walker as they exited the building. The two of them said nothing until they had walked the half block to where her car was parked. When they were buckled in and headed out of the city, Reggie let out a large sigh. Only now was her pulse returning to normal.

"Damn, you are one audacious woman," Walker said. "I can't believe you pulled that off."

She grinned at him, relief flooding her veins. "'Audacious' has a very nice ring to it. So, you got what we need?"

Walker was checking his cell phone but looked up at her question and smiled. "It says there's a Best Buy in San Rafael; we can pick up a player there."

"Next stop: Best Buy."

Chapter Thirty-Six

Armed with a new microcassette player and a take and bake pizza from Lindy's, Reggie and Walker returned to The Grove and settled in at the kitchen table to cull through the tapes.

Sandi had said it all began about four months earlier. Luckily, Frank Hatteras had labeled each one by date, so that by starting five months back, they made sure they'd catch the interview they were hoping he'd recorded with Chris Fung.

Reggie was impressed. Hatteras might have been sloppy in his living habits, but he was quite articulate when it came to what he called his "deals." At the end of each interview, presumably after the client had left the room, the fixer gave a summary of what he'd been asked to do in recaps that would have made the Sopranos proud.

"Can you believe this guy?" said Walker. "In the course of six weeks' time he helped two businessmen and one supervisor—a gay Latina, no less—pay off mistresses; fronted two ridiculously high interest-rate loans to cover gambling debts and paid off three building inspectors for a low-income housing developer."

"He was an equal opportunity shark, you've got to give him that," Reggie said dryly. "Plus, there was that one IT guy who wanted Frank to get rid of somebody, but he politely told the guy to look elsewhere. I guess he had some standards."

Walker smirked. "I suppose you could say that." At Reggie's suggestion, he'd worn the gloves again as he handled the tapes. He put the next microcassette in the machine.

"Yo, Chris, good to see you. Have a seat." The fixer's voice came through loud and clear.

"Bingo," Walker said.

They listened to the fifteen-minute conversation which began with Chris Fung asking if they were being recorded.

"Come on, what do you take me for?" There was the grating sound of a chair being scooted back.

"Hey, you wanna feel me up?" Hatteras said. "I'm all yours, kid. I'm not wired. I give you my word."

Chris Fung laughed nervously and explained that he represented "a person in government."

"Yo, kid, you're gonna have to do better than that," Hatteras chided.

"Let's just say, the client is in a highly sensitive governmental position..."

"City, state, federal or otherwise?" Hatteras prodded.

"Otherwise."

"Our government or somebody else's?"

There was a prolonged silence, until Chris said, "I ... I am not at liberty to tell you."

"Well then, I'm not at liberty to help you, am I?"

A pause, then, "She would...they would..."

"Tell you what. Write the name of the client on this card and slide it over. That way you can honestly say you never told me a thing."

"But that's the card I just gave you. That's my card."

"So it is. Trust me on this."

More silence, then...

"See, that wasn't so hard, was it? I figured as much but I wanted you to confirm it. Your kind does tend to stick together. Always has. Now tell me what your 'highly sensitive government official' wants with little old me."

Chris Fung proceeded to lay out much of what Reggie had already learned from Sandi: Hatteras would set up the victim—in this case Allen Willis—in a sting operation, preying on the man's ego and gambling habit. He was free to structure it however he pleased, but he'd need someone who looked like Willis's niece to be part of the scam. His team would "extract" the jade earrings along with two other pieces for the fake "loan collateral" from Willis's bank vault and send them to the address that Chris would give him. Approximately three weeks later, they'd receive the same jewelry back and return it to the vault. No one would know the difference, not even Willis, and Frank Hatteras would be sixty thousand dollars richer.

"So how do we keep in touch?" Hatteras asks.

Easy, according to Chris. All Frank had to do was join the Facebook Group called "The Jade Hunters" and check it daily, as well as open a P.O. box to receive the goods and cash.

"I don't do that social media shit," Hatteras says.

"Well, it's not that difficult. For sixty grand, maybe you could learn."

Hatteras chuckled. "You got a point there, kid. A very good point. By the way, what's in it for you?"

"Well, it's much less than your fee, but adequate for my needs."

"Lemme guess. Five Grand."

"Ten."

"Whoa. Your client doesn't mess around. I like that. It's a deal. And to show you good faith, I'm getting rid of your card, see?"

They could hear paper being chewed up by the shredder. The two men said goodbye, Chris Fung apparently left, and Hatteras could be heard dialing a phone. "Hey, babe. We got a nice big fat one, but I'm gonna need your help with that Facebook crap you're always checking ... yeah, and you may need to do a little tug and tickle at some point—nothing you can't handle— plus we're gonna need one of your girls as a lookalike ... yeah, he gave me a picture ... okay, I'll fill you in tonight."

The recording stopped at that point.

"Where's the summary laying it all out?" Reggie asked.

"I don't know." Walker fast-forwarded the tape a bit to see if Hatteras added something later, but the tape was silent until yet another "client" began to talk.

"Maybe he figured he had what he needed, or he'd use the Facebook messages as a record. But I think we've got enough to show how Chris Fung fits into all this, don't you? Maybe that'll convince Detective Liu that he's got something other than a garden variety serial killer on his hands."

"If this doesn't convince him, I don't know what will," Walker said. The question is, what about all these other tapes? They point to a hell of a lot of crimes. What do we do with them?"

"Good question. I think maybe we ought to bring Gabe in on this."

Walker agreed and was about to call the detective when the back door opened, and Axel and Kaitlyn walked in. Axel carried his usual backpack and she carried what looked like a large sketch pad. They were holding hands.

"There's some pizza if you're interested," Reggie offered.

"Uh, no thanks. We've got some ... stuff to do." They barely broke stride. Walker glanced at Reggie before saying. "Where you going?"

"My room," Axel said.

"Uh, no, the library's available," Walker said.

"What? No, man, my laptop's up there, and—"

"You can bring it downstairs."

Axel rolled his eyes. "Come on."

"You heard me," Walker said.

"Oh, man, this is *bogus*." He gave his father a look that all but screamed *What are you doing to me in front of my girl?*

"Sorry. You're part of this family, you follow the rules."

"Come on, Kaitlyn, let's get out of here."

The girl, whom Reggie was already beginning to appreciate, tugged back on Axel's hand. "No, the library's fine. Come on, A.J., just get your laptop and we'll look it up down there."

Axel hesitated and shot daggers at his father one more time before acquiescing. In a small act of defiance, he scooped up two pieces of pizza and carried them out without benefit of napkins or plates as he and Kaitlyn left the room.

Walker took a deep breath as if to swallow his annoyance before it got the better of him.

"Hey, don't you remember what it was like to be sixteen and in love?" Reggie asked him with a smile.

Walker's response was dour. "I remember *exactly* what it was like to be sixteen, and love had nothing to do with it."

Reggie chuckled. "Just keep in mind, he's a good kid."

"Yeah, and even good kids do dumb stuff."

Their conversation was cut short by another couple who entered holding hands, only this time it was Brit and Jenna, just back from a gallery opening in Bellam's Cove.

"How was the show?" Reggie asked.

"Great, if you love looking at splotches of paint thrown against a canvas filled with squares, rectangles and triangles," Brit said.

"Oh, it wasn't that bad," Jenna said. "Okay, maybe it was. The artist hit us up to be an artist-in-residence. I gave him your cousin's name, since she'll be managing that program once The Grove officially opens."

"One more thing," Brit added. "They had some great microbrew flights. We've got to get some 'Mountain Goat Amber.'"

"Mountain Goat?" Walker sounded dubious.

Brit shrugged and reached for the last piece of pizza in the box. "I know. Sounds bad but tasted good."

He and Jenna headed up the stairs arm in arm. Watching them, Reggie heaved a sigh. "I can't wait until the foremost thing on my mind is remembering the taste of a good brew."

"Dammit, we talked about this, but he still treats me like a fucking kid," Axel groused to Kaitlyn. They were sitting closely together on the couch in the library, his laptop and her sketch pad set up side by side.

"Um, I think he made us come down here because he doesn't think you're a kid at all," she said.

"What do you mean?"

She rolled her eyes. "You know."

It took a second, but he finally got it. As soon as he did, he could feel himself getting red. Of course! That's what his father had pretty much accused him of the other morning. God, he wasn't ready for all *that*. "Oh, oh yeah. Well, still, he should give me more credit." He watched her flip through her sketches. She was really good. There were some sketches of him, which he liked, and some birds they'd seen on one of their hikes. She was super talented.

"Maybe, but he's a dad, so whaddya expect?" Kaitlyn reached a blank page. "Now show me what you want me to do."

Glad to change the subject, Axel booted up and went to the file he'd been working on for the past several days. He'd narrowed down the secret societies to those who had anything to do with tigers, and who existed in some form or another today. Some were pretty recent, but others seemed to have started way back, maybe a hundred years or more. Once he narrowed it down, he could pay his gray hat with an AGC code to find specifics, like where they operated out of and shit like that. It'd probably cost a few bucks, but he was flush right now with working at The Grove. It would help if that detective could spill the beans on the dead guys' marks.

He showed Kaitlyn what he had so far. "I've collected these photos of guys in various old Chinatown gangs and they're covered in tats, see. Most of it is run of the mill shit, but some of them are symbols of their secret triad. I want to get bigger pictures of those partic-ular tats and see if they mean anything."

"How come?" Kaitlyn asked. "Is this for your museum or something?"

I don't want you spilling your gut to Kaitlyn. She doesn't need to be involved in something that could turn dangerous at some point. His dad was right. "Uh, yeah, we're just looking into that aspect of the story is all."

They worked in companionable silence for the better part of an hour; Axel would point out a certain symbol he wanted Kaitlyn to reproduce. She was super good at recreating it. He was playing with her hair a little bit while she did it, and she smiled, which was making him hot. He was about to go ahead and kiss her when, bam —his dad popped into the room, scaring the shit out of him.

"Now what?" Axel blurted.

"Now it's a little after nine and you're working tomorrow, so it's time to take Kaitlyn home." His dad held up the keys to the Explorer. "You can use this if you want."

Axel couldn't believe it. "Really?"

"Really. Just get yourself back here by ten and put the key on the rack by the back door."

As they left the house, Kaitlyn wrapped her arm around Axel's waist. "See what I mean? Your pop wouldn't let you have the car if he thought you were just a kid."

"Maybe you're right." He couldn't help but grin as he unlocked the car door and they drove down the hill.

Walker returned to the kitchen, took Reggie's hand, and headed upstairs. *Damn, this woman is fine: her instincts about Axe are the best.* "You really are brilliant, you know that?"

Regina let out a melodramatic sigh. "That's certainly true. But more important, I know you just scored some big time points with your son."

Walker raised his eyebrows. "Maybe I'll score with someone else, too."

"Perhaps," Regina said, but her look told him the odds were greatly in his favor.

Chapter Thirty-Seven

Tonight, Thomas's keepers were sitting in the next room drinking some kind of beer. It smelled delicious, sweet and yeasty. He wondered if he would ever experience the taste again. Although he was not warm by any stretch, he took a moment to imagine the cool liquid sliding down his throat, quenching his thirst, for a drink, but more than that—for freedom. The fantasy kept despair at bay.

After an hour or so—it was difficult to keep track of time in his underground prison—Chow Li Jun came into his chamber and sat on his haunches in front of Thomas.

"How is the carving?" he asked.

Yes. He is intrigued. "I have finished two of them. They are initial carvings, but of course still good enough for you to sell. Now I am beginning to carve your talismans." He handed over two medallions with the sign that had been tattooed on Chow's upper arm. It was a stylized rendition of the character for the word "king," but employed lines to symbolize "rising." "It feels like the white jade of the tigers," he explained as the guard examined the carvings, "which is why it will be highly valued, aside from the fact that I carved it."

Chow looked at him and pulled out his cell phone. "What is the name of that dealer you mentioned?"

"Dr. Leo Brunt," Thomas said. "He has an office at the University of San Francisco, in the art department, but he is also an art dealer. Tell him I have something he would be very interested in and he will talk to you."

"Will he pay?"

"Not immediately. He will check with his buyers first. Perhaps he will want to take the piece, but do not give it to him. Tell him I only authorized him to take a picture of it. Tell him there are very few like it in the world."

The guard seemed skeptical. "What if he knows you were ... arrested? Won't he be suspicious?"

The young man is thinking, which is not good. "You misunderstand. Dr. Brunt deals in a wide range of art objects, not just Asian carvings, and he has specific buyers for each type of art. He could not possibly keep track of all the artists he brokers. However, I tell you this..." Thomas lowered his voice. "... he does not kow tow to law enforcement. He is his own man through and through." *Please let that be only a partial lie.*

That seemed to placate Chow. "When will mine and my brother's amulets be ready?"

"It will take a while," Thomas said, not knowing if he needed to stall or not. "I want them to be perfect."

"Well, it had better be soon. Your time here is coming to an end." With that, the guard rose and returned to the other room.

The lantern's light, dim though it was, would be extinguished soon, Thomas knew. It would be better to begin working; every minute counted. But what did Chow mean, "coming to an end"? It sounded so ... so *final.* He thought again of his mother and his eyes began to well with tears.

This will never do, he told himself fiercely. He reached for the stones and his carving pouch and willed his hands to stop shaking. Never had he wished so fervently for greed to overtake a man's heart and propel him forward. Never had he set all his hopes upon the actions of a *laowai.* But foreigner or no, Dr. Brunt was all Thomas had.

He took a deep breath and began to carve.

Chapter Thirty-Eight

"You cannot be serious," Walker said to Gabe the next morning. If blood could really boil while it was inside the body, it was surely happening to him. The detective had stopped by The Great House and had just finished listening to the tape of Chris Fung proposing the jewelry theft to Frank Hatteras.

"Yep, afraid I am," Gabe said, taking a sip of his coffee. "You can't walk this into Detective Liu's office and expect him to be able to use it. If it wasn't obtained through a warrant, then it wouldn't be admissible, and there'd be no usable evidence to go after the consul general, who seems to be implicated here. Besides, how do you know Hatteras didn't turn around and run the sting just to get the proceeds for himself?"

"But it's the connection that matters, isn't it?" Regina said. "Detective Liu has four unsolved murders to deal with and they're linked by some sort of mark on the victim. This tape shows how all four are connected, and by the sound of it, it all started with someone on Jiang Wei's staff running interference for him."

"Let's say you're right," Gabe said. "Your theory is that the consul general, who wanted the jade tigers, either for himself or for his country, set this plan into motion and has proceeded to cover his tracks by systematically eliminating the players. The first logical question is why? He knows he's leaving in a few weeks; without ironclad evidence that he stole the pieces, he wouldn't even be interviewed, much less charged. His diplomatic status protects him. He could just pocket the tigers and head off into the sunset. No one on his staff or involved in the theft itself is going to rat him out."

Regina opened her mouth to argue, but he continued.

"Then you've got to look into the 'how.' I mean, you aren't suggesting the consul general himself is committing murder, are you? That just doesn't make any sense."

"When does murdering someone ever make sense?" Walker asked, "but regardless, how do we at least get Liu to look in that direction?"

"You're not going to like it, but the first thing you need to do is return those microcassettes so that we can get a warrant and collect them legally. It goes without saying that you don't want your prints showing up anywhere."

"Do we have to?" Regina protested. "I don't want to get Sandi Bollocks in trouble."

"Look, as far as we know, she's just an accessory at

this point, and if she were needed to make the case down the road, she could cooperate with the state. Besides, she's flown the coop, right? My guess is, wherever she ends up, they aren't going to know her as Ms. Bollocks."

Walker couldn't help but snicker. "That would take a lot of balls, for sure." He and Gabe shared a grin.

Regina was not impressed. "Okay, we put the tapes back and then what? We leave an anonymous message on the police tip line?"

Gabe shrugged. "Believe it or not, yes. You could even drop off the key—wiped clean, of course. Liu's not going to like it because you're forcing him to open a huge can of worms. The crimes chronicled in those tapes will keep him busy for quite a while, and it wouldn't surprise me if a lot of them mysteriously fall through the cracks because of the big names involved."

"That's despicable," Walker said. "You can't use proof that someone's broken the law unless you've dotted all the i's and crossed all the T's, but even when you go through the hoops to do all that, the bad guys still get away with murder, depending on who they know. That totally sucks."

"Yeah, it does. But bad guys don't get off *all* the time, and the system, with all its flaws, is still the best there is." Gabe finished his cup and got up to leave. "Oh," he said to Regina, "Off topic, but when this thing is over—and sooner or later it will be—would you be available to design a ring for me?"

Regina glanced at Walker before responding. "Sure. What kind of ring?"

Gabe sent her a slow smile. "*That* kind. Being the good Catholics we are, Dani and I want to start making babies, and I'd like us to be wearing rings when it happens."

Regina unabashedly hugged him. "I am so happy for you!"

Walker extended his hand. "That's great news. Congratulations."

"She hasn't officially said yes yet."

"She'd be a fool to say no, and Dani's no fool," Regina said.

Gabe was halfway out the door when he said, "The one thing I can follow up on is finding out if there were any large payments made to Chris Fung's personal account shortly before he was killed and where they might have come from. If something turns up, that might light a fire under Detective Liu."

"That and a certain forthcoming anonymous tip," Regina said.

After Gabe left, Walker started to straighten up the kitchen. Ridiculous, but tidying up the place gave him a small feeling of accomplishment in the midst of all the uncertainty. "Well, that was a study in frustration," he said.

"I know. It seems we're hampered at every turn. But I have an answer to your unspoken question."

He'd been wondering what she felt about marriage and kids and all that. She was genuinely happy for

Gabe; did she wish something similar for her life? But she couldn't be that much of a mind-reader, could she?

"Ah, what question is that?" he said.

"What's next, of course! I say we take the tapes back, leave the tip for Detective Liu, and swing by Vihaan Chaudhry's studio. He's got something for me."

"And that would be…?"

"Another pair of jade tiger earrings."

It had been in the back of Walker's mind to wonder: if Frank Hatteras had been killed last Saturday night, why hadn't the law immediately swooped down to his "back office"? Surely, they knew about it. He said as much to Regina as they headed back to the Tenderloin to "replant" the microcassettes. They were still in Regina's car, but this time Walker was driving so she could make phone calls.

"It's a good question," she said. "You'd think someone would have said, 'Hey, he has an office near City Hall, but the real action takes place on Eddy Street.' I have a theory, though."

"Let's hear it."

"Frank Hatteras was a fixer, and the reason he was never busted was because he knew too much about the city's movers and shakers, right? It stands to reason he and Sandi had proof of what they knew, and that the proof was in his office."

Walker nodded to the little box that held the micro-cassettes. "Well, we're living proof of that."

"So, who's going to volunteer to tell the police where all the evidence was? Certainly, nobody who might get busted in the sweep."

"That makes sense. But the law had to know where he did business even if they looked the other way while he did it. Why didn't they go in and clean house?"

Regina shrugged. "There's probably evidence *they'd* prefer didn't see the light of day, either. Maybe they figured it would all end up being thrown out in the trash." He could tell she'd set her jaw. "But too bad for them."

Their talk of Hatteras's office remaining unperturbed was premature. Once more donning gloves, they entered the premises to find it had been thoroughly ransacked in the same methodical way as Regina's cottage; it was a good bet that not a drawer or a file or a closet shelf had been left unsearched.

"Well, that's one sliver of good luck," Regina said. "At least we got here first. Do you think it was one of the consul's minions, or maybe someone wanting to play the blackmail game?"

Walker opened the lateral file. "It has to be our guy, because they didn't touch these files. There's a lot of dirt here too." Wiping off the box of tapes, he put it back in the desk drawer exactly where he'd found it. As he did so, he saw that the ugly cat statue had been knocked over and was broken in half. "All good things must come to an end," he muttered.

They were back in the hallway, locking the door, when a young Hispanic man, barely out of his teens, opened the door to Jorge Mendoza's place at the same time. He looked startled to see them. *Here we go again*, Walker thought.

"Hello," Regina offered. "Hey, is your dad Jorge Mendoza? Tell him Gina says hi."

"I would, but he's in a coma," the young man said bitterly. "I'm goin' to the hospital now to see him."

Regina couldn't hide her shock. "Oh, how terrible! What happened?"

"He caught someone trashing your place and he ... he tried to stop it. The guy bashed him with my dad's own bat and cracked his skull."

The boy was obviously distraught, and Regina touched his arm in comfort. "That is horrible. You tell him when he wakes up that we'll find out who did it, and—"

"No, you won't. The police don't touch this place."

"Oh, they will this time," Regina said, her voice cold and determined. "I guarantee it."

Hearing about poor Jorge Mendoza tore Reggie up, and learning that the police, even now, were reluctant to get involved, pushed her deeper into misery.

The devastation the consul general had no doubt set in motion obliterated the hopeful spirits she'd enjoyed at the start of the day. She understood the value of her grandmother's little jade tigers, both as art and as arti-facts. But did they warrant such death and destruction? Absolutely not. More than ever, she was determined to bring the bastard who started all this to justice, even if she had to mete out that justice herself.

She was so immersed in the gloom of her thoughts that she didn't hear Walker's request.

"So, want to go?" he asked.

She glanced at him. "Sorry, wool gathering again. I have a habit of doing that. What were you saying?"

"It's one o'clock, I'm hungry, and I heard there's a new cafe at the top of the Fremont Center. Forty-second floor. Probably has killer views. It's between here and your diamond cutter. You said he was in North Beach, right?"

Ugh. The idea of having to be so high up was just one more stress she didn't need. "Um, the answer to that would be 'Yes and No.' Yes to the fact that Vihaan's in North Beach, and no to having lunch at the Fremont Center."

"You're not hungry?"

"I could eat, but food has nothing to do with it. I just … well, it's that height thing I told you about. I abso-lutely hate being too high up." She smiled ruefully. "I'm not sure why, but I don't like flying and I don't like elevators, especially glass ones. I can't even go out on viewing platforms. Forget ferris wheels or roller coast-ers. I try not to let it rule my life, but I must confess, it's crippling sometimes."

Rather than belittle her, Walker sent her a sympathetic glance. "I'm sorry. I forgot. And hey, we've all got our quirks. I told you, tight spaces are mine; they freak me out. So, I guess you never made it to the Top of the Mark?"

Reggie sighed. "No, but I've heard it's lovely."

"Yes, it is. But there are plenty of ground-level places with great food. How about Pier 39?"

How does he do that? Begin to pull me out of a funk even when we're talking about one of my worst short-comings? She smiled at him. "That sounds delicious."

Boudin's classic clam chowder served in a sourdough boulé was just what the doctor ordered; creamy, not too "fishy," and washed down with a crisp Chardonnay. During their lunch, Walker seemed to realize Reggie needed a break from the frustration of their quest, so he took the conversation in a different direction, asking her about her work, where it had taken her, and where she still wanted to go with it. She found herself sharing thoughts and aspirations she hadn't even voiced before —notions of passing along her expertise through teaching, maybe finding time for other pursuits. She didn't expressly mention "family," although admittedly that had been on her mind for some time. In turn she asked Walker where he was in his career, and surprisingly, he was in a similar place. The difference was, he already had a child. She envied him that, just as she envied her cousin Ava having a little girl.

But those kinds of wishes will have to wait, she told herself. *Now is not the time*.

She concentrated instead on the here and now, which was the scrumptious but calorie-laden meal before her. Sighing with pleasure, she chewed the very last bite she was going to take of the world's finest bread before leaving half the tasty vessel on the plate. Of course, Walker demolished his.

"Want the rest of mine?" she asked.

"Thanks, but I'm sufficiently stuffed." He swallowed the rest of his Anchor Steam beer. "What do you say we walk some of this off? As I recall, Chaudhry's studio isn't that far from here."

"I love it," Reggie said.

In a romantic gesture, Walker took Reggie's hand as they headed down Stockton and then turned west on Francisco. As they walked, he asked, deceptively casual, "How come you didn't mention you were having another set of earrings made?"

It was a fair question. "I'm not sure. I guess I didn't want you to think I was going too far overboard with all this intrigue." She paused. "So, do you think I am?"

Walker paused before answering. "I see why you did it; you can't very well pretend to have two pairs of earrings, one being the originals, if you only possess one pair."

Reggie pressed his hand. "Exactly!"

"But..."

She stopped and gazed at him. "But?"

He took her hand up to his lips and kissed it. "I truly

think we're playing with fire here. It's a good bet that whoever's behind all this—"

"You mean Jiang Wei."

"—perhaps. If it *is* him, he's obviously a powerful man, willing to do anything and everything to make sure he has the right set. That means he's coming after you. The fact that he's leaving the city in a few weeks means he's going to make a move sooner rather than later."

Reggie's hackles rose, not against Walker, but against her adversary. "I say the sooner the better. If we can catch his henchman in the act, or better yet, unmask Jiang Wei himself, then we'll have the proof we need to stop him from leaving and hopefully recover the jade."

Walker didn't look convinced. "I can't help but worry about you," he said gently. "I don't want anything to happen to you. I've said it before: nothing is worth that."

The moments stretched as they looked at each other, communicating on a level that didn't require any more words. Finally, she broke the connection. "We're here," she said.

Chapter Thirty-Nine

Regina Firestone was beautiful, stubborn, principled, and fearless—and Walker was falling more deeply in love with her than he thought possible. His chest tightened to a greater degree than ever before. *How can I keep her safe?* The thought that he might fail at that task sent shards of cold, bitter dread throughout his body.

He tried to shake it off as they entered Vihaan Chaudhry's studio and waited until the diamond cutter finished with what looked like a very wealthy, well-fed, middle-aged client.

When the man left, Vihaan smiled serenely. "He just ordered a seven-carat round brilliant cut for an internally flawless stone in a platinum setting. It is for 'a special friend.' I wonder if she will sign a pre-nuptial agreement?"

Regina chuckled. "With a ring like that, she won't need one."

After Regina introduced the men, Chaudhry invited them into his workshop by pressing a button that opened a secure door behind the counter. When they had passed through, the door closed behind them with a *whooshing* sound.

"I was quite impressed with the hotan jade carving Dr. Brunt's colleague created for you," he remarked as he handed her the latest iteration of the white jade tigers. "Per your instructions, I used rose cuts for the eyes and I faceted the culet; as a result they display the more diffused warmth of the originals as opposed to the bright edginess of the counterfeits—the first counterfeits, that is."

"I just hope we can tell them apart," Walker said.

"The carver of this pair uses a tiny twisting vine as her mark, which I verified before I attached the eyes. So, you should be able to tell the three pairs from one another by both the marks and the cut of the eyes." He pulled out a small velvet pouch.

"What color is that pouch?" Regina asked Walker.

"Green."

"Right." She pulled out the pouch that had protected the original earrings, but now housed the switched pair. "And this one?"

"Also green."

"Nope, it's red," she said, letting out a sigh.

Walker shrugged. "All right. Give both pouches to me, one at a time. First the red." She did so and he carefully felt each of them before returning them to her. "I'm going to turn around while you mix them up. Now hand me one of them." She did that as well, and Walker said, "This is the green one."

Chaudhry was watching the strange interlude and exclaimed, "You did it by feel."

Walker nodded and caught Regina's eye. "You see—"

She beamed. "It's only a problem when other people tell you it's a problem. I get it. *Now* our problem is not knowing if the originals have their own pouch or not."

"Here's another one, in case you need it," said Chaudhry, handing it to her.

"How about this one?" she asked Walker.

"That one's easy. Black."

"All right, we're good to go."

They said their goodbyes and were halfway to Regina's car when Walker reminded her that they needed to file the anonymous tip at Detective Liu's office. "Have you got the Eddy Street key on you, or did you leave it in the car?"

Regina reached into her jacket pocket. "Ahh. We've got one more thing to do first."

"And that is?"

She pulled out the post office box key. "How long would it take to walk to Pine Street from here?"

Walker checked his phone. "Too long. Let's get your car and drive over."

They did so, and within twenty minutes, they were standing in front of a huge wall of post office boxes. Number 1711 was three rows from the bottom on the right-hand side. Regina opened it and pulled out the usual stack of junk mail: flyers, brochures, announcements, fake invoices that were really pleas for donations...

And one more envelope.

It was addressed to Francis Hatteras and the return address was ... Francis Hatteras at 482 Eddy Street.

"Well lookee here," she said.

Walker once again put on his gloves, removed the letter from the box, and carefully opened it. Inside a tri-folded piece of blank typing paper was the business card of Christopher Fung, legislative aide to San Francisco City Supervisor Amy Jin.

And on that card a phrase was printed. It read "Jiang Wei via Sharilyn Huang."

"This was Hatteras's insurance," Walker said. "He pulled one over on Chris Fung and didn't actually shred the thing."

Regina's voice was cold. "And now we have what we need to take the next step."

"Yes, the link Detective Liu needs to get the ball rolling on the investigation."

"No," she said, "It's what we're going to take directly to the consul general right this very minute."

Seeing the proof they'd been looking for lit a fire in Reggie. She was sick to death of this cat and mouse game; now she had something tangible to use against Jiang Wei. A kind of frantic exultation sped through her.

Walker, by contrast, was measured. "You cannot go over there, guns blazing, with just a business card to prove your point. At best he'll be insulted; at worst, he'll call the cops on you—that's if he'll even let you through in the first place."

"Watch me," Reggie growled. "All I have to do is mention the tigers and he'll see me."

Walker continued to reason against it, but Reggie was having none of it. "How many times do I have to tell you? You don't have to come with me. It's my fight, not yours."

The ferocious look he gave her would have stopped anyone else in their tracks, but by now Reggie knew the truth behind it: Walker Banks cared for her, probably far more than he was willing to admit. And the idea of her being in any kind of danger was driving him crazy. Knowing that filled her with both joy and resolve. Impulsively she reached up and kissed him deeply. "I'm sorry I said that. Please see this through with me. Please."

Walker resisted for approximately a nanosecond before returning her embrace. "I don't know what to do with you," he finally murmured.

Just love me, she wanted to say, but didn't. "Just take me to the consulate," she said instead.

Chapter Forty

With dour resignation, Walker drove to the Consulate General of the People's Republic of China on Laguna Street; it took less time getting there than it did finding a place to park. By the time he and Regina walked through the doors, it was two twenty; the consulate closed at two thirty.

An efficient-looking receptionist with short dark hair and large tortoise-shell glasses tried to bar their entry, explaining that if they were looking for a visa, they'd best come back the next day.

"Please tell the consul general that Regina Firestone is here to see him about the tigers," Regina said in a voice devoid of all warmth and congeniality. "Tell him it's in his best interest to talk to me right now."

The woman looked rather startled at the barely leashed command and spoke to someone on the intercom. "Yes, all right," she said, after hanging up. She hit a buzzer under her desk which unlocked the door heading to the back offices. Her voice was flat as she said, "Through that door, please. Mr. Long will see you."

"I don't want to see Mr. Long," Regina started, "I—"

"That's fine. Thank you," Walker said firmly and took Regina gently by the arm. "He's just the next gate-keeper," he murmured as they walked down the hall. "Hold your fire."

Regina nodded and took a deep breath. *She's a warrior*, Walker thought. *I want her on my side on the battlefield.*

Daniel Long, the consul general's chief of staff, walked swiftly up to them, but was no match for Regina, who barreled past him through the double doors leading to the consul general's office suite.

Once inside, they saw that a smaller office on the left—presumably Daniel's—was open, but that the large door at the rear was closed. From within they heard the unmistakable sounds of two people indulging in some "afternoon delight." Under different circumstances it might have been cause for a sheepish retreat and a rescheduled appointment, but the sounds only seemed to infuriate Regina more. She no doubt remembered how Lily Quan had characterized the bureaucrat's extramarital activities; it was one thing to confront a thief and a murderer, but a cheater on top of that? Walker could almost read her mind: *Three strikes and you're out, asshole!*

Regina wasted no time before knocking loudly on

the door. "Mr. Jiang. It's Regina Firestone. I need to speak to you immediately!"

Horrified, Daniel Long stared beseechingly at Walker, who could only shrug in return. In truth, Regina was magnificent, and he had to remind himself that in the valiant pursuit of her own small tigers, she was poking a very large, powerful one.

The rhythmic sounds had stopped immediately after Regina's pounding, and were replaced by what were certainly curses in Cantonese. The door opened a minute later and Sharilyn Huang came out, smoothing down her skirt and looking extremely embarrassed before she escaped to what must have been her side office and shut the door. Jiang Wei came out after her, putting on his suit jacket. Walker could tell that he hadn't buttoned his rather tight-fitting pants after zipping them up.

"What is the meaning of this?" Jiang Wei demanded. "Daniel, why didn't you—"

"Don't blame him," Regina said. "We forced our way in here because I need to talk to you about my grandmother's jade earrings."

Jiang brightened immediately, which was odd. "So, you have decided to part with them? I'm sure I can make you an offer that—"

"Make me an offer? No, I'll make *you* an offer: you return the pair of earrings you stole and I'll make sure you don't rot in hell for it."

Walker winced at Regina's rhetoric, but Jiang had a worse reaction. As he absorbed her accusation, he grew red in the face, his anger causing his already fleshy cheeks to expand, reminding Walker of a frilled dragon lizard that he'd seen once while filming in northern Australia. When those lizards got mad, the flaps on the sides of their little heads stuck straight out, no doubt instilling fear and trembling in their enemies. *Please don't blow a gasket*, Walker thought. *The last thing we need is for you to stroke out.*

"What are you talking about?" Jiang bellowed. "How dare you accuse me of such a thing! I would never steal something that I could purchase."

His blustery denial had no impact on Regina. She whipped out the business card and thrust it at him. "Then explain why your *interpreter* set up a sting on your behalf using that poor sap Chris Fung—who is now dead—to dupe my Uncle Allen, who is also dead! Fung's deal with Frank Hatteras is all on tape. Oh, and did I mention that Hatteras is dead, too? Why would you do such a horrendous, hideous thing ... and all for a pair of fake earrings?" She pulled out the two pouches. "You see, I have the real ones, and I have the fakes you tried to foist upon me. But I want the third pair because you will *not* get away with trying to pass them off as real. I won't let it happen."

Regina seemed to run out of words, but her glare took up the slack. She was breathing hard and Walker wanted to do something—anything—to make it easier for her. But he knew she wouldn't want him stepping in. Right now, she didn't need him. She was in the arena and it was her battle to fight.

Jiang looked at the card again, his mind obviously

still processing all that Regina had accused him of. Finally, in a surprisingly calm voice, he said, "Daniel, tell Sharilyn to come out here and clear this up." As Daniel went to the side office, Jiang addressed Regina directly. "I swear to you on my honor that I had nothing to do with this. I am many things, but I am not a thief and I am certainly not a murderer. I—"

"Sharilyn's gone," Daniel said. "She must have left through the outer door of her office."

Jiang instructed Daniel to ask the receptionist to come back and talk with them.

"Yes, sir?" the woman said a few moments later.

"Did Sharilyn leave the building?"

"Yes, sir, I'm pretty sure she did. She seemed to be in a hurry and had her briefcase and purse with her; I assume she had an appointment."

"Do you know a man named Chris Fung?" Jiang asked her.

She nodded sadly. "I did. Poor fellow. He was attacked near his house and died."

Jiang's face was passive. "Did Sharilyn know him?"

The receptionist paused, probably sensing it might be a trick question.

"The truth," Jiang barked.

"Y ... yes. Yes, she did."

"How well?"

The woman swallowed, pushed her large eyeglasses back up onto her rather small nose. "They had lunch a lot. They seemed ... close. I think he had a crush on her."

Everyone in the room was able to do the math on that one. Apparently Sharilyn had seduced Chris Fung and gotten him to liaison with Frank Hatteras; in the process she'd gotten both men killed. But how? Surely, she couldn't have done it herself. She had to be working with someone else.

The look on Jiang's face telegraphed both anger and disappointment, and perhaps a little sadness, but not a shred of guilt. By the looks of things, his mistress had two-timed him, possibly with criminal intent. Walker wondered if the man felt worse about the deaths or about the fact that he'd no longer be getting some on the side.

"Daniel," Jiang said, "You know where Miss Huang lives. Please inform her she needs to contact me and explain her actions immediately." He said it with the air of one who knows his order won't be carried out to his satisfaction.

"Yes, sir," Daniel said, and left along with the receptionist.

When it was just the three of them, Jiang addressed Regina directly once more. "I believe I understand how you might think I committed this crime, but I assure you I did not. I will, however, do all I can to help you find the perpetrator. That my interpreter is caught up in this imbroglio pains me greatly, but I cannot have someone in my employ bringing dishonor and shame upon our mission, no matter the nature of our relationship. Our countries have enough problems already without this type of wretchedness. Please. call whichever authorities you feel you need to in order to clear up the situation. I will wait here while you do it."

He sat heavily at his desk and gazed out the window. It was only mid-afternoon, and the sky was clear with no fog to speak of, at least outside. Inside, the mists of uncertainty were swirling.

Walker looked at Regina, who seemed shell-shocked. "But it was on the tape," she said, as if she were still puzzling it out.

"No, it wasn't," Walker said gently. "Sharilyn may very well have told Chris that she was an intermediary, too, when in fact she was the source."

Regina nodded, then turned to Jiang. "I don't know what to say."

"Let's not concern ourselves with words at the moment. I would much rather have this matter dealt with quickly and suggest we alert the authorities as soon as possible."

"We've been working with Detective Liu from the Investigations Bureau," Walker said.

"Then by all means, let's go see him together."

"It is over!" Sharilyn Huang cried into her cell phone as she rode in a hastily flagged taxi to her apartment on Taylor Street. The cab driver was Hispanic, so she wasn't worried that he'd understand her native tongue. Still, he glared at her through the rearview mirror. She wanted to bash his head in.

"No, I'm not exaggerating. I'm telling you it's over! Regina Firestone burst into the office and told Jiang Wei everything. She even offered proof that Chris Fung and I had set up the theft, but she thought Jiang had directed us to do it—as if he would ever have the balls to try such a bold act! You should have seen her, waving the originals and the pair that we put in their place, demanding that he give her the second counterfeit pair so he couldn't pass it off as real." Sharilyn let out a strangled laugh. "I wish I could have captured the look on his fat face!"

She listened for a moment and clung to a sliver of hope. "Do you really think that will work? It's not quite the way we planned it, but .... yes ... yes, I trust you. You are my brother. You are the only one I *can* trust ... Fifteen minutes? I am almost home. Of course, I will be ready."

Just as Sharilyn ended the call, the sour-faced taxi driver reached the address she'd given him. She tossed him a ten-dollar bill, which barely covered the fare, slammed the door, and hurried inside her apartment. Pulling her suitcase from the hall closet, she began to fill it with the items she would need for her journey back to the homeland.

There would not be much. Unlike Jiang Wei, Sharilyn had only pretended to be a collector; for as long as she could remember, the only objects she had coveted were the pieces she was now in danger of losing forever.

In the bathroom, she slid her cosmetics into their travel pouch, noticing the hammered bronze necklace that Jiang Wei had insisted she wear to the reception. In a rage, she flung it across the small space, where it clanged against the tile. In the same vein she hastily removed her tanzanite earrings, another gift from him. Those she flushed down the toilet. "At least I will never have to spread my legs for you again," she muttered.

She felt the small dragon necklace around her neck that Daniel had given her and sought the only other piece of jewelry that mattered. From the bottom of her lingerie drawer she pulled the soft black pouch and poured its contents into her hand. The white jade tigers had caused her no end of grief, from the moment she had heard the first stories about them. Part of her wanted to throw them out the window, but that would have been no different than flinging herself out as well. She was born, she'd been told, for one purpose and one purpose only: to recover the honor of her family by recovering the lost jungle cats.

She looked at them again. They seemed real enough. Who would know?

The answer was, *she* would know, and so would her brother, who was as dedicated as she to their cause— perhaps even more so. Together, they had decided it would be best to examine all of them, the real and the counterfeit, and have Thomas Ling determine which was which.

Then they would have to kill him. That part of this entire business was particularly distressing.

She finished packing and took a deep breath. Her brother had a new plan to accomplish their goal and they would see it through. Then they would leave the country forever.

She would never return.

She would never see Daniel again.

The thought sent a sob coursing through her body. When she began her quest, she was prepared for the repeated sacrifice, of her body, of her dignity. Yes, and even the "collateral damage" as some called it. It was all for the sake of honor.

But she had never planned on surrendering her heart.

If she thought about losing him too much, she would shatter, and that she could not do. So, when her doorbell rang, she gripped her bag and opened the door, assuming her brother had arrived early.

She could not believe it. Was she dreaming?

Daniel Long stood there, out of breath and carrying a small duffle bag. He took her face in his hands and kissed her fiercely.

"Take me with you," he said.

Chapter Forty-One

After four grueling hours spent going over every detail of the case with Detective Liu, Reggie and Walker were finally on the road back to The Grove. Thank God she wasn't driving this time around; she wasn't sure she'd have enough energy left to make it to the Great House, much less the second floor and her oh so comfortable bed.

She looked over at the man she realized she was falling in love with. He had been by her side throughout this entire screwed up mess, arguing his case, but letting her make the decisions and being there to support and protect her, even when he didn't agree with her actions. He was the kind of man worth making a major change for ... was he willing to do the same?

At the moment he was quiet but alert, his eyes on the road. "Feel better now that the professionals are finally taking over?" she asked.

He sent her a warm glance and reached his right

hand over to cover hers. "I absolutely do. The question is, are you okay with it?"

"For the most part, yes. It's good to know Detective Liu is totally on board now. He'd never say it, but I think he's glad we found evidence that he could actually use to connect all four killings."

"You were smart to call Gabe and have him meet us there, by the way. You have him to thank for letting you keep the counterfeits."

"Don't I know it." She lowered her voice to imitate their friend. "Detective Liu, I can assure you that the carvings will be far safer at The Grove Center than could ever be achieved in an SFPD evidence room."

"You sound just like him," he teased. "Your build isn't quite the same, though, which I'm grateful for.'

She chuckled, but it was fleeting; her thoughts succumbed to the melancholy beginning to overtake her. Walker picked up on it immediately.

"Tell me," he said.

"I don't know. Maybe they'll be able to pick up Sharilyn Huang soon and she'll turn on whoever she's working with."

"But?"

"It's just that she or whoever she's working with have the tigers, and they're so small, and she could do anything with them, especially if she thinks they're fake. With my brilliant idea of drawing her out, I may have unwittingly played a role in losing them forever."

Walker squeezed her hand reassuringly. "As my mother always says, 'You don't know what's going to happen, so don't borrow worry.' But I'll say this: Your family would be very proud of you for all you've done. I know *I* am. Despite the gray hairs you've given me, I think you're incredible." Then, as if what he'd just said was no big deal, he followed it with, "Listen, I know you're tired, but what do you say we stop by the Milk and Honey and grab some dinner? Lunch is a distant memory and 'Man cannot live by vending machine crap alone.'"

No two ways about it—this man makes me smile inside. "Okay, but you've got to let me pay this time."

Walker grinned back. "We'll thumb-war for it."

They drove the rest of the way to Little Eden in comfortable silence, and just before she drifted off, Reggie thought, *I may have lost the tigers, but maybe I gained something—or someone—my grandmama would have considered far more important.*

Walker dug into his bacon cheeseburger and thought about the last one he'd had at the cozy hometown diner. It was the day he'd picked Axel up from the airport, and he couldn't believe it had barely been three weeks earlier. So much had happened since then, yet it felt like he'd had Axe and Regina in his life forever.

With the case of the stolen tigers now turned over to the authorities, and Axel getting ready to go back to school, everything was going to change again. Did he want that to happen?

No, his brain shot back. *You do not.*

He made a mental note to talk to Axe tomorrow about possibly transferring to Little Eden High. It didn't have the cachet that his college prep school in New York had, and it probably wasn't what Caroline wanted, but too bad. Walker just couldn't imagine his son living clear across the country when the two of them could find a place right here in Little Eden and be perfectly content.

The two of them. That didn't sound right, either. There ought to be three. He gazed at Regina munching on her salad and checking her phone.

Damn, there *had* to be three.

The idea of Regina moving back down the peninsula instead of staying with him was just ... unimaginable. But what did she think about it? It unsettled him that he didn't know the extent of her feelings.

But he planned on getting the answer soon. He'd talk to Axel and once that was figured out, he'd broach the topic with her and find out where she stood, find out if she wanted to give it a go as much as he did.

She looked up at that moment and caught him staring at her. "What?" she said with a half-smile.

"Nothing. I—"

At that moment her phone buzzed and she checked the screen. "It's Leo."

Walker suppressed a reaction that he knew was childish and nodded for her to answer it.

"Hi, Leo ... *Really*?" It must have been interesting because she sat up straighter in her chair, infused with renewed energy. "Oh my God. It must have come from him," she said. "Thank God he's alive! ... No, I'm not sure the authorities even know he's gone. His mother thinks the authorities *took* him! You didn't let on about that, did you? ... Good; better to let him think you're in the dark about that ... Okay, text it to me. I'll tell Gabe about it right away. In the meantime, tell the guy you've found some interested buyers and that you'd like to see more from him. Quote him whatever price you think he'll believe and see if you can get any more details ...Yes, I totally agree ... All right, call me."

She hung up and reached for Walker's hand over the table. "Leo met with some young guy today who said he was sent by Thomas Ling. He showed Leo a medallion and insisted Ling had recently carved it. Leo could only take a picture of it and he's supposed to get back with the guy to let him know if there are interested buyers."

Her phone pinged with a text alert. "Here it is." She handed Walker her phone and scooted over next to him in the booth. Another image popped up. "See, that's the back." She squinted, then enlarged the image. "Yes, there it is. Ling's mark." She looked up at Walker, bubbling with excitement. "Leo figures it's a sign that Thomas Ling meant to show us. It may be a clue as to who's behind all this."

Walker examined the medallion image. "It's a kind of symbol, for sure. Axe might have seen it. Let's check with him when we get back."

They finished up and Walker let Regina win the thumb war so she could pay the bill. If he had his way, soon enough it wouldn't matter who paid because it would all be coming out of the same till.

Once they reached The Grove, they stopped at the main museum building to drop off the two pairs of earrings in the secure storage room. Whoever the thief was, he or she knew that Reggie was staying here, which meant they should treat the earrings as if they were the originals.

As a result, it was just after ten when they pulled up in front of the Great House. Walker noticed that Axel's bike was not in its usual place or visible anywhere nearby. He frowned, yet was determined this time not to jump to conclusions. "I don't see Axe's bike."

"I don't either," Regina said, looking around. "Why don't you give him a call? Maybe he's got a flat."

Walker dialed his son's phone, but it went straight to voicemail, which he didn't bother with, because Axel admitted he rarely listened to messages. "Or maybe he's playing a game, turned off his phone, and forgot about the time."

Regina gently touched Walker's arm. "Well it is Friday night, you know. No matter what, it's not worth a shouting match, right?" She smiled sweetly. "Save that for the really big stuff, like, oh, armed robbery."

Walker gave Regina a quick but satisfying kiss. *This woman is good for me in too many ways to count.* "I got it," he said. "You go on inside; I'll just take a spin and see if you're right about the flat. Maybe he needs a ride."

"All right, dad," she chided him. Then, in a flirtatious move of her own, she reached up and caressed the back of Walker's neck, tugging it down for a much longer, much more satisfying kiss.

The intimate darkness, coupled with the sweet, womanly scent of her and the softness of her lips conspired to bring Walker almost to his knees with lust. He engulfed her curves completely and began nibbling her neck, whispering, "I can't get enough of you, you know."

Regina let him feast for a few more minutes before playfully pushing him away. "Go find your son. Maybe later we'll see what you consider 'enough.'"

"Yes, ma'am," he said.

Getting out of the car, she turned around to wave at him before entering the house. He rolled down the driver's window and grinned at her with the barely checked glee of someone who's about to receive a very special treat. "Hold that thought, Ms. Firestone."

Still smiling, Walker drove down the hill. He spent the next twenty minutes checking the sites in Little Eden where he imagined Axel (and no doubt Kaitlyn) might be: the Milk and Honey Cafe; Lindy's; the Hang Out. He even drove by the nearby trailhead where he knew Kaitlyn and Axe often hiked.

No kids. No bike.

He'd left his smile behind several minutes ago. A twinge of worry ran through his head, but he ineffectually slapped it away. No way could he go from a "barely there" to a "helicopter" parent that fast. Except that he could, and he was.

But just in case he *was* overreacting, he decided to return to the Great House. Maybe Axel was already home. Barring that, he could call Kaitlyn's parents and see what was happening with those two.

He was about a third of the way back up the hill when he saw it glinting off the beam of his headlights. Something metal. A wheel. A bike's wheel. It was perched precariously on the steep side of the road.

No. No, he thought, and screeched to a halt on the shoulder. Turning off his headlights, he reached into the glove compartment for the small but powerful flashlight he'd bought for the car. He'd been caught in the dark out in the boonies once and swore never again. Taking a deep breath, he ventured over to the edge of the cliff to investigate. His shoes crunched on the gravel between the pavement and the scrub.

Yes, it was Axel's beater bike.

His heart pounding in his chest, he leaned over as far as he could to see if Axel was down there somewhere and if so, how they could get him out. The beam of the light was strong, but only showed a narrow swath of the terrain. The area on either side was rimmed with shadows. He looked carefully but couldn't make out anything that looked like Axel down the hillside.

Neither did he hear the crunching of the ground behind him.

Nor did he see the cudgel bearing down on the back of his head just before it struck.

One second he could barely see, and the next, he couldn't see or hear anything at all.

Chapter Forty-Two

Reggie checked the kitchen clock again. Where were they? Little Eden wasn't all that big. Walker had been gone for forty-five minutes and by now he should have found Axel and given him a lift, or at least figured out where he was. She was about to call his cell phone when Axel himself walked in the door.

"Somebody stole my bike," he announced. "It pisses me off. On top of everything else, that hill is steep, and it's hella dark out there."

"Oh. That's a bummer. We thought maybe you had a flat or something. Where's your dad?"

"I dunno; I thought he was with you."

Reggie reached once more for her phone. "No, he left about forty-five minutes ago to see if he could find you."

"Is he mad at me?" He glanced up at the same clock. "I know it's after ten, but…"

"No, not at all," she said, dialing the phone. "He was

just concerned, with everything that's been going on. Speaking of which, remind me to show you something we found out that you might be interested in." As she spoke, she listened to Walker's phone go to voicemail. When the message prompt came on, she said, "Hey, it's me. Your prodigal son has returned. All is well. Come on home."

"No answer, huh? That's weird; he's always getting on my case for turning my phone off, and now he goes and does the same thing."

Reggie was open to the idea of unexplainable phenomena such as "sixth" senses; she'd come across many stones throughout her career that individuals swore enabled them to feel things beyond the physical world. Unfortunately, she was feeling something along those lines right now, a niggling sense that something was terribly off. Walker should have been back by now or called to say where he was. He wasn't the type to get distracted or stop off for a drink or a chat without alerting the person waiting for him. Not wanting to alarm Axel, she tried her best to ignore the tendrils of dread coiling around her nerve endings. It didn't help that the boy was showing signs of worry, too.

"Maybe he got stuck someplace," Axel said. "Maybe we ought to go out and see if we can find *him*."

Reggie was reaching for her car keys on the rack when the back door to the kitchen opened and Brit and Jenna entered. The expression on their faces told her that her sixth sense was right all along. "What is it?" she asked in a rush. "What's happened?"

Jenna saw Axel standing there and said, "Thank God. We thought—"

"What's going on?" Axel asked, his face betraying anxiety and alarm.

"We found the Explorer down the hill a ways," Britt said. "The door was open, and your bike was on the side of the road. It looks like Walker saw the bike and stopped to see what was going on."

Reggie began to shiver. "Well, where is he? Did he get hit? Is he hurt? What?"

"That's just it," Jenna said with a touch of panic. We saw some blood on the side of the road, and a flashlight, but we couldn't see any trace of Walker. He's disappeared."

As exhausted as she'd been earlier in the evening, Reggie was now wired. The coffee that Jenna kept flowing was part of it, but the intensity of her fear for Walker kept her coiled and taut—a snake ready to strike as soon a target presented itself. The problem was finding the target.

Within an amazingly short period of time, the library of the Great House had been transformed into the command post for the search and rescue of Walker Banks and possibly Thomas Ling as well. Detective Gabe de la Torre was in charge, and he was in constant contact with Detective Liu, who had already sent an officer to investigate the supposed "arrest" of Ling.

Everybody now understood that this was no ordinary missing person case. They'd sent a team to the bottom of the hill and an accident—Walker falling down the mountainside while searching for his son in the dark—was quickly ruled out.

But knowing that Walker hadn't had a terrible accident left the far more sinister possibility: that he had been kidnapped for the express purpose of putting the squeeze on Reggie to turn over her "original" tigers.

Another search was underway as well. Both Sharilyn Huang and Daniel Long had disappeared; the consul general had not been able to reach either of them for the past several hours. His latest missive to Detective Liu, shared with the team at The Grove, said that he was "completely taken by surprise" that his second in command had somehow fallen in with the woman. He'd had no idea that he'd been cuckolded by his mistress not once, but twice (this was of course implied, not stated).

"Serves him right," Reggie said. But such retribution meant little when compared to the shocking reality that at least two very bad people, with no compunction about killing others, were still at large.

"We will find them," Gabe tried to reassure her. "It's just a matter of when."

"And what will be left of Walker and Thomas Ling when you do," she shot back, careful to express her fear out of Axel's earshot.

The wait for a ransom demand began. Everyone assumed that a call would come in from Walker's phone to hers, but nothing transpired until Reggie realized, after watching so many laptops at work, that she hadn't checked The Jade Hunters Facebook group since the crisis began. *I am an idiot*, she thought as she logged on to her own computer. Yes, she had been deemed worthy of joining the group, and yes, there was a direct message from a certain "Cheri Lynn:"

I would like to see both sets of your collectible. Are you interested in a swap for something from my collection?

Without asking Gabe for instructions, Reggie typed back:

Yes. But first I must have proof of yours.

There was no immediate response, and Reggie suffered the beginnings of a panic attack that had nothing to do with being high off the ground. She quickly showed the information to Gabe in the hope that he would bring her down from her mental precipice. He, in turn, brought one of his team members over to check the IP address of "Cheri Lynn."

"Can't do it," the IT expert said when he saw the message. "Facebook protects its users' addresses with impenetrable firewalls. You can't breach 'em."

"I didn't think we could, but thought I'd ask," Gabe said. "At least she knows we want to deal, so now we wait."

They were doing just that when Axel, who'd been

quiet and watchful throughout the night, came over. Even though he was almost grown, she wanted to hug him as a mom would; how awful to know your own father is in danger! But she felt Axe would probably feel weird, so she refrained. Instead she concentrated on maintaining her own equilibrium by revisiting every-thing she knew about the theft and the subsequent deaths. It was now four in the morning.

"Uh, Regina, before we heard about my dad being missing, you said you had something to show me."

Yes, indeed, a complete idiot. She'd forgotten all about Leo's call and text. "Yes. Gabe? You'll be inter-ested in this, too."

Gabe came over again and they flanked her on the couch as she called up the images on her phone.

"Leo Brunt was approached by a young Asian man who tried to sell him a medallion he said was carved by the well-known jade carver Ling Qiang Mao."

"The same guy who's missing?" Gabe asked.

"Yes. Leo sent me pictures of the medallion the man was peddling." She showed Axel and Gabe the images.

"That looks very similar to the mark that was found on the four victims," Gabe said. "Could be the link that ties this whole case together."

"What do you think, Axel? Have you seen this in your research?"

"Maybe. I'm not sure. Would you mind sending it to me?" He told her his phone number and she texted the image to him. His phone chirped.

"Got it," he said. "I'd like to go upstairs for a while."

Poor kid; as much tension as I'm feeling, it must be ten times worse for him. "Sure. Maybe you could get some sleep. We'll let you know if there's an update."

She squeezed his arm gently in support and watched him almost jog out of the room. Maybe playing one of his video games would help take his mind off things. But as she watched him bound up the stairs, it struck her that he looked much more like a man on a mission.

Axel was shaking as he got to his room and shut the door. *This could be it.* He turned on his laptop and opened his tong research file. Then he reached for the pages that Kaitlyn had given him with the various tattoos he'd wanted her to sketch. Flipping through them, he searched for the one he knew looked a freakin' lot like the photo Regina had sent him.

There it was. The sign of the New Rising Tigers Triad. From what little he'd learned so far, the triad was some kind of fringe group that started way back when the last emperor got kicked out of China. The group had fizzled when the Communists took over after World War Two, but lately there'd been signs it was rebooting itself. A lot of Chinese millennials who weren't that well-off saw how screwed up the Chinese government was today; like how come, if everybody's supposed to be the same, the top guys are super rich? Maybe they figured things would be better if they could go back to being part of a dynasty. Even though the NRTT was small, it already had a toehold in places like California and New York, where there was a lot more money around to get the ball rolling again. The San Francisco cell was supposedly only a few months old.

Axel reached into his backpack and pulled out the clamshell phone, along with some of those thin gloves his dad used; he'd bought them with cash at the Target in Bellam Cove. Then he pulled the hundred-dollar Amazon gift card, also bought with cash, out of his wallet.

Now came the moment of truth. He logged on to Discord as Wiseapple, his online name, and direct messaged his gray hat hacking buddy, Bystander:

I need a location for a hundred bucks. That still cool?

It didn't take long for a response.

Bystander: **Yeah, who do u want 2 find**

Wiseapple: **New RisingTigers Triad - Need coordinates of S.F. HQ ASAP AGC 042-306-417-8994**

Bystander: **One moment.**

. . .

The minutes seemed to crawl by. Come on. Come *on.* Finally...

> Bystander: **37.8890 degrees N**
> **122.6108 degrees W**
> **some old bunker**
> **You know the drill.**

Then they both logged off.

Axel knew the drill, all right. To avoid him or his family being completely eviscerated online, he had to erase any digital trail between him, Bystander and a third party, especially if that third party happened to be the law.

That's where the clamshell came in. He'd use his smartphone's Google Earth app to drive to the location of the NRTT. *Please don't let it be too far away.* When he got there, he'd use the clamshell phone, which couldn't be traced back to him, to call the cops. He wouldn't identify himself, but he'd tell them the hostages were near. Hopefully they'd pick up on the cell tower pings from the phone and trace them to the loca-tion. By then he'd be long gone. They'd show up and with luck be able to get his dad and the other guy out of there without them getting hurt.

All his dad had to do was hold on until then.

Axel hastily wiped the tears that had begun to well up. *Shit. Just hold on.*

He quickly put the coordinates Bystander had given him into his regular smart phone and deleted the information on his laptop. Then he put the other stuff he needed in his backpack and laid down on the bed, fully dressed. The keys to the Explorer jangled in his pocket. At sunrise he'd slip downstairs and head out.

Two hours to go.

Chapter Forty-Three

The night was moonless, which was always a good omen as far as Huang Hu was concerned. The darker, the better. The musty old ranger's cabin, which he'd rented for the past six months, was lit only by two battery-operated lanterns. Because the hour was late, their power was running low, leaving the tiny living room looking dim and sad. The place had few other amenities to offer, but its location was perfect. Located just beyond the boundary of Mount Tamalpais State Park, it was only a twenty-minute hike from the future nerve center for the New Rising Tiger Triad.

Huang Hu, who had gone by the name Hugh for the past two years in San Francisco, was ready for this assignment to be over. He had done all that was asked of him by his superiors in Shanghai. He'd located a secure base of operations; recruited some foot soldiers; and most importantly, deceived his sister into helping retrieve the all-important symbol of their cause, the almost mythical jade tigers. It wasn't his fault there'd been complications. Players had talked too much and had to be eliminated; doubts about the tigers' authenticity had to be addressed. Now he was forced to deal with Daniel Long, whom he'd hoped to avoid dealing with altogether. Despite all of that, he could almost smell victory and he was glad of it. It was time to go home.

He watched out the cabin's front window as Daniel waited for Sharilyn to plead his case. It was full on dark, but he could see the burning tip of the man's cigarette, a firefly bobbing in the gloom. The man was agitated, as well he should be; he wouldn't like what was going on inside Hugh's head.

Sharilyn, looking uncomfortable in hiking clothes and a sweater, mirrored her paramour's anxiety and paced in front of Hugh. "I love him," she told her brother defiantly. "And he loves me. Didn't he prove it by coming with me? He sacrificed his career for me, and he even brought his passport! There will be room for one more in the boat, I'm sure. He can come with us, can't he?"

"We'll see." In fact, Daniel would not be coming with them, nor would the Chow brothers, nor that photographer Walker Banks. And certainly, once Regina Firestone gave up the tigers and Thomas Ling was able to determine their authenticity, they would go the way of the others, too.

Revolution was a messy business. Sometimes you

had to lie, even to your own family, in service to the cause. And sometimes you had to kill for it.

But the rewards? They were incalculable; worth every sacrifice. Huang Hu would bring his country back to its former glory or die trying.

He nodded to Sharilyn's laptop. "Has she responded yet?"

Sharilyn checked her computer and this time she sat up, looking excited. "Yes. She says she needs proof of life first."

"All right, then. We will have Walker Banks tell her something only he would know." He opened the front door of the cabin. "Daniel, we are all going to take a little walk."

"It's pretty dark out here," Long said.

"Are you scared?" Hugh asked lightly. *You ought to be.*

Walker's brain throbbed like a speedbag that was still being punched. *It could be worse,* he thought. *I could be dead.*

He opened his eyes, or so he thought, to another horrific reality. He couldn't see a damn thing. Reaching up, he felt for his eyes. Were they still in his sockets? They were, thank God. *Something else to be grateful for.*

But where the hell was he? Lying on a cold stone floor

on a stinking mat, by the smell and feel of it. *Oh God, not a crypt.* Immediately his chest started pounding in time with his head, the all too familiar sense of barely leashed terror threatening to overtake him. He flailed his arms about to check the size of his cell when he hit another body.

The body grunted, then said something in Chinese.

"Do you speak English?" Walker asked the voice.

"Yes. I am Thomas Ling. Who are you?"

"Walker Banks. Where the hell are we? Why is it so damn dark in here?" *And thank you for being something to concentrate on instead of this ridiculous fear of small spaces.*

"We are in a bunker of sorts, I believe. Underground."

Shit. Walker willed himself to stay in control. "Are we alone? I mean, are there guards nearby right now?"

"No. They generally leave late at night and return around midday."

Wait. Thomas Ling? "Hey, I met your mother."

Ling's voice perked up. "You did?"

"Yes. I'm working with Regina Firestone."

"Ah. The tigers. Now I understand. How was my mother?"

He wasn't about to tell the man how frightened the old woman had sounded. "Oh, well, she's a feisty little thing. She thought we were more of the so-called government agents."

"'So-called' is correct. I did not think your government was involved in this escapade. The men who came to my door dressed as if they belong to your FBI are the same men who periodically check up on me."

"You did carve the counterfeit tigers, though, didn't you?"

Ling hesitated. "It was under duress. But how did you know?"

"There's an art broker, Leo Brunt—"

"I know him."

"Well, he said that even though it wasn't obvious, you might have somehow left your mark. Regina figured out where you put it."

"I am glad," he said. "I left it to let someone know that I did not intend to deceive. I was forced into carving the tigers; otherwise they said my mother and I would be deported in disgrace."

"'They'?"

"A woman from the Chinese consulate. But I have not seen her since."

"I don't get it: if you did what she asked, what are you doing here? Not to alarm you, but by rights you should be dead. That's how they've dealt with virtually every other player in this game."

Ling's voice took on a desperate quality. "That's just it, I do not know why I am here! My captor said that my expertise was needed. That's all he would tell me."

Walker took a moment to ponder the situation. Apparently, Regina's plan had worked better than they knew.

"Here's what I think is happening," he said and shared

his theory. Afterwards, they discussed the carver's ploy of alerting Leo Brunt through the medallions; Walker assured him it had succeeded and that the authorities would hopefully now be looking into his disappearance.

Much as he wished she'd stay away, Walker assumed Regina would eventually bring the other two sets of tigers in exchange for his safety. He knew that about her as surely as he knew the softness of her skin. The question was, how were they going to get out of this hellhole after that? Was she working with Gabe and Detective Liu? And would they be able to save the original tigers in the process?

An idea came to him regarding the artifacts and he asked Ling if his handlers had used a pouch of any kind for the counterfeit earrings he'd created.

"Yes, it was a small black one. Why? Is that important?"

"If we're lucky, it might be," Walker said, and laid out his plan. Then he asked the carver, "Do you think you can do it?"

Walker could hear the smile in Thomas Ling's voice as the man replied, "I believe so. I am very good with my hands."

"I'm counting on it," Walker said. "I—"

A hand reached out to touch him in the darkness. "Shhh, they are coming."

Shortly after that he could tell someone had entered the room. He feigned sleep but a minute later, the pointed beam of a cellphone light assaulted Walker's eyes and a harsh voice whispered, "Get up."

At first light, Axel headed softly down the stairs and past the agents still working in the library. There was a woman talking on the phone who had the same kind of darkish red hair as Regina, and a couple of guys who were tapping away at their laptops. The real Regina had fallen asleep on the couch. She was pretty cool, but he was glad he didn't have to explain himself. He left a note on his bed addressed to her saying he'd gone to visit Kaitlyn; that should satisfy her for a while.

When he walked outside, it felt cold and clammy; a bummed-looking policeman in uniform was keeping watch, blowing into his hands to keep warm. Axel waived to him and nonchalantly walked to his dad's SUV, which had been driven back up the hill after being dusted for fingerprints. Once he was down in Little Eden, he opened the Google Earth/Maps app and put in the coordinates he'd gotten from Bystander.

The result surprised and pleased him; it was less than an hour away, which meant he wouldn't even have to drive over the bridge and into the city. *Sweet.* It was stressful enough just driving around town, much less in San Francisco!

He drove through the village, which was practically dead so early in the morning, and was headed south on Shoreline Highway when it hit him. What if something went wrong? He knew he had to get as close as possible to the entrance of the underground location in order to lead the police there. But what if there were sentries or even snipers guarding the place? What if one of them thought he looked suspicious and shot him?

He swallowed hard. As it was now, no one would know where he'd gone. They might steal his dad's car and the police wouldn't even find that. Axel's imagination went from one catastrophic scenario to another until he began to shiver from dread.

Wait. He could just go back to The Grove and show the police what he had. But if it got out what he'd done, he'd be in deep shit. His family could be marked. Having every bit of personal and financial information out there in the public and worse, in the hands of black hatters, was no small thing; in fact, with his dad's money, that could be a total clusterfuck.

Keep your shit together. Just keep going.

He decided on a sort of compromise and sent a text to Kaitlyn:

Checking out a lead on my dad's location. If I don't text you by noon, send somebody to 37.8890 degrees N /122.6108 degrees W. Then start looking for someplace underground. But not before. Luv u, A.J.

He hesitated before hitting the "send" button. Was it too much to say, "luv u"? But he felt that way, dammit, and if that was the last thing she got from him, then that was worth sending. He hit "send."

Fifty minutes later he was homing in on the location. The road to the park was open, so he went in, not bothering to pay at the entry station because he wasn't planning on being there that long.

Where to park? After driving around a while, he found a small parking lot near a trailhead with two cars in it. They probably belonged to some early morning hikers or runners. He parked alongside one of the cars, pulled out his backpack and changed the mode of transportation on his app from "drive" to "walk." It was like he was geocaching or something, only the treasure at the end of the hunt was a cache of scumbags. *I'm going to find you fuckers*, he thought. *You can't hide from me.*

Chapter Forty-Four

R eggie woke from the couch in the library with a stiff neck. Some kind soul had draped a blanket over her, but she still shivered in the early morning chill. She checked her watch; she'd been out for about two hours. Quickly she opened her laptop and logged onto the Facebook Group. "Cheri" had responded:

> **Our mutual collector friend says to tell you he's wondering about your eye color. He also asked you to tell A.J. he should take that sign language class because it will be an easy A.**

Cheri had also attached a picture of a scruffy Walker. He was sitting with one knee bent and his elbow resting on that knee. It was close enough that all Reggie could see was a stone wall behind him. He was not smiling.

Relief surged through her as tears welled up. *My eye color*. Blinking rapidly, she quickly typed back:

Where and when?

As Reggie waited for the reply, she looked for Gabe. He was standing in the kitchen drinking coffee, talking with Diana, the female agent who had come with the rest of the team. They were going over some notes. Had he been here all night?

"She got back to me," Reggie told him, and he quickly came to peer over her shoulder.

"Walker looks like shit," Gabe said.

"Yes, but consider the alternative. And she definitely got that message from him."

"What's with the eye color and what does he mean about the sign language?"

"Oh, it's ... it's a private joke. And Walker knows Axel's been researching those gang signs. I'd shown him the medallion photo that Leo sent me, so I'm hoping it means Thomas Ling is with him."

"Or that the carving can tell us something. Let's get Axel down here and ask him," Gabe suggested.

Reggie threw off the blanket and stood up. "Let me take a quick shower and change, okay? Then I'll wake him up. He's got to be exhausted."

"Fair enough."

But ten minutes later, when she knocked on Axel's door, she found his room empty and a note that said he was visiting Kaitlyn.

Back downstairs, Gabe and Diana were gathered over Reggie's laptop. He called Reggie over. "Your Facebook pal has set the drop point. It's a pullout about a half mile north of Muir Beach. And she added a little something else."

The message read:

Bring your collectibles by eleven a.m. and we will set a price.

"What?!" Reggie was incensed. "The price is Walker!"

"She probably wants to see the goods first. So, we'll need to give Diana here something that looks like the tigers."

"What do you mean, Diana? They're expecting *me* to show up."

Gabe shook his head. "There's no way we're going to let a civilian make the swap, Reggie. Diana's an old hand at this. She'll be wearing a hat and glasses, and she'll be armed. But if you can get me something to stand in for the tigers, a couple of pouches, maybe, we can get close enough to take down whoever's making the trade. We have to move fast, though, to get our guys in place beforehand. You with me on this?"

Reggie was growing more recalcitrant by the minute, but she nodded tersely. "I'll get you something from the storage facility." After grabbing her purse and phone, she stepped out the back door, only to surprise

Kaitlyn, who was about to knock on the door and jumped back with an "Oh!"

Reggie's voice softened. "Hey, Kaitlyn." She looked over the girl's shoulder. "Where's Axel? He left a note saying he was with you."

Kaitlyn looked visibly upset. "That's what I want to talk to you about." She glanced at the uniformed guard and whispered, "In private."

"Come with me," Reggie said, and the two headed down the trail to the museum. Once they entered the warmth of the building, she drew Kaitlyn to a row of chairs.

The poor girl was close to tears. She immediately pulled out her phone and scrolled until she found what she was looking for, then showed the screen to Reggie.

"How did Axel get this?"

"I don't know. But he could be in real danger, so I don't care if he hates me."

Reggie gave her a squeeze. "You did the right thing, and he's not going to hate you, I promise. I've got to get something out of storage. Have you got a paper and pencil?"

"Sure." Kaitlyn pulled a sketch pad out of her satchel along with a mechanical pencil. "This okay?"

"Perfect. From what I've learned lately, it's not a good idea to send private stuff electronically. So please sit here and write down the coordinates from the text. Make sure it's accurate. Then we'll head back toward the Great House together, okay? And don't worry: our goal is to keep Axel safe."

While Kaitlyn copied the text, Reggie went through the biometric security protocol and hurried to the safe containing the jewels. Her mind was revving at a hundred miles an hour. What if the police botched up the exchange and Walker got killed in the cross fire? What if he wasn't even at the drop point and was still underground? What if, God forbid, he was already dead…and what if Axel got caught up in all of it?

There seemed to be only one way to find the answers, and that was to see for herself. If Axel's information was correct, she now had the location. She could go there and check things out. If the worst happened, she'd give up the tigers—all of them—to ensure Walker and Thomas Ling's safety. But the best way to avoid that was to get some protection, and she knew right where to get it.

Relieved to finally have a plan, she removed both pairs of tigers, still in their pouches, and stuffed them into the slightly larger black pouch that Vihaan Chaudhry had given her. Then she emptied the two little red bags protecting the citrine and emerald necklaces, leaving the gems exposed in the box. "You won't be cold for long, I promise," she said as she closed the safe.

She looked around the storage area. What could she stick in the empty bags to simulate the earrings? There wasn't much, and she was about to look elsewhere when she noticed a magnetic bulletin board with two small magnets in the shape of California. She found a couple of paper clips in a drawer, twisted them open, and stuck one in each pouch, hoping they'd cling to the magnets and feel like the wire attached to the earrings.

Then she texted Axel, hoping against hope that he hadn't yet done whatever he was planning on doing, and telling him to wait for her; she was on her way.

Kaitlyn was sitting where Reggie had left her. At least now she seemed less frantic; she was looking around and biting her fingernails.

Reggie smiled at her. "Have you got that paper for me?"

Kaitlyn handed her the coordinates and Reggie checked them against Axel's text before having Kaitlyn delete it. Then Reggie gave the girl the "magnetic tigers." "Can you go back to the Great House and give these to Detective de la Torre? He's expecting them. And please tell him that I went to visit the professor."

"Sure, okay." Kaitlyn seemed glad just to have something to do.

Reggie gave her a hug. "Thank you so much for letting me know about Axel, but no need to share it with anyone else until I tell you, okay? I want to make sure Axel stays out of harm's way."

Reggie and Kaitlyn parted ways and Reggie walked farther down toward Ethan's cabin, a larger edifice known as the Firestone Cottage because it had been built especially for Will Firestone, the man who ultimately became Reggie's grandpapa.

Just as she walked up, the professor was locking his door. He saw her and smiled grimly. "Any word?"

"We've been given instructions to meet and 'set a price.' Ethan, I have a very big favor to ask."

"What is it, my dear?"

"I'd like to borrow your Sig Sauer."

The old man frowned. "You would?"

"Yes," she continued. "I still have my permit, so you wouldn't be doing anything wrong by letting me carry it."

"I'm not worried about that, but why do you feel you need it?"

Time for a slightly different version of the truth. "I ... I may be meeting with the kidnappers and I'd feel more secure if I were armed, that's all."

Ethan regarded her without speaking and she tried hard not to squirm. At last he nodded, turned back to his front door and unlocked it. "I know the feeling very well," he said. "Wait just a moment."

And ten minutes later she was on the road, pushing the speed limit, and praying that this latest idea of hers wouldn't be her last.

The terrain Axel followed started out kind of rolling, but then it grew steeper, and there were clumps of boulders sticking up here and there, and more and more trees. It was growing warmer and the sun was rising, which was both good and bad: good that he could see better, but bad that he could more easily be seen.

He kept his eyes peeled for any sign of an opening,

like a mine shaft or something, but there was nothing he could readily see. Yet his app was telling him he was virtually right on the spot.

He stood at ground zero and slowly turned around in a circle.

Nobody.

Nothing.

Fuck, he thought. *I can't call the police from here. They'd think I was just a nut job yanking their chain.*

And then he saw it. A rustling in the trees. A shift in the light. He quickly dropped down behind one of the rock outcroppings and watched as three guys emerged from what seemed like a small stand of trees. They weren't dressed for hiking; in fact, the two larger guys were wearing nice street clothes and one of them stopped to brush himself off. Thank God they were headed away from Axel.

He waited a bit longer to see if anyone else emerged, but no one did, so he crept closer toward the trees. There, wedged between some large rocks, was a large bush that didn't seem natural up close. And it wasn't, because something metal glinted underneath the green leaves of it.

Axel had seen enough. He scrambled back to his place behind the rocks and waited for his heart to stop hammering before he pulled out the flip phone. Then he pulled out Detective de la Torre's card. Pausing a minute to practice his spiel, he was about to dial the number when his regular phone pinged. It was a text from Regina:

. . .

SUPER IMPORTANT: WAIT FOR ME BEFORE DOING ANYTHING!! ON MY WAY; WILL TEXT WHEN CLOSE

"Fuck," he muttered. He hesitated. Should he go ahead and make the call, or should he wait? After some internal debate, he decided to hold off. Maybe everyone came up with a plan to smoke them out or something. No, she would have told him that, wouldn't she? *Shit*.

He worked his way carefully back to the Explorer, got inside and leaned his chair way back so no one looking casually at the car would see that it was occu-pied. Even though the sun was rising, he still tucked his hands inside his sweatshirt to warm up. As the minutes passed, he thought of Kaitlyn and tried to be mad at her for not doing what he'd asked her to do.

But try as he might, he couldn't do it. He knew she'd told Regina because she was afraid for him, and that made him feel really good. And he assumed she didn't tell the cops because none of them had sent him any messages. So maybe, when Regina got here, he could still pull this off the way he planned.

He settled down, thinking of his dad, who might be super close by. Was he okay? No, he *had* to be okay. Because otherwise, the jitters that had started to over-take his body might never stop.

Walker must have dozed off after his captor's visit because when he woke up again, there was a dim light in the room. He felt the back of his head to see if the lump back there was as big as he imagined it was. Yep, it was. Fortunately, the throbbing had subsided into a dull ache.

He looked over to see the man behind the voice in the darkness. Thomas Ling looked to be in his mid-forties with a slight build, short black hair, and a scraggly beard. Right now, he was scratching it.

"I don't know how you *laowei* can enjoy such a hirsute existence," Thomas said, smiling slightly. "My mother would not approve of this."

Walker felt his own beard, which was rough after only two days. "Tell me about it," he said. He noticed the bandage on Ling's foot. "What happened to you?"

"I was a bit too zealous in trying to avoid being incarcerated," he explained. "Fortunately, it only hurts when I put weight on it."

Looking around, Walker was gratified to see that he was not in a tiny cell. Though stark and chilly, the chamber was normal size. A rusted metal table with two equally decrepit chairs provided the only furniture, and on the far wall, an old-fashioned radiator stood silent, the promise of heat unfulfilled.

"How big do you think this place is?" he asked Thomas.

"I am not sure, but I think it has many rooms," came the reply. "At some point it no doubt served as a—"

Sharilyn Huang entered the room. She was wearing jeans, a turtleneck, and sweater, a far cry from the last time he'd seen her. Objectively she was a beautiful woman, but masked anger and anxiety made her appear brittle. She carried two bags which she handed to the men along with bottles of water.

"Some breakfast, gentlemen."

Walker looked inside and saw a burrito along with some soggy-looking fries. He went for the water instead. "What's this all about?" he asked her, hoping she'd spill something that would help them get out of their predicament.

"You know very well what this is about," she said. "You are lucky that your lady friend loves you very much. She's agreed to meet with Hugh and the Chow brothers at eleven a.m. with the tigers."

Walker frowned. "Aren't you supposed to exchange me for them?"

Sharilyn shrugged. "Hugh thought it would be better to bring her here."

This was not good. Not good at all. He fervently hoped that Regina wouldn't allow herself to be brought down here to what he now referred to as "hell." He had a feeling that Hugh liked to "tidy up" as he went along, and that meant eliminating those who had outlived their usefulness. Once she gave up the tigers, they would both fall squarely into that category.

Daniel Long, the young man who had apparently

thrown in his lot with Sharilyn, came into the room. Maybe he had some sense left.

"How did you get involved with all this?" Walker asked him. "Is this really the way you want to end your career?"

Daniel surprised him by chuckling. "Oh, there's a lot you don't know, Mr. Banks. A lot." He turned to Sharilyn. "There's a lot you don't know, too."

Sharilyn was taken aback. "What do you mean? What don't I know?"

"Your brother is not who you think he is."

Chapter Forty-Five

As soon as she entered the state park, Reggie texted Axel, who directed her to the Dipsea Trailhead parking lot. There she found Walker's Explorer with Axel reclining in it. The teen looked annoyed, but it couldn't be helped.

Reggie climbed into the passenger seat with her messenger bag containing the gun and the tigers. "Listen, I know you're probably mad at Kaitlyn for contacting me, but she did the right thing. She's worried. You haven't tried to go in, have you?"

"No. I was never gonna do that," Axel said. "I was just going to call the cops and get the SWAT team to storm the place."

Reggie relaxed a little. "Why not just tell Detective de la Torre back at The Grove? He could set something up."

"And then he'd ask me how I got the location." He

showed her the clamshell phone. "This way I do it anonymously and there's no way to trace it."

"Okay, I'm not going to ask how you got the location either, except to say, are you absolutely sure of your information?"

"As sure as I can be, given what I know about this freakin' group that's doin' all this shit. And I know from my own eyes that three guys came out of a hatch hidden in the bushes over there a while back."

"Was one of them your dad?"

"No."

Figures. However many there are in that bunker, there are three fewer right now. If I'm going to do this... "All right. Listen. Detective de la Torre is setting a trap for the kidnappers using a body double for me. It's not that far from here, and it doesn't look like the bad guys are keeping their part of the bargain and bringing your dad to exchange. I'm going to go inside this place you've found and assess the situation, maybe try to help your dad and the other fellow they're keeping."

"Are you crazy? We don't know how many are down there. You could get yourself killed!"

"Look, I'm not going to make myself known until I know what the situation is." Reggie patted her bag. "Besides, I'm armed, and I have what they want."

Axel's face told the whole story: fierce love and fear coupled with hope. "If you think it'll work."

She took his arm. "Axel, I don't know anything for sure. What I do know is that I'm going to do all I can to get your dad out of there."

"What do you want me to do?"

She checked her watch. "I think you should wait no more than twenty minutes. If I don't come out again, make your call."

Axel nodded. Before she shut the door, he said, "Wait" and checked the glove compartment. "Here, take this," he said, handing her the flashlight that someone must have put back after they found it by his bike. "My dad says you should always carry one in the car in case you ever need it. I'd say you're gonna need it."

Reggie smiled her thanks and headed in the direction Axel had pointed out. Following his description, it didn't take her long to find the concealed hatch. Lifting it, she saw a tunnel completely devoid of light.

"Here we go," she muttered, and shut the hatch behind her.

She turned on Walker's flashlight to get a sense of the cave, or whatever the heck it was. It was long, low and narrow, the sides shored up with boards like you'd see in an old mine shaft. The passage sloped down, turned left, then slanted even more for about sixty feet before stopping abruptly at a ledge. Rather than lead into an abyss, however, the edge was illuminated by a weak light.

As she drew closer, she realized the cliff was a high retaining wall; iron rungs set in the concrete served as a ladder leading below. She couldn't hear anybody, so she quickly climbed down the rungs to find herself in a bunker of sorts. It was large and seemed to head in several different directions. Here and there a lantern had been stuck on a hook along the passageway, but the light was meager at best.

Reggie continued to explore the complex, poking her head into rooms if the doors were opened, quietly testing the door knobs if they weren't. By and large the place seemed abandoned.

She encountered a flight of stairs and took them down to yet another level. Along a hall lit by a single sputtering lantern, more rooms awaited, but these were even less inhabitable than the ones above, without the courtesy of a coat of plaster or a military-green paint job.

At the far end of the lower hall she saw a door unlike all the rest. It was reinforced by metal sheeting that rose nearly to the ceiling, attached with grommets rusty and discolored with age. Over the flashing, three horizontal bars set on hinges further discouraged entry.

When she opened the door, she was met with a two-foot high barrier, also metal, that she had to step over to enter the room. The room itself was nothing, small and neglected. But on the opposite wall was another rein-forced metal door, more of a hatch, really, equipped with a wheel that looked like the same mechanism that might secure a bank vault. Logic told her the barrier was designed to keep something contained, either fire or ... water.

Water. It must be. They were underground and near the coastline. The bunker—left over from World War II, maybe?— was probably carved from an already existing cave system. At that point she noticed a clipboard next to the far door that contained several pages of columns and numbers. She held her light up to it. It was a tides chart, dated 1962. They'd probably kept the place operational during the Cold War. "Must be the back door," she murmured.

She was about to open the hatch to see where it led when she heard distant voices. Carried by the water on the other side of the barrier, maybe? Retracing her path up the stairs to the main hallway, she continued until the sounds grew loud enough that she could make out Sharilyn Huang talking. Who was she speaking to? Walker? No, it was Daniel. She made a move to edge even closer before another sound made her freeze.

Footsteps. From behind her. Someone had returned.

Heart pounding like a kettle drum, she ducked into the closest room, a supply closet by the looks of it, and shut the door, hoping desperately for the footsteps to pass her by.

Sharilyn looked at her lover with disbelief. "What are you talking about, Daniel? My brother has helped me every step of the way."

Daniel took her hand. "Did you ever wonder why your brother felt the need for this place? Why would he, if all he was doing was helping you?"

Sharilyn swallowed, the first feelings of doubt slithering up her spine. "No... I wondered, but I never asked. I assumed he had his reasons."

"He has his reasons, all right. He's not working for your family's honor; he's working for a very dangerous organization who wants the tigers for themselves. They intend to sell them and use the fakes to raise even more money for terrorist activities. They are vicious dreamers. They want to install a new dynasty in China."

Sharilyn looked around the room for someplace to sit down and absorb what Daniel was telling her. "How do you know all this?"

Daniel looked sheepish. "I ... well, I care about you, so I did some research. This group he's part of, this NRTT is bad news, Sharilyn. You shouldn't be associated with it, or with him. He's a liar of the first order."

"Don't listen to him, Sharilyn. He's the one who's been lying to you."

Hugh had returned.

Something is terribly wrong, she thought. *Why is Hugh back so early, and where is Regina Firestone?*

"What's happened?" she asked anxiously.

Hugh scrubbed his face; never had he seemed so agitated. "It was a set up by the police; I should have taken more precautions. It was a good thing I hung back, but unfortunately the brothers had to be sacrificed."

"'Sacrificed'? Are you saying they're dead?"

"Shots were fired," her brother said without emotion. "I assume the worst."

"Then what do we do?" She eyed the men in the room—her brother, her lover, even the two prisoners along the wall. What was going to happen to all of them? Panic threatened to overwhelm her.

"We're going to revise our plans," her brother said calmly. He checked his watch. "The boat will pick us up below as soon we are finished here and we'll have to make do with what we have."

"*Wait!* You are moving much too quickly. First tell me what Daniel is talking about, that you belong to some secret group. What is this nonsense about selling the tigers? That was never the plan. The plan was to bring them home where they belong, to restore honor to our family. And to do that we must make sure we have the right ones!"

"Little Sister, you are beautiful and clever, but you are not wise. It would only be a matter of time before you sacrificed your treasure for love, like our ancestor Chen Li Bao." Hugh pointed contemptuously to Daniel. "This man, this Long Da, you think he returns your affection? Then you are a fool. He has clung to you like a parasite, unwilling to do the work himself, but waiting for you to gain the treasure he too has sought—the treasure our group must have."

Sharilyn's mind began to race. Could there be truth in Hugh's words? She had always held a whisper of doubt; if Daniel truly wanted her, how could he have been content to have Jiang on top of her, and so often in the next room with just an office door between them?

"Don't listen to him," Daniel said. "I want only you."

Hugh smirked. "Then you must let your wife and

little son know that back in Hong Kong." He looked over at Sharilyn. "You look shocked. You mean he didn't tell you about his other family? Look at his wallet. I guarantee you will not find a picture of you inside it."

"He's lying," Daniel said. "Just like he lied to you about the tigers."

Sharilyn looked from one to the other. Daniel had a family? It couldn't be. And her brother had as much as admitted his duplicity. "Why did you lie to me, brother? Haven't you done exactly what you accuse Daniel of doing?"

Hugh's eyes burned with fervor. "Lying is nothing. I have *killed* for those tigers, many times over. And not to have them gather dust in some box back in our family home in Tianjin. They hold power, and that power will be used to right the wrongs the West has perpetrated upon our country for nearly two hundred years. We will return to the glory days of a new Imperial China."

Much to Sharilyn's shock, Daniel's veneer of innocence seemed to crack under the pressure of Hugh's diatribe. "Power," he sneered. "You're right about one thing. The power is in the wrong hands. But you're the fool if you think a new dynasty will change that. My ancestors suffered immeasurably under your decadent monarchy; the only way some of them could survive was to cut off their very manhood and serve their oppressors. So, don't talk to me about 'glory days.' The only power those tigers bring is the power of money, and you can only get that by selling them to the highest bidder, who is undoubtedly a westerner—the very race you claim to despise."

"You are only half-correct, insect." Hugh curled his hands into fists. "Imagine one of these hands contains the real and true tigers ... and one does not. Who is to say which is which?" He pounded his chest. "*I* am to say, that is who. If we cannot secure the originals, we will make a copy of the copy, like we did before. One I will sell as genuine. You remember the collector whose house we visited? He is willing to buy it. It's true he's not of our race, but his money is green, and that is all I care about. After the money is transferred, the other pair will be 'discovered' as the true relic of the Qing dynasty. It will become the symbol of the reborn New Rising Tigers Triad."

How could I have missed this? Sharilyn wondered. *Was I so blinded by my own quest that I didn't see his?*

"You can't be serious, Hugh," she said.

The glint in his eyes was feral. "Do you think I am joking, little sister? Our members are rising everywhere. In every country that matters. They are waiting for the sign. They are waiting to destroy the current order, one sycophant at a time. They just need a symbol to believe in. When that happens, I would not want to be a member of the ruling party, because no one, no matter where they are, will be safe.

"And *you*," he addressed Daniel contemptuously "You and your pathetic People's Dragon Movement. Your kind thinks to return to the weak democracy of

Sun Yat Sen; it is a pipe dream; it will never happen, but even if it did, you will never live to see it."

Hugh is losing it, Sharilyn thought. *I don't know if I can stop him...or if I even want to. Daniel has another family?*

"Let me see your wallet," she asked her lover.

Daniel paused, and in that pause, she had her answer. Yet, he persisted. "You don't trust me? Can't you see? Your brother has gone mad. If you stop him, you and I can be together." He reached out to her, a feeble attempt.

"But we can't be together, can we, Daniel?" Sharilyn's own words sounded flat to her, as if a robot were speaking, certainly not a woman who had a heart capable of breaking. "You used me. You made me fall in love with you when all the time you were committed to someone else. You didn't care about me at all. You are no better than my brother."

"But Sharilyn ..." Daniel pleaded.

She turned to her brother. "I think you need to deal with him."

"As you wish." Hugh calmly walked up to Daniel, as if to take him by the arm. Daniel reached for something but wasn't quick enough to avoid the stiletto that Hugh plunged into his stomach.

"My God!" cried Thomas Ling as Daniel crumpled to the floor.

You betrayed me, Sharilyn thought as she dispassionately watched her lover fall. *You should not have done that.*

"You," Hugh said to Walker Banks. "Put him in the storage room across the hall. We'll deal with him later."

"But the man is bleeding out!" Thomas cried.

"That is the plan, yes," Hugh replied calmly, and gestured to Banks, who must have felt the better part of honor was to obey. He hefted Daniel into a fireman's lift and carried him to the other room.

When he returned, he was not alone.

Chapter Forty-Six

It had been eighteen minutes and Axel was about ready to jump out of his skull. Where was she? What had she found down there? Why wasn't she coming back up? He checked his phone again. Nineteen minutes. *Okay. That's it.*

He stuffed he gear into his back pack and was ready to hop out of the car when there was a tap on the window. Axel's heart leaped into his throat; he almost wet his pants.

It was a park ranger. He looked like he was maybe ten years older than Axel, all tan and built, with short blonde hair and a Dudley Do-Right attitude.

Shiiiit.

He rolled down the window. "Uh, yes sir? Something the matter?"

"May I see your license and car registration, please?"

Shit and double shit.

What the hell was going on? Axel reached into the glove compartment for the registration slip, then fished out his wallet to show the ranger. The man looked at it, held it up to the light, flipped it over, then read the car registration information.

"Would you step out of the car, please, sir?"

Oh, man. This can't be happening. Not now! Should I tell this guy what's going on? No - he's going to think I'm a perv or something. Okay, Okay. Just play it cool.

Axel stepped out of the car.

"Turn around please and place your hands on the hood."

"Hey, what's going on? What'd I do?" *Geez, maybe this guy is a perv and he's only pretending to be a park ranger, and he kidnaps guys, and—"*

"Is this your car, sir?"

"No, it's my dad's."

"Your last name and the name on the registration don't match."

"That's 'cause our names don't match. But he's my dad." *Whether he wants to be or not.*

"Your addresses don't match either. It says your father lives in Idaho. Does your dad know you've taken the car?"

Uh oh. "Uh, technically, no, but I don't think he'd mind. We're staying north of here for a few weeks. He lets me take the car all the time." *Okay, maybe that's a stretch, but...*

"May I ask what you're doing here this early in the morning?"

The guy was *relentless.*

"Uh, well, getting ready to go on a hike?"

He didn't look impressed. "We've had a report that a car matching your description has been parked here for quite some time and that it was occupied. We don't allow overnight parking, and you can imagine, those who use this park are leery when they see vehicles whose occupants are acting strangely."

Axel mentally counted to ten. *I haven't done a fucking thing! This guy's probably getting off on being such a dick. Now I can try being a dick myself, or I can keep kissing his ass in the hope that he loses interest.* "Well, I really wasn't doing anything, but if you'd like me to leave, then..."

The ranger handed Axel the registration and his license. "That might be a good idea," he said, and stood back.

Burning with shame and more than a little panic, Axel started up the car. *I can call from down the road,* he thought, *as soon as I get this fucker off my tail.*

As he pulled out of the lot, he could hear a siren in the distance. At least police were somewhere nearby; imagine if they'd been out in the middle of nowhere?

He left the boundaries of the park and pulled off to the side of the road, deciding to text Regina first to see if he even had to call the cops; maybe she'd been able to take care of things on her own. He pulled out his phone and texted:

A ranger kicked me out of the park B4 I could call. U still need it?

He waited for an answer. Minutes ticked by and there was nothing.

Nothing.

And Axel started to shake all over again.

"I'm here to negotiate," Regina said, pointing the Sig Sauer directly at Sharilyn Huang. "Your lives for all the tigers."

Walker couldn't believe the guts of this amazing woman. Five minutes earlier she'd nearly scared the shit out of him when she popped up from behind one of the racks in the storage room.

"What in the hell are you doing here?" he'd whispered fiercely, torn between utter relief and abject fear for her safety.

Other than a brief kiss, she'd wasted no time on a response, directing him to place Daniel on the floor, using her own jacket as a pillow. The man was bleeding but still breathing, and she'd quickly pressed a wad of paper towels against the wound, taking an unopened box of some kind of industrial cleaner and putting it right on top of the pad to apply some pressure. Then she'd gestured for Walker to precede her back to the larger room.

Hugh now kept his eyes on Regina as he slowly moved toward his sister and Thomas Ling. "It's nice to meet you again, Miss Firestone."

She frowned until recognition apparently set in. "It was you that day in the high rise. You looked like an accountant."

The monster smiled. "One of my many personas."

"Let me see your copy of the tigers," Regina said to Sharilyn. Apparently, the chit chat was over.

Sharilyn brought out a black pouch and laid it on the table. Regina, her gun still trained on Sharilyn, reached for them. As she did so, her phone must have buzzed and surprised her, because she reached into her pocket and glanced down; unfortunately it was enough of a distraction that when she raised her head again, Hugh had the tip of his stiletto poised at the neck of Thomas Ling.

"You know I will not hesitate."

Both of them froze: Regina in the act of pointing her gun, Hugh in the act of murdering yet another innocent victim. No one said a word.

Give it up, Regina. The bastard means what he says. It's not worth another death. Walker only thought the words but hoped somehow Regina heard them.

She did, and gently laid the gun on the table. Hugh picked it up. "And your phone as well," he said.

Reggie saw that the text was from Axel; he hadn't been able to make the call, which meant no SWAT team was on its way. Maybe he was right, and Regina *was* crazy to think she could walk away with all three sets of tigers along with Walker and Thomas.

But dammit, she had to try. How did the saying go? "If you don't try, a failure rate of one hundred percent is guaranteed." She'd assumed help was on the way; possibly she could have stacked the odds even more in her favor. But none of that mattered now. Now it was a matter of surviving, pure and simple. She had to wait for an opportunity and grab it.

"Now, given whom I know *you* to be, I assume you brought your own tigers," Hugh said.

Reggie nodded, second guessing the wisdom of that decision as well. No, it was an insurance policy, in case something like this were to happen. They were the ultimate bargaining chips.

"Good. Now let's get this matter taken care of. I have a boat to catch." Hugh instructed Thomas to sit at the metal table, then asked his sister to give up the sweater she'd been wearing to cover the table's scarred surface.

"But it's cold in here, and the table is filthy."

"Do it," he said sharply, "and put your pair of tigers on top of it."

Once Sharilyn had done so, Hugh instructed Reggie to do the same. She handed Thomas the black bag from which he withdrew the red and green pouches holding their sets.

"I need more light," Thomas said. "And I could really use a ten-magnification loupe."

"You've got what you've got. Get on with it," Hugh said.

Thomas sat quietly observing the three pairs of tigers, picking them up and holding them to the light of the lantern that Sharilyn had brought to the table. It was the only light available and kept the rest of the room in gloom. After a few minutes he said, "The eyes are the first tell- tale sign."

"Why?" Sharilyn asked.

"Because their cut determines their age. The diamond eyes for this pair have faceted culets." He held up the second pair. "As do these. Whereas the third—the pair that I carved—do not. The diamond cutter should have used an older style but failed to do so." He set the tigers close to the others.

"Is that how you determined the tigers were counterfeit, by the eyes?" Sharilyn asked Reggie.

"Partly yes, but I wasn't entirely sure even then."

"Probably because of the jade itself," Thomas said. He held up one earring from each of the pairs, his hands caressing, turning, showing them in the light. His love of the ancient stone showed in his every practiced move.

"Two factors play a role: one, the quality of the stone, the other, the quality of the carving." He held up one. "This one presents very well; the tiger is carved in near perfect detail. But look at the jade itself." He presented the back side of the earring, which had a pale green streak that was ever so slightly darker than the rest of the stone. "This you do not see in older mutton fat jade from Hotan." He picked up a tiger from the other pair. "You see here? These tigers are well carved, but not quite as precisely as the first. This is because of the limited carving tools used prior to and during the seventeenth century. The jade as well is blemish free, indicative of earlier, higher quality stone extractions."

Oh. my. God. Reggie couldn't believe what she was hearing. She caught Walker's eyes; he kept his gaze steady, silently talking to her.

Sharilyn pointed to the pair on Thomas's left. "So, you're saying these are the originals?"

"That is what I'm saying. I want to live, madam. I have a mother who is frantic without me and whom I care for. You told me to carve a copy of the earrings you provided to me and I did so. And now you have told me to confirm to you which are the true originals as the price of my freedom. I have done that as well. Now will you uphold your part of the bargain?"

During this time Hugh had been looking at the tigers. "I'm not sure I agree," he said slowly. He seemed to be weighing all the factors. "I think it might be the other."

Now's the time, Reggie thought. "You should listen to your brother," she said to Sharilyn.

Thomas Ling smiled gently. "You may believe what you like. Of course, there is a final method of determination."

"What is that?" Sharilyn said.

"The mark. The earliest carvers left symbols so

that others would know it was their work, but later ones felt their work should stand on its own merits. I left my own mark in keeping with that ancient practice."

Sharilyn picked up one of the earrings. She squinted at the piece from all sides. "Where is this mark?"

Reggie dared not say a word. She had no idea if the original had a mark or not. If it was found to have one, this whole exercise would be pointless.

"It is behind the eye, but one cannot see it without removing the eyes with the proper tool, otherwise the piece will be irrevocably damaged. When you take it back home, have a professional remove the eyes and you will see." Thomas began to put the earrings back in their pouches. "I guarantee you that the originals will have a mark." He held Hugh's gaze. "Tell me which ones you want," he said quietly. "I will oblige."

Hugh returned the stare, and then looked at his sister.

"That is the one!" she cried, pointing to the pair on the left.

"Fine. Put the original in the black pouch," Hugh said.

Thomas did as he was told, placing the others in the red and green bags.

"Hand them over," Hugh ordered.

Thomas rose to do so but wobbled on his injured leg and knocked the lantern off the table. The room was briefly cast into shadows before Sharilyn rushed forward to pick it up.

"You idiot," Hugh said to Thomas, leveling his gun to shoot the man.

"No, that would be *you*," came a strained voice from around the corner. Daniel Long, pressing one hand to his stomach, pointed his own weapon at Hugh and fired.

Chapter Forty-Seven

S hit! As soon as he heard the shot, Walker looked to see if Regina was all right. She had ducked, but Sharilyn, standing next to her brother, screamed shrilly as Hugh dropped to the floor, a bullet entering his skull right between the eyes.

It was instant chaos. Sharilyn grabbed a black pouch, picked up the gun that Hugh had dropped, and waved it wildly before running down the hall. At the same time, Daniel once more collapsed and Regina ran to help him. The wad of paper she had pressed against his knife wound was soaked in blood.

"We need something else to stop the bleeding," she cried. Walker quickly tore the shirt from Hugh's body and brought it over, applying pressure to the wound.

"Stay with us, Daniel," Regina said to him. "We're going to get help as soon as we can." Once Walker was in place, she rocked back on her heels, hesitated a second, then cried "Dammit!" before jumping up running after Sharilyn.

"No, Regina—wait!" Walker called, his hands still occupied with the bleeding man on the ground.

"Go after her," Thomas said, limping over to Daniel and tossing Walker the remaining pouches. "She doesn't know. I will stay and gladly help the man who saved us."

"She *does* know. The little fool wants them all," Walker said.

"Take ... take this," Daniel hissed, handing Walker his revolver. "You might need it."

"A Colt?"

Daniel winced rather than smiled. "I like old Westerns."

"Thanks." Walker took the remaining three bullets out of the chamber to avoid an accident and stuck the pistol in the back of his waistband, then started running down the various halls of the bunker. Where the fuck were they? Where was the exit? He followed the sound of pounding footsteps, every few seconds calling "Regina! It's not worth it!" He could hear her in turn calling out "Wait!" to her quarry. Shots were fired and then there was no more shouting.

God, what was happening?

Finally, he found the stairs. What *was* this place? He ran down to the lower level and caught a glimpse of Regina entering a room at the end of the hall.

Thank you. Thank you.

By the time he made it to the room, Regina was

standing at the opening of what looked like a submarine hatch. Of course. They were near the water. She was catching her breath and waiting for him.

"Come on," she said. "She's getting away."

"Where does that lead?"

"To a cave," she said. "It's got to be an exit; otherwise they would have boarded it up." She held out her hand. "Please, we can't lose her. Let's go."

"I can't," he said.

"You can. Come on. We're losing time!"

The panic that was never far away at times like this reared its ugly head. "I can't do it. I told you I can't handle small spaces. I can't ..."

Regina placed her hands firmly on the sides of his face as she looked deep within him. "This is not a long cave; it can't be, because it's very close to the water and is subject to the tides." She pointed to the other side of the hatch. "You can see the tide is coming in. We must go and I need your help. You have always been there for me and I know you'll be there for me now. Just as I'm going to be there for you, every step of the way. I will not let you go, I promise."

Walker stared at Regina's beautiful, earnest face. It had all come down to this. It was too important for her to stop, and too dangerous to let her go on her own. She needed him, and he wasn't going to let a crippling phobia stand in his way. He could do this, if not for his sake, then for hers. Taking a deep breath and exhaling through his mouth, he summoned courage from God knew where. Then he took her hand in his and kissed her palm. "*Sei la mia luce*," he said at last. "Lead on."

Regina was comfortable in the darkness. She pulled out a flashlight, and when she turned it on, he recognized it.

"You can thank your resourceful son for this, and a whole lot more," she said.

"What do you mean, 'a whole lot more'?"

"Oh, I'll let him tell you. You have a lot to be proud of, though."

They had walked a hundred yards or so and now had to bend over; the passage had become low and narrow, no more than four feet at its widest and at times barely four feet high. It continued to gently twist and turn so that he could not see the proverbial light at the end of the tunnel. As they made their way cautiously along, it was obvious the tide was coming in. Water was beginning to slosh around their ankles, soaking his boots. As far as either of them knew, it could go on like this for miles, eventually filling with water and trapping them in a watery grave. Panic began a full-on assault of his body. *Please don't let me scream or yell or whimper or, God forbid, pee myself.*

All the while Regina held his hand firmly, guiding him, letting him know he was not alone. She hadn't chided him or belittled him or made light of something that even he knew was ridiculous. She simply carried on.

"Why are you hell-bent on going after her?" he

asked to avoid thinking about where he was. "You have what you need."

"Do I? Sharilyn may not have pulled the trigger or used the knife, but she indirectly caused the deaths of five people, maybe six, if Daniel doesn't make it. For heaven's sake, her own brother is dead! It has to end, because if she believes her pair is counterfeit, she'll return to steal again. I can't go through this anymore and neither can you. Besides, she has the professor's gun."

He could tell the last part was said in jest, but she was deadly serious about the rest of it. He realized how he could help her, even now.

"Then you'll need this," he said, handing her one of the pouches Thomas had given him.

She smiled slowly at him and aimed the flashlight on the pouch. "What color is it?"

He smiled back. "Black."

She reached up and kissed him quickly. "Who says you're color blind?"

He was about to respond when they turned another corner and saw a glimmer of light.

Hallelujah.

As they drew closer, the entrance widened a bit and he could see sunlight glinting off the water that was pulsing and undulating into the cave. Whatever happened, they would not be going back the way they came.

At the far end of the little cove they saw Sharilyn, no doubt waiting for the boat that Hugh had promised would come. When she saw Regina and Walker, she once again brandished the gun. "It's too late!" she cried. "I've got the tigers!"

"Are you sure?" Regina called back. "She held up her black pouch. "You might want to check."

Much as I hate to, I have to do this, Reggie thought. She walked purposefully toward a defiant Sharilyn.

"Don't come any closer," the woman said.

"I have to," Reggie said, hiding her fear that she was staring down the barrel of Ethan's gun held by an unstable woman. "I want to see your face when you open the pouch you think is so very precious."

Reggie's words had the desired effect; Sharilyn's demeanor changed from haughty to puzzled. She reached into her jeans pocket and pulled out the black pouch.

Walker calmly stepped to Sharilyn's side so that her view of them was split too wide.

"Stay where you are!" she ordered, swinging the gun in Walker's direction.

"Or you'll what?" he asked, slowly pulling out Daniel's pistol and aiming it at her.

"Please," Reggie said, as if they were playing good cop/bad cop. "There's no need for violence. Haven't we had enough of that? What say we both put down our weapons and lay our cards—or rather our jewels—on the table."

Sharilyn shifted her gaze nervously between them. Walker made to lay down his gun on a large piece of driftwood and waited for her to do the same. After a moment's hesitation, she did, and used both hands to open her pouch. She poured the contents into her hand and gasped.

"What are these?" she sputtered. "These are not the tigers—they aren't anything!"

Reggie barely masked her own surprise. She looked at Walker in shock. What in the hell had just happened? She was expecting one of the fake pairs, but *this!*

"They're just tiger amulets made from alabaster," Walker said. "Compliments of Thomas Ling."

Sharilyn's anger escaped its restraints. "Why that little prick!" She turned to Reggie. "Let's see yours," she demanded.

Now Reggie was filled with uncertainty. Were these the right ones? Would she be able to tell the difference easily? The answer was no. So, could she do what she meant to do? She looked to Walker for guidance and he nodded ever so slightly.

Then she thought of her grandmother, and what she would have done. Mandy Firestone would have done whatever was necessary to keep her loved ones safe. She could almost feel her grandmama whispering in her ear, "You need to do this. You need to let go."

Reggie took a step forward and poured the contents of her own pouch into her hand. A lovely pair of crouching white tigers, made of hotan jade with diamond eyes, spilled into her palm. She held them out for Sharilyn to see.

"Yes," the woman said, reaching for them.

"No," Reggie said. "These tigers have caused you nothing but agony your entire life. People have died because of you and your family's obsession. That's going to stop right here. No matter how beautiful they are, no matter how much power you think they have, they aren't worth the nightmare you have put so many people through."

With that she handed one to Walker, took the remaining tiger, and hurled it as far as she could into the ocean. Then she nodded to Walker, who threw his even farther out.

"No!" Sharilyn cried, turning to watch them disappear into the churning sea.

At that moment they heard the chug and rumble of a boat motor, maneuvering into the cove. As it rounded the corner, Reggie quickly picked up both weapons and gestured to the boat. "There's your ride, Sharilyn. Better take it."

Sharilyn stood, frozen, until the futility of further action seemed to penetrate her will. "I can't believe it's over. I failed."

"No, you're free," Reggie said. "Perhaps at some point you'll even thank me for it."

"I do not think so," she said bitterly. Then she turned and waded out to the boat her brother had hired. Once she was aboard, its captain quickly reversed direction and sped out of the cove.

"Maybe you will someday," Reggie murmured as she and Walker watched the vessel head for the horizon.

"Ah, Regina?" Walker said.

She turned to him, this man whom she knew now she could not live without. "Yes?"

"We need to leave this cove fairly quickly because the tide is rolling in."

"I agree. Let's go."

He shook his head. "Unfortunately, we can't go back the way we came."

Reggie looked back at the entrance to the cave: the opening was now flooding more with every wave. She looked around and saw that the sides of the cove shot out too far into the water to go around them.

And there was no path to the cliffs above.

Fear completely overwhelmed the satisfaction she'd felt after throwing the tigers into the sea. She turned to Walker with alarm. "What are we going to do?"

"We're going to go up."

Gotta call, gotta call. Sweating and shivering from nerves, Axel waited until he thought the ranger was gone, then drove back into the park and found a place along the road that was as close as he could get to the entrance of the underground bunker. He flipped open the clamshell phone, and once again started to dial the number for Detective de la Torre. He wasn't even going to pretend this time. He was gonna make sure they fucking knew they had to get in there *now*!

Except that this time, he was stopped by the sound and fury of half a dozen police cars and vans converging on the very place he was about to swat. Had he made the call earlier in some kind of trance? No, he couldn't have. Maybe Regina made the call from inside the bunker. But wouldn't she have texted him, too? Okay, so maybe Kaitlyn decided to contact the police after all.

He didn't know the right answer, but he was smart enough to figure out that right now wasn't the time to ask anybody about it. They looked like they were about to do some serious shit in there and were already setting up a perimeter. If he didn't move, he was going to get caught in it.

He started the Explorer again and resumed driving, thanking whoever had made the call. Then he heard a siren and looked in his rearview mirror. An ambulance had just arrived.

Axel's throat closed up and he fought the overwhelming urge to cry. The shakes continued and he kept up a steady mantra of *No, please God, don't let it be them. Please don't let it be them* all the way back to The Grove.

Chapter Forty-Eight

There is no way. Reggie looked up at the cliff forming one side of the cove and nearly went catatonic with anxiety. She was bad at estimating such things, but it seemed to be at least forty feet high and Almost. Straight. Up.

"No," she said. "I can't do that. Can't we just wait until the tide goes out again?"

Walker had taken the pistols from Reggie, emptied Ethan's, and put them in his back waistband. Then he gestured to the small beach that was increasingly covered with water. "Where would you suggest we stay for the next six hours? No rocks are high enough to keep us out of harm's way, and the temperature is going to be dropping soon." He stepped closer to Reggie and took her gently by the shoulders, capturing her gaze much as she had secured his earlier. "I'm scared shitless of caves, but this I can do. I know how to climb, and I can get us up that cliff."

She was beginning to shiver with fear. "But how? We don't have any ropes or anything. It's got to be slippery, and what if I—"

"Fall? You're not going to fall. I'm not going to let you fall. If you trust me and listen to what I tell you, I will get you up that wall."

Reggie looked around the cove, hoping to see *any* alternative. But the water was starting to rise, and she knew there was no other way out of their predicament. She started to hyperventilate and worked on getting her breathing under control, when really, all she wanted to do was cry.

No time for that, either. There was only Walker, who had supported her from the beginning, and who was there now to help her.

"Okay," she finally said. "What do I do.?"

They walked to the cliff face and Walker pointed out to her the texture of the wall. He said they were lucky because it was a good wall for climbing.

Reggie snorted. "Uh huh. Right."

"I'm serious," he said. "You see these rough protrusions? They're like small steps right up to the top. And these cracks are great for handholds, which you'll be able to take advantage of because you're dexterous and have strong hands from manipulating the metals for your jewelry. Now, there are two things I want you to remember."

"Only two?"

He smiled. "Well, to start, anyway. The first thing is, this is not a race. You can take your time finding handholds that feel comfortable, and more importantly, good footholds that let you use your big toe, the ball of your foot, and the muscles in your beautiful legs to propel yourself up to the next level." He demonstrated and easily climbed up ten feet before dropping back down to the sand.

"What's the second thing?" she asked.

He reached over and kissed her. "The second thing is that I'm going to be right here with you every step of the way."

Reggie took several more deep breaths. "Okay, then. Let's do this."

And they did. Slowly, sometimes a foot at a time, they crawled up the cliff together. At about the halfway point Reggie caught a glimpse of how far they were off the ground and was almost crushed by a sense of futility and panic.

"I can't do this," she whimpered. "I can't do this!"

Walker responded with a firm "Hey ... *Hey*. Look at me. "Look ... at ... me." She turned to him and he continued. "Forget where you've been. That's gone. That's yesterday's news. You are right where you need to be in this very moment. The only thing on your mind right now should be the next handhold and the next foothold and making sure you don't stretch yourself too much. Nothing matters except where you're going and conserving your strength enough to get there."

The stress of focusing on just the next little step was so great that Reggie started tearing up, which blurred her vision. Walker paused, easily held on with his feet and one hand, and wiped her tears away with his thumb. "None of that, now," he said gently. "You've got plenty of time for that once we reach the top, which we're very close to, by the way."

Reggie nodded and refocused her efforts. Sure enough, fifteen excruciating minutes later they were almost to the edge. But by now her muscles were quivering with the strain and she knew, she just knew she wasn't going to be able to pull herself over the top. She said as much to Walker.

"I know, so this is what we're going to do. I'm going to climb the rest of the way and then pull you up from above."

"How can you do that?" she asked, concern for him battling with fear. "You've got to be as tired as I am. What if you can't do it?"

Once again, he let go with one hand, perhaps to show her his strength, but maybe to further encourage her by touching her cheek. "Regina Firestone, I am telling you here without a doubt or hesitation, that *nothing* will stop me from bringing you up and into my arms. Nothing."

She took a tremulous breath and nodded, watching Walker as he climbed the rest of the way to the top of the cliff.

Now she was on the cliff face all by herself. It was up to her to get her body high enough that Walker could reach her. Willing herself not to look down, she found two new sets of holds, one after the other, until she'd brought herself within his reach.

Once he propelled himself over the top, he lay down on his stomach, his arms extended down below the edge of the cliff toward her. "Ready to trust me one more time?" he asked. "When I take your arms, at the count of three, you find some traction and push with your legs with everything you've got. All right?"

"All right."

He grasped her slender arms in his muscular ones and said, "One ... two ... three ... now!" and with a giant pull and scramble, he hauled Regina over the edge.

"Oh, Oh!" she cried and really did start bawling as she lay flat on the tufted grass. The tension that had wrapped itself around her was no match for her tears and began to melt away.

Walker, still breathing hard from the effort, chuckled and took her in his arms. "Cry all you want, sweetheart. You were magnificent." He kissed her wet cheeks and she responded with her lips on his, and even though she knew it was all about surviving, it was also about something deeper.

"I know I'm not supposed to say this right now, but I can't help it," she said. "I love you. And it's not just because you saved my life. It's so, so much more, and I hope you feel just a little bit of what I feel, what I've been feeling for a while. But if you don't, that's okay, that's—"

Walker rose up over her, brushing her hair back and stopping her confession with his own. "I love you, too. But I need to tell you, as soon as we get back, I'm going to ask Axel not to go away to school. I'm going to be a full-time dad to him, and I want to be a full-time partner to you ... and a husband, if you're willing. I hope you're okay with that, because I don't know what I'm going to do if you aren't."

Reggie started crying again, but laughing, too. "I'm okay with that."

Walker lay down again and they both gazed at the blue of the sky, feeling the solid earth beneath them, holding hands and absorbing the momentous shift their lives had just taken. After a little while Reggie heard Walker chuckle.

"What?" she asked.

"I was just thinking, between my fear of closed spaces and your fear of heights, we may have a devil of a time deciding on family vacations."

Reggie rolled over so that she was looking into Walker's eyes. "If there's one thing we've learned, it's that we can disagree about a lot of things and still make it work. And one more thing."

"What's that?"

"My eyes are green."

Walker smiled ear to ear and took her face in his. "No matter what color they are, I adore you, Regina Firestone." Then he kissed her to prove his point.

It was the end of a *very* long day. Without a cell phone between them, Walker and Regina had walked half a mile in wet boots before they found someone to relay the message to Gabe de la Torre that they were all right. Hours of debriefing back at the Department of Investigations in Lagunitas followed.

Although he'd touched base with Axel on the phone, Walker was anxious to get home and talk to him face to face about the future. But when he and Regina finally made it back to The Grove, his son had already gone upstairs for the night. Walker couldn't blame him; it had to be incredibly stressful thinking your father's gone and maybe not coming back.

Gabe had given Regina and Walker a ride back and stayed to talk informally with everyone about the case. "*Dio Mio*," he said to the small group gathered in the library. "Talk about stressful. First, we get one of the Chow brothers to sing about the location where Walker and Thomas Ling were being kept. Fantastic. Then we arrive, only to find out Regina has gotten there before us." He looked directly at Regina. "By the way, are you ever going to tell us how you knew about that place?"

Regina smiled like the cat that ate the canary. "I told you back at the station: intuition, pure and simple."

Gabe rolled his eyes. "Right, and you've got a bridge to sell me, too. Anyway, there we were, thinking we'd blown it. According to Thomas Ling, three people had gone downstairs and all three had disappeared. By the time we cleared the premises down to that level, we had to shut the hatch because the room was flooding. Thank God we heard from you before we contacted Axel."

"How was Daniel doing when you first got there?" Regina asked.

"Hanging in there. We got him to the hospital right away, so I think he's going to be fine. By the way, it looks like he won't be charged for killing Huang Hu. If we need to, we assume Ling, not to mention you two, will testify that it was self-defense."

Walker agreed. "We owe Daniel our lives. But man, that guy must be dedicated to his cause, going through all that just to make sure the NRTT didn't get the symbol or the money it needed. Seducing Sharilyn Huang the way he did, just to stay close to the operation —that's pretty low."

"That's essentially the life of an undercover cop," said Gabe. "Nasty stuff, but a means to an end."

"I think it went beyond that for Daniel," said Regina. "Apparently, some of his ancestors had been screwed over by the monarchy. But what about Sharilyn —think they'll ever catch her?"

Gabe was skeptical. "Maybe, but I doubt ICE will spend many resources on it given they can't pin the theft or any of the killings directly on her. My guess is she'll find another sugar daddy in China."

"Maybe not," Regina countered. "She wasn't a mistress by choice; I think her brother convinced her it was the only way to restore the family honor, strange as that sounds. I hope whatever happens, she finds some peace."

"Detective Liu must be one happy camper tonight," said Brit. "I bet he was sweating bullets trying to figure out who the killer was and why he was leaving those marks on every victim."

"That guy Hugh—talk about a man who got way too into his mission," Jenna said. "It turned him into a monster! Axel deserves a lot of credit for figuring out what he and his group were all about."

"You're right," Gabe said. "Turns out the NRTT is based in Shanghai and had the money to finance the entire operation. Sharilyn must have been too focused on her own plans to worry about where her brother's resources came from."

"In the end, it was all about the tigers." Regina filled everyone in on the pouches and their surprising contents.

"So, how on earth did Mr. Ling exchange them?" Ethan asked. "That must have been quite a performance."

"He told me he could do it if he got the opportunity," Walker said. "It helped that Regina had brought the extra pouch. I imagine he did it when he knocked over the lantern, but I sure as hell didn't see him do it. Bottom line is, he made it happen."

"But did he?" Regina asked. "I'm still not entirely sure which two are left."

Walker pulled out the red and green pouches from his pocket and handed them to her. After inspecting them, she sighed with apparent satisfaction. "Both pairs have faceted culets, which means one is the original and one is the copy that Vihaan Chaudhry helped make for me."

"What's a culet?" Gabe asked.

Regina showed Gabe one of the earrings. "It's hard to see here, but it's the very bottom of the diamond; in this case, the tiny diamonds that form the tigers' eyes. Centuries ago they made them flat like other parts of the cut stone. They called them 'little faces' or 'facets.' Probably because the diamonds would sit better in their settings, or because they didn't have the skill to keep them pointed like most cutting styles use today. So, we know at least one of these pairs is very old."

Brit took the earring from Gabe and examined it. "So, between the two, how do you tell one from the other?"

"A couple of ways." Reggie held one earring up. "You can see that this one has a pale green streak on the belly; I happen to know that my tigers had that same streak. Thomas Ling led Sharilyn and her brother to believe the opposite as part of his shell game.

"But let's say I wasn't as familiar with the characteristics of the stone. When I remove the eyes, I'll see the jade carver's mark on at least one pair. It'll be a tiny twisting vine. The other pair—the true originals—may or may not have a mark."

"Speaking of that, Thomas said he would love to meet the 'Liane' that Leo Brunt hired for the job," Walker said. "He told me she must be beautiful to have carved such a lovely rendition of the tigers."

Regina grinned. "If she's single and interested, I hope she's strong enough to handle Thomas Ling's very protective mama." Everyone laughed at the near universal horror of an overbearing in-law.

More conversation followed, but eventually the hour grew late and Ethan prevailed upon Gabe to give him a lift back to his cottage on his way home to Dani. Gabe obliged, and shortly thereafter Brit and Jenna said good-night and went upstairs.

Walker wasted no time. He took Regina in his arms and kissed her deeply. "I can't wait to start the new chapter of our lives together," he murmured. "We have a lot of decisions to make."

"Such as..."

"Such as where to live ... where's the best place to establish your studio and mine ... where Axel's going to go to school ... If we want to..."

Regina gazed at him, a serious look on her face. "If we want to what? Have kids?"

He nodded. "Yes. We didn't talk about it, but, well, I'd like to know. Do you?"

He felt her stiffen in his arms. Was she not interested?

"Do *you*?" she asked. "You're the one with all the experience."

Walker scoffed. "Hardly. These past weeks have given me a glimpse of what it's really like to be a func-tioning parent. It's aggravating, and at times downright petrifying, when you realize just how much you love somebody and fear for them. But not wanting kids with you would be the same as not wanting you—just unthinkable. So, yes, I'm up for it." He chuckled. "Yeah, definitely that."

Regina put her arms around his neck. "A while back I had some regrets that I didn't stay in the relationship with Curtis long enough to have a child. I envy Ava her little girl Nia. I very much want to be a mother. But now I'm more than glad I waited. I just hope some of grand-mama's fertility got passed down to me."

"Her beauty certainly did." Walker kissed her again before stepping back and pulling her toward the stairs.

"I want to check on Axel, and if he's still awake I'd love to have the conversation I need to have with him. After that, I want to come to your bed and have you tell me in great detail about your lovely green eyes and the color of your hair. And then I want to do things with you and to you that require no conversation whatsoever."

A light knocking on the door drew Axel halfway out of his shallow sleep. Once he'd gotten the call from his dad saying that he and Regina were all right, his jitters had thankfully subsided. But waiting for the two of them to come home had driven him so far up the wall that he decided to play a video game. He lay down wearing his headphones and tried to play, but he couldn't concentrate, and he gave up after getting killed about a gazillion times. He must have dropped off eventually because when he did, he had visions of the police banging on his door, telling him he had to leave because his father had lost everything to black hat hackers and the only place left to live was a deep, cold, windowless basement that you entered from the middle of an amusement park.

Axel's bedroom was dark, so he felt rather than saw his father come in and lean over him, taking the headphones off and putting them on the nightstand. Then he took the blanket and pulled it up to Axel's chin, a move that that made Axel want to cry, because he felt safe and cared for in a way he hadn't felt for a very long time.

He didn't want his dad to leave the room. Ever.

"You're back," he said sleepily.

"I'm back." He sat down on the bed. "Axel," he said quietly. "Son."

And Axel, without thinking, put his arms around his father and held on, and he didn't care that some people might say he was too old to do such a sappy thing, because his dad, at least the man he had always considered his dad, was safe and unhurt, and cared about him.

After a bit his father said, "I need to ask you a question. Do you mind us talking right now? Or would you rather sleep?"

He didn't want his father to leave, so he scooted up in the bed. "What do you want to ask?"

"It's about Regina. And it's about school."

Oh. That's what it's all about. Now I get it. Now that Regina was in the picture, there was no more room for Axel. Time to ship him out. Time to—

"I've asked Regina to live with me and at some

point here soon we're probably going to get married. I want to know what you think about that."

The anger just lurking off stage stepped into the spotlight. "You want to know how soon I'm leaving, is that it?" He swallowed to get the lie out. "I don't give a crap. Just buy the fucking ticket and I'm out of here."

Instead of getting mad, his dad just smiled, which was weird as shit. "No. I want to know if you're going to be okay with living with her, because I told her that as much as I love her, I can't give you up. Look, I know you don't think I'm your real father, and maybe you don't realize I'm completely aware that your mother was sleeping with another person when you were conceived.

"But there's one thing you need to be absolutely clear about. I don't give a crap about whether our DNA matches or not. You are my son. Period. I love you and want to be a real father to you, which means I don't want you going to school on the other side of the country when you could just as easily go to school here. I want the three of us to make our own family, right here in Little Eden, if you want. Regina wants that, too. And maybe someday, she and I will make our family bigger. But I promise you, with all that's in me, that you will never, *ever*, feel like an outsider again. What do you say?"

For once in his life, Axel didn't know how to respond. He just sat there, like a lump, stupid tears spilling over, not quite believing, but wanting more than he'd ever wanted anything in his whole friggin' life for what his dad just said to be true.

His dad was sitting there, tears rolling down his cheeks too, not ashamed at all, just waiting and hoping for an answer, like it really meant something to him what that answer was going to be.

And in that moment Axel got it. It was better than getting his license, better than kissing Kaitlyn, better than any Christmas morning, real or imagined. And the words finally came.

"Yeah, I think I'd like that. Like, more than anything."

Chapter Forty-Nine

The New Grove Center for American Art

Mid-October

By nature, Reggie Firestone wasn't a fan of big parties, but today was an exception. She was thrilled that Opening Day for The New Grove Center for American Art had arrived and that she was sharing it with Walker Banks, the love of her life; his son, whom she had also come to love; and several Firestone family members, who were finally going to see the full story of their incredible matriarch, Mandy Culpepper.

The morning was clear and crisp with the promise of warmer temperatures as the day unfolded. Every building had been checked and double-checked, including the museum and gallery; the conference rooms and workshops; and the refurbished guest cottages that would soon house both artists and the occasional patron. The main and auxiliary exhibits had been installed and the shop, refreshment outlets and special event caterers were all in place to introduce The Grove to a new audience of art lovers everywhere.

Earlier, Reggie, Walker and Axel had walked through the Amelia Firestone Exhibit to check it one last time. Axel's research on the Chinese immigrant culture had added depth to the displays, and Walker's photographic treatment of both the historic photos of Mandy as well as Reggie's modern interpretations was somehow both nostalgic and edgy. He truly was a gifted visual artist. And the gems from her grandmother's unique collection were on display as well, including the original jade tiger earrings that had once been the gift of an emperor.

But the absolute best part of the walk hadn't been the setting; it had been the simple pleasure of talking about their upcoming activities. Axel was now attending Little Eden High and loving it; he was meeting Kaitlyn later in the morning to work a shift directing guests throughout the complex. Walker was telling Reggie about some of the items he wanted Brit to address the following day regarding the renovation of Puerta Del Mar, which Walker and Reggie had purchased. And Reggie was developing a metal casting class for future art students at The Grove. Life was good. No, life was *great.*

After their museum run-though they headed to the Great House, where Professor Ethan Wolff was gathering family and friends for one final pep talk. Brit and

Jenna were there, of course, along with Jenna's brother Jason, who was home from college for the event. Dr. Leo Brunt had come, and Detective Gabe de la Torre had arrived with Dani, who was proudly wearing the elegant engagement ring Gabe had commissioned from Reggie. The happy couple was planning a Christmas wedding at the Havenwood Inn; several of their friends from Verona, Italy would be attending.

"I am so very glad to share this wonderful day with each and every one of you," Ethan declared. "There were times I feared this day would never come, days when Brit and Jenna seemed to be holding everything together with chewing gum and chicken wire." Everyone chuckled along with the architect and the art teacher who had rekindled their love while fighting to save the retreat earlier in the summer. Their Thanksgiving wedding reception, in fact, would be one of the first private functions hosted at The Grove.

Jason, tall and blond like his sister, called out, "You provided the glue, Da," and the rest of the group heartily agreed.

"That's very kind of you to say, dear boy. I like to think I've played a small but useful part in bringing you all together for this grand project of ours. Despite the rocky road, we made it in time to celebrate a new Grove Center for American Art. A place that will carry on the noble traditions of its founders, August and Amelia Wolff. An oasis of creativity that will foster a new generation of talented artists in every medium as they interpret our great country and our culture in their own unique ways. I thank you all for your help over the years and months and days, for coming together as family, extended though it might be, to see it through. Now let's show the world that the place they know as Sinner's Grove is in reality the fantastic New Grove Center for American Art."

And with that, they all went outside and opened the gates.

Thank You

Thank you so much for reading *The Jade Hunters*. Readers like you are powerful, and you would be doing me a great favor by posting an objective review on Amazon, Goodreads, or other platforms based on the e-reader you use. In today's publishing world, those reviews are golden to authors like me.

Sharing your thoughts with others (including me!) on social media would be wonderful as well. You'll find me on **Twitter, Facebook, and Pinterest.** And don't forget to stop by my website (**abmichaels.com**) to learn more about my work. There you can join my Readers Group and receive a welcome gift along with monthly updates and special content.

Other Titles By A.B. Michaels

The contemporary series, "Sinner's Grove Suspense," follows a number of descendants from "The Golden City" historical series as they work to re-open the famous artists' retreat north of San Francisco known as "The Grove." A brief excerpt from the first and second novels in the suspense series, *Sinner's Grove* and *The Lair,* follows, as well as introductions to all five novels from "The Golden City" series.

Each novel is a stand-alone read.

SINNER'S GROVE
(Book One of the "Sinner's Grove Suspense" series)

A startling discovery when she was fourteen left San Francisco artist Jenna Bergstrom estranged from her family; unforeseen tragedy only sharpened her loneliness. But now her ailing grandfather needs her expertise to re-open the family's once-famous artists' retreat on the California coast. The problem? She'll have to face architect Brit Maguire, the ex-love of her life.

Seven years ago, Maguire spent a magical time with the woman of his dreams, only to have her disappear from his life completely. Now she's back, helping with the biggest historic renovation of Brit's career. No matter how deep his feelings still run, Brit can't afford the distraction of Jenna Bergstrom, because something is going terribly wrong with the project at Sinner's Grove.

An excerpt from *Sinner's Grove:*

"What the hell?!" Brit turned around when a second explosion followed on the heels of the first. He immediately wrapped his arms protectively around Jenna.

"My God, was that a bomb?" she cried. She couldn't believe what was happening. She quickly dropped her leg and straightened her dress, fear turning her passion into panic.

"I don't know," Brit said grimly. "Let's find out."

They ran out of the building, passing several workers and a few investors rushing in different directions with terror-stricken faces. The street lights had not gone out, and Jenna saw her brother across the lawn.

"Jason! Do you know what happened?"

"It looks like the equipment barn blew up!" he called as he ran in that direction. "I just called 911."

"Anybody hurt?" Brit yelled.

"Don't know yet!"

Brit took Jenna by the shoulders. "Go back to the Great House. I'll check it out."

"Not in your life," she shot back. "I'm staying with you."

Brit set his jaw and started running toward the maintenance area. Thankful she'd worn flats to the presentation, Jenna easily kept up with him. As they crested the hill, Brit stopped short and stuck out his arm to keep Jenna from running past him.

"Too dangerous!" he yelled.

She grabbed onto his arm to stop her momentum. *Oh my God— this is hell on earth.* The front two-thirds of the huge barn was a fireball shooting flames a hundred feet into the sky. And the heat was so intense, she felt as if even her blood was boiling. Smoke was everywhere, sucking the oxygen from the air. Men were shouting and running back and forth, trying to be heard over the roar of the inferno. *Please keep Jason and Da away from this*, Jenna prayed, her breathing harsh and labored.

"How's it looking, Jack?" Brit called out to the man he'd pegged to help manage the crew.

"Not good." Jack, looking disgusted, tossed a hose on the ground where it joined several others coiled haphazardly in the gloom like somnolent snakes. "Whoever did this cut the hoses. We can't get any pressure, so we're down to a bucket brigade until the fire trucks get here."

"Everybody accounted for?"

"I think so, but it's pretty crazy right now. Maybe we oughta do a head count."

Brit looked around in frustration. In the distance sirens could be heard. "Good idea," he said. "Maybe—"

"Mr. Maguire! Mr. Maguire!" Parker Bishop and Kyle Summers ran up to the group.

"What's wrong?" Jenna cried.

"I think…I think—" Parker seemed to be particularly anxious.

"Spit it out, man," Brit barked.

Jenna glared at Brit. "Give him a chance to calm down!"

"We think…we think maybe that guy Lester's still in the building!" Kyle said.

"How do you know?" Brit asked sharply.

"We were on litter patrol down around the lower bungalows. Parker said he saw him go inside."

"How could you see in the dark?" Jenna asked.

"I think it was him, but I don't know for sure," Parker hedged.

"The light wasn't that good, but we saw *somebody* go inside and close the slider. You can tell when that big sucker closes," Kyle explained. "I didn't think much of it and kept working."

"Me too," Parker said.

"No, you were on the phone, dude, remember?"

Parker nodded. "Yeah, that's right. My dad called. And then, *Kablam*! So we started running back here."

Brit didn't waste a second. "Anybody seen Lester?" he yelled to the members of the makeshift fire crew.

A chorus of "no's" came back.

"Jack, you got a master key on you?" he called out.

The man shook his head.

"Get one!" Brit yelled. He then headed toward the back of the barn.

"Where do you think you're going?" Jenna cried, grabbing his arm.

"If he's in there, there's a chance he's in the back and can't get out," Brit said. "He may not be able to get to the side door. We've got to get it open and help him out."

"But you're not going in after him, right?"

Brit paused and looked at Jenna, running his fingertip down the side of her cheek. "Don't worry." With that he took off, glancing back once before he turned the corner of the building.

Speechless, Jenna watched his retreating figure as if in slow motion. She noticed vaguely that Kyle and Parker had walked up on either side of her. Kyle put his arm around her shoulders.

"It's all right," he said soothingly. "We're here."

Jenna turned and looked up at the large, muscular young man. He had the same glittery look he'd had the last day of school. Then she looked at Parker. He was staring at Kyle and his eyes burned fiercely, just as they had that same day. Fear, slippery and cold, slid over her.

"We need to help Brit," she said neutrally, hoping her voice wouldn't betray the anxiety threatening to overtake her.

By the time she worked her way safely around to the

side of the burning barn, several burly workmen were in the process of battering the side door with what looked like a large fence post. The door was already starting to buckle from the heat. When it finally gave way, smoke billowed out and Jenna watched in horror as Brit tore off his jacket, tie and shirt, soaking the latter in a nearby bucket and wrapping it around his nose and mouth.

"Don't go in there—please!" Jenna cried.

Brit looked at her briefly, his eyes communicating what words could not. Then he disappeared inside the carnage. Moments later another deafening explosion ripped apart the air.

"Nooooo!" Jenna screamed. Tears streaming down her face, arms wrapped around herself to keep from falling apart, Jenna stared in shock at the burning, crumbling building, her only words a mantra-like "please God, please God, please God."

She felt someone—Parker, perhaps—urge her back from the heat of the fire, but she couldn't seem to move. Her entire focus was on the jagged hole into which Brit had run. She couldn't believe he was gone. Wouldn't believe it. He was going to walk out again. Any second now. Any second. Any second.

THE LAIR
(Book Two of the "Sinner's Grove Suspense" series)

After her father dies in a boating incident, innkeeper Daniela Dunn must travel from Northern California's Sinner's Grove back to Verona, Italy and her childhood home, an estate called the Panther's Lair. It's a mansion full of frightful memories and deeply buried secrets, where appearances are deceiving and the price of honesty is death. As Dani is drawn further into her family's intrigues, she has an unlikely ally in handsome Marin County investigator Gabriele de la Torre. He says he's come along merely to support her, but his actions show he has an agenda all his own.

Gabe de la Torre needs to settle old family debts before starting fresh with the woman he feels could be The One. But once Dani finds out whom he's beholden to, all bets might be off. When a mystery woman reveals that Dani's father may have been murdered, the stakes rise dramatically and Gabe realizes they're now players in a dangerous game. Protecting Dani becomes his top priority, even as she strives to figure out whom she can trust: her relatives, Gabe, or even herself.

An excerpt from *The Lair:*

"Nothing like a wide awake drunk," Gabe muttered an hour later. They'd gotten back to La Tana and as usual Fausta had grudgingly let them in. "Hey, you can always give us a key," he'd joked, but his aunt had simply turned around and gone back to her room.

Once in their suite, Dani had been asleep on her feet, which were a little unsteady at best, so he'd pointed her in the direction of her bedroom and reluctantly bid her good night.

God she was beautiful. So elegant, so feminine, even though she didn't put on airs *at all*. He'd spent the entire evening fighting the impulse to touch her everywhere, even in places that demanded privacy at the very least. He'd known instinctively that she'd get along great with Marco and Gina, and she hadn't disappointed him. Man, she was driving him crazy. He heaved a sigh. Both tired and wired, he couldn't tell which was more to blame, the alcohol or the stress of keeping his desire in check.

He reflexively reached into the small refrigerator for a beer before he realized he was already half pickled, so he opted for water instead. Unscrewing the cap, he drank half the bottle while pulling his shirt out of his slacks. To keep his libido in check he decided to focus on something decidedly unsexy. Reaching for the jacket he'd tossed on the back of the sofa, he pulled out the report that Marco had given him earlier that evening.

"I think we're on to something," Marco had told him quietly. "We found a match."

He was just beginning to scan the document when the bedroom door opened and Dani appeared. Her hair was tousled and she walked a bit uncertainly, as if she were slogging through mud in high heels, even though she was barefoot. She wore an ivory-colored cover-up of some kind and she looked nervous. "I'm ready," she said.

He looked at her quizzically. "Ready for what, bella?"

"For us…you know." He didn't have a chance to reply before she tottered up to him and threw her slender arms around his neck, locking her lips with his.

After his initial shock, Gabe took a moment to enjoy

the feel of Dani's curves against him. Jesus, after all that booze his body still reacted immediately, hardening in response to her softness. She felt so damn good—like falling into the most luxurious bed when you've been sleeping on the floor all your life. He smiled inwardly at her inexperienced but earnest attempt at seduction and cursed his inner cop—the prig who wouldn't let him take advantage of her while she was intoxicated. Reluctantly he took her by the upper arms and peeled her away from his body. "Uh, sweetheart, I don't think this is a good thing to be doing…"

"What?" she asked softly but defensively. "Don't I measure up to your other women friends? Don't I? Just a little?" She stepped back and before he could stop her she dropped the cover-up, revealing a perfect—and perfectly naked—female form encased in a 5 foot two inch frame. She was biting her full lower lip, practically screaming for his approval.

An image flashed before him of Dani pregnant. She was ripe and luscious—the epitome of Woman. Instead of cooling him off, the thought of her big with child —*his* child—only made him hotter and made what he had to do all the more difficult. He looked at her a long time, so long that he could see uncertainty, followed by embarrassment, overtake her. He reached down and picked up the wrap, putting it around her shoulders.

"I…I'm sorry," she mumbled. "I thought ..." She turned to go, but Gabe took her shoulders and turned her back toward him.

"If you think for one second that I don't want to

bury myself in you right now, you are sadly mistaken," he said roughly. "When you and I make love, I am going to be all over you. You are going to feel me everywhere and know when I've taken you higher than you've ever been before." He tore himself away and covered her back up. "And the next morning, you're going to remember everything I did to you and want me to do it all over again. Count on it. Now go to bed."

"But—"

"Please," he said firmly, turning her around and practically pushing her back into the bedroom. It took several minutes after her door shut for Gabe's upper brain to start functioning again. "Keep your eye on the prize," he repeated like a mantra. "Keep your eye on the prize." The prize, in this case, was a Dani who felt no regrets about whatever physical gymnastics they might partake in together. He'd waited this long for the timing to be right; he could wait a little longer, even though it was damn near going to kill him.

"The Golden City"
Historical Series

"The Golden City" series includes *The Art of Love, The Depth of Beauty, The Promise, The Price of Compassion* and *Josephine's Daughter*.

Each of these novels is also a stand-alone read.

THE ART OF LOVE
(Book One of "The Golden City" series)

At the end of the Gilded Age, the "Golden City" of San Francisco offers everything a man could want — except the answers August Wolff desperately needs to find.

After digging a fortune in gold from the frozen fields of the Klondike, Gus head south, hoping to start over and put the baffling disappearance of his wife and daughter behind him. The turn of the century brings him even more success, but the distractions of a city some call the new Sodom and Gomorrah can't fill the gaping hole in his life.

Amelia Starling is a wildly talented artist caught in the straightjacket of Old New York society. Making a heart-breaking decision, she moves to San Francisco to further her career, all while living with the pain of a sacrifice no woman should ever have to make.

Brought together by the city's flourishing art scene, Gus and Lia forge a rare connection. But the past, shrouded in mystery, prevents the two of them from moving forward as one. Unwilling to face society's scorn, Lia leaves the city and vows to begin again in Europe.

Gus can't bear to let her go, but unless he can set his ghosts to rest, he and Lia have no chance for happiness at all.

THE DEPTH OF BEAUTY

(Book Two of "The Golden City" series)

In San Francisco's Chinatown circa 1903, slavery, polygamy and rampant prostitution are thriving – just blocks away from the Golden City's elite.

Wealthy and well-connected, Will Firestone enters the mysterious enclave with an eye toward expanding his shipping business. What he finds there will astonish him. With the help of an exotic young widow and a gifted teenage orphan, he embarks on a journey of self-discovery, where lust, love and tragedy will change his life forever.

The Depth of Beauty was nominated for a RITA award in 2017 in the category of general fiction.

THE PROMISE
(Book Three of "The Golden City" series)

April 18, 1906. A massive earthquake has decimated much of San Francisco, leaving thousands without food, water or shelter. Patrolling the streets to help those in need, Army corporal Ben Tilson meets a young woman named Charlotte who touches his heart, making him think of a future with her in it. In the heat of the moment he makes a promise to her family that even he realizes will be almost impossible to keep.

Because on the heels of the earthquake, a much worse disaster looms: a fire that threatens to consume everything and everyone in its path.

It will take everything Ben's got to make it back to

the woman he's fallen for—and even that may not be enough.

THE PRICE OF COMPASSION
(Book Four of "The Golden City" series)

April 18, 1906. San Francisco has just been shattered by a massive earthquake and is in the throes of an even more deadly fire. During the chaos, gifted surgeon Tom Justice makes a life-changing decision that wreaks havoc on his body, mind and spirit. Leaving the woman he loves, he embarks on a quest to regain his sanity and self-worth. Yet just when he finds some answers, he's arrested for murder—a crime he may very well be guilty of. The facts of the case are troubling; they'll have you asking the question: "Is he guilty?" Or even worse …"What would I have done?"

JOSEPHINE'S DAUGHTER
(Book Five of "The Golden City" series)

In the late nineteenth century, wealthy and headstrong Kit Firestone chafes under the strictures of The Golden City's high society, especially the interference of her charming but overbearing mother, Josephine. Kit's secret rebellion leads to potentially catastrophic results and keeps her from finding happiness.

When her brother nearly dies from a dangerous infection, Kit defied convention and becomes a working nurse. Through her troubled romance with a young doctor and a series of dramatic events, including a natural disaster and her mother's own critical illness, Kit begins to understand who her mother truly is and what their relationship is all about. She may not get the chance to appreciate their bond, however, because through no fault of her own, a madman has Kit in his crosshairs.

Set amidst the backdrop of the Gilded Age and beyond, Josephine's Daughter explores many of the social and medical issues facing women of that era— issues that resonate today. Independence, reproductive rights, birth control, childbirth and parenting are all put to the test in *Josephine's Daughter*.

About the Author

A native of California, A.B. Michaels holds masters' degrees in history (UCLA) and broadcasting (San Francisco State University). After working for many years as a promotional writer and editor, she decided it was time to focus on writing the kind of fiction she likes to read.

A.B. and her husband currently live in Boise, Idaho. On any given day you might see them on the golf course, the bocce court, or walking their four-legged "sons" along the Boise River. More than likely, however, you'll find her hard at work on her next book.

https://abmichaels.com